The Anthem Guide to Short Fiction

The Anthem Guide to Short Fiction

Edited by
Christopher Linforth

ANTHEM PRESS
LONDON · NEW YORK · DELHI

Anthem Press
An imprint of Wimbledon Publishing Company
www.anthempress.com

This edition first published in UK and USA 2011
by ANTHEM PRESS
75-76 Blackfriars Road, London SE1 8HA, UK
or PO Box 9779, London SW19 7ZG, UK
and
244 Madison Ave. #116, New York, NY 10016, USA

British Library Cataloguing in Publication Data
A catalogue record for this book is available from the British Library.

Library of Congress Cataloging-in-Publication Data

The Anthem guide to short fiction / [edited by] Christopher Linforth.
p. cm. – (Anthem learning)
Includes bibliographical references.
ISBN-13: 978-0-85728-769-4 (pbk.)
ISBN-10: 0-85728-769-9 (pbk.)
1. Short stories, American. 2. American fiction–19th century. 3. American fiction–20 century. 4. Short stories, English. 5. English fiction–19th century. 6. English fiction–20 century. 7. Short story. I. Linforth, Christopher.
PS648.S5A6125 2011
813'.0108–dc22
2011012832

ISBN-13: 978 0 85728 769 4 (Pbk)
ISBN-10: 0 85728 769 9 (Pbk)

This title is also available as an eBook.

Table of Contents

Acknowledgments

The Anthem Guide to Short Fiction would not be possible without the help and guidance of Tej P. S. Sood and his staff at Anthem Press, especially Janka Romero. In preparing this edition, I am grateful to my readers, Molly Emmett, Colin Clancy, Marilyn Brock, Jennifer Poon, Anna Rose Welch, Kirsten Dean, Maria D'Alessandro, and Leah Wisroth, for all the feedback and suggestions they have given me during the book's development. In particular, I thank M. K. Foster and Eve Marie Blasinsky for their generous emotional and intellectual support over the last few months. Lastly, I would like to dedicate this book to the memory of Emily Landis, a dear friend and poet, who sadly passed away.

Christopher Linforth
Blacksburg, Virginia

Preface

The premise of *The Anthem Guide to Short Fiction* originated from years of teaching writing and literature with monolithic textbooks and crammed anthologies. In the modern classroom, I believe, there is a need for something different: a helpful book, a guide as we have named it, which takes classic literature as its base and contextualizes and interrogates it to foster discussion and engagement. In inception and execution, the guide is more than a simple anthology; it goes beyond a series of stories, static within their pages. Indeed, the guide has been designed for students and their instructors to critically think about texts and their construction, and how, indeed, those same texts could be creatively examined and even re-envisioned. Therefore, this book is especially useful as a text for college-level composition, literature, and creative writing classes, and as part of AP English and International Baccalaureate curricula.

The Anthem Guide to Short Fiction contains 20 classic short stories by well-known and respected authors. Some of the stories included are rarely anthologized in the contemporary publishing market. Accordingly, the selection presented within these pages provides a fresh perspective on each author and his or her place in the literary canon. Further, the guide features individual biographical notes and a brief introduction to each author's work. Following every one of the stories is a "Thinking About the Story" section and incisive discussion questions, formulated for students to respond to the text as a piece of literature. Similarly, the creative activities have been devised to stimulate critical and imaginative thinking in the reader. The aim: to give student writers agency, and an understanding of authorship and the creative process. At the back of the book you will find a concise glossary of literary terms designed for optimal and regular use.

Introduction

I find that most people know what a story is until they sit down to write one.
Flannery O'Connor — "The Nature and Aim of Fiction" (1969)

An astute commentator on fiction, O'Connor's aphorism exemplifies a central strand of this book's purpose: to create engaged readers who understand the aims, practices, and craft of fiction. Yes, you will find in this volume, analytical questions about plot, character, theme, and so forth. However, as O'Connor indicates, writing, or in this book's case *re-writing*, fiction will enable a different understanding of how stories operate.

In accordance with the demands of the modern classroom, *The Anthem Guide to Short Fiction* seeks to equip students with the tools to become seasoned interpreters and writers of fiction. It is generally agreed upon that there is a close connection between well-versed readers and skilled writers. This relationship suggests that literature is not separate from the people who read it, but is part of an impassioned personal literacy. Developing this idea further, it should be understood that stories are not written in a vacuum; they emerge from a purposeful world of art and entertainment. Yet stories also reflect the social conditions within which they were created. The reader takes part in a long-established conversation with the writer and the text, transcending the time and place of creation to find meaning and value in the work.

The Art of Short Fiction

For art, we need artists—in this case, writers. Yet we also need readers. Between the two roles, and the inherent acts of writing and reading, emerges a symbiotic relationship—each feeding the other in a constant loop. The result is a deeper understanding of literature and the manifest forms it appears in. As in other creative fields, writing is a *discipline.* I use that word in two ways: writing is a specialized field of study and scholarship, and it is a skill that requires practice and commitment. The writers you will encounter in this volume are masters of the short form genre—all experts in telling a good story. "Good" is, of course, a subjective term. What I imply here is that successful fiction operates on several levels at the same time, whether that is in terms of language, narrative complexity, thematic resonance, or strong characterization. Usually all of these elements, and more, are present in a piece of short fiction.

In reviewing the title of this book, the question arises: why *short fiction*? This larger term encompasses what we know today as the short story, but also its historical relations: allegories, tales, fables, and myths. Over the centuries, there has been a progression of short form fiction, one text influencing another, driving innovation and standardization. In *The Anthem Guide to Short Fiction* we see the modern era of the short story emerge through a variety of texts. From Nathaniel Hawthorne's allegorical "Young Goodman Brown" to Robert E. Howard's pulp story "Circus Fists," the best qualities of the short form are evident. Within this book's 20 stories is a continuum of prose styles and genres, all technically proficient in their own way, which serves to highlight the vast diversity of literature produced in the last two hundred years.

Reading Stories

When reading a story you should take your time. You should also read each one twice: the first time for enjoyment, the second time to see how the story works. Post-reading, it is often helpful to write down your thoughts, allowing you to assess what you understood about the story. For you, there may be a clash of meaning between what you thought the story was about and the intentions of the writer. Do not worry; this is a natural outcome. To help you navigate this uncertain terrain, you can use the following concepts: *the act of interpretation* and *the understanding of craft*. These two practices can be highlighted by the simple questions below.

Interpretative Questions

How do you interpret the events of the story?
What themes emerge from the story?
Does the protagonist change? Why does he change?
Why does the story have a particular setting?
What elements within the story are symbolic?

Craft Questions

How is the story structured?
Does the story have a conflict?
From whose point of view is the story being told?
Who are the main characters?
What is the story's setting?
What is the story's climax?

In using the above questions and the relevant ones that follow each story, you will analyze and interpret fiction in terms of its elements. This is a useful skill and will help you to be a more active reader. Remember, though, it is also important to view each story as a holistic whole, as something more than the individual components. In almost all cases, short stories are textured; they contain ideas, locations, characters, and questions, which all permeate through the narrative. Therefore, it is difficult to clearly prove one thing means this or that. The best writing works on more than one level. Although, at first, this might prove frustrating, it is a fact that you will come to appreciate and enjoy the more you read. You, as a reader, can only *interpret*. To successfully complete this act in a scholarly fashion, it is necessary to reference passages of text to support your contentions. Doing so will help you to become a close and studious reader, one equally up to the task of creating your own stories.

Writing Stories

One of the unique features of this book is the series of creative activities. These task you to rewrite another author's story. Although this might seem strange, it demands you understand the events of the story and the characters' behaviors and actions. In addition, the act of *becoming* a creative writer will initiate a deep appreciation of the challenges and complexities a professional author faces.

Broadly speaking, the activities fall into two camps: direct and indirect. The former refers to a manipulation or transformation of the original text, while the latter concerns the creation of subsidiary material that does not alter the original text.

Direct

Rewriting the story from another character's point of view.
Rewriting the end of the story.
Continuing on the story.

Indirect

Creating a character's journal.
Composing a newspaper article based on the events in the story.
Creating a musical soundtrack for the story.

The above examples are not exhaustive, but serve to highlight the types of activities that follow each story. Completing a combination of these activities will provide you with several writing skills: narrative construction, consistency in point of view, understanding tone and atmosphere, to name a few. Once the entire book has been read and the activities and discussion questions completed, you will have acquired a strong foundation for reading and understanding literature. Moreover, you will have learned and practiced the requisite tools to write your own original works of fiction.

How to Use This Book

The Anthem Guide to Short Fiction has been specifically designed for ease of use. The book has a simple format: the chapters are arranged chronologically by author's year of birth. Each chapter begins with a biographical note and a short summary of each writer's major works and some of the ideas explored in his or her writing. Following this is the story and then a helpful "Thinking About the Story" section, which lends an intellectual context to the discussion questions and the creative activities. Lastly, at the back of the book is a glossary of literary terms.

The post-story questions exist to foment in-class discussion and analytical thought on behalf of the students. Instructors should consider using a range of individual, pair, and group designations when utilizing the discussion questions. In contrast, the creative activities are more in-depth and provide opportunities for extended classroom activities and individual homework assignments. Further, the activities can be graded assignments, ones that require multiple drafts. Over the semester, it is advisable to give several quizzes on literary terms to encourage students to learn and understand the specialized vocabulary of the discipline.

Nathaniel Hawthorne

We must not always talk in the market place of what happens to us in the forest.
Nathaniel Hawthorne — *The Scarlet Letter* (1850)

A contemporary of Edgar Allan Poe and Henry Wadsworth Longfellow, Nathaniel Hawthorne (1804–1864) is considered one of the preeminent novelists and short story writers of the nineteenth century. Born in Salem, Massachusetts, to a historically Puritan New England family, the young Hawthorne suffered two catastrophes: his father's death (1808), and a lame leg (1813). Hawthorne's time as an invalid allowed him to read widely, especially William Shakespeare's plays and John Bunyan's *Pilgrim's Progress*. Later, he attended Bowdoin College and, after graduating, published his first novel, *Fanshawe* (1828). In 1842, after a three-year engagement, he married a talented painter and linguist, Sophia Peabody. The couple moved to Concord and had three children. After working as a Custom House worker for several years, Hawthorne and his family moved to the Berkshires. In 1853, college friend Franklin Pierce appointed him as a United States consul, and for seven years, Hawthorne and his family lived in Liverpool, England. On their return to the U.S. they moved back to Concord. Four years later, he died after a period of ill health.

During Hawthorne's career, he became friends with the writers Henry David Thoreau and Herman Melville, and he wrote several landmark novels, *The Scarlet Letter* (1850), *The House of the Seven Gables* (1851), and *The Marble Faun* (1860). The historic background for these books allowed Hawthorne to explore past guilt and sin in an innovative context. In tandem with the themes of his novels, Hawthorne's short fiction often comes in the moral tale form, as allegories that exist on two levels: characters and situations are set up to illustrate "good" and "bad" actions. Yet at the same time the stories are replete with bleak romanticism and historical allusion. Collections such as *Twice-Told Tales* (1837) and *Mosses From an Old Manse* (1846), from which "Young Goodman Brown" (1835) was later republished in, should be seen in this dual light. The narrative revels in a concoction of episodic drama and Gothic romance, highlighting a moral center examined and replayed through the main characters. Readers should consider temptation and rebellion, public good and private evil, as touchstones for interpretation. Hawthorne's Puritan past, and his guilt for his ancestors' actions during the Salem Witch Trials, combines within this story to provide a narrative complexity that demands multiple readings.

Young Goodman Brown

Nathaniel Hawthorne

Young Goodman Brown came forth at sunset into the street at Salem village; but put his head back, after crossing the threshold, to exchange a parting kiss with his young wife. And Faith, as the wife was aptly named, thrust her own pretty head into the street, letting the wind play with the pink ribbons of her cap while she called to Goodman Brown.

"Dearest heart," whispered she, softly and rather sadly, when her lips were close to his ear, "prithee put off your journey until sunrise and sleep in your own bed tonight. A lone woman is troubled with such dreams and such thoughts that she's afeard of herself sometimes. Pray tarry with me this night, dear husband, of all nights in the year."

"My love and my Faith," replied young Goodman Brown, "of all nights in the year, this one night must I tarry away from thee. My journey, as thou callest it, forth and back again, must needs be done 'twixt now and sunrise. What, my sweet, pretty wife, dost thou doubt me already, and we but three months married?"

"Then God bless you!" said Faith, with the pink ribbons; "and may you find all well when you come back."

"Amen!" cried Goodman Brown. "Say thy prayers, dear Faith, and go to bed at dusk, and no harm will come to thee."

So they parted; and the young man pursued his way until, being about to turn the corner by the meeting-house, he looked back and saw the head of Faith still peeping after him with a melancholy air, in spite of her pink ribbons.

"Poor little Faith!" thought he, for his heart smote him. "What a wretch am I to leave her on such an errand! She talks of dreams, too. Methought as she spoke there was trouble in her face, as if a dream had warned her what work is to be done tonight. But no, no; 't would kill her to think it. Well, she's a blessed angel on earth; and after this one night I'll cling to her skirts and follow her to heaven."

With this excellent resolve for the future, Goodman Brown felt himself justified in making more haste on his present evil purpose. He had taken a dreary road, darkened by all the gloomiest trees of the forest, which barely stood aside to let the narrow path creep through, and closed immediately behind. It was all as lonely as could be; and there is this peculiarity in such a solitude, that the traveler knows not who may be concealed by the innumerable trunks and the thick boughs overhead; so that with lonely footsteps he may yet be passing through an unseen multitude.

"There may be a devilish Indian behind every tree," said Goodman Brown to himself; and he glanced fearfully behind him as he added, "What if the devil himself should be at my very elbow!"

His head being turned back, he passed a crook of the road, and, looking forward again, beheld the figure of a man, in grave and decent attire, seated at the foot of an old tree. He arose at Goodman Brown's approach and walked onward side by side with him.

"You are late, Goodman Brown," said he. "The clock of the Old South was striking as I came through Boston, and that is full fifteen minutes agone."

"Faith kept me back a while," replied the young man, with a tremor in his voice, caused by the sudden appearance of his companion, though not wholly unexpected.

It was now deep dusk in the forest, and deepest in that part of it where these two were journeying. As nearly as could be discerned, the second traveler was about fifty years old, apparently in the same rank of life as Goodman Brown, and bearing a considerable resemblance to him, though perhaps more in expression than features. Still they might have been taken for father and son. And yet, though the elder person was as simply clad as the younger, and as simple in manner too, he had an indescribable air of one who knew the world, and who would not have felt abashed at the governor's dinner table or in King William's court, were it possible that his affairs should call him thither. But the only thing about him that could be fixed upon as remarkable was his staff, which bore the likeness of a great black snake, so curiously wrought that it might almost be seen to twist and wriggle itself like a living serpent. This, of course, must have been an ocular deception, assisted by the uncertain light.

"Come, Goodman Brown," cried his fellow traveler, "this is a dull pace for the beginning of a journey. Take my staff, if you are so soon weary."

"Friend," said the other, exchanging his slow pace for a full stop, "having kept covenant by meeting thee here, it is my purpose now to return whence I came. I have scruples touching the matter thou wot'st of."

"Sayest thou so?" replied he of the serpent, smiling apart. "Let us walk on, nevertheless, reasoning as we go; and if I convince thee not thou shalt turn back. We are but a little way in the forest yet."

"Too far! Too far!" exclaimed the goodman, unconsciously resuming his walk. "My father never went into the woods on such an errand, nor his father before him. We have been a race of honest men and good Christians since the days of the martyrs; and shall I be the first of the name of Brown that ever took this path and kept"—

"Such company, thou wouldst say," observed the elder person, interpreting his pause. "Well said, Goodman Brown! I have been as well acquainted with your family as with ever a one among the Puritans; and that's no trifle to say. I helped your grandfather, the constable, when he lashed the Quaker woman so smartly through the streets of Salem; and it was I that brought your father a pitch-pine knot, kindled at my own hearth, to set fire to an Indian village, in King Philip's war. They were my good friends, both; and many a pleasant walk have we had along this path, and returned merrily after midnight. I would fain be friends with you for their sake."

"If it be as thou sayest," replied Goodman Brown, "I marvel they never spoke of these matters; or, verily, I marvel not, seeing that the least rumor of the sort would have driven them from New England. We are a people of prayer, and good works to boot, and abide no such wickedness."

"Wickedness or not," said the traveler with the twisted staff, "I have a very general acquaintance here in New England. The deacons of many a church have drunk the communion wine with me; the selectmen of divers towns make me their chairman; and a majority of the Great and General Court are firm supporters of my interest. The governor and I, too—But these are state secrets."

"Can this be so?" cried Goodman Brown, with a stare of amazement at his undisturbed companion. "Howbeit, I have nothing to do with the governor and council; they have their own ways, and are no rule for a simple husbandman like me. But, were I to go on with thee, how should I meet the eye of that good old man, our minister, at Salem village? Oh, his voice would make me tremble both Sabbath day and lecture day."

Thus far the elder traveler had listened with due gravity; but now burst into a fit of irrepressible mirth, shaking himself so violently that his snake-like staff actually seemed to wriggle in sympathy.

"Ha! Ha! Ha!" shouted he again and again; then composing himself, "Well, go on, Goodman Brown, go on; but, prithee, don't kill me with laughing."

"Well, then, to end the matter at once," said Goodman Brown, considerably nettled, "there is my wife, Faith. It would break her dear little heart; and I'd rather break my own."

"Nay, if that be the case," answered the other, "e'en go thy ways, Goodman Brown. I would not for twenty old women like the one hobbling before us that Faith should come to any harm."

As he spoke he pointed his staff at a female figure on the path, in whom Goodman Brown recognized a very pious and exemplary dame, who had taught him his catechism in youth, and was still his moral and spiritual adviser, jointly with the minister and Deacon Gookin.

"A marvel, truly, that Goody Cloyse should be so far in the wilderness at nightfall," said he. "But with your leave, friend, I shall take a cut through the woods until we have left this Christian woman behind. Being a stranger to you, she might ask whom I was consorting with and whither I was going."

"Be it so," said his fellow traveler. "Betake you to the woods, and let me keep the path."

Accordingly the young man turned aside, but took care to watch his companion, who advanced softly along the road until he had come within a staff's length of the old dame. She, meanwhile, was making the best of her way, with singular speed for so aged a woman, and mumbling some indistinct words—a prayer, doubtless—as she went. The traveler put forth his staff and touched her withered neck with what seemed the serpent's tail.

"The devil!" screamed the pious old lady.

"Then Goody Cloyse knows her old friend?" observed the traveler, confronting her and leaning on his writhing stick.

"Ah, forsooth, and is it your worship indeed?" cried the good dame. "Yes, truly is it, and in the very image of my old gossip, Goodman Brown, the grandfather of the silly fellow that now is. But—would your worship believe it?—my broomstick hath strangely disappeared, stolen, as I suspect, by that unhanged witch, Goody Cory, and that, too, when I was all anointed with the juice of smallage, and cinquefoil, and wolf's bane"—

"Mingled with fine wheat and the fat of a new-born babe," said the shape of old Goodman Brown.

"Ah, your worship knows the recipe," cried the old lady, cackling aloud. "So, as I was saying, being all ready for the meeting, and no horse to ride on, I made up my mind to foot it; for they tell me there is a nice young man to be taken into communion tonight. But now your good worship will lend me your arm, and we shall be there in a twinkling."

"That can hardly be," answered her friend. "I may not spare you my arm, Goody Cloyse; but here is my staff, if you will."

So saying, he threw it down at her feet, where, perhaps, it assumed life, being one of the rods which its owner had formerly lent to the Egyptian magi. Of this fact, however, Goodman Brown could not take cognizance. He had cast up his eyes in astonishment, and, looking down again, beheld neither Goody Cloyse nor the serpentine staff, but his fellow traveler alone, who waited for him as calmly as if nothing had happened.

"That old woman taught me my catechism," said the young man; and there was a world of meaning in this simple comment.

They continued to walk onward, while the elder traveler exhorted his companion to make good speed and persevere in the path, discoursing so aptly that his arguments seemed rather to spring up in the bosom of his auditor than to be suggested by himself. As they went, he plucked a branch of maple to serve for a walking stick, and began to strip it of the twigs and little boughs, which were wet with evening dew. The moment his fingers touched them they became strangely withered and dried up as with a week's sunshine. Thus the pair proceeded, at a good free pace, until suddenly, in a gloomy hollow of the road, Goodman Brown sat himself down on the stump of a tree and refused to go any farther.

"Friend," said he, stubbornly, "my mind is made up. Not another step will I budge on this errand. What if a wretched old woman do choose to go to the devil when I thought she was going to heaven: is that any reason why I should quit my dear Faith and go after her?"

"You will think better of this by and by," said his acquaintance, composedly. "Sit here and rest yourself a while; and when you feel like moving again, there is my staff to help you along."

Without more words, he threw his companion the maple stick, and was as speedily out of sight as if he had vanished into the deepening gloom. The young man sat a few moments by the roadside, applauding himself greatly, and thinking with how clear a conscience he should meet the minister in his morning walk, nor shrink from the eye of good old Deacon Gookin. And what calm sleep would be his that very night, which was to have been spent so wickedly, but so purely and sweetly now, in the arms of Faith! Amidst these pleasant and praiseworthy meditations, Goodman Brown heard the tramp of horses along the road, and deemed it advisable to conceal himself within the verge of the forest, conscious of the guilty purpose that had brought him thither, though now so happily turned from it.

On came the hoof tramps and the voices of the riders, two grave old voices, conversing soberly as they drew near. These mingled sounds appeared to pass along the road, within a few yards of the young man's hiding-place; but, owing doubtless to the depth of the gloom at that particular spot, neither the travelers nor their steeds were visible. Though their figures brushed the small boughs by the wayside, it could not be seen that they intercepted, even for a moment, the faint gleam from the strip of bright sky athwart which they must have passed. Goodman Brown alternately crouched and stood on tiptoe, pulling aside the branches and thrusting forth his head as far as he durst without discerning so much as a shadow. It vexed him the more, because he could have sworn, were such a thing possible, that he recognized the voices of the minister and Deacon Gookin, jogging along quietly, as they were wont to do, when bound to some ordination or ecclesiastical council. While yet within hearing, one of the riders stopped to pluck a switch.

"Of the two, reverend sir," said the voice like the deacon's, "I had rather miss an ordination dinner than tonight's meeting. They tell me that some of our community are to be here from Falmouth and beyond, and others from Connecticut and Rhode Island, besides several of the Indian powwows, who, after their fashion, know almost as much deviltry as the best of us. Moreover, there is a goodly young woman to be taken into communion."

"Mighty well, Deacon Gookin!" replied the solemn old tones of the minister. "Spur up, or we shall be late. Nothing can be done, you know, until I get on the ground."

The hoofs clattered again; and the voices, talking so strangely in the empty air, passed on through the forest, where no church had ever been gathered or solitary Christian prayed. Whither, then, could these holy men be journeying so deep into the heathen wilderness? Young Goodman Brown caught hold of a tree for support, being ready to sink down on the ground, faint and overburdened with the heavy sickness of his heart. He looked up to the sky, doubting whether there really was a heaven above him. Yet there was the blue arch, and the stars brightening in it.

"With heaven above and Faith below, I will yet stand firm against the devil!" cried Goodman Brown.

While he still gazed upward into the deep arch of the firmament and had lifted his hands to pray, a cloud, though no wind was stirring, hurried across the zenith and hid the brightening stars. The blue sky was still visible, except directly overhead, where this black mass of cloud was sweeping swiftly northward. Aloft in the air, as if from the depths of the cloud, came a confused and doubtful sound of voices. Once the listener fancied that he could distinguish the accents of towns-people of his own, men and women, both pious and ungodly, many of whom he had met at the communion table, and had seen others rioting at the tavern. The next moment, so indistinct were the sounds, he doubted whether he had heard aught but the murmur of the old forest, whispering without a wind. Then came a stronger swell of those familiar tones, heard daily in the sunshine at Salem village, but never until now from a cloud of night. There was one voice of a young woman, uttering lamentations, yet with an uncertain sorrow, and entreating for some favor, which, perhaps, it would grieve her to obtain; and all the unseen multitude, both saints and sinners, seemed to encourage her onward.

"Faith!" shouted Goodman Brown, in a voice of agony and desperation; and the echoes of the forest mocked him, crying, "Faith! Faith!" as if bewildered wretches were seeking her all through the wilderness.

The cry of grief, rage, and terror was yet piercing the night, when the unhappy husband held his breath for a response. There was a scream, drowned immediately in a louder murmur of voices, fading into far-off laughter, as the dark cloud swept away, leaving the clear and silent sky above Goodman Brown. But something fluttered lightly down through the air and caught on the branch of a tree. The young man seized it, and beheld a pink ribbon.

"My Faith is gone!" cried he, after one stupefied moment. "There is no good on earth; and sin is but a name. Come, devil; for to thee is this world given."

And, maddened with despair, so that he laughed loud and long, did Goodman Brown grasp his staff and set forth again, at such a rate that he seemed to fly along the forest path rather than to walk or run. The road grew wilder and drearier and more faintly traced, and vanished at length, leaving him in the heart of the dark wilderness, still rushing onward with the instinct that guides mortal man to evil. The whole forest was peopled with frightful sounds—the creaking of the trees, the howling of wild beasts, and the yell of Indians; while sometimes the wind tolled like a distant church bell, and sometimes gave a broad roar around the traveler, as if all Nature were laughing him to scorn. But he was himself the chief horror of the scene, and shrank not from its other horrors.

"Ha! Ha! Ha!" roared Goodman Brown when the wind laughed at him. "Let us hear which will laugh loudest. Think not to frighten me with your deviltry. Come witch, come wizard, come Indian powwow, come devil himself, and here comes Goodman Brown. You may as well fear him as he fear you."

In truth, all through the haunted forest there could be nothing more frightful than the figure of Goodman Brown. On he flew among the black pines, brandishing his staff with frenzied gestures, now giving vent to an inspiration of horrid blasphemy, and now shouting forth such laughter as set all the echoes of the forest laughing like demons around him. The fiend in his own shape is less hideous than when he rages in the breast of man. Thus sped the demoniac on his course, until, quivering among the trees, he saw a red light before him, as when the felled trunks and branches of a clearing have been set on fire, and throw up their lurid blaze against the sky, at the hour of midnight. He paused, in a lull of the tempest that had driven him onward, and heard the swell of what seemed a hymn, rolling solemnly from a distance with the weight of many voices. He knew the tune; it was a familiar one in the choir of the village meetinghouse. The verse died heavily away, and was lengthened by a chorus, not of human voices, but of all the sounds of the benighted wilderness pealing in awful harmony together. Goodman Brown cried out, and his cry was lost to his own ear by its unison with the cry of the desert.

In the interval of silence he stole forward until the light glared full upon his eyes. At one extremity of an open space, hemmed in by the dark wall of the forest, arose a rock, bearing some rude, natural resemblance either to an alter or a pulpit, and surrounded by four blazing pines, their tops aflame, their stems untouched, like candles at an evening meeting. The mass of foliage that had overgrown the summit of the rock was all on fire, blazing high into the night and fitfully illuminating the whole field. Each pendent twig and leafy festoon was in a blaze. As the red light arose and fell, a numerous congregation alternately shone forth, then disappeared in shadow, and again grew, as it were, out of the darkness, peopling the heart of the solitary woods at once.

"A grave and dark-clad company," quoth Goodman Brown.

In truth they were such. Among them, quivering to and fro between gloom and splendor, appeared faces that would be seen next day at the council board of the province, and others, which, Sabbath after Sabbath, looked devoutly heavenward, and benignantly over the crowded pews, from the holiest pulpits in the land. Some affirm that the lady of the governor was there. At least there were high dames well known to her, and wives of honored husbands, and widows, a great multitude, and ancient maidens, all of excellent repute, and fair young girls, who trembled lest their mothers should espy them. Either the sudden gleams of light flashing over the obscure field bedazzled Goodman Brown, or he recognized a score of the church members of Salem village famous for their especial sanctity. Good old Deacon Gookin had arrived, and waited at the skirts of that venerable saint, his revered pastor. But, irreverently consorting with these grave, reputable, and pious people, these elders of the church, these chaste dames and dewy virgins, there were men of dissolute lives and women of spotted fame, wretches given over to all mean and filthy vice, and suspected even of horrid crimes. It was strange to see that the good shrank not from the wicked, nor were the sinners abashed by the saints. Scattered also among their pale-faced enemies were the Indian priests, or powwows, who had often scared their native forest with more hideous incantations than any known to English witchcraft.

"But where is Faith?" thought Goodman Brown; and, as hope came into his heart, he trembled.

Another verse of the hymn arose, a slow and mournful strain, such as the pious love, but joined to words which expressed all that our nature can conceive of sin, and darkly hinted at far more. Unfathomable to mere mortals is the lore of fiends. Verse after verse was sung; and still the chorus of the desert swelled between like the deepest tone of a mighty organ; and with the final peal of that dreadful anthem there came a sound, as if the roaring wind, the rushing streams, the howling beasts, and every other voice of the unconcerted wilderness were mingling and according with the voice of guilty man in homage to the prince of all. The four blazing pines threw up a loftier flame, and obscurely discovered shapes and visages of horror on the smoke wreaths above the impious assembly. At the same moment the fire on the rock shot redly forth and formed a glowing arch above its base, where now appeared a figure. With reverence be it spoken, the figure bore no slight similitude, both in garb and manner, to some grave divine of the New England churches.

"Bring forth the converts!" cried a voice that echoed through the field and rolled into the forest.

At the word, Goodman Brown stepped forth from the shadow of the trees and approached the congregation, with whom he felt a loathful brotherhood by the sympathy of all that was wicked in his heart. He could have well nigh sworn that the shape of his own dead father beckoned him to advance, looking downward from a smoke wreath, while a woman, with dim features of despair, threw out her hand to warn him back. Was it his mother? But he had no power to retreat one step, nor to resist, even in thought, when the minister and good old Deacon Gookin seized his arms and led him to the blazing rock. Thither came also the slender form of a veiled female, led between Goody Cloyse, that pious teacher of the catechism, and Martha Carrier, who had received the devil's promise to be queen of hell. A rampant hag was she. And there stood the proselytes beneath the canopy of fire.

"Welcome, my children," said the dark figure, "to the communion of your race. Ye have found thus young your nature and your destiny. My children, look behind you!"

They turned; and flashing forth, as it were, in a sheet of flame, the fiend worshippers were seen; the smile of welcome gleamed darkly on every visage.

"There," resumed the sable form, "are all whom ye have reverenced from youth. Ye deemed them holier than yourselves, and shrank from your own sin, contrasting it with their lives of righteousness and prayerful aspirations heavenward. Yet here are they all in my worshipping assembly. This night it shall be granted you to know their secret deeds: how hoary-bearded elders of the church have whispered wanton words to the young maids of their households; how many a woman, eager for widows' weeds, has given her husband a drink at bedtime and let him sleep his last sleep in her bosom; how beardless youths have made haste to inherit their fathers' wealth; and how fair damsels—blush not, sweet ones—have dug little graves in the garden, and bidden me, the sole guest to an infant's funeral. By the sympathy of your human hearts for sin ye shall scent out all the places—whether in church, bedchamber, street, field, or forest—where crime has been committed, and shall exult to behold the whole earth one stain of guilt, one mighty blood spot. Far more than this. It shall be yours to penetrate, in every bosom, the deep mystery of sin, the fountain of all wicked arts, and which inexhaustibly supplies more evil impulses than human power—than my power at its utmost—can make manifest in deeds. And now, my children, look upon each other."

They did so; and, by the blaze of the hell-kindled torches, the wretched man beheld his Faith, and the wife her husband, trembling before that unhallowed altar.

"Lo, there ye stand, my children," said the figure, in a deep and solemn tone, almost sad with its despairing awfulness, as if his once angelic nature could yet mourn for our miserable race. "Depending upon one another's hearts, ye had still hoped that virtue were not all a dream. Now are ye undeceived. Evil is the nature of mankind. Evil must be your only happiness. Welcome again, my children, to the communion of your race."

"Welcome," repeated the fiend worshippers, in one cry of despair and triumph.

And there they stood, the only pair, as it seemed, who were yet hesitating on the verge of wickedness in this dark world. A basin was hollowed, naturally, in the rock. Did it contain water, reddened by the lurid light? Or was it blood? Or, perchance, a liquid flame? Herein did the shape of evil dip his hand and prepare to lay the mark of baptism upon their foreheads, that they might be partakers of the mystery of sin, more conscious of the secret guilt of others, both in deed and thought, than they could now be of their own. The husband cast one look at his pale wife, and Faith at him. What polluted wretches would the next glance show them to each other, shuddering alike at what they disclosed and what they saw!

"Faith! Faith!" cried the husband, "look up to heaven, and resist the wicked one."

Whether Faith obeyed he knew not. Hardly had he spoken when he found himself amid calm night and solitude, listening to a roar of the wind, which died heavily away through the forest. He staggered against the rock, and felt it chill and damp; while a hanging twig, that had been all on fire, besprinkled his cheek with the coldest dew.

The next morning young Goodman Brown came slowly into the street of Salem village, staring around him like a bewildered man. The good old minister was taking a walk along the graveyard to get an appetite for breakfast and meditate his sermon, and bestowed a blessing, as he passed, on Goodman Brown. He shrank from the venerable saint as if to avoid an anathema. Old Deacon Gookin was at domestic worship, and the holy words of his prayer were heard through the open window. "What God doth the wizard pray to?" quoth Goodman Brown. Goody Cloyse, that excellent old Christian, stood in the early sunshine at her own lattice, catechizing a little girl who had brought her a pint of morning's milk. Goodman Brown snatched away the child as from the grasp of the fiend himself. Turning the corner by the meetinghouse, he spied the head of Faith, with the pink ribbons, gazing anxiously forth, and bursting into such joy at sight of him that she skipped along the street and almost kissed her husband before the whole village. But Goodman Brown looked sternly and sadly into her face, and passed on without a greeting.

Had Goodman Brown fallen asleep in the forest and only dreamed a wild dream of a witch-meeting?

Be it so if you will; but, alas! It was a dream of evil omen for young Goodman Brown. A stern, a sad, a darkly meditative, a distrustful, if not a desperate man did he become from the night of that fearful dream. On the Sabbath day, when the congregation were singing a holy psalm, he could not listen because an anthem of sin rushed loudly upon his ear and drowned all the blessed strain. When the minister spoke from the pulpit with power and fervid eloquence, and, with his hand on the open Bible, of the sacred truths of our religion, and of saint-like lives and triumphant deaths, and of future bliss or misery unutterable, then did Goodman Brown turn pale, dreading lest the roof should thunder down upon the gray blasphemer and his hearers. Often, waking suddenly at midnight, he shrank from the bosom of Faith; and at morning or eventide, when the family knelt down at prayer, he scowled and muttered to himself, and gazed sternly at his wife, and turned away. And when he had lived long, and was borne to his grave a hoary corpse, followed by Faith, an aged woman, and children and grandchildren, a goodly procession, besides neighbors not a few, they carved no hopeful verse upon his tombstone, for his dying hour was gloom.

Thinking About the Story

Over the years, scholars have disputed the meaning of "Young Goodman Brown" and the lesson that Nathaniel Hawthorne wanted to impart upon his readers. One thing, though, is clear: Hawthorne invokes through symbolism and allusion the Puritan tenets of male self-doubt and examination. After reading the story, you should research the historical nature of Puritanism to further deepen your understanding of Hawthorne's work. Moreover, when considering the manner in which you are going to interpret this story, it's important to know you can read Brown's journey into the forest in three distinct ways: as a dream, as a trick played by the devil, or as an actual occurrence. Whichever way you interpret this section, understanding the whole story as part of the moral allegory tradition is essential. To broaden your knowledge of this genre, compare and contrast "Young Goodman Brown" with Rudyard Kipling's "Mowgli's Brothers" and with Leo Tolstoy's "How Much Land Does a Man Need?"

Discussion Questions

1. Underline specific parts of the story that you consider emblematic of Puritan values. Next, bearing your discoveries in mind, what are the moral themes that emerge in the story?

2. What are your thoughts on Goodman Brown's encounters with (a) the man with the walking stick? (b) Goody Cloyse? and (c) Faith? Next, discuss the forest setting. In what ways is it a necessary part of the story?

3. Consider Young Goodman Brown's statement: "My Faith is gone!" What are the possible meanings and repercussions of his outburst?

Further, what significance do you read into the character's names and titles of address?

4. Formulate your thoughts on the behavior and actions of Goodman Brown. Do you think Goodman Brown is deluding himself? Why is he so obsessed with sin and guilt? What are his feelings toward women?

5. How do you interpret the story's last sentence? Do you find the story's end to be ambiguous or clear-cut? Explain your answer.

Activities

1. Look again at the first ten instances of dialogue. The language used is an attempt at seventeenth-century English. Convert the dialogue into what you consider to be modern-day speech.

2. Imagine yourself as a newspaper reporter. Write a short article on the events that occur in the forest. Remember to be impartial, to stick to the facts, and to consider incorporating "interviews" with the characters.

3. Create your own moral tale. First, list examples of contemporary injustices. For example, human trafficking, the blood diamond trade, or Third World poverty. Second, choose one of your own injustices and identify a moral that can be personified through a fictional character or situation.

Edgar Allan Poe

I became insane, with long intervals of horrible sanity.
Edgar Allan Poe — *Private letter* (1846)

Master of the Gothic tale and innovator of the detective story, Edgar Allan Poe (1809-1849) had a profound influence upon nineteenth-century literature. Born in Boston, Massachusetts, to a family of stage actors, Poe's parents died when he was a young child. He was taken in by the Allan family, tobacco merchants in Richmond, Virginia. When the Allans' moved to Britain, Poe was schooled in Irvine and London. Later, he continued his education in the U. S. and excelled in Latin, Greek, and French. After accruing significant gambling debts at the University of Virginia, he enlisted in the U. S. Army. Within three years he had been promoted to sergeant major and accepted into West Point. In 1836 he married his young cousin, Virginia Clemm. She, though, died in 1847, and this event exacerbated Poe's alcoholism and depression. Poe died in strange circumstances. In Baltimore, he was found unconscious and dressed in someone else's clothes. He was taken to a hospital where he died a few days later.

During his life Poe was a noted poet, who also completed one novel, *The Narrative of Arthur Gordon Pym of Nantucket* (1838). Unquestionably, his fame and influence lies in the quality and complexity of his short stories. Collections such as *Tales of the Grotesque and Arabesque* (1840) cement his reputation as a master of the form. Poe's fiction surpasses his Gothic influences, creating a new urban configuration that re-envisions the world of doubles, buried secrets, and murderous crime. Using the excesses of urban density and the chaos of the crowd, Poe leads the reader to psychological terror and unexplained madness. Characters are forced to view themselves; exposed are their exterior movements and interior mental processes. In his later work, Poe fashions the struggle between the irrational mind and the rational world into the detective story. Clues to this artistic development are seen in "The Man of the Crowd" (1840). No doubt influenced by Charles Dickens' society sketches, the story transcends the parameters of Dickens' intentions. In the story's second half, Poe moves into new territory: the obsessive voyeur. Seen in the light of Victorian social and cultural sensibilities, the narrator emerges attuned to the minutiae of society, but also intrigued by the potential of the individual.

The Man of the Crowd

Edgar Allan Poe

Ce grand malheur, de ne pouvoir être seul. — La Bruyère

It was well said of a certain German book that *"es lässt sich nicht lesen"*—it does not permit itself to be read. There are some secrets which do not permit themselves to be told. Men die nightly in their beds, wringing the hands of ghostly confessors, and looking them piteously in the eyes—die with despair of heart and convulsion of throat, on account of the hideousness of mysteries which will not *suffer themselves* to be revealed. Now and then, alas, the conscience of man takes up a burthen so heavy in horror that it can be thrown down only into the grave. And thus the essence of all crime is undivulged.

Not long ago, about the closing in of an evening in autumn, I sat at the large bow window of the D—— Coffee House in London. For some months I had been ill in health, but was now convalescent, and, with returning strength, found myself in one of those happy moods which are so precisely the converse of *ennui*—moods of the keenest appetency, when the film from the mental vision departs—*achlus os prin epeen*—and the intellect, electrified, surpasses as greatly its everyday condition, as does the vivid yet candid reason of Leibnitz, the mad and flimsy rhetoric of Gorgias. Merely to breathe was enjoyment; and I derived positive pleasure even from many of the legitimate sources of pain. I felt a calm but inquisitive interest in everything. With a cigar in my mouth and a newspaper in my lap, I had been amusing myself for the greater part of the afternoon, now in poring over advertisements, now in observing the promiscuous company in the room, and now in peering through the smoky panes into the street.

This latter is one of the principal thoroughfares of the city, and had been very much crowded during the whole day. But, as the darkness came on, the throng momently increased; and, by the time the lamps were well lighted, two dense and continuous tides of population were rushing past the door. At this particular period of the evening I had never before been in a similar situation, and the tumultuous sea of human heads filled me, therefore, with a delicious novelty of emotion. I gave up, at length, all care of things within the hotel, and became absorbed in contemplation of the scene without.

At first my observations took an abstract and generalizing turn. I looked at the passengers in masses, and thought of them in their aggregate relations. Soon, however, I descended to details, and regarded with minute interest the innumerable varieties of detail, dress, air, gait, visage, and expression of countenance.

By far the greater number of those who went by had a satisfied business-like demeanour, and seemed to be thinking only of making their way through the press. Their brows were knit, and their eyes rolled quickly; when pushed against by fellow-wayfarers they evinced no symptom of impatience, but adjusted their clothes and hurried on. Others, still a numerous class, were restless in their movements, had flushed faces, and talked and gesticulated to themselves, as if feeling in solitude on account of the very denseness of the company around. When impeded in their progress, these people suddenly ceased muttering, but redoubled their gesticulations, and awaited, with an absent and overdone smile upon the lips, the course of the persons impeding them. If jostled, they bowed profusely to the jostlers, and appeared overwhelmed with confusion. There was nothing very distinctive about these two large classes beyond what I have noted. Their habiliments belonged to that order which is pointedly termed the decent. They were undoubtedly noblemen, merchants, attorneys, tradesmen, stock-jobbers—the Eupatrids and the commonplaces of society—men of leisure and men actively engaged in affairs of their own, conducting business upon their own responsibility. They did not greatly excite my attention.

The tribe of clerks was an obvious one; and here I discerned two remarkable divisions. There were the junior clerks of flash houses—young gentlemen with tight coats, bright boots, well-oiled hair, and supercilious lips. Setting aside a certain dapperness of carriage, which may be termed *deskism* for want of a better word, the manner of these persons seemed to me an exact facsimile of what had been the perfection of *bon ton* about twelve or eighteen months before. They wore the cast-off graces of the gentry; and this, I believe, involves the best definition of the class.

The division of the upper clerks of staunch firms, or of the "steady old fellows," it was not possible to mistake. These were known by their coats and pantaloons of black or brown, made to sit comfortably, with white cravats and waistcoats, broad solid-looking shoes, and thick hose or gaiters. They had all slightly bald heads, from which the right ears, long used to pen-holding, had an odd habit of standing off on end. I observed that they always removed or settled their hats with both hands, and wore watches, with short gold chains of a substantial and ancient pattern. Theirs was the affectation of respectability; if indeed there be an affectation so honourable.

There were many individuals of dashing appearance, whom I easily understood as belonging to the race of swell pick-pockets, with which all great cities are infested. I watched these gentry with much inquisitiveness, and found it difficult to imagine how they should ever be mistaken for gentlemen by gentlemen themselves. Their voluminousness of wristband, with an air of excessive frankness, should betray them at once.

The gamblers, of whom I described not a few, were still more easily recognizable. They wore every variety of dress, from that of the desperate thimble-rig bully, with velvet waistcoat, fancy neckerchief, gilt chains, and filigreed buttons, to that of the scrupulously inornate clergyman than which nothing could be less liable to suspicion. Still all were distinguished by a certain sodden swarthiness of complexion, a filmy dimness of eye, and pallor and compression of lip. There were two other traits, moreover, by which I could always detect them; a guarded lowness of tone in conversation, and a more than ordinary extension of the thumb in a direction at right angles with the fingers. Very often, in company with these sharpers, I observed an order of men somewhat different in habits, but still birds of a kindred feather. They may be defined as the gentlemen who live by their wits. They seem to prey upon the public in two battalions—that of the dandies and that of the military men. Of the first grade the leading features are long locks and smiles; of the second frogged coats and frowns.

Descending in the scale of what is termed gentility, I found darker and deeper themes for speculation. I saw Jew pedlars, with hawk eyes flashing from countenances whose every other feature wore only an expression of abject humility; sturdy professional street beggars scowling upon mendicants of a better stamp, whom despair alone had driven forth into the night for charity; feeble and ghastly invalids, upon whom death had placed a sure hand, and who sidled and tottered through the mob, looking every one beseechingly in the face, as if in search of some chance consolation, some lost hope; modest young girls returning from long and late labour to a cheerless home, and shrinking more tearfully than indignantly from the glance of ruffians, whose direct contact, even, could not be avoided; women of the town of all kinds and of all ages—the unequivocal beauty in the prime of her womanhood, putting one in mind of the statue in Lucian, with the surface of Parthian marble, and the interior filled with filth—the loathsome and utterly lost leper in rags—the wrinkled, bejewelled, and paint-begrimed beldame, making a last effort at youth—the mere child of immature form, yet, from long association, an adept in the dreadful coquetries of her trade, and burning with a rabid ambition to be ranked the equal of her elders in vice; drunkards innumerable and indescribable—some in shreds and patches, reeling, inarticulate, with bruised visage and lack-lustre eyes—some in whole although filthy garments, with a slightly-unsteady swagger, thick sensual lips, and hearty-looking rubicund faces—others clothed in materials which had once been good, and which even now were scrupulously well brushed—men who walked with a more than naturally firm and springy step, but whose countenances were fearfully pale, whose eyes hideously wild and red, and who clutched with quivering fingers, as they strode through the crowd, at every object which came within their reach; beside these, pie-men, porters, coal-heavers, sweeps; organ-grinders, monkey-exhibitors, and ballad-mongers, those who vended with those who sang; ragged artisans and exhausted labourers of every description, and all full of a noisy and inordinate vivacity which jarred discordantly upon the ear, and gave an aching sensation to the eye.

As the night deepened, so deepened to me the interest of the scene; for not only did the general character of the crowd materially alter (its gentler features retiring in the gradual withdrawal of the more orderly portion of the people, and its harsher ones coming out into bolder relief, as the late hour brought forth every species of infamy from its den), but the rays of the gas-lamps, feeble at first in their struggle with the dying day, had now at length gained ascendancy, and threw over everything a fitful and garish lustre. All was dark yet splendid—as that ebony to which has been likened the style of Tertullian.

The wild effects of the light enchained me to an examination of individual faces; and although the rapidity with which the world of light flitted before the window, prevented me from casting more than a glance upon each visage, still it seemed that, in my then peculiar mental state, I could frequently read, even in that brief interval of a glance, the history of long years.

With my brow to the glass, I was thus occupied in scrutinizing the mob, when suddenly there came into view a countenance (that of a decrepit old man, some sixty-five or seventy years of age)—a countenance that at once arrested and absorbed my whole attention, on account of the absolute idiosyncrasy of its expression. Anything even remotely resembling that expression I had never seen before. I well remember that my first thought, upon beholding it, was that Retszch, had he viewed it, would have greatly preferred it to his own pictural incarnations of the fiend. As I endeavoured, during the brief minute of my original survey, to form some analysis of the meaning conveyed, there arose confusedly and paradoxically within my mind, the ideas of vast mental power, of caution, of penuriousness, of avarice, of coolness, of malice, of blood-thirstiness, of triumph, of merriment, of excessive terror, of intense—of extreme despair. I felt singularly aroused, startled, fascinated. "How wild a history," I said to myself, "is written within that bosom!" Then came a craving desire to keep the man in view—to know more of him. Hurriedly putting on an overcoat, and seizing my hat and cane, I made my way into the street, and pushed through the crowd in the direction which I had seen him take; for he had already disappeared. With some little difficulty I at length came within sight of him, approached, and followed him closely, yet cautiously, so as not to attract his attention.

I had now a good opportunity of examining his person. He was short in stature, very thin, and apparently very feeble. His clothes, generally, were filthy and ragged; but as he came, now and then, within the strong glare of a lamp, I perceived that his linen, although dirty, was of beautiful texture;

and my vision deceived me, or, through a rent in a closely-buttoned and evidently second-handed *roquelaure* which enveloped him, I caught a glimpse both of a diamond and of a dagger. These observations heightened my curiosity, and I resolved to follow the stranger whithersoever he should go.

It was now fully nightfall, and a thick humid fog hung over the city, soon ending in a settled and heavy rain. This change of weather had an odd effect upon the crowd, the whole of which was at once put into new commotion, and overshadowed by a world of umbrellas. The waver, the jostle, and the hum increased in a tenfold degree. For my own part I did not much regard the rain—the lurking of an old fever in my system rendering the moisture somewhat too dangerously pleasant. Tying a handkerchief about my mouth, I kept on. For half an hour the old man held his way with difficulty along the great thoroughfare; and I here walked close at his elbow through fear of losing sight of him. Never once turning his head to look back, he did not observe me. By and by, he passed into a cross street, which, although densely filled with people, was not quite so much thronged as the main one he had quitted. Here a change in his demeanour became evident. He walked more slowly and with less object than before—more hesitatingly. He crossed and re-crossed the way repeatedly without apparent aim; and the press was still so thick, that, at every such movement, I was obliged to follow him closely. The street was a narrow and long one, and his course lay within it for nearly an hour, during which the passengers had gradually diminished to about that number which is ordinarily seen at noon in Broadway near the Park—so vast a difference is there between a London populace and that of the most frequented American city. A second turn brought us into a square, brilliantly lighted, and, overflowing with life. The old manner of the stranger reappeared. His chin fell upon his breast, while his eyes rolled wildly from under his knit brows, in every direction, upon those who hemmed him in. He urged his way steadily and perseveringly. I was surprised, however, to find, upon his having made the circuit of the square, that he turned and retraced his steps. Still more was I astonished to see him repeat the same walk several times—once nearly detecting me as he came round with a sudden movement.

In this exercise he spent another hour, at the end of which we met with far less interruption from passengers than at first. The rain fell fast;

the air grew cool; and the people were retiring to their homes. With a gesture of impatience, the wanderer passed into a by-street comparatively deserted. Down this, some quarter of a mile long, he rushed with an activity I could not have dreamed of seeing in one so aged, and which put me to much trouble in pursuit. A few minutes brought us to a large and busy bazaar, with the localities of which the stranger appeared well acquainted, and where his original demeanour again became apparent, as he forced his way to and fro, without aim, among the host of buyers and sellers.

During the hour and a half, or thereabouts, which we passed in this place, it required much caution on my part to keep him within reach without attracting his observation. Luckily I wore a pair of caoutchouc over-shoes, and could move about in perfect silence. At no moment did he see that I watched him. He entered shop after shop, priced nothing, spoke no word, and looked at all objects with a wild and vacant stare. I was now utterly amazed at his behaviour, and firmly resolved that we should not part until I had satisfied myself in some measure respecting him.

A loud-toned clock struck eleven, and the company were fast deserting the bazaar. A shop-keeper, in putting up a shutter, jostled the old man, and at the instant I saw a strong shudder come over his frame. He hurried into the street, looked anxiously around him for an instant, and then ran with incredible swiftness through many crooked and people-less lanes, until we emerged once more upon the great thoroughfare whence we had started: the street of the D—— Hotel. It no longer wore, however, the same aspect. It was still brilliant with gas; but the rain fell fiercely, and there were few persons to be seen. The stranger grew pale. He walked moodily some paces up the once populous avenue, then, with a heavy sigh, turned in the direction of the river, and, plunging through a great variety of devious ways, came out, at length, in view of one of the principal theatres. It was about being closed, and the audience were thronging the doors. I saw the old man gasp as if for breath while he threw himself amid the crowd; but I thought that the intense agony of his countenance had, in some measure, abated. His head again fell upon his breast; he appeared as I had seen him at first. I observed that he now took the course in which had gone the greater number of the audience—but, upon the whole, I was at a loss to comprehend the waywardness of his actions.

As he proceeded, the company grew more scattered, and his old uneasiness and vacillation were resumed. For some time he followed closely a party of some ten or twelve roisterers; but from this number one by one dropped off, until three only remained together, in a narrow and gloomy lane little frequented. The stranger paused, and, for a moment, seemed lost in thought, then, with every mark of agitation, pursued rapidly a route which brought us to the verge of the city, amid regions very different from those we had hitherto traversed. It was the most noisome quarter of London, where everything wore the worst impress of the most deplorable poverty, and of the most desperate crime. By the dim light of an accidental lamp, tall, antique, worm-eaten, wooden tenements were seen tottering to their fall, in directions so many and capricious that scarce the semblance of a passage was discernible between them. The paving-stones lay at random, displaced from their beds by the rankly-growing grass. Horrible filth festered in the dammed-up gutters. The whole atmosphere teemed with desolation. Yet, as we proceeded, the sounds of human life revived by sure degrees, and at length large bands of the most abandoned of a London populace were seen reeling to and fro. The spirits of the old man again flickered up, as a lamp, which is near its death-hour. Once more he strode onward with elastic tread. Suddenly a corner was turned, a blaze of light burst upon our sight, and we stood before one of the huge suburban temples of Intemperance—one of the palaces of the fiend, Gin.

It was now nearly daybreak; but a number of wretched inebriates still pressed in and out of the flaunting entrance. With a half shriek of joy the old man forced a passage within, resumed at once his original bearing, and stalked backward and forward, without apparent object, among the throng. He had not been thus long occupied, however, before a rush to the doors gave token that the host was closing them for the night. It was something even more intense than despair that I then observed upon the countenance of the singular being whom I had watched so pertinaciously. Yet he did not hesitate in his career, but, with a mad energy, retraced his steps at once, to the heart of the mighty London. Long and swiftly he fled, while I followed him in the wildest amazement, resolute not to abandon a scrutiny in which I now felt an interest all-absorbing. The sun arose while we proceeded, and, when we had once again reached the most thronged part of the populous town, the street of the D—— Hotel, it presented an appearance of human bustle and activity scarcely inferior to what I had seen on the evening before. And here, long, amid the momently increasing confusion, did I persist in my pursuit of the stranger. But, as usual, he walked to and fro, and during the day did not pass from out the turmoil of that street. And, as the shades of the second evening came on, I grew wearied unto death, and, stopping fully in front of the wanderer, gazed at him steadfastly in the face. He noticed me not, but resumed his solemn walk, while I, ceasing to follow, remained absorbed in contemplation. "This old man," I said at length, "is the type and the genius of deep crime. He refuses to be alone. *He is the man of the crowd*. It will be in vain to follow; for I shall learn no more of him, nor of his deeds. The worst heart of the world is a grosser book than the *Hortulus Animae*, and perhaps it is but one of the great mercies of God that *'es lässt sich nicht lesen.'*"

Thinking About the Story

Edgar Allan Poe's story frames a descent into the physical underworld of London, describing various classes of workers and their characteristics. You should consider Poe's purpose in presenting his story in this manner. In particular, you should take stock of the La Bruyère epigraph, which translates as, "This great misfortune, not to be able to be alone." You should look for the resonances of this quote, including the strange quality of its phrasing, and how it relates to the old man and the crowd. As you further weigh the story, consider the questions: What is crime? Does it have an essence? It is perhaps beneficial to note that in life, as in fiction, a single crime can be solved, but crime itself cannot be. Accordingly, you will it interesting to scrutinize Poe's notions of crime in relation to Arthur Conan Doyle's "A Scandal in Bohemia."

Discussion Questions

1. Speculate on why the narrator watches the crowd. Do you consider his watching to be a passive act or one of more active voyeurism?
2. What is the narrator's purpose in following the man? Are there any clues as to his motivations? How do you interpret the narrator's

Leo Tolstoy

It is amazing how complete is the delusion that beauty is goodness.
Leo Tolstoy — *The Kreutzer Sonata* (1889)

A wealth of transcendent prose marks out Leo Tolstoy (1828–1910) as Russia's greatest novelist, and, consequently, as a major influence on several writers that includes James Joyce, William Faulkner, and Marcel Proust. Born into Russian nobility in western Russia, both of Tolstoy's parents died when he was young. Raised by female relatives in Kazan, he attended the local university, where he studied oriental languages and law. In 1847, he left without graduating and returned to his home estate. Soon after, he began to write autobiographical narratives, many of which were published. After living in Moscow and St. Petersburg, he served in the Crimean War. His experiences in the war transformed his views on death and spirituality. In 1862, he married Sophia Bers and the couple had thirteen children. Over the next twenty years, Tolstoy focused on his writing and his spiritual life, practicing a form of Christianity that championed universal love, nonviolence, and pacifism. Aged 82, he fled his estate to become a traveling ascetic, but he died at the nearby railroad station.

Like his influential predecessors Alexander Pushkin and Nikolai Gogol, Tolstoy's contribution to literature is vast and rich. His major works include *War and Peace* (1865–69), *Anna Karenina* (1873–77), and *The Death of Ivan Ilyich* (1886). He also wrote several nonfiction books on morality, philosophy, and religion, over a dozen seminal short stories, and three plays. Despite his occasional didactic use of exposition, the moral humanity within his fiction still engages the reader. Perhaps because of his fully realized characters, which range from the peasantry to the nobility, Tolstoy manages to transcend facile sermonizing. In his writing, what Tolstoy makes clear is the complicated nature of relationships and the important role played by dramatic crises in these human equations. This is evident in "How Much Land Does a Man Need?" (1887). This short story or modern-day parable, as some have read it, highlights the competing forces of capitalism and feudalism, and the accumulation of wealth and land corrupting the higher values of family and religious purpose.

How Much Land Does a Man Need?

Leo Tolstoy

Translated by Louise and Aylmer Maude

I

An elder sister came to visit her younger sister in the country. The elder was married to a tradesman in town, the younger to a peasant in the village. As the sisters sat over their tea talking, the elder began to boast of the advantages of town life: saying how comfortably they lived there, how well they dressed, what fine clothes her children wore, what good things they ate and drank, and how she went to the theater, promenades, and entertainments.

The younger sister was piqued, and in turn disparaged the life of a tradesman, and stood up for that of a peasant.

"I would not change my way of life for yours," she said. "We may live roughly, but at least we are free from anxiety. You live in better style than we do, but though you often earn more than you need, you are very likely to lose all you have. You know the proverb, 'Loss and gain are brothers twain.' It often happens that people who are wealthy one day are begging their bread the next. Our way is safer. Though a peasant's life is not a fat one, it is a long one. We shall never grow rich, but we shall always have enough to eat."

The elder sister said: "Enough? Yes, if you like to share with the pigs and calves! What do you know of elegance or manners! However much your good man may slave, you will die as you are living—on a dung heap—and your children the same."

"Well, what of that?" replied the younger. "Of course our work is rough and coarse. But, on the other hand, it is sure, and we need not bow to anyone. But you, in your towns, are surrounded by temptations; today all may be right, but tomorrow the Evil One may tempt your husband with card, wine, or women, and all will go to ruin. Don't such things happen often enough?"

Pahóm, the master of the house, was lying on the top of the stove and he listened to the women's chatter.

"It is perfectly true," he thought. "Busy as we are from childhood tilling mother earth, we peasants have no time to let any nonsense settle in our heads. Our only trouble is that we haven't land enough. If I had plenty of land, I shouldn't fear the Devil himself!"

The women finished their tea, chatted a while about dress, and then cleared away the tea-things and lay down to sleep.

But the Devil had been sitting behind the stove, and had heard all that was said. He was pleased that the peasant's wife had led her husband into boasting, and that he had said that if he had plenty of land he would not fear the Devil himself.

"All right," thought the Devil. "We will have a tussle. I'll give you land enough; and by means of that land I will get you into my power."

II

Close to the village there lived a lady, a small landowner who had an estate of about three hundred acres. She had always lived on good terms with the peasants until she engaged as her steward an old soldier, who took to burdening the people with fines. However careful Pahóm tried to be, it happened again and again that now a horse of his got among the lady's oats, or a cow strayed into her garden, or his calves found their way into her meadows—and he always had to pay a fine.

Pahóm paid up, but grumbled and, going home in a temper, was rough with his family. All through that summer, Pahóm had much trouble because of this steward, and he was even glad when winter came and the cattle had to be stabled. Though he grudged the fodder when they could no longer graze on the pastureland, at least he was free from anxiety about them.

In the winter the news got about that the lady was going to sell her land and that the keeper of the inn on the high road was bargaining for it. When the peasants heard this they were very much alarmed.

"Well," they thought, "if the innkeeper gets the land, he will worry us with fines worse than the lady's steward. We all depend on that estate."

So the peasants went on behalf of their Commune, and asked the lady not to sell the land to the innkeeper, offering her a better price for it. The lady agreed to let them have the land. Then the peasants tried to arrange for the Commune to buy the whole estate, so that it might be held by them all in common. They met twice to discuss it, but could not settle the matter; the Evil One sowed discord among them and they could not agree. So they decided to buy the land individually, each according to his means; and the lady agreed to this plan as she had to the other.

Presently Pahóm heard that a neighbor of his was buying fifty acres, and that the lady had consented to accept one half in cash and to wait a year for the other half. Pahóm felt envious.

"Look at that," he thought, "the land is all being sold, and I shall get none of it." So he spoke to his wife.

"Other people are buying," he said, "and we must also buy twenty acres or so. Life is becoming impossible. That steward is simply crushing us with his fines."

So they put their heads together and considered how they could manage to buy it. They had one hundred rubles laid by. They sold a colt and one half of their bees, hired out one of their sons as a laborer and took his wages in advance; borrowed the rest from a brother-in-law, and so scraped together half the purchase money.

Having done this, Pahóm chose out a farm of forty acres, some of it wooded, and went to the lady to bargain for it. They came to an agreement, and he shook hands with her upon it and paid her a deposit in advance. Then they went to town and signed the deeds; he paying half the price down, and undertaking to pay the remainder within two years.

So now Pahóm had land of his own. He borrowed seed, and sowed it on the land he had bought. The harvest was a good one, and within a year he had managed to pay off his debts both to the lady and to his brother-in-law. So he became a landowner, plowing and sowing his own land, making hay on his own land, cutting his own trees, and feeding his cattle on his own pasture. When he went out to plough his fields, or to look at his growing corn, or at his grass-meadows, his heart would fill with joy. The grass that grew and the glowers that bloomed there seemed to him unlike any that grew elsewhere. Formerly, when he had passed by that land, it had appeared the same as any other land, but now it seemed quite different.

III

So Pahóm was content, and everything would have been right if the neighboring peasants would only not have trespassed on his cornfields and meadows. He appealed to them most civilly, but they still went on: now the Communal herdsmen would let the village cows stray into his meadows, then horses from the night pasture would get among his corn. Pahóm turned them out again and again, and forgave their owners, and for a long time he forbore to prosecute any one. But at last he lost patience and complained to the District Court. He knew it was the peasants' want of land, and no evil intent on their part, that caused the trouble, but he thought:

"I cannot go on overlooking it or they will destroy all I have. They must be taught a lesson."

So he had them up, gave them one lesson, and then another, and two or three of the peasants were fined. After a time Pahóm's neighbors began to bear him a grudge for this, and would now and then let their cattle on to his land on purpose. One peasant even got into Pahóm's wood at night and cut down five young lime trees for their bark. Pahóm passing through the wood one day noticed something white. He came nearer and saw the stripped trunks lying on the ground, and close by stood the stumps where the trees had been. Pahóm was furious.

"If he had only cut one here and there it would have been bad enough," thought Pahóm, "but the rascal has actually cut down a whole clump. If I could only find out who did this, I would pay him out."

He racked his brain as to who it could be. Finally he decided: "It must be Simon—no one else could have done it." So he went to Simon's homestead to have a look round, but he found nothing, and only had an angry scene. However, he now felt more certain than ever that Simon had done it, and he lodged a complaint. Simon was summoned. The case was tried, and retried, and at the end of it all Simon was acquitted, there being no evidence against him. Pahóm felt still more aggrieved, and let his anger loose upon the Elder and the Judges.

"You let thieves grease your palms," he said. "If you were honest folk yourselves you would not let a thief go free."

So Pahóm quarreled with the Judges and with his neighbors. Threats to burn his building began to be uttered. So though Pahóm had more land, his place in the Commune was much worse than before.

About this time a rumor got about that many people were moving to new parts.

"There's no need for me to leave my land," thought Pahóm. "But some of the others might leave our village and then there would be more room for us. I would take over their land myself and make my estate a bit bigger. I could then live more at ease. As it is, I am still too cramped to be comfortable."

One day Pahóm was sitting at home when a peasant, passing through the village, happened to call in. He was allowed to stay the night, and supper was given him. Pahóm had a talk with this peasant and asked him where he came from. The stranger answered that he came from beyond the Volga, where he had been working. One word led to another, and the man went on to say that many people were settling in those parts. He told how some people from his village had settled there. They had joined the Commune, and had twenty-five acres per man granted them. The land was so good, he said, that the rye sown on it grew as high as a horse, and so thick that five cuts of a sickle made a sheaf. One peasant, he said, had brought nothing with him but his bare hands, and now he had six horses and two cows of his own.

Pahóm's heart kindled with desire. He thought:

"Why should I suffer in this narrow hole, if one can live so well elsewhere? I will sell my land and my homestead here, and with the money I will start afresh over there and get everything new. In this crowded place one is always having trouble. But I must first go and find out all about it myself."

Towards summer he got ready and started. He went down the Volga on a steamer to Samara, then walked another three hundred miles on foot, and at last reached the place. It was just as the stranger had said. The peasants had plenty of land: every man had twenty-five acres of Communal land given him for his use, and any one who had money could buy, besides, at a ruble an acre as much good freehold land as he wanted.

Having found out all he wished to know, Pahóm returned home as autumn came on, and began selling off his belongings. He sold his land at a profit, sold his homestead and all his cattle, and withdrew from membership in the commune. He only waited till the spring, and then started with his family for the new settlement.

IV

As soon as Pahóm and his family reached their new abode, he applied for admission into the Commune of a large village. He stood treat to the Elders and obtained the necessary documents. Five shares of Communal land were given him for his own and his sons' use: that is to say, 125 acres (not all together, but in different fields) besides the use of the Communal pasture. Pahóm put up the buildings he needed, and bought cattle. Of the Communal land alone he had three times as much as at his former home, and the land was good corn-land. He was ten times better off than he had been. He had plenty of arable land and pasturage, and could keep as many head of cattle as he liked.

At first, in the bustle of building and settling down, Pahóm was pleased with it all, but when he got used to it he began to think that even here he had not enough land. The first year, he sowed wheat on his share of the Communal land and had a good crop. He wanted to go on sowing wheat, but had not enough Communal land for the purpose, and what he had already used was not available; for in those parts wheat is only sown on virgin soil or on fallow land. It is sown for one or two years, and then the land lies fallow till it is again overgrown with prairie grass. There were many who wanted such land and there was not enough for all. So people quarreled about it. Those who were better off wanted it for growing wheat, and those who were poor wanted it to let to dealers, so that they might raise money to pay their taxes. Pahóm wanted to sow more wheat, so he rented land from a dealer for a year. He sowed much wheat and had a fine crop, but the land was too far from the village—the wheat had to be carted more than ten miles.

After a time Pahóm noticed that some peasant-dealers were living on separate farms and were growing wealthy; and he thought:

"If I were to buy some freehold land and have a homestead on it, it would be a different thing altogether. Then it would all be nice and compact."

The question of buying freehold land recurred to him again and again.

He went on in the same way for three years, renting land and sowing wheat. The seasons turned out well and the crops were good, so that he began to lay money by. He might have gone on living contentedly, but he grew tired of having to rent other people's land every year, and having to scramble for it. Wherever there was good land to be had, the peasants would rush for it and it was taken up at once, so that unless you were sharp about it you got none. It happened in the third year that he and a dealer together rented a piece of pasture-land from some peasants; and they had already ploughed it up, when there was some dispute and the peasants went to law about it, and things fell out so that the labor was all lost.

"If it were my own land," thought Pahóm, "I should be independent, and there would not be all this unpleasantness."

So Pahóm began looking out for land that he could buy; and he came across a peasant who had bought thirteen hundred acres, but having got into difficulties was willing to sell again cheap. Pahóm bargained and haggled with him, and at last they settled the price at 1,500 rubles, part in cash and part to be paid later. They had all but clinched the matter when a passing dealer happened to stop at Pahóm's one day to get a feed for his horses. He drank tea with Pahóm and they had a talk. The dealer said that he was just returning from the land of the Bashkirs, far away, where he had bought thirteen thousand acres of land, all for 1,000 rubles. Pahóm questioned him further, and the tradesman said:

"All one need do is to make friends with the chiefs. I gave away about one hundred rubles' worth of silk robes and carpets, besides a case of tea, and I gave wine to those who would drink it; and I got the land for less than a penny an acre." And he showed Pahóm the title deeds, saying:

"The land lies near a river, and the whole prairie is virgin soil."

Pahóm plied him with questions, and the tradesman said:

"There is more land there than you could cover if you walked a year, and it all belongs to the Bashkirs. They are as simple as sheep, and land can be got almost for nothing."

"There now," thought Pahóm, "with my one thousand rubles, why should I get only thirteen hundred acres, and saddle myself with a debt besides? If I take it out there, I can get more than ten times as much for the money."

V

Pahóm inquired how to get to the place, and as soon as the tradesman had left him, he prepared to go there himself. He left his wife to look after the homestead, and started on his journey taking his man with him. They stopped at a town on their way and bought a case of tea, some wine, and other presents, as the tradesman had advised. On and on they went until they had gone more than three hundred miles, and on the seventh day they came to a place where the Bashkirs had pitched their tents. It was all just as the tradesman had said. The people lived on the steppes, by a river, in felt-covered tents. They neither tilled the ground, nor ate bread. Their cattle and horses grazed in herds on the steppe. The colts were tethered behind the tents, and the mares were driven to them twice a day. The mares were milked, and from the milk kumiss was made. It was the women who prepared kumiss, and they also made cheese. As far as the men were concerned, drinking kumiss and tea, eating mutton, and playing on their pipes, was all they cared about. They were all stout and merry, and the summer long they never thought of doing any work. They were quite ignorant, and knew no Russian, but were good-natured enough.

As soon as they saw Pahóm, they came out of their tents and gathered round their visitor. An interpreter was found, and Pahóm told them he had come about some land. The Bashkirs seemed very glad; they took Pahóm and led him into one of the best tents, where they made him sit on some down cushions placed on a carpet, while they sat round him. They gave him some tea and kumiss, and had a sheep killed, and gave him mutton to eat. Pahóm took presents out of his cart and distributed them among the Bashkirs, and divided the tea amongst them. The Bashkirs were delighted. They talked a great deal among themselves, and then told the interpreter to translate.

"They wish to tell you," said the interpreter, "that they like you, and that it is our custom to do all we can to please a guest and to repay him for his gifts. You have given us presents, now tell us which of the things we possess please you best, that we may present them to you."

"What pleases me best here," answered Pahóm, "is your land. Our land is crowded and the soil is exhausted; but you have plenty of land and it is good land. I never saw the like of it."

The interpreter translated. The Bashkirs talked among themselves for a while. Pahóm could not understand what they were saying, but saw that they were much amused and that they shouted and laughed. Then they were silent and looked at Pahóm while the interpreter said:

"They wish me to tell you that in return for your presents they will gladly give you as much land as you want. You have only to point it out with your hand and it is yours."

The Bashkirs talked again for a while and began to dispute. Pahóm asked what they were disputing about, and the interpreter told him that some of them thought they ought to ask their Chief about the land and not act in his absence, while others thought there was no need to wait for his return.

VI

While the Bashkirs were disputing, a man in a large fox-fur cap appeared on the scene. They all became silent and rose to their feet. The interpreter said, "This is our Chief himself."

Pahóm immediately fetched the best dressing gown and five pounds of tea, and offered these to the Chief. The Chief accepted them, and seated himself in the place of honor. The Bashkirs at once began telling him something. The Chief listened for a while, then made a sign with his head for them to be silent, and addressing himself to Pahóm, said in Russian:

"Well, let it be so. Choose whatever piece of land you like; we have plenty of it."

"How can I take as much as I like?" thought Pahóm. "I must get a deed to make it secure, or else they may say 'It is yours,' and afterwards may take it away again."

"Thank you for your kind words," he said aloud. "You have much land, and I only want a little. But I should like to be sure which bit is mine. Could it not be measured and made over to me? Life and death are in God's hands. You good people give it to me, but your children might wish to take it away again."

"You are quite right," said the Chief. "We will make it over to you."

"I heard that a dealer had been here," continued Pahóm, "and that you gave him a little land, too, and signed title-deeds to that effect. I should like to have it done in the same way."

The Chief understood.

"Yes," he replied, "that can be done quite easily. We have a scribe, and we will go to town with you and have the deed properly sealed."

"And what will be the price?" asked Pahóm.

"Our price is always the same: one thousand rubles a day."

Pahóm did not understand.

"A day? What measure is that? How many acres would that be?"

"We do not know how to reckon it out," said the Chief. "We sell it by the day. As much as you can go round on your feet in a day is yours, and the price is one thousand rubles a day."

Pahóm was surprised.

"But in a day you can get round a large tract of land," he said.

The Chief laughed.

"It will all be yours!" he said. "But there is one condition: If you don't return on the same day to the spot whence you started, your money is lost."

"But how am I to mark the way that I have gone?"

"Why, we shall go to any spot you like, and stay there. You must start from that spot and make your round, taking a spade with you. Wherever you think necessary, make a mark. At every turning, dig a hole and pile up the turf; then afterwards we will go round with a plough from hole to hole. You may make as large a circuit as you please, but before the sun sets you must return to the place you started from. All the land you cover will be yours."

Pahóm was delighted. It was decided to start early next morning. They talked a while, and after drinking some more kumiss and eating some more mutton, they had tea again, and then the night came on. They gave Pahóm a feather-bed to sleep on, and the Bashkirs dispersed for the night, promising to assemble the next morning at daybreak and ride out before sunrise to the appointed spot.

VII

Pahóm lay on the feather bed, but could not sleep. He kept thinking about the land. "What a large tract I will mark off!" he thought. "I can easily do thirty-five miles in a day. The days are long now, and within a circuit of thirty-five miles what a lot of land there will be! I will sell the poorer land, or let it to peasants, but I'll pick out the best and farm it. I will buy two ox teams, and hire two more laborers. About a hundred and fifty acres shall be plough-land, and I will pasture cattle on the rest."

Pahóm lay awake all night, and dozed off only just before dawn. Hardly were his eyes closed when he had a dream. He thought he was lying in that same tent and heard somebody chuckling outside. He wondered who it could be, and rose and went out, and he saw the Bashkir Chief sitting in front of the tent holding his sides and rolling about with laughter. Going nearer to the Chief, Pahóm asked: "What are you laughing at?" But he saw that it was no longer the Chief, but the dealer who had recently stopped at his house and had told him about the land. Just as Pahóm was going to ask, "Have you been here long?" he saw that it was not the dealer, but the peasant who had come up from the Volga, long ago, to Pahóm's old home. Then he saw that it was not the peasant either, but the Devil himself with hoofs and horns, sitting there and chuckling, and before him lay a man barefoot, prostrate on the ground, with only trousers and a shirt on. And Pahóm dreamed that he looked more attentively to see what sort of a man it was that was lying there, and he saw that the man was dead, and that it was himself! He awoke horror-struck.

"What things one does dream," he thought.

Looking around he saw through the open door that the dawn was breaking.

"It's time to wake them up," he thought. "We ought to be starting."

He got up, roused his man (who was sleeping in his cart), bade him harness; and went to call the Bashkirs.

"It's time to go to the steppe to measure the land," he said.

The Bashkirs rose and assembled, and the Chief came too. Then they began drinking kumiss again, and offered Pahóm some tea, but he would not wait.

"If we are to go, let us go. It is high time," he said.

VIII

The Bashkirs got ready and they all started: some mounted on horses, and some in carts. Pahóm drove in his own small cart with his servant and took a spade with him. When they reached the steppe, the morning red was beginning to kindle. They ascended a hillock (called by the Bashkirs a shikhan) and dismounting from their carts and their horses, gathered in one spot. The Chief came up to Pahóm and stretching out his arm towards the plain:

"See," he said, "all this, as far as your eye can reach, is ours. You may have any part of it you like."

Pahóm's eyes glistened: it was all virgin soil, as flat as the palm of your hand, as black as the seed of a poppy, and in the hollows different kinds of grasses grew breast high.

The Chief took off his fox-fur cap, placed it on the ground and said:

"This will be the mark. Start from here, and return here again. All the land you go round shall be yours."

Pahóm took out his money and put it on the cap. Then he took off his outer coat, remaining in his sleeveless under-coat. He unfastened his girdle and tied it tight below his stomach, put a little bag of bread into the breast of his coat, and tying a flask of water to his girdle, he drew up the tops of his boots, took the spade from his man, and stood ready to start. He considered for some moments which way he had better go—it was tempting everywhere.

"No matter," he concluded, "I will go towards the rising sun."

He turned his face to the east, stretched himself, and waited for the sun to appear above the rim.

"I must lose no time," he thought, "and it is easier walking while it is still cool."

The sun's rays had hardly flashed above the horizon, before Pahóm, carrying the spade over his shoulder, went down into the steppe.

Pahóm started walking neither slowly nor quickly. After having gone a thousand yards he stopped, dug a hole, and placed pieces of turf one on another to make it more visible. Then he went on; and now that he had walked off his stiffness he quickened his pace. After a while he dug another hole.

Pahóm looked back. The hillock could be distinctly seen in the sunlight, with the people on it, and the glittering tires of the cartwheels. At a rough guess Pahóm concluded that he had walked three miles. It was growing warmer; he took off his under-coat, flung it across his shoulder, and went on again. It had grown quite warm now and the sun made him think of breakfast.

"The first shift is done, but there are four in a day, and it is too soon yet to turn. But I will just take off my boots," he said to himself.

He sat down, took off his boots, stuck them into his girdle, and went on. It was easy walking now.

"I will go on for another three miles," he thought, "and then turn to the left. This spot is so fine, that it would be a pity to lose it. The further one goes, the better the land seems."

He went straight on for a while, and when he looked round, the hillock was scarcely visible and the people on it looked like black ants, and he could just see something glistening there in the sun.

"Ah," thought Pahóm, "I have gone far enough in this direction, it is time to turn. Besides I am in a regular sweat, and very thirsty."

He stopped, dug a large hole, and heaped up pieces of turf. Next he untied his flask, had a drink, and then turned sharply to the left. He went on and on; the grass was high, and it was very hot.

Pahóm began to grow tired: he looked at the sun and saw that it was noon.

"Well," he thought, "I must have a rest."

He sat down, and ate some bread and drank some water; but he did not lie down, thinking that if he did he might fall asleep. After sitting a little while, he went on again. At first he walked easily: the food had strengthened him; but it had become terribly hot and he felt sleepy, still he went on, thinking: "An hour to suffer, a life-time to live."

He went a long way in this direction also, and was about to turn to the left again, when he perceived a damp hollow: "It would be a pity to leave that out," he thought. "Flax would do well there." So he went on past the hollow, and dug a hole on the other side of it before he turned the corner. Pahóm looked towards the hillock. The heat made the air hazy: it seemed to be quivering, and through the haze the people on the hillock could scarcely be seen.

"Ah!" thought Pahóm, "I have made the sides too long; I must make this one shorter." And he went along the third side, stepping faster. He looked at the sun: it was nearly halfway to the horizon, and he had not yet done two miles of the third side of the square. He was still ten miles from the goal.

"No," he thought, "though it will make my land lop-sided, I must hurry back in a straight line now. I might go too far, and as it is I have a great deal of land."

So Pahóm hurriedly dug a hole, and turned straight towards the hillock.

IX

Pahóm went straight towards the hillock, but he now walked with difficulty. He was done up with the heat, his bare feet were cut and bruised, and his legs began to fail. He longed to rest, but it was impossible if he meant to get back before sunset. The sun waits for no man, and it was sinking lower and lower.

"Oh dear," he thought, "if only I have not blundered trying for too much! What if I am too late?"

He looked towards the hillock and at the sun. He was still far from his goal, and the sun was already near the rim. Pahóm walked on and on; it was very hard walking but he went quicker and quicker. He pressed on, but was still far from the place. He began running, threw away his coat, his boots, his flask, and his cap, and kept only the spade that he used as a support.

"What shall I do," he thought again, "I have grasped too much and ruined the whole affair. I can't get there before the sun sets."

And this fear made him still more breathless. Pahóm went on running, his soaking shirt and trousers stuck to him and his mouth was parched. His breast was working like a blacksmith's bellows, his heart was beating like a hammer, and his legs were giving way as if they did not belong to him. Pahóm was seized with terror lest he should die of the strain.

Though afraid of death, he could not stop. "After having run all that way they will call me a fool if I stop now," he thought. And he ran on and on, and drew near and heard the Bashkirs yelling and shouting to him, and their cries inflamed his heart still more. He gathered his last strength and ran on.

The sun was close to the rim, and cloaked in mist looked large, and red as blood. Now, yes now, it was about to set! The sun was quite low, but he was also quite near his aim. Pahóm could already see the people on the hillock waving their arms to hurry him up. He could see the fox-fur cap on the ground and the money on it, and the Chief sitting on the ground holding his sides. And Pahóm remembered his dream.

"There is plenty of land," he thought, "but will God let me live on it? I have lost my life, I have lost my life! I shall never reach that spot!"

Pahóm looked at the sun, which had reached the earth: one side of it had already disappeared. With all his remaining strength he rushed on, bending his body forward so that his legs could hardly follow fast enough to keep him from falling. Just as he reached the hillock it suddenly grew dark. He looked up—the sun had already set! He gave a cry: "All my labor has been in vain," he thought, and was about to stop, but he heard the Bashkirs shouting, and remembered that though to him, from below, the sun seemed to have set, they on the hillock could still see it. He took a long breath and ran up the hillock. It was still light there. He reached the top and saw the cap. Before it sat the Chief laughing and holding his sides. Again Pahóm remembered his dream, and he uttered a cry: his legs gave way beneath him; he fell forward and reached the cap with his hands.

"Ah, that's a fine fellow!" exclaimed the Chief. "He has gained much land!"

Pahóm's servant came running up and tried to raise him, but he saw that blood was flowing from his mouth. Pahóm was dead!

The Bashkirs clicked their tongues to show their pity.

His servant picked up the spade and dug a grave long enough for Pahóm to lie in, and buried him in it. Six feet from his head to his heels was all he needed.

Thinking About the Story

Leo Tolstoy's story has often been interpreted as a parable, a term that can be defined as a short and simple allegorical tale. Others have read the work as a modern-day story, containing only allegorical elements. Therefore, you should take your time in reflecting upon how you read "How Much Land Does a Man Need?" For you, is it a parable? A story of the fantastic? Or a narrative of social drama? In considering these questions, think about the depth of characterization, the sophistication of the plot, and the inferred purpose of the story. Whatever the results of your initial thoughts are, it is useful to compare Tolstoy's work with Nathaniel Hawthorne's "Young Goodman Brown." It would be helpful for you to flesh out the similarities and differences between these two stories and to formulate your thoughts on the nature and purpose of allegorical fiction.

Discussion Questions

1. Evaluate Pahóm as a character. Does he seem like a real person or an embodiment of an underlying moral weakness? If you decide upon the latter, what is that moral weakness? Further analyze Pahóm's behavior? Does it change throughout the story? What causes it to change?

2. What is the relationship between Pahóm's dream and the events in his life? How does the Devil's appearance make you rethink the story?

3. Use the story as a touchstone for a philosophical discussion. In particular, compare and contrast notions of individual gain and communal good. Do these two ideas always have to conflict? What role does land and its acquisition play in the story?

4. Discuss your thoughts on the behavior of the Bashkirs. How are their lives different from the peasants who live in the settlement beyond the Volga?

5. Make a note of all the different instances of irony in the story. What is the cumulative effect? In reference to the last line, what is ironic about the story's outcome?

Activities

1. Write a new scene that shows the Chief talking to the Bashkirs behind Pahóm's back.

2. Imagine you're Pahóm's wife. Compose a letter to Pahóm, addressing her concerns for his behavior, his long travels, and not spending time with his family.

3. Write down three examples of obsessive behavior you have seen in fiction. For each, write a paragraph on the form it takes, speculating on the character's motives and the psychology driving the obsession.

Mark Twain

The reports of my death have been greatly exaggerated.
Mark Twain — *Cable Message* (1897)

Samuel Langhorne Clemens (1835–1910), who wrote under the pen name Mark Twain, created Huck Finn and Tom Sawyer, two of the most memorable characters in American literature. Born in Florida, Missouri, Twain and his large family moved a few years later to the town of Hannibal on the Mississippi River. As a child, he swam in the river, built rafts, and played in the woods—all experiences he would later recreate in his fiction. After his father died, he went to work for his brother's newspaper company. Starting in 1857, he worked on a Mississippi steamboat until the Civil War (1861–65) closed the waterway. In between journalistic assignments and his evasion of lawsuits, Twain panhandled for gold in Nevada, and in 1870 married Olivia Langdon. The couple moved from New York to Connecticut, where they had one son (who died in infancy) and two daughters. Due to Twain's bad investments, including his use of subscription-based publishing, his fortunes fluctuated between wealth and near-poverty. At the age of 74, after many years on the lecture circuit, he died from an angina-related heart problem.

Twain wrote dozens of books, including the classics *The Innocents Abroad* (1869), *The Adventures of Tom Sawyer* (1876), *Adventures of Huckleberry Finn* (1884), and *A Connecticut Yankee in King Arthur's Court* (1889). He wrote in several genres—nonfiction, novel, short story, journalism, playwriting—yet the subject of his work often came back to the Mississippi River and the frontier of the American West. Commonly, his writing uses innovative narrative construction, irreverent humor, and biting satire, to parlay his ideas and his characters to great effect. In terms of Twain's oeuvre, "The Californian's Tale" (1893) is one of his most straightforward stories.

Rather than his usual fare, the story is a more traditional narrative. Shaped by vivid descriptions of the landscape, the story's themes mirror the desolation of the environment. At the story's center is a mystery, one cloaked in the isolation of the mountains, a claustrophobic location for madness to ferment.

The Californian's Tale

Mark Twain

Thirty-five years ago I was out prospecting on the Stanislaus, tramping all day long with pick and pan and horn, and washing a hatful of dirt here and there, always expecting to make a rich strike, and never doing it. It was a lovely region, woodsy, balmy, delicious, and had once been populous, long years before, but now the people had vanished and the charming paradise was a solitude. They went away when the surface diggings gave out. In one place, where a busy little city with banks and newspapers and fire companies and a mayor and aldermen had been, was nothing but a wide expanse of emerald turf, with not even the faintest sign that human life had ever been present there. This was down toward Tuttletown. In the country neighborhood thereabouts, along the dusty roads, one found at intervals the prettiest little cottage homes, snug and cozy, and so cobwebbed with vines snowed thick with roses that the doors and windows were wholly hidden from sight—a sign that these were deserted homes, forsaken years ago by defeated and disappointed families who could neither sell them nor give them away. Now and then, half an hour apart, one came across solitary log cabins of the earliest mining days, built by the first gold-miners, the predecessors of the cottage-builders. In some few cases these cabins were still occupied; and when this was so, you could depend upon it that the occupant was the very pioneer who had built the cabin; and you could depend on another thing, too—that he was there because he had once had his opportunity to go home to the States rich, and had not done it; had rather lost his wealth, and had then in his humiliation resolved to sever all communication with his home relatives and friends, and be to them thenceforth as one dead. Round about California in that day were scattered a host of these living dead men—pride-smitten poor fellows, grizzled and old at forty, whose secret thoughts were made all of regrets and longings—regrets for their wasted lives, and longings to be out of the struggle and done with it all.

It was a lonesome land! Not a sound in all those peaceful expanses of grass and woods but the drowsy hum of insects; no glimpse of man or beast; nothing to keep up your spirits and make you glad to be alive. And so, at last, in the early part of the afternoon, when I caught sight of a human creature, I felt a most grateful uplift. This person was a man about forty-five years old, and he was standing at the gate of one of those cozy little rose-clad cottages of the sort already referred to. However, this one hadn't a deserted look; it had the look of being lived in and petted and cared for and looked after; and so had its front yard, which was a garden of flowers, abundant, gay, and flourishing. I was invited in, of course, and required to make myself at home—it was the custom of the country.

It was delightful to be in such a place, after long weeks of daily and nightly familiarity with miners' cabins—with all which this implies of dirt floor, never-made beds, tin plates and cups, bacon and beans and black coffee, and nothing of ornament but war pictures from the Eastern illustrated papers tacked to the log walls. That was all hard, cheerless, materialistic desolation, but here was a nest which had aspects to rest the tired eye and refresh that something in one's nature which, after long fasting, recognizes, when confronted by the belongings of art, howsoever cheap and modest they may be, that it has unconsciously been famishing and now has found nourishment. I could not have believed that a rag carpet could feast me so, and so content me; or that there could be such solace to the soul in wall-paper and framed lithographs, and bright-colored tidies and lamp-mats, and Windsor chairs, and varnished what-nots, with sea-shells and books and china vases on them, and the score of little unclassifiable tricks and touches that a woman's hand distributes about a home, which one sees without knowing he sees them, yet would miss in a moment if they were taken away. The delight that was in my heart showed in my face, and the man saw it and was pleased; saw it so plainly that he answered it as if it had been spoken.

"All her work," he said, caressingly; "she did it all herself—every bit," and he took the room in with a glance which was full of affectionate worship. One of those soft Japanese fabrics with which women drape with careful negligence the upper part of a picture-frame was out of adjustment. He noticed it, and rearranged it with cautious pains, stepping back several times to gauge the effect before he got it to suit him. Then he gave it a light finishing pat or two with his hand, and said: "She always does that. You can't tell just what it lacks, but it does lack something until you've done that—you can see it yourself after it's done, but that is all you know; you can't find out the law of it. It's like the finishing pats a mother gives the child's hair after she's got it combed and brushed, I reckon. I've seen her fix all these things so much that I can do them all just her way, though I don't know the law of any of them. But she knows the law. She knows the why and the how both; but I don't know the why; I only know the how."

He took me into a bedroom so that I might wash my hands; such a bedroom as I had not seen for years: white counterpane, white pillows, carpeted floor, papered walls, pictures, dressing-table, with mirror and pin-cushion and dainty toilet things; and in the corner a wash-stand, with real china-ware bowl and pitcher, and with soap in a china dish, and on a rack more than a dozen towels—towels too clean and white for one out of practice to use without some vague sense of profanation. So my face spoke again, and he answered with gratified words:

"All her work; she did it all herself—every bit. Nothing here that hasn't felt the touch of her hand. Now you would think—But I mustn't talk so much."

By this time I was wiping my hands and glancing from detail to detail of the room's belongings, as one is apt to do when he is in a new place, where everything he sees is a comfort to his eye and his spirit; and I became conscious, in one of those unaccountable ways, you know, that there was something there somewhere that the man wanted me to discover for myself. I knew it perfectly, and I knew he was trying to help me by furtive indications with his eye, so I tried hard to get on the right track, being eager to gratify him. I failed several times, as I could see out of the corner of my eye without being told; but at last I knew I must be looking straight at the thing—knew it from the pleasure issuing in invisible waves from him. He broke into a happy laugh, and rubbed his hands together, and cried out:

"That's it! You've found it. I knew you would. It's her picture."

I went to the little black-walnut bracket on the farther wall, and did find there what I had not yet noticed—a daguerreotype-case. It contained the sweetest girlish face, and the most beautiful, as it seemed to me, that I had ever seen. The man drank the admiration from my face, and was fully satisfied.

"Nineteen her last birthday," he said, as he put the picture back; "and that was the day we were married. When you see her—ah, just wait till you see her!"

"Where is she? When will she be in?"

"Oh, she's away now. She's gone to see her people. They live forty or fifty miles from here. She's been gone two weeks today."

"When do you expect her back?"

"This is Wednesday. She'll be back Saturday, in the evening—about nine o'clock, likely."

I felt a sharp sense of disappointment.

"I'm sorry, because I'll be gone then," I said, regretfully.

"Gone? No—why should you go? Don't go. She'll be disappointed."

She would be disappointed—that beautiful creature! If she had said the words herself they could hardly have blessed me more. I was feeling a deep, strong longing to see her—a longing so supplicating, so insistent, that it made me afraid. I said to myself: "I will go straight away from this place, for my peace of mind's sake."

"You see, she likes to have people come and stop with us—people who know things, and can talk—people like you. She delights in it; for she knows—oh, she knows nearly everything herself, and can talk, oh, like a bird—and the books she reads, why, you would be astonished. Don't go; it's only a little while, you know, and she'll be so disappointed."

I heard the words, but hardly noticed them, I was so deep in my thinkings and strugglings. He left me, but I didn't know. Presently he was back, with the picture case in his hand, and he held it open before me and said:

"There, now, tell her to her face you could have stayed to see her, and you wouldn't."

That second glimpse broke down my good resolution. I would stay and take the risk. That night we smoked the tranquil pipe, and talked till late about various things, but mainly about her; and certainly I had had no such pleasant and restful time for many a day. The Thursday followed and slipped comfortably away. Toward twilight a big miner from three miles away came—one of the grizzled, stranded pioneers—and gave us warm salutation, clothed in grave and sober speech. Then he said:

"I only just dropped over to ask about the little madam, and when is she coming home. Any news from her?"

"Oh, yes, a letter. Would you like to hear it, Tom?"

"Well, I should think I would, if you don't mind, Henry!"

Henry got the letter out of his wallet, and said he would skip some of the private phrases, if we were willing; then he went on and read the bulk of it—a loving, sedate, and altogether charming and gracious piece of handiwork, with a postscript full of affectionate regards and messages to Tom, and Joe, and Charley, and other close friends and neighbors.

As the reader finished, he glanced at Tom, and cried out:

"Oho, you're at it again! Take your hands away, and let me see your eyes. You always do that when I read a letter from her. I will write and tell her."

"Oh no, you mustn't, Henry. I'm getting old, you know, and any little disappointment makes me want to cry. I thought she'd be here herself, and now you've got only a letter."

"Well, now, what put that in your head? I thought everybody knew she wasn't coming till Saturday."

"Saturday! Why, come to think, I did know it. I wonder what's the matter with me lately? Certainly I knew it. Ain't we all getting ready for her? Well, I must be going now. But I'll be on hand when she comes, old man!"

Late Friday afternoon another gray veteran tramped over from his cabin a mile or so away, and said the boys wanted to have a little gaiety and a good time Saturday night, if Henry thought she wouldn't be too tired after her journey to be kept up.

"Tired? She tired! Oh, hear the man! Joe, you know she'd sit up six weeks to please any one of you!"

When Joe heard that there was a letter, he asked to have it read, and the loving messages in it for him broke the old fellow all up; but he said he was such an old wreck that that would happen to him if she only just mentioned his name. "Lord, we miss her so!" he said.

Saturday afternoon I found I was taking out my watch pretty often. Henry noticed it, and said, with a startled look:

"You don't think she ought to be here soon, do you?"

I felt caught, and a little embarrassed; but I laughed, and said it was a habit of mine when I was in a state of expectancy. But he didn't seem quite satisfied; and from that time on he began to show uneasiness. Four times he walked me up the road to a point whence we could see a long distance; and there he would stand, shading his eyes with his hand, and looking. Several times he said:

"I'm getting worried, I'm getting right down worried. I know she's not due till about nine o'clock, and yet something seems to be trying to warn me that something's happened. You don't think anything has happened, do you?"

I began to get pretty thoroughly ashamed of him for his childishness; and at last, when he repeated that imploring question still another time, I lost my patience for the moment, and spoke pretty brutally to him. It seemed to shrivel him up and cow him; and he looked so wounded and so humble after that, that I detested myself for having done the cruel and unnecessary thing. And so I was glad when Charley, another veteran, arrived toward the edge of the evening, and nestled up to Henry to hear the letter read, and talked over the preparations for the welcome. Charley fetched out one hearty speech after another, and did his best to drive away his friend's bodings and apprehensions.

"Anything happened to her? Henry, that's pure nonsense. There isn't anything going to happen to her; just make your mind easy as to that. What did the letter say? Said she was well, didn't it? And said she'd be here by nine o'clock, didn't it? Did you ever know her to fail of her word? Why, you know you never did. Well, then, don't you fret; she'll be here, and that's absolutely certain, and as sure as you are born. Come, now, let's get to decorating—not much time left."

Pretty soon Tom and Joe arrived, and then all hands set about adorning the house with flowers. Toward nine the three miners said that as they had brought their instruments they might as well tune up, for the boys and girls would soon be arriving now, and hungry for a good, old-fashioned break-down. A fiddle, a banjo, and a clarinet—these were the instruments. The trio took their places side by side, and began to play some rattling dance-music, and beat time with their big boots.

It was getting very close to nine. Henry was standing in the door with his eyes directed up the road, his body swaying to the torture of his mental distress. He had been made to drink his wife's health and safety several times, and now Tom shouted:

"All hands stand by! One more drink, and she's here!"

Joe brought the glasses on a waiter, and served the party. I reached for one of the two remaining glasses, but Joe growled under his breath:

"Drop that! Take the other."

Which I did. Henry was served last. He had hardly swallowed his drink when the clock began to strike.

He listened till it finished, his face growing pale and paler; then he said:

"Boys, I'm sick with fear. Help me—I want to lie down!"

They helped him to the sofa. He began to nestle and drowse, but presently spoke like one talking in his sleep, and said: "Did I hear horses' feet? Have they come?"

One of the veterans answered, close to his ear: "It was Jimmy Parish come to say the party got delayed, but they're right up the road a piece, and coming along. Her horse is lame, but she'll be here in half an hour."

"Oh, I'm so thankful nothing has happened!"

He was asleep almost before the words were out of his mouth. In a moment those handy men had his clothes off, and had tucked him into his bed in the chamber where I had washed my hands. They closed the door and came back. Then they seemed preparing to leave; but I said: "Please don't go, gentlemen. She won't know me; I am a stranger."

They glanced at each other. Then Joe said:

"She? Poor thing, she's been dead nineteen years!"

"Dead?"

"That or worse. She went to see her folks half a year after she was married, and on her way back, on a Saturday evening, the Indians captured her within five miles of this place, and she's never been heard of since."

"And he lost his mind in consequence?"

"Never has been sane an hour since. But he only gets bad when that time of year comes round. Then we begin to drop in here, three days before she's due, to encourage him up, and ask if he's heard from her, and Saturday we all come and fix up the house with flowers, and get everything ready for a dance. We've done it every year for nineteen years. The first

Saturday there was twenty-seven of us, without counting the girls; there's only three of us now, and the girls are gone. We drug him to sleep, or he would go wild; then he's all right for another year—thinks she's with him till the last three or four days come round; then he begins to look for her, and gets out his poor old letter, and we come and ask him to read it to us. Lord, she was a darling!"

Thinking About the Story

As noted in this chapter's introduction, "The Californian's Tale" does not contain the biting satire usually associated with Mark Twain. However, like his iconic novels, the story takes place on the American frontier. You should consider the implications of this quintessentially American setting. Moreover, answering the following questions will lead you to consider the ramifications of this time and place: How were the spaces of the frontier gendered? Are there such things as men and women's jobs? Has this situation changed over the years? In examining the spheres of male life and work, and conversely the place women take within these areas, it is helpful to read Twain's "The Californian's Tale" in conjunction with Ambrose Bierce's "An Occurrence at Owl Creek Bridge." A second analytical route can be to compare Twain's themes of madness and obsession with the similarly wrought manifestations found in Edgar Allan Poe's "The Man of the Crowd" and H. P. Lovecraft's "The Outsider."

Discussion Questions

1. Using evidence from the text, characterize Henry's personality. In what ways is Henry a solitary man? Why does he want the narrator to stay with him at the cabin?

2. Compare and contrast the representations of male and female space in the story. What do your answers suggest was prevalent about each gender at this time? Further, what does the absence of women suggest about these spaces?

3. List, and then analyze, the narrator's motives for staying at the cabin. How do you understand the narrator's phrase "living dead men"? Does the narrator empathize with Henry's situation? If not, speculate on why that might be the case.

4. Underline passages that describe the setting. In weighing the results, how would you best describe the setting? Further, how do ideas about the western frontier manifest themselves in the story?

5. Do you like the ending? Were you expecting the story to end this way? Looking back, how does the ending resonate through the rest of the narrative?

Activities

1. Twain mentions a daguerreotype, an early form of the photograph. Accordingly, find a photograph of the American West and write about the person in it. Using the details you can see, describe for a page what you think the person's life was like.

2. Using details from the story and your own imagination, write an obituary for Henry's wife. To help you in your task, read some detailed obituaries from a selection of local and national newspapers.

3. Write a new ending to the story using one of the following scenarios:

   a. The wife is alive and comes back to the cabin.

   b. The wife is still dead, but Henry acts differently.

   c. The other miners do something unexpected.

Ambrose Bierce

War: A by-product of the arts of peace.
Ambrose Bierce — *The Devil's Dictionary* (1911)

Like Ernest Hemingway decades later, Ambrose Bierce (1842–1914?) started his career as a journalist, writing newspaper articles and short stories for several publications. His path in becoming one of America's greatest short story writers began in the rural settlement of Horse Cave Creek, Ohio. With his literary-minded parents, and a dozen brothers and sisters, he grew up in neighboring Indiana. Although poor, he enjoyed a close family life and on the advice of his father worked for an anti-slavery newspaper. At age seventeen, he received a short, but well-rounded education at Kentucky Military Institute before enlisting in the Union Army in 1861. During the Civil War, he was wounded and discharged, and he moved to San Francisco to recuperate. There he met his wife, Mary Ellen Day, and the two of them—with money from her father—immigrated to England for several years. They returned to San Francisco with their two boys, who later died in tragic circumstances. Either at the end of 1913, or the beginning of 1914, Bierce died in Mexico.

When Bierce disappeared he enjoyed observer status with Pancho Villa's revolutionary troops. In many ways his death is emblematic of his fiction. In his short stories, he writes regularly about the graphic nature of war and the consequences it has upon individual soldiers. These facets can be seen in his most famous story, "An Occurrence at Owl Creek Bridge." First published in 1890, the story contains several narrative elements that would be copied by later writers. Bierce's insistence on dramatic tension and an attention to realistic detail drives the reader through the innovative use of narrative time and plot structure. Moreover, emulating his predecessor Edgar Allan Poe, Bierce forges a unity of theme that is emboldened by his clinical aesthetic. In "An Occurrence at Owl Creek Bridge" and many of his other stories, Bierce consistently brings to the surface the terror of war and the comprehension of death, elements that often leave the reader to recoil and meditate upon what has just transpired.

An Occurrence at Owl Creek Bridge

Ambrose Bierce

I

A man stood upon a railroad bridge in northern Alabama, looking down into the swift water twenty feet below. The man's hands were behind his back, the wrists bound with a cord. A rope closely encircled his neck. It was attached to a stout cross-timber above his head and the slack fell to the level of his knees. Some loose boards laid upon the ties supporting the rails of the railway supplied a footing for him and his executioners—two private soldiers of the Federal army, directed by a sergeant who in civil life may have been a deputy sheriff. At a short remove upon the same temporary platform was an officer in the uniform of his rank, armed. He was a captain. A sentinel at each end of the bridge stood with his rifle in the position known as "support," that is to say, vertical in front of the left shoulder, the hammer resting on the forearm thrown straight across the chest—a formal and unnatural position, enforcing an erect carriage of the body. It did not appear to be the duty of these two men to know what was occurring at the center of the bridge; they merely blockaded the two ends of the foot planking that traversed it.

Beyond one of the sentinels nobody was in sight; the railroad ran straight away into a forest for a hundred yards, then, curving, was lost to view. Doubtless there was an outpost farther along. The other bank of the stream was open ground—a gentle slope topped with a stockade of vertical tree trunks, loopholed for rifles, with a single embrasure through which protruded the muzzle of a brass cannon commanding the bridge. Midway up the slope between the bridge and fort were the spectators—a single company of infantry in line, at "parade rest," the butts of their rifles on the ground, the barrels inclining slightly backward against the right shoulder, the hands crossed upon the stock. A lieutenant stood at the right of the line, the point of his sword upon the ground, his left hand resting upon his right. Excepting the group of four at the center of the bridge, not a man moved. The company faced the bridge, staring stonily, motionless. The sentinels, facing the banks of the stream, might have been statues to adorn the bridge. The captain stood with folded arms, silent, observing the work of his subordinates, but making no sign. Death is a dignitary who when he comes announced is to be received with formal manifestations of respect, even by those most familiar with him. In the code of military etiquette silence and fixity are forms of deference.

The man who was engaged in being hanged was apparently about thirty-five years of age. He was a civilian, if one might judge from his habit, which was that of a planter. His features were good—a straight nose, firm mouth, broad forehead, from which his long, dark hair was combed straight back, falling behind his ears to the collar of his well fitting frock coat. He wore a moustache and pointed beard, but no whiskers; his eyes were large and dark gray, and had a kindly expression which one would hardly have expected in one whose neck was in the hemp. Evidently this was no vulgar assassin. The liberal military code makes provision for hanging many kinds of persons, and gentlemen are not excluded.

The preparations being complete, the two private soldiers stepped aside and each drew away the plank upon which he had been standing. The sergeant turned to the captain, saluted and placed himself immediately behind that officer, who in turn moved apart one pace. These movements left the condemned man and the sergeant standing on the two ends of the same plank, which spanned three of the cross-ties of the bridge. The end upon which the civilian stood almost, but not quite, reached a fourth. This plank had been held in place by the weight of the captain; it was now held by that of the sergeant. At a signal from the former the latter would step aside, the plank would tilt and the condemned man go down between two ties. The arrangement commended itself to his judgment as simple and effective. His face had not been covered nor his eyes bandaged. He looked a moment at his "unsteadfast footing," then let his gaze wander to the swirling water of the stream racing madly beneath his feet. A piece of dancing driftwood caught his attention and his eyes followed it down the current. How slowly it appeared to move! What a sluggish stream!

He closed his eyes in order to fix his last thoughts upon his wife and children. The water, touched to gold by the early sun, the brooding mists under the banks at some distance down the stream, the fort, the soldiers, the piece of drift—all had distracted him. And now he became conscious of a new disturbance. Striking through the thought of his dear ones was a sound which he could neither ignore nor understand, a sharp, distinct, metallic percussion like the stroke of a blacksmith's hammer upon the anvil; it had the same ringing quality. He wondered what it was, and whether immeasurably distant or nearby—it seemed both. Its recurrence was regular, but as slow as the tolling of a death knell. He awaited each new stroke with impatience and—he knew not why—apprehension. The intervals of silence grew progressively longer; the delays became maddening. With their greater infrequency the sounds increased in strength and sharpness. They hurt his ear like the trust of a knife; he feared he would shriek. What he heard was the ticking of his watch.

He unclosed his eyes and saw again the water below him. "If I could free my hands," he thought, "I might throw off the noose and spring into the stream. By diving I could evade the bullets and, swimming vigorously, reach the bank, take to the woods and get away home. My home, thank God, is as yet outside their lines; my wife and little ones are still beyond the invader's farthest advance."

As these thoughts, which have here to be set down in words, were flashed into the doomed man's brain rather than evolved from it, the captain nodded to the sergeant. The sergeant stepped aside.

II

Peyton Fahrquhar was a well-to-do planter, of an old and highly respected Alabama family. Being a slave owner and like other slave owners a politician, he was naturally an original secessionist and ardently devoted to the Southern cause. Circumstances of an imperious nature, which it is unnecessary to relate here, had prevented him from taking service with that gallant army which had fought the disastrous campaigns ending with the fall of Corinth, and he chafed under the inglorious restraint, longing for the release of his energies, the larger life of the soldier, the opportunity for distinction. That opportunity, he felt, would come, as it comes to all in wartime. Meanwhile he did what he could. No service was too humble for him to perform in the aid of the South, no adventure too perilous for him to undertake if consistent with the character of a civilian who was at heart a soldier, and who in good faith and without too much qualification assented to at least a part of the frankly villainous dictum that all is fair in love and war.

One evening while Fahrquhar and his wife were sitting on a rustic bench near the entrance to his grounds, a gray-clad soldier rode up to the gate and asked for a drink of water. Mrs. Fahrquhar was only too happy to serve him with her own white hands. While she was fetching the water her husband approached the dusty horseman and inquired eagerly for news from the front.

"The Yanks are repairing the railroads," said the man, "and are getting ready for another advance. They have reached the Owl Creek bridge, put it in order and built a stockade on the north bank. The commandant has issued an order, which is posted everywhere, declaring that any civilian caught interfering with the railroad, its bridges, tunnels, or trains will be summarily hanged. I saw the order."

"How far is it to the Owl Creek bridge?" Fahrquhar asked.

"About thirty miles."

"Is there no force on this side of the creek?"

"Only a picket post half a mile out, on the railroad, and a single sentinel at this end of the bridge."

"Suppose a man—a civilian and student of hanging—should elude the picket post and perhaps get the better of the sentinel," said Fahrquhar, smiling, "what could he accomplish?"

The soldier reflected. "I was there a month ago," he replied. "I observed that the flood of last winter had lodged a great quantity of driftwood against the wooden pier at this end of the bridge. It is now dry and would burn like tinder."

The lady had now brought the water, which the soldier drank. He thanked her ceremoniously, bowed to her husband and rode away. An hour later, after nightfall, he repassed the plantation, going northward in the direction from which he had come. He was a Federal scout.

III

As Peyton Fahrquhar fell straight downward through the bridge he lost consciousness and was as one already dead. From this state he was awakened—ages later, it seemed to him—by the pain of a sharp pressure upon his throat, followed by a sense of suffocation. Keen, poignant agonies seemed to shoot from his neck downward through every fiber of his body and limbs. These pains appeared to flash along well defined lines of ramification and to beat with an inconceivably rapid periodicity. They seemed like streams of pulsating fire heating him to an intolerable temperature. As to his head, he was conscious of nothing but a feeling of fullness—of congestion. These sensations were unaccompanied by thought. The intellectual part of his nature was already effaced; he had power only to feel, and feeling was torment. He was conscious of motion. Encompassed in a luminous cloud, of which he was now merely the fiery heart, without material substance, he swung through unthinkable arcs of oscillation, like a vast pendulum. Then all at once, with terrible suddenness, the light about him shot upward with the noise of a loud splash; a frightful roaring was in his ears, and all was cold and dark. The power of thought was restored; he knew that the rope had broken and he had fallen into the stream. There was no additional strangulation; the noose about his neck was already suffocating him and kept the water from his lungs. To die of hanging at the bottom of a river!—the idea seemed to him ludicrous. He opened his eyes in the darkness and saw above him a gleam of light, but how distant, how inaccessible! He was still sinking, for the light became fainter and fainter until it was a mere glimmer. Then it began to grow and brighten, and he knew that he was rising toward the surface—knew it with reluctance, for he was now very comfortable. "To be hanged and drowned," he thought, "that is not so bad; but I do not wish to be shot. No, I will not be shot; that is not fair."

He was not conscious of an effort, but a sharp pain in his wrist apprised him that he was trying to free his hands. He gave the struggle his attention, as an idler might observe the feat of a juggler, without interest in the outcome. What splendid effort!—what magnificent, what superhuman strength! Ah, that was a fine endeavor! Bravo! The cord fell away; his arms parted and floated upward, the hands dimly seen on each side in the growing light. He watched them with a new interest as first one and then the other pounced upon the noose at his neck. They tore it away and thrust it fiercely aside, its undulations resembling those of a water snake. "Put it back, put it back!" He thought he shouted these words to his hands, for the undoing of the noose had been succeeded by the direst pang that he had yet experienced. His neck ached horribly; his brain was on fire, his heart, which had been fluttering faintly, gave a great leap, trying to force itself out at his mouth. His whole body was racked and wrenched with an insupportable anguish! But his disobedient hands gave no heed to the command. They beat the water vigorously with quick, downward strokes, forcing him to the surface. He felt his head emerge; his eyes were blinded by the sunlight; his chest expanded convulsively, and with a supreme and crowning agony his lungs engulfed a great draught of air, which instantly he expelled in a shriek!

He was now in full possession of his physical senses. They were, indeed, preternaturally keen and alert. Something in the awful disturbance of his organic system had so exalted and refined them that they made record of things never before perceived. He felt the ripples upon his face and heard their separate sounds as they struck. He looked at the forest on the bank of the stream, saw the individual trees, the leaves and the veining of each leaf—he saw the very insects upon them: the locusts, the brilliant bodied flies, the gray spiders stretching their webs from twig to twig. He noted the prismatic colors in all the dewdrops upon a million blades of grass. The humming of the gnats that danced above the eddies of the stream, the beating of the dragon flies' wings, the strokes of the water spiders' legs, like oars which had lifted their boat—all these made audible music. A fish slid along beneath his eyes and he heard the rush of its body parting the water.

He had come to the surface facing down the stream; in a moment the visible world seemed to wheel slowly round, himself the pivotal point, and he saw the bridge, the fort, the soldiers upon the bridge, the captain, the sergeant, the two privates, his executioners. They were in silhouette against the blue sky. They shouted and gesticulated, pointing at him. The captain had drawn his pistol, but did not fire; the others were unarmed. Their movements were grotesque and horrible, their forms gigantic.

Suddenly he heard a sharp report and something struck the water smartly within a few inches of his head, spattering his face with spray. He heard a second report, and saw one of the sentinels with his rifle at his shoulder, a light cloud of blue smoke rising from the muzzle. The man in the water saw the eye of the man on the bridge gazing into his own through the sights of the rifle. He observed that it was a gray eye and remembered having read that gray eyes were keenest, and that all famous marksmen had them. Nevertheless, this one had missed.

A counter-swirl had caught Fahrquhar and turned him half round; he was again looking at the forest on the bank opposite the fort. The sound of a clear, high voice in a monotonous singsong now rang out behind him and came across the water with a distinctness that pierced and subdued all other sounds, even the beating of the ripples in his ears. Although no soldier, he had frequented camps enough to know the dread significance of that deliberate, drawling, aspirated chant; the lieutenant on shore was taking a part in the morning's work. How coldly and pitilessly—with what an even, calm intonation, presaging, and enforcing tranquility in the men—with what accurately measured interval fell those cruel words:

"Company! . . . Attention! . . . Shoulder arms! . . . Ready! . . . Aim! . . . Fire!"

Fahrquhar dived—dived as deeply as he could. The water roared in his ears like the voice of Niagara, yet he heard the dull thunder of the volley and, rising again toward the surface, met shining bits of metal, singularly flattened, oscillating slowly downward. Some of them touched him on the face and hands, then fell away, continuing their descent. One lodged between his collar and neck; it was uncomfortably warm and he snatched it out.

As he rose to the surface, gasping for breath, he saw that he had been a long time under water; he was perceptibly farther downstream, nearer to safety. The soldiers had almost finished reloading; the metal ramrods flashed all at once in the sunshine as they were drawn from the barrels, turned in the air, and thrust into their sockets. The two sentinels fired again, independently and ineffectually.

The hunted man saw all this over his shoulder; he was now swimming vigorously with the current. His brain was as energetic as his arms and legs; he thought with the rapidity of lightning:

"The officer," he reasoned, "will not make that martinet's error a second time. It is as easy to dodge a volley as a single shot. He has probably already given the command to fire at will. God help me, I cannot dodge them all!"

An appalling splash within two yards of him was followed by a loud, rushing sound, *diminuendo*, which seemed to travel back through the air to the fort and died in an explosion which stirred the very river to its deeps! A rising sheet of water curved over him, fell down upon him, blinded him, strangled him! The cannon had taken a hand in the game. As he shook his head free from the commotion of the smitten water he heard the deflected shot humming through the air ahead, and in an instant it was cracking and smashing the branches in the forest beyond.

"They will not do that again," he thought. "The next time they will use a charge of grape. I must keep my eye upon the gun; the smoke will apprise me—the report arrives too late; it lags behind the missile. That is a good gun."

Suddenly he felt himself whirled round and round—spinning like a top. The water, the banks, the forests, the now distant bridge, fort and men, all were commingled and blurred. Objects were represented by their colors only; circular horizontal streaks of color—that was all he saw. He had been caught in a vortex and was being whirled on with a velocity of advance and gyration that made him giddy and sick. In few moments he was flung upon the gravel at the foot of the left bank of the stream—the southern bank—and behind a projecting point which concealed him from his enemies. The sudden arrest of his motion, the abrasion of one of his hands on the gravel, restored him, and he wept with delight. He dug his fingers into the sand, threw it over himself in handfuls and audibly blessed it. It looked like diamonds, rubies, emeralds; he could think of nothing beautiful which it did not resemble. The trees upon the bank were giant garden plants; he noted a definite order in their arrangement, inhaled the fragrance of their blooms. A strange roseate light shone through the spaces among their trunks and the wind made in their branches the music of Aeolian harps. He had not wish to perfect his escape—he was content to remain in that enchanting spot until retaken.

A whiz and a rattle of grapeshot among the branches high above his head roused him from his dream. The baffled cannoneer had fired him a random farewell. He sprang to his feet, rushed up the sloping bank, and plunged into the forest.

All that day he traveled, laying his course by the rounding sun. The forest seemed interminable; nowhere did he discover a break in it, not even a woodman's road. He had not known that he lived in so wild a region. There was something uncanny in the revelation.

By nightfall he was fatigued, footsore, famished. The thought of his wife and children urged him on. At last he found a road which led him in what he knew to be the right direction. It was as wide and straight as a city street, yet it seemed untraveled. No fields bordered it, no dwelling anywhere. Not so much as the barking of a dog suggested human habitation. The black bodies of the trees formed a straight wall on both sides, terminating on the horizon in a point, like a diagram in a lesson in perspective. Overhead, as he looked up through this rift in the wood, shone great golden stars looking unfamiliar and grouped in strange constellations. He was sure they were arranged in some order which had a secret and malign significance. The wood on either side was full of singular noises, among which—once, twice, and again—he distinctly heard whispers in an unknown tongue.

His neck was in pain and lifting his hand to it found it horribly swollen. He knew that it had a circle of black where the rope had bruised it. His eyes felt congested; he could no longer close them. His tongue was swollen with thirst; he relieved its fever by thrusting it forward from between his teeth into the cold air. How softly the turf had carpeted the untraveled avenue—he could no longer feel the roadway beneath his feet!

Doubtless, despite his suffering, he had fallen asleep while walking, for now he sees another scene—perhaps he has merely recovered from a delirium. He stands at the gate of his own home. All is as he left it, and all bright and beautiful in the morning sunshine. He must have traveled the entire night. As he pushes open the gate and passes up the wide white walk, he sees a flutter of female garments; his wife, looking fresh and cool and sweet, steps down from the veranda to meet him. At the bottom of the steps she stands waiting, with a smile of ineffable joy, an attitude of matchless grace and dignity. Ah, how beautiful she is! He springs forwards with extended arms. As he is about to clasp her he feels a stunning blow upon the back of the neck; a blinding white light blazes all about him with a sound like the shock of a cannon—then all is darkness and silence!

Peyton Fahrquhar was dead; his body, with a broken neck, swung gently from side to side beneath the timbers of the Owl Creek bridge.

Thinking About the Story

Ambrose Bierce's story takes place at the time of the Civil War, a critical juncture in American history. As the historical period is intertwined with the unusual use of narrative structure, the story demands that you read it a second time. Indeed post-reading, it is beneficial for you to run through a few comprehension questions: Whose side is Peyton Fahrquhar on? Is he being set up by the Union Army? What exactly takes place in part III of the story? Remember the three parts of this story conspire in narrative disjunction; thus, forcing you to infer and to make assumptions about what is going on and to whom actions are affecting. In terms of style and use of scene building, you should compare "An Occurrence at Owl Creek Bridge" to Stephen Crane's "The Open Boat," and in terms of plot twists compare to O. Henry's "The Ransom of Red Chief."

Discussion Questions

1. Why is it necessary for the story to be told through an omniscient point of view? Consider, then explain, other ways this story could be told. What would be gained? What would be lost?

2. How do the story's structural shifts in time relate to (a) your sense of Peyton Fahrquhar's character? (b) his backstory? and (c) his fate?

3. If the hallucination in part III were not included in the story, how would the dramatic tension be affected?

4. Consider the story's prose style. Do you think it is effective? How do the descriptions of the environment aid Bierce's attempts at Realism? Explain how the realistic detail amplifies the descriptions of war and death.

5. Formulate the themes of the story, annotating passages in the book that support your views. Using these themes, infer from the story Bierce's view of the military. Is he a realist, fatalist, or nihilist? Or none of the above?

Activities

1. Note the main events and essential information in each part. Rearrange the story's structure into chronological order and assess the impact this has upon your reading of the narrative.

2. Rewrite one part of the story from the following characters' perspectives:

    a. The Federal scout

    b. The captain

    c. Peyton Fahrquhar in the first-person ("I")

3. The landscape of Alabama plays a crucial role in the story. Underline Bierce's descriptions, and then replace them with an area or state you know well. What are the effects of changing the setting? Is there a link between regionalism and cultural identity?

Sarah Orne Jewett

The growth of true friendship may be a lifelong affair.
Sarah Orne Jewett — *The Country of the Pointed Firs* (1896)

By the end of the nineteenth century, Sarah Orne Jewett (1849–1909) was an accomplished New England novelist and short story writer. Born in South Berwick, Maine, Jewett grew up a sickly child. Her father, a country doctor, encouraged her to play outside for the perceived health benefits. Although at school she was an average student, Jewett read voraciously and often accompanied her father on his medical rounds. Her observations and interactions with local people gave her the material that she would later write about. A few years after graduation, she moved to Boston and was introduced by William Dean Howells to literary society. Here, Jewett met the wife of her publisher, Annie Adams Fields. The two became close friends, and lived and traveled together, independent of male support. In 1902, Jewett was seriously injured in a road accident that ended her writing career. Seven years later, aged 59, she died of a cerebral hemorrhage.

Influenced by the writers Leo Tolstoy, Henry James, and Gustave Flaubert, Jewett became one of New England's finest writers. She produced over a dozen books, including *Deephaven* (1877), *A White Heron and Other Stories* (1886), and her masterpiece novel, *The Country of the Pointed Firs* (1896). Jewett writes in a suspenseful, matter-of-fact style, which lends her work a pointed edge. Often she describes rural locations and communities in and around Maine and New Hampshire, giving her settings a sense of spiritual isolation. Local color and dialect is a common feature in her fiction and enlivens the prose with rich exactitude. These qualities are also present in her short story, "A White Heron" (1886), a tale that broaches the relationship between humans and nature, and men and women. Though readers may be seduced by the story's lush descriptions of the landscape, they should be aware of the themes simmering within the text: female freedom, power, and knowledge.

A White Heron

Sarah Orne Jewett

I

The woods were already filled with shadows one June evening, just before eight o'clock, though a bright sunset still glimmered faintly among the trunks of the trees. A little girl was driving home her cow, a plodding, dilatory, provoking creature in her behavior, but a valued companion for all that. They were going away from whatever light there was, and striking deep into the woods, but their feet were familiar with the path, and it was no matter whether their eyes could see it or not.

There was hardly a night the summer through when the old cow could be found waiting at the pasture bars; on the contrary, it was her greatest pleasure to hide herself away among the high huckleberry bushes, and though she wore a loud bell she had made the discovery that if one stood perfectly still it would not ring. So Sylvia had to hunt for her until she found her, and call Co'! Co'! with never an answering Moo, until her childish patience was quite spent. If the creature had not given good milk and plenty of it, the case would have seemed very different to her owners. Besides, Sylvia had all the time there was, and very little use to make of it. Sometimes in pleasant weather it was a consolation to look upon the cow's pranks as an intelligent attempt to play hide and seek, and as the child had no playmates she lent herself to this amusement with a good deal of zest. Though this chase had been so long that the wary animal herself had given an unusual signal of her whereabouts, Sylvia had only laughed when she came upon Mistress Moolly at the swamp-side, and urged her affectionately homeward with a twig of birch leaves. The old cow was not inclined to wander farther. She even turned in the right direction for once as they left the pasture, and stepped along the road at a good pace. She was quite ready to be milked now, and seldom stopped to browse. Sylvia wondered what her grandmother would say because they were so late. It was a great while since she had left home at half-past five o'clock, but everybody knew the difficulty of making this errand a short one. Mrs. Tilley had chased the horned torment too many summer evenings herself to blame any one else for lingering, and was only thankful as she waited that she had Sylvia, nowadays, to give such valuable assistance. The good woman suspected that Sylvia loitered occasionally on her own account; there never was such a child for straying about out-of-doors since the world was made! Everybody said that it was a good change for a little maid who had tried to grow for eight years in a crowded manufacturing town, but, as for Sylvia herself, it seemed as if she never had been alive at all before she came to live at the farm. She thought often with wistful compassion of a wretched geranium that belonged to a town neighbor.

"'Afraid of folks,'" old Mrs. Tilley said to herself, with a smile, after she had made the unlikely choice of Sylvia from her daughter's houseful of children, and was returning to the farm. "'Afraid of folks,' they said! I guess she won't be troubled no great with 'em up to the old place!" When they reached the door of the lonely house and stopped to unlock it, and the cat came to purr loudly, and rub against them, a deserted pussy, indeed, but fat with young robins, Sylvia whispered that this was a beautiful place to live in, and she never should wish to go home.

* * *

The companions followed the shady wood-road, the cow taking slow steps and the child very fast ones. The cow stopped long at the brook to drink, as if the pasture were not half a swamp, and Sylvia stood still and waited, letting her bare feet cool themselves in the shoal water, while the great twilight moths struck softly against her. She waded on through the brook as the cow moved away, and listened to the thrushes with a heart that beat fast with pleasure. There was a stirring in the great boughs overhead. They were full of little birds and beasts that seemed to be wide awake, and going about their world, or else saying goodnight to each other in sleepy twitters. Sylvia herself felt sleepy as she walked along. However, it was not much farther to the house, and the air was soft and sweet. She was not often in the woods so late as this, and it made her feel as if she were a part of the gray shadows and the moving leaves. She was just thinking how long it seemed since she first came to the farm a year ago, and wondering if everything went on in the noisy town just the same as when she was there, the thought of the great red-faced boy who used to chase and frighten her made her hurry along the path to escape from the shadow of the trees.

Suddenly this little woods-girl is horror-stricken to hear a clear whistle not very far away. Not a bird's-whistle, which would have a sort of friendliness, but a boy's whistle, determined, and somewhat aggressive. Sylvia left the cow to whatever sad fate might await her, and stepped discreetly aside into the bushes, but she was just too late. The enemy had discovered her, and called out in a very cheerful and persuasive tone, "Halloa, little girl, how far is it to the road?" and trembling Sylvia answered almost inaudibly, "A good ways."

She did not dare to look boldly at the tall young man, who carried a gun over his shoulder, but she came out of her bush and again followed the cow, while he walked alongside.

"I have been hunting for some birds," the stranger said kindly, "and I have lost my way, and need a friend very much. Don't be afraid," he added gallantly. "Speak up and tell me what your name is, and whether you think I can spend the night at your house, and go out gunning early in the morning."

Sylvia was more alarmed than before. Would not her grandmother consider her much to blame? But who could have foreseen such an accident as this? It did not seem to be her fault, and she hung her head as if the stem of it were broken, but managed to answer "Sylvy," with much effort when her companion again asked her name.

Mrs. Tilley was standing in the doorway when the trio came into view. The cow gave a loud moo by way of explanation.

"Yes, you'd better speak up for yourself, you old trial! Where'd she tucked herself away this time, Sylvy?" But Sylvia kept an awed silence; she knew by instinct that her grandmother did not comprehend the gravity of the situation. She must be mistaking the stranger for one of the farmer-lads of the region.

The young man stood his gun beside the door, and dropped a lumpy game-bag beside it; then he bade Mrs. Tilley good-evening, and repeated his wayfarer's story, and asked if he could have a night's lodging.

"Put me anywhere you like," he said. "I must be off early in the morning, before day; but I am very hungry, indeed. You can give me some milk at any rate, that's plain."

"Dear sakes, yes," responded the hostess, whose long slumbering hospitality seemed to be easily awakened. "You might fare better if you went out to the main road a mile or so, but you're welcome to what we've got. I'll milk right off, and you make yourself at home. You can sleep on husks or feathers," she proffered graciously. "I raised them all myself. There's good pasturing for geese just below here towards the ma'sh. Now step round and set a plate for the gentleman, Sylvy!" And Sylvia promptly stepped. She was glad to have something to do, and she was hungry herself.

It was a surprise to find so clean and comfortable a little dwelling in this New England wilderness. The young man had known the horrors of its most primitive housekeeping, and the dreary squalor of that level of society which does not rebel at the companionship of hens. This was the best thrift of an old-fashioned farmstead, though on such a small scale that it seemed like a hermitage. He listened eagerly to the old woman's quaint talk, he watched Sylvia's pale face and shining gray eyes with ever growing enthusiasm, and insisted that this was the best supper he had eaten for a month, and afterward the new-made friends sat down in the door-way together while the moon came up.

Soon it would be berry-time, and Sylvia was a great help at picking. The cow was a good milker, though a plaguy thing to keep track of, the hostess gossiped frankly, adding presently that she had buried four children, so Sylvia's mother, and a son (who might be dead) in California were all the children she had left. "Dan, my boy, was a great hand to go gunning," she explained sadly. "I never wanted for pa'tridges or gray squer'ls while he was to home. He's been a great wand'rer, I expect, and he's no hand to write letters. There, I don't blame him, I'd ha' seen the world myself if it had been so I could.

"Sylvy takes after him," the grandmother continued affectionately, after a minute's pause. "There ain't a foot o' ground she don't know her way over, and the wild creatures counts her one o' themselves. Squer'ls she'll tame to come an' feed right out o' her hands, and all sorts o' birds.

Last winter she got the jaybirds to bangeing here, and I believe she'd 'a' scanted herself of her own meals to have plenty to throw out amongst 'em, if I hadn't kep' watch. Anything but crows, I tell her, I'm willin' to help support—though Dan he had a tamed one o' them that did seem to have reason same as folks. It was round here a good spell after he went away. Dan an' his father they didn't hitch—but he never held up his head ag'in after Dan had dared him an' gone off."

The guest did not notice this hint of family sorrows in his eager interest in something else.

"So Sylvy knows all about birds, does she?" he exclaimed, as he looked round at the little girl who sat, very demure but increasingly sleepy, in the moonlight. "I am making a collection of birds myself. I have been at it ever since I was a boy." (Mrs. Tilley smiled.) "There are two or three very rare ones I have been hunting for these five years. I mean to get them on my own ground if they can be found."

"Do you cage 'em up?" asked Mrs. Tilley doubtfully, in response to this enthusiastic announcement.

"Oh no, they're stuffed and preserved, dozens and dozens of them," said the ornithologist, "and I have shot or snared every one myself. I caught a glimpse of a white heron a few miles from here on Saturday, and I have followed it in this direction. They have never been found in this district at all. The little white heron, it is," and he turned again to look at Sylvia with the hope of discovering that the rare bird was one of her acquaintances.

But Sylvia was watching a hop-toad in the narrow footpath.

"You would know the heron if you saw it," the stranger continued eagerly. "A queer tall white bird with soft feathers and long thin legs. And it would have a nest perhaps in the top of a high tree, made of sticks, something like a hawk's nest."

Sylvia's heart gave a wild beat; she knew that strange white bird, and had once stolen softly near where it stood in some bright green swamp grass, away over at the other side of the woods. There was an open place where the sunshine always seemed strangely yellow and hot, where tall, nodding rushes grew, and her grandmother had warned her that she might sink in the soft black mud underneath and never be heard of more. Not far beyond were the salt marshes just this side the sea itself, which Sylvia wondered and dreamed much about, but never had seen, whose great voice could sometimes be heard above the noise of the woods on stormy nights.

"I can't think of anything I should like so much as to find that heron's nest," the handsome stranger was saying. "I would give ten dollars to anybody who could show it to me," he added desperately, "and I mean to spend my whole vacation hunting for it if need be. Perhaps it was only migrating, or had been chased out of its own region by some bird of prey."

Mrs. Tilley gave amazed attention to all this, but Sylvia still watched the toad, not divining, as she might have done at some calmer time, that the creature wished to get to its hole under the door-step, and was much hindered by the unusual spectators at that hour of the evening. No amount of thought, that night, could decide how many wished-for treasures the ten dollars, so lightly spoken of, would buy.

* * *

The next day the young sportsman hovered about the woods, and Sylvia kept him company, having lost her first fear of the friendly lad, who proved to be most kind and sympathetic. He told her many things about the birds and what they knew and where they lived and what they did with themselves. And he gave her a jack-knife, which she thought as great a treasure as if she were a desert-islander. All day long he did not once make her troubled or afraid except when he brought down some unsuspecting singing creature from its bough. Sylvia would have liked him vastly better without his gun; she could not understand why he killed the very birds he seemed to like so much. But as the day waned, Sylvia still watched the young man with loving admiration. She had never seen anybody so charming and delightful; the woman's heart, asleep in the child, was vaguely thrilled by a dream of love. Some premonition of that great power stirred and swayed these young creatures who traversed the solemn woodlands with soft-footed silent care. They stopped to listen to a bird's song; they pressed forward again eagerly, parting the branches, speaking to each other rarely and in whispers; the young man going first and Sylvia following, fascinated, a few steps behind, with her gray eyes dark with excitement.

She grieved because the longed-for white heron was elusive, but she did not lead the guest, she only followed, and there was no such thing as speaking first. The sound of her own unquestioned voice would have terrified her—it was hard enough to answer yes or no when there was need of that. At last evening began to fall, and they drove the cow home together, and Sylvia smiled with pleasure when they came to the place where she heard the whistle and was afraid only the night before.

II

Half a mile from home, at the farther edge of the woods, where the land was highest, a great pine-tree stood, the last of its generation. Whether it was left for a boundary mark, or for what reason, no one could say; the woodchoppers who had felled its mates were dead and gone long ago, and a whole forest of sturdy trees, pines and oaks and maples, had grown again. But the stately head of this old pine towered above them all and made a landmark for sea and shore miles and miles away. Sylvia knew it well. She had always believed that whoever climbed to the top of it could see the ocean; and the little girl had often laid her hand on the great rough trunk and looked up wistfully at those dark boughs that the wind always stirred, no matter how hot and still the air might be below. Now she thought of the tree with a new excitement, for why, if one climbed it at break of day, could not one see all the world, and easily discover from whence the white heron flew, and mark the place, and find the hidden nest?

What a spirit of adventure, what wild ambition! What fancied triumph and delight and glory for the later morning when she could make known the secret! It was almost too real and too great for the childish heart to bear.

All night the door of the little house stood open and the whippoorwills came and sang upon the very step. The young sportsman and his old hostess were sound asleep, but Sylvia's great design kept her broad awake and watching. She forgot to think of sleep. The short summer night seemed as long as the winter darkness, and at last when the whippoorwills ceased, and she was afraid the morning would after all come too soon, she stole out of the house and followed the pasture path through the woods, hastening toward the open ground beyond, listening with a sense of comfort and companionship to the drowsy twitter of a half-awakened bird, whose perch she had jarred in passing. Alas, if the great wave of human interest which flooded for the first time this dull little life should sweep away the satisfactions of an existence heart to heart with nature and the dumb life of the forest!

There was the huge tree asleep yet in the paling moonlight, and small and silly Sylvia began with utmost bravery to mount to the top of it, with tingling, eager blood coursing the channels of her whole frame, with her bare feet and fingers, that pinched and held like bird's claws to the monstrous ladder reaching up, up, almost to the sky itself. First she must mount the white oak tree that grew alongside, where she was almost lost among the dark branches and the green leaves heavy and wet with dew; a bird fluttered off its nest, and a red squirrel ran to and fro and scolded pettishly at the harmless housebreaker. Sylvia felt her way easily. She had often climbed there, and knew that higher still one of the oak's upper branches chafed against the pine trunk, just where its lower boughs were set close together. There, when she made the dangerous pass from one tree to the other, the great enterprise would really begin.

She crept out along the swaying oak limb at last, and took the daring step across into the old pine-tree. The way was harder than she thought; she must reach far and hold fast, the sharp dry twigs caught and held her and scratched her like angry talons, the pitch made her thin little fingers clumsy and stiff as she went round and round the tree's great stem, higher and higher upward. The sparrows and robins in the woods below were beginning to wake and twitter to the dawn, yet it seemed much lighter there aloft in the pine-tree, and the child knew she must hurry if her project were to be of any use.

The tree seemed to lengthen itself out as she went up, and to reach farther and farther upward. It was like a great main-mast to the voyaging earth; it must truly have been amazed that morning through all its ponderous frame as it felt this determined spark of human spirit wending its way from higher branch to branch. Who knows how steadily the least twigs held themselves to advantage this light, weak creature on her way! The old pine must have loved his new dependent. More than all the hawks, and bats, and moths, and even the sweet voiced thrushes, was the brave, beating heart of the solitary gray-eyed child. And the tree stood still and frowned away the winds that June morning while the dawn grew bright in the east.

Sylvia's face was like a pale star, if one had seen it from the ground, when the last thorny bough was past, and she stood trembling and tired but wholly triumphant, high in the treetop. Yes, there was the sea with the dawning sun making a golden dazzle over it, and toward that glorious east flew two hawks with slow-moving pinions. How low they looked in the air from that height when one had only seen them before far up, and dark against the blue sky. Their gray feathers were as soft as moths; they seemed only a little way from the tree, and Sylvia felt as if she too could go flying away among the clouds. Westward, the woodlands and farms reached miles and miles into the distance; here and there were church steeples, and white villages, truly it was a vast and awesome world.

The birds sang louder and louder. At last the sun came up bewilderingly bright. Sylvia could see the white sails of ships out at sea, and the clouds that were purple and rose-colored and yellow at first began to fade away. Where was the white heron's nest in the sea of green branches, and was this wonderful sight and pageant of the world the only reward for having climbed to such a giddy height? Now look down again, Sylvia, where the green marsh is set among the shining birches and dark hemlocks; there where you saw the white heron once you will see him again; look, look! a white spot of him like a single floating feather comes up from the dead hemlock and grows larger, and rises, and comes close at last, and goes by the landmark pine with steady sweep of wing and outstretched slender neck and crested head. And wait! wait! do not move a foot or a finger, little girl, do not send an arrow of light and consciousness from your two eager eyes, for the heron has perched on a pine bough not far beyond yours, and cries back to his mate on the nest and plumes his feathers for the new day!

The child gives a long sigh a minute later when a company of shouting cat-birds comes also to the tree, and vexed by their fluttering and lawlessness the solemn heron goes away. She knows his secret now, the wild, light, slender bird that floats and wavers, and goes back like an arrow presently to his home in the green world beneath. Then Sylvia, well satisfied, makes her perilous way down again, not daring to look far below the branch she stands on, ready to cry sometimes because her fingers ache and her lamed feet slip. Wondering over and over again what the stranger would say to her, and what he would think when she told him how to find his way straight to the heron's nest.

* * *

"Sylvy, Sylvy!" called the busy old grandmother again and again, but nobody answered, and the small husk bed was empty and Sylvia had disappeared.

The guest waked from a dream, and remembering his day's pleasure hurried to dress himself that might it sooner begin. He was sure from the way the shy little girl looked once or twice yesterday that she had at least seen the white heron, and now she must really be made to tell. Here she comes now, paler than ever, and her worn old frock is torn and tattered, and smeared with pine pitch. The grandmother and the sportsman stand in the door together and question her, and the splendid moment has come to speak of the dead hemlock-tree by the green marsh.

But Sylvia does not speak after all, though the old grandmother fretfully rebukes her, and the young man's kind, appealing eyes are looking straight in her own. He can make them rich with money; he has promised it, and they are poor now. He is so well worth making happy, and he waits to hear the story she can tell.

No, she must keep silence! What is it that suddenly forbids her and makes her dumb? Has she been nine years growing and now, when the great world for the first time puts out a hand to her, must she thrust it aside for a bird's sake? The murmur of the pine's green branches is in her ears, she remembers how the white heron came flying through the golden air and how they watched the sea and the morning together, and Sylvia cannot speak; she cannot tell the heron's secret and give its life away.

* * *

Dear loyalty, that suffered a sharp pang as the guest went away disappointed later in the day, that could have served and followed him and loved him as a dog loves! Many a night Sylvia heard the echo of his whistle haunting the pasture path as she came home with the loitering cow. She forgot even her sorrow at the sharp report of his gun and the sight of thrushes and sparrows dropping silent to the ground, their songs hushed and their pretty feathers stained and wet with blood. Were the birds better friends than their hunter might have been—who can tell? Whatever treasures were lost to her, woodlands and summer time, remember! Bring your gifts and graces and tell your secrets to this lonely country child!

Thinking About the Story

The celebration of the natural environment is omnipresent within Sarah Orne Jewett's story. You can read her pastoral descriptions as a proposal of women's space, a gendered landscape that is destabilized by the hunter's arrival. In further assessing the story, you should consider the assumptions writers and scholars articulate on women and nature: In literature, what's unique about forests? Are they symbolic? Do they represent safety or danger? Are they places of darkness and the unknown? In debating some of your answers, it is helpful to compare "A White Heron" with the representation of the forest in Nathaniel Hawthorne's "Young Goodman Brown." In particular, consider in both stories whether the forest is a place for men and what actions men perform within these carefully delineated spaces.

Discussion Questions

1. Discuss the setting of the story. How important are time and place to understanding the actions and attitudes of the characters? Would you class this story an allegory or not? Are these characters archetypes? If so, of what?
2. Is it a coincidence that Sylvia, her grandmother, and the cow are all females? And that the hunter is a man? Is he a threat to the women? Does he present a form of salvation for them? How does Sylvia change over the course of the story? What are her feelings toward the hunter?
3. Using examples from the story to support your ideas, assess the motivation(s) of the hunter. Why does he kill and stuff birds? Why does Jewett use different words to describe him?
4. Discuss the importance of the white heron. Why does Sylvia prefer to keep the bird's location secret? What are the symbolic resonances of the heron's color?
5. Speculate on the purpose(s) and function(s) of the last paragraph. Do you read Sylvia's actions as submissive? Does Sylvia regret her decision? Would she have lost something had she chosen to go with the hunter?

Activities

1. Make a list of five animals and then speculate on the symbolic connotations of each one. Remember to explain why you feel each animal represents what you have suggested.

2. Think back to your childhood and to a realization you had about the adult world. Write a journal entry describing what the realization was and what sparked it at the time.
3. Free-writing challenge: imagine you are the white heron flying over the woods. What do you see, smell, and hear? Where do you go? What do you do?

Kate Chopin

Perhaps it is better to wake up after all, even to suffer, rather than to remain a dupe to illusions all one's life.
Kate Chopin — *The Awakening* (1899)

Like her contemporary Charlotte Perkins Gilman, Kate Chopin (1850–1904) is known for her proto-feminist writing. She was born Catherine O'Flaherty in St. Louis, Missouri. After her father died when she was four, the family moved to Louisiana. There, Chopin had a Creole upbringing, which included her family owning slaves until the American Civil War (1861–65). Later, in 1870, she married Oscar Chopin, a cotton merchant. Over a period of eight years they had five sons and one daughter. In 1882, Oscar died, leaving her with substantial debt. Her mother's death a year later left Chopin suffering from depression. By 1888, she had financially recovered and bought a house in St. Louis. The proceeds from her wise investments and from her writing allowed Chopin to travel widely across Europe and Mexico. In the following decade (1890–1900) she produced many of her finest works. In 1904, she died in St. Louis from a brain hemorrhage, aged 54.

Influenced by Walt Whitman, Guy De Maupassant, and Émile Zola, Chopin is best known for her book *The Awakening* (1899), a novel that explores women's sexuality and women's hidden lives. Chopin also published one other novel, *At Fault* (1890), and two short story collections, *Bayou Folk* (1894), and *A Night in Acadie* (1897). Since the 1960s, Chopin's work has been intensively re-read and studied. Although in her life she was not actively involved with social justice movements, she used her writing and her painting to illuminate issues of inequality in American society. In recent decades, stories such as "The Story of an Hour" (1894) have become an integral part of the feminist movement's canon.

In this particular story, its importance does not lie in the fine prose and skillfully wrought irony alone; rather, the work is a singular piece of art, compressed into a striking vision, much like Edvard Munch's contemporaneous painting *The Scream*. In Chopin's case, the primal urges are for independence and freedom; however, her artistic impulses filter ambiguity and contradiction into her story, thereby showing a masterful reluctance in permitting an easy resolution.

The Story of an Hour

Kate Chopin

Knowing that Mrs. Mallard was afflicted with a heart trouble, great care was taken to break to her as gently as possible the news of her husband's death.

It was her sister Josephine who told her, in broken sentences; veiled hints that revealed in half concealing. Her husband's friend Richards was there, too, near her. It was he who had been in the newspaper office when intelligence of the railroad disaster was received, with Brently Mallard's name leading the list of "killed." He had only taken the time to assure himself of its truth by a second telegram, and had hastened to forestall any less careful, less tender friend in bearing the sad message.

She did not hear the story as many women have heard the same, with a paralyzed inability to accept its significance. She wept at once, with sudden, wild abandonment, in her sister's arms. When the storm of grief had spent itself she went away to her room alone. She would have no one follow her.

There stood, facing the open window, a comfortable, roomy armchair. Into this she sank, pressed down by a physical exhaustion that haunted her body and seemed to reach into her soul. She could see in the open square before her house the tops of trees that were all aquiver with the new spring life. The delicious breath of rain was in the air. In the street below a peddler was crying his wares. The notes of a distant song, which some one was singing, reached her faintly, and countless sparrows were twittering in the eaves.

There were patches of blue sky showing here and there through the clouds that had met and piled one above the other in the west facing her window.

She sat with her head thrown back upon the cushion of the chair, quite motionless, except when a sob came up into her throat and shook her, as a child who has cried itself to sleep continues to sob in its dreams.

She was young, with a fair, calm face, whose lines bespoke repression and even a certain strength. But now there was a dull stare in her eyes, whose gaze was fixed away off yonder on one of those patches of blue sky. It was not a glance of reflection, but rather indicated a suspension of intelligent thought.

There was something coming to her and she was waiting for it, fearfully. What was it? She did not know; it was too subtle and elusive to name. But she felt it, creeping out of the sky, reaching toward her through the sounds, the scents, the color that filled the air.

Now her bosom rose and fell tumultuously. She was beginning to recognize this thing that was approaching to possess her, and she was striving to beat it back with her will—as powerless as her two white slender hands would have been. When she abandoned herself a little whispered word escaped her slightly parted lips. She said it over and over under her breath: "free, free, free!" The vacant stare and the look of terror that had followed it went from her eyes. They stayed keen and bright. Her pulses beat fast, and the coursing blood warmed and relaxed every inch of her body.

She did not stop to ask if it were or were not a monstrous joy that held her. A clear and exalted perception enabled her to dismiss the suggestion as trivial. She knew that she would weep again when she saw the kind, tender hands folded in death; the face that had never looked save with love upon her, fixed and gray and dead. But she saw beyond that bitter moment a long procession of years to come that would belong to her absolutely. And she opened and spread her arms out to them in welcome.

There would be no one to live for during those coming years; she would live for herself. There would be no powerful will bending hers in that blind persistence with which men and women believe they have a right to impose a private will upon a fellow-creature. A kind intention or a cruel intention made the act seem no less a crime as she looked upon it in that brief moment of illumination.

And yet she had loved him—sometimes. Often she had not. What did it matter! What could love, the unsolved mystery, count for in the face of this possession of self-assertion, which she suddenly recognized as the strongest impulse of her being!

"Free! Body and soul free!" she kept whispering.

Josephine was kneeling before the closed door with her lips to the keyhole, imploring for admission. "Louise, open the door! I beg; open the door—you will make yourself ill. What are you doing, Louise? For heaven's sake open the door."

"Go away. I am not making myself ill." No; she was drinking in a very elixir of life through that open window.

Her fancy was running riot along those days ahead of her. Spring days, and summer days, and all sorts of days that would be her own. She breathed a quick prayer that life might be long. It was only yesterday she had thought with a shudder that life might be long.

She arose at length and opened the door to her sister's importunities. There was a feverish triumph in her eyes, and she carried herself unwittingly like a goddess of Victory. She clasped her sister's waist, and together they descended the stairs. Richards stood waiting for them at the bottom.

Someone was opening the front door with a latchkey. It was Brently Mallard who entered, a little travel-stained, composedly carrying his gripsack and umbrella. He had been far from the scene of the accident, and did not even know there had been one. He stood amazed at Josephine's piercing cry; at Richards' quick motion to screen him from the view of his wife.

When the doctors came they said she had died of heart disease—of the joy that kills.

Thinking About the Story

When sifting through the ramifications of Kate Chopin's story, it's important to note the context in which it was written. In the last decade of the nineteenth century, American women were considered by men to be intellectually and physically inferior, often assigned to domestic chores and a life of child-rearing. Accordingly, women did not have the right to vote, and were often accountable to their husbands. In assessing the importance, then, of this story, consider why Louise Mallard is always inside her house, looking out at the world. How is her life reflected in the struggles women faced at that time? Why do you think women did not have the vote? For a deeper analysis of these issues, an intelligent comparison can be made between "The Story of an Hour" and Charlotte Perkins Gilman's "The Yellow Wallpaper." In reviewing these stories, it's useful to bear in mind the following question: Are woman writers in a special position to circumvent the patriarchal power structure that surrounds them?

Discussion Questions

1. Why is the protagonist, Louise Mallard, so concerned about being free? How does her sense of freedom relate to the line "that blind persistence with which men and women believe they have a right to impose a private will upon a fellow-creature"?
2. What are the story's themes? How does the setting emphasize these themes?
3. What are the symbolic implications of Louise Mallard's heart condition?
4. Discuss the relationship between Louise and her sister, Josephine. What are the similarities and the differences between the two of them?
5. Comment on the use of irony in the story. What kind of irony exists at the story's end? Do you find the ending improbable? How do you interpret the final words "the joy that kills"?

Activities

1. Write a new scene from Brently Mallard's point of view when he comes back to the house. What does he see? How does he react? What happens next?
2. Make a list of confined settings. What are the physical features of each setting? Speculate on how the features would influence a character's psychology and behavior.
3. Create a playlist to accompany the story. Include at least ten tracks and a short written explanation of how each selected song relates to the text.

Arthur Conan Doyle

Where there is no imagination there is no horror.
Arthur Conan Doyle — "A Study in Scarlet" (1887)

A prolific writer, Sir Arthur Conan Doyle (1859–1930) is best known for his Sherlock Holmes detective stories. He was born in Edinburgh, Scotland, to a distinguished, yet poverty-stricken, family. His father, Charles, was a civil servant and occasional artist, who suffered from alcoholism, while his mother, Mary, kept the family together and impressed the importance of literature upon the young Conan Doyle. At the University of Edinburgh he studied medicine, which eventually led him to question and then renounce Christianity. Following his marriage to Louisa Hawkins in 1862 and the birth of his two children, Mary and Kingsley, he gave up his medical practice to write full-time. In 1900, Conan Doyle assisted the British Army as a doctor in the Boer War. After Louisa died in 1906, Conan Doyle cultivated an interest in Spiritualism, which intensified when Kingsley was killed in the First World War. Despite the sadness over his son's death, Doyle married again and had three more children. He died, aged 71, of a heart attack.

Although associated with detective fiction, Conan Doyle wrote in several genres: romance, science fiction, and historical drama, to name a few. His important works include *The White Company* (1891), *The Lost World* (1912), and four novels and 56 short stories featuring Sherlock Holmes. With Holmes, Conan Doyle built on Edgar Allan Poe's fictional detective, Monsieur Dupin, and incorporated the forensic science developments of his university mentor, Joseph Bell. In these Victorian era stories, Holmes and his confidant, Doctor Watson, explore the mysterious, the exotic, and the macabre. Conan Doyle, however, felt his Holmes stories detracted from his other writing. Nevertheless, the unique friendship of Holmes and

Watson are firmly entrenched within the literary canon. Holmes, a master of keen observation and logical deduction, and the brave, sentimental Watson, still delight audiences today. "A Scandal in Bohemia" (1891) introduces Irene Adler, a criminal, like Professor Moriarty, who is Holmes' equal. The story sets up an intellectual contest between the two characters, a dynamic that sustains the narrative action.

A Scandal in Bohemia

Arthur Conan Doyle

I

To Sherlock Holmes she is always *the* woman. I have seldom heard him mention her under any other name. In his eyes she eclipses and predominates the whole of her sex. It was not that he felt any emotion akin to love for Irene Adler. All emotions, and that one particularly, were abhorrent to his cold, precise, but admirably balanced mind. He was, I take it, the most perfect reasoning and observing machine that the world has seen; but, as a lover, he would have placed himself in a false position. He never spoke of the softer passions, save with a gibe and a sneer. They were admirable things for the observer—excellent for drawing the veil from men's motives and actions. But for the trained reasoner to admit such intrusions into his own delicate and finely adjusted temperament was to introduce a distracting factor which might throw a doubt upon all his mental results. Grit in a sensitive instrument, or a crack in one of his own high-power lenses, would not be more disturbing than a strong emotion in a nature such as his. And yet there was but one woman to him, and that woman was the late Irene Adler, of dubious and questionable memory.

I had seen little of Holmes lately. My marriage had drifted us away from each other. My own complete happiness, and the home-centred interests which rise up around the man who first finds himself master of his own establishment, were sufficient to absorb all my attention; while Holmes, who loathed every form of society with his whole Bohemian soul, remained in our lodgings in Baker Street, buried among his old books, and alternating from week to week between cocaine and ambition, the drowsiness of the drug, and the fierce energy of his own keen nature. He was still, as ever, deeply attracted by the study of crime, and occupied his immense faculties and extraordinary powers of observation in following out those clues, and clearing up those mysteries, which had been abandoned as hopeless by the official police. From time to time I heard some vague account of his doings: of his summons to Odessa in the case of the Trepoff murder, of his clearing up of the singular tragedy of the Atkinson brothers at Trincomalee, and finally of the mission which he had accomplished so delicately and successfully for the reigning family of Holland. Beyond these signs of his activity, however, which I merely shared with all the readers of the daily press, I knew little of my former friend and companion.

One night—it was on the 20th of March, 1888—I was returning from a journey to a patient (for I had now returned to civil practice), when my way led me through Baker Street. As I passed the well-remembered door, which must always be associated in my mind with my wooing, and with the dark incidents of the Study in Scarlet, I was seized with a keen desire to see Holmes again, and to know how he was employing his extraordinary powers. His rooms were brilliantly lit, and, even as I looked up, I saw his tall spare figure pass twice in a dark silhouette against the blind. He was pacing the room swiftly, eagerly, with his head sunk upon his chest and his hands clasped behind him. To me, who knew his every mood and habit, his attitude and manner told their own story. He was at work again. He had risen out of his drug-created dreams and was hot upon the scent of some new problem. I rang the bell, and was shown up to the chamber which had formerly been in part my own.

His manner was not effusive. It seldom was; but he was glad, I think, to see me. With hardly a word spoken, but with a kindly eye, he waved me to an armchair, threw across his case of cigars, and indicated a spirit case and a gasogene in the corner. Then he stood before the fire and looked me over in his singular introspective fashion.

"Wedlock suits you," he remarked. "I think, Watson, that you have put on seven and a half pounds since I saw you."

"Seven," I answered.

"Indeed, I should have thought a little more. Just a trifle more, I fancy, Watson. And in practice again, I observe. You did not tell me that you intended to go into harness."

"Then, how do you know?"

"I see it, I deduce it. How do I know that you have been getting yourself very wet lately, and that you have a most clumsy and careless servant girl?"

"My dear Holmes," said I, "this is too much. You would certainly have been burned, had you lived a few centuries ago. It is true that I had a country walk on Thursday and came home in a dreadful mess; but, as I have changed my clothes, I can't imagine how you deduce it. As to Mary Jane, she is incorrigible, and my wife has given her notice; but there again I fail to see how you work it out."

He chuckled to himself and rubbed his long nervous hands together.

"It is simplicity itself," said he; "my eyes tell me that on the inside of your left shoe, just where the firelight strikes it, the leather is scored by six almost parallel cuts. Obviously they have been caused by someone who has very carelessly scraped round the edges of the sole in order to remove crusted mud from it. Hence, you see, my double deduction that you had been out in vile weather, and that you had a particularly malignant boot-slitting specimen of the London slavey. As to your practice, if a gentleman walks into my rooms smelling of iodoform, with a black mark of nitrate of silver upon his right fore-finger, and a bulge on the side of his top-hat to show where he has secreted his stethoscope, I must be dull indeed, if I do not pronounce him to be an active member of the medical profession."

I could not help laughing at the ease with which he explained his process of deduction. "When I hear you give your reasons," I remarked, "the thing always appears to me to be so ridiculously simple that I could easily do it myself, though at each successive instance of your reasoning I am baffled until you explain your process. And yet I believe that my eyes are as good as yours."

"Quite so," he answered, lighting a cigarette, and throwing himself down into an armchair. "You see, but you do not observe. The distinction is clear. For example, you have frequently seen the steps which lead up from the hall to this room."

"Frequently."

"How often?"

"Well, some hundreds of times."

"Then how many are there?"

"How many! I don't know."

"Quite so! You have not observed. And yet you have seen. That is just my point. Now, I know that there are seventeen steps, because I have both seen and observed. By the way, since you are interested in these little problems, and since you are good enough to chronicle one or two of my trifling experiences, you may be interested in this." He threw over a sheet of thick, pink-tinted notepaper which had been lying open upon the table. "It came by the last post," said he. "Read it aloud."

The note was undated, and without either signature or address.

"There will call upon you tonight, at a quarter to eight o'clock," it said, "a gentleman who desires to consult you upon a matter of the very deepest moment. Your recent services to one of the royal houses of Europe have shown that you are one who may safely be trusted with matters which are of an importance which can hardly be exaggerated. This account of you we have from all quarters received. Be in your chamber then at that hour, and do not take it amiss if your visitor wear a mask."

"This is indeed a mystery," I remarked. "What do you imagine that it means?"

"I have no data yet. It is a capital mistake to theorise before one has data. Insensibly one begins to twist facts to suit theories, instead of theories to suit facts. But the note itself. What do you deduce from it?"

I carefully examined the writing, and the paper upon which it was written.

"The man who wrote it was presumably well to do," I remarked, endeavouring to imitate my companion's processes. "Such paper could not be bought under half a crown a packet. It is peculiarly strong and stiff."

"Peculiar—that is the very word," said Holmes. "It is not an English paper at all. Hold it up to the light."

I did so, and saw a large E with a small g, a P, and a large G with a small t woven into the texture of the paper.

"What do you make of that?" asked Holmes.

"The name of the maker, no doubt; or his monogram, rather."

"Not at all. The G with the small t stands for 'Gesellschaft,' which is the German for 'Company.' It is a customary contraction like our 'Co.' P, of course, stands for 'Papier.' Now for the Eg. Let us glance at our Continental Gazetteer." He took down a heavy brown volume from his shelves. "Eglow, Eglonitz—here we are, Egria. It is in a German-speaking country—in Bohemia, not far from Carlsbad. 'Remarkable as being the scene of the death of Wallenstein, and for its numerous glass factories and paper mills.' Ha, ha, my boy, what do you make of that?" His eyes sparkled, and he sent up a great blue triumphant cloud from his cigarette.

"The paper was made in Bohemia," I said.

"Precisely. And the man who wrote the note is a German. Do you note the peculiar construction of the sentence: 'This account of you we have from all quarters received.' A Frenchman or Russian could not have written that. It is the German who is so uncourteous to his verbs. It only remains, therefore, to discover what is wanted by this German who writes upon Bohemian paper, and prefers wearing a mask to showing his face. And here he comes, if I am not mistaken, to resolve all our doubts."

As he spoke there was the sharp sound of horses' hoofs and grating wheels against the curb, followed by a sharp pull at the bell. Holmes whistled.

"A pair, by the sound," said he. "Yes," he continued, glancing out of the window. "A nice little brougham and a pair of beauties. A hundred and fifty guineas apiece. There's money in this case, Watson, if there is nothing else."

"I think that I had better go, Holmes."

"Not a bit, Doctor. Stay where you are. I am lost without my Boswell. And this promises to be interesting. It would be a pity to miss it."

"But your client—"

"Never mind him. I may want your help, and so may he. Here he comes. Sit down in that armchair, Doctor, and give us your best attention."

A slow and heavy step, which had been heard upon the stairs and in the passage, paused immediately outside the door. Then there was a loud and authoritative tap.

"Come in!" said Holmes.

A man entered who could hardly have been less than six feet six inches in height, with the chest and limbs of a Hercules. His dress was rich with a richness which would, in England, be looked upon as akin to bad taste. Heavy bands of Astrakhan were slashed across the sleeves and fronts of his double-breasted coat, while the deep blue cloak which was thrown over his shoulders was lined with flame-coloured silk, and secured at the neck with a brooch which consisted of a single flaming beryl. Boots which extended half way up his calves, and which were trimmed at the tops with rich brown fur, completed the impression of barbaric opulence which was suggested by his whole appearance. He carried a broad-brimmed hat in his hand, while he wore across the upper part of his face, extending down past the cheek-bones, a black vizard mask, which he had apparently adjusted that very moment, for his hand was still raised to it as he entered. From the lower part of the face he appeared to be a man of strong character, with a thick, hanging lip, and a long, straight chin suggestive of resolution pushed to the length of obstinacy.

"You had my note?" he asked, with a deep harsh voice and a strongly marked German accent. "I told you that I would call." He looked from one to the other of us, as if uncertain which to address.

"Pray take a seat," said Holmes. "This is my friend and colleague, Dr. Watson, who is occasionally good enough to help me in my cases. Whom have I the honour to address?"

"You may address me as the Count Von Kramm, a Bohemian nobleman. I understand that this gentleman, your friend, is a man of honour and discretion, whom I may trust with a matter of the most extreme importance. If not, I should much prefer to communicate with you alone."

I rose to go, but Holmes caught me by the wrist and pushed me back into my chair. "It is both, or none," said he. "You may say before this gentleman anything which you may say to me."

The Count shrugged his broad shoulders. "Then I must begin," said he, "by binding you both to absolute secrecy for two years, at the end of that time the matter will be of no importance. At present it is not too much to say that it is of such weight it may have an influence upon European history."

"I promise," said Holmes.

"And I."

"You will excuse this mask," continued our strange visitor. "The august person who employs me wishes his agent to be unknown to you, and I may confess at once that the title by which I have just called myself is not exactly my own."

"I was aware of it," said Holmes dryly.

"The circumstances are of great delicacy, and every precaution has to be taken to quench what might grow to be an immense scandal and seriously compromise one of the reigning families of Europe. To speak plainly, the matter implicates the great House of Ormstein, hereditary kings of Bohemia."

"I was also aware of that," murmured Holmes, settling himself down in his armchair and closing his eyes.

Our visitor glanced with some apparent surprise at the languid, lounging figure of the man who had been no doubt depicted to him as the most incisive reasoner, and most energetic agent in Europe. Holmes slowly reopened his eyes, and looked impatiently at his gigantic client.

"If your Majesty would condescend to state your case," he remarked, "I should be better able to advise you."

The man sprang from his chair and paced up and down the room in uncontrollable agitation. Then, with a gesture of desperation, he tore the mask from his face and hurled it upon the ground. "You are right," he cried, "I am the King. Why should I attempt to conceal it?"

"Why, indeed?" murmured Holmes. "Your Majesty had not spoken before I was aware that I was addressing Wilhelm Gottsreich Sigismond von Ormstein, Grand Duke of Cassel-Felstein, and hereditary King of Bohemia."

"But you can understand," said our strange visitor, sitting down once more and passing his hand over his high white forehead, "you can understand that I am not accustomed to doing such business in my own person. Yet the matter was so delicate that I could not confide it to an agent without putting myself in his power. I have come incognito from Prague for the purpose of consulting you."

"Then, pray consult," said Holmes, shutting his eyes once more.

"The facts are briefly these: Some five years ago, during a lengthy visit to Warsaw, I made the acquaintance of the well-known adventuress, Irene Adler. The name is no doubt familiar to you."

"Kindly look her up in my index, Doctor," murmured Holmes, without opening his eyes. For many years he had adopted a system of docketing all paragraphs concerning men and things, so that it was difficult to name a subject or a person on which he could not at once furnish information. In this case I found her biography sandwiched in between that of a Hebrew Rabbi and that of a staff-commander who had written a monograph upon the deep sea fishes.

"Let me see?" said Holmes. "Hum! Born in New Jersey in the year 1858. Contralto—hum! La Scala, hum! Prima donna Imperial Opera of Warsaw—yes! Retired from operatic stage—ha! Living in London—quite so! Your Majesty, as I understand, became entangled with this young person, wrote her some compromising letters, and is now desirous of getting those letters back."

"Precisely so. But how—"

"Was there a secret marriage?"

"None."

"No legal papers or certificates?"

"None."

"Then I fail to follow your Majesty. If this young person should produce her letters for blackmailing or other purposes, how is she to prove their authenticity?"

"There is the writing."

"Pooh, pooh! Forgery."

"My private notepaper."

"Stolen."

"My own seal."

"Imitated."

"My photograph."

"Bought."

"We were both in the photograph."

"Oh, dear! That is very bad! Your Majesty has indeed committed an indiscretion."

"I was mad—insane."

"You have compromised yourself seriously."

"I was only Crown Prince then. I was young. I am but thirty now."

"It must be recovered."

"We have tried and failed."

"Your Majesty must pay. It must be bought."

"She will not sell."

"Stolen, then."

"Five attempts have been made. Twice burglars in my pay ransacked her house. Once we diverted her luggage when she travelled. Twice she has been waylaid. There has been no result."

"No sign of it?"

"Absolutely none."

Holmes laughed. "It is quite a pretty little problem," said he.

"But a very serious one to me," returned the King, reproachfully.

"Very, indeed. And what does she propose to do with the photograph?"

"To ruin me."

"But how?"

"I am about to be married."

"So I have heard."

"To Clotilde Lothman von Saxe-Meningen, second daughter of the King of Scandinavia. You may know the strict principles of her family. She is herself the very soul of delicacy. A shadow of a doubt as to my conduct would bring the matter to an end."

"And Irene Adler?"

"Threatens to send them the photograph. And she will do it. I know that she will do it. You do not know her, but she has a soul of steel. She has the face of the most beautiful of women, and the mind of the most resolute of men. Rather than I should marry another woman, there are no lengths to which she would not go—none."

"You are sure that she has not sent it yet?"

"I am sure."

"And why?"

"Because she has said that she would send it on the day when the betrothal was publicly proclaimed. That will be next Monday."

"Oh, then we have three days yet," said Holmes, with a yawn. "That is very fortunate, as I have one or two matters of importance to look into just at present. Your Majesty will, of course, stay in London for the present?"

"Certainly. You will find me at the Langham, under the name of the Count Von Kramm."

"Then I shall drop you a line to let you know how we progress."

"Pray do so. I shall be all anxiety."

"Then, as to money?"

"You have carte blanche."

"Absolutely?"

"I tell you that I would give one of the provinces of my kingdom to have that photograph."

"And for present expenses?"

The King took a heavy chamois leather bag from under his cloak, and laid it on the table.

"There are three hundred pounds in gold, and seven hundred in notes," he said.

Holmes scribbled a receipt upon a sheet of his note-book, and handed it to him.

"And mademoiselle's address?" he asked.

"Is Briony Lodge, Serpentine Avenue, St. John's Wood."

Holmes took a note of it. "One other question," said he. "Was the photograph a cabinet?"

"It was."

"Then, good night, your Majesty, and I trust that we shall soon have some good news for you. And good night, Watson," he added, as the wheels of the Royal brougham rolled down the street.

"If you will be good enough to call tomorrow afternoon at three o'clock, I should like to chat this little matter over with you."

II

At three o'clock precisely I was at Baker Street, but Holmes had not yet returned. The landlady informed me that he had left the house shortly after eight o'clock in the morning. I sat down beside the fire, however, with the intention of awaiting him, however long he might be. I was already deeply interested in his inquiry, for, though it was surrounded by none of the grim and strange features which were associated with the two crimes which I have already recorded, still, the nature of the case and the exalted station of his client gave it a character of its own. Indeed, apart from the nature of the investigation which my friend had on hand, there was something in his masterly grasp of a situation, and his keen, incisive reasoning, which made it a pleasure to me to study his system of work, and to follow the quick, subtle methods by which he disentangled the most inextricable mysteries. So accustomed was I to his invariable success that the very possibility of his failing had ceased to enter into my head.

It was close upon four before the door opened, and a drunken-looking groom, ill-kempt and side-whiskered, with an inflamed face and disreputable clothes, walked into the room. Accustomed as I was to my friend's amazing powers in the use of disguises, I had to look three times before I was certain that it was indeed he. With a nod he vanished into the bedroom, whence he emerged in five minutes tweed-suited and respectable, as of old. Putting his hands into his pockets, he stretched out his legs in front of the fire, and laughed heartily for some minutes.

"Well, really!" he cried, and then he choked; and laughed again until he was obliged to lie back, limp and helpless, in the chair.

"What is it?"

"It's quite too funny. I am sure you could never guess how I employed my morning, or what I ended by doing."

"I can't imagine. I suppose that you have been watching the habits, and perhaps the house, of Miss Irene Adler."

"Quite so, but the sequel was rather unusual. I will tell you, however. I left the house a little after eight o'clock this morning, in the character of a groom out of work. There is a wonderful sympathy and freemasonry among horsey men. Be one of them, and you will know all that there is to know. I soon found Briony Lodge. It is a bijou villa, with a garden at the back, but built out in front right up to the road, two stories. Chubb lock to the door. Large sitting-room on the right side, well furnished, with long windows almost to the floor, and those preposterous English window fasteners which a child could open. Behind there was nothing remarkable, save that the passage window could be reached from the top of the coach-house. I walked round it and examined it closely from every point of view, but without noting anything else of interest.

"I then lounged down the street, and found, as I expected, that there was a mews in a lane which runs down by one wall of the garden. I lent the ostlers a hand in rubbing down their horses, and I received in exchange twopence, a glass of half-and-half, two fills of shag tobacco, and as much information as I could desire about Miss Adler, to say nothing of half a dozen other people in the neighbourhood in whom I was not in the least interested, but whose biographies I was compelled to listen to."

"And what of Irene Adler?" I asked.

"Oh, she has turned all the men's heads down in that part. She is the daintiest thing under a bonnet on this planet. So say the Serpentine-mews, to a man. She lives quietly, sings at concerts, drives out at five every day, and returns at seven sharp for dinner. Seldom goes out at other times, except when she sings. Has only one male visitor, but a good deal of him. He is dark, handsome, and dashing; never calls less than once a day, and often twice. He is a Mr. Godfrey Norton, of the Inner Temple. See the advantages of a cabman as a confidant. They had driven him home a dozen times from Serpentine-mews, and knew all about him. When I had listened to all they had to tell, I began to walk up and down near Briony Lodge once more, and to think over my plan of campaign.

"This Godfrey Norton was evidently an important factor in the matter. He was a lawyer. That sounded ominous. What was the relation between them, and what the object of his repeated visits? Was she his client, his friend, or his mistress? If the former, she had probably transferred the photograph to his keeping. If the latter, it was less likely. On the issue of this question depended whether I should continue my work at Briony Lodge, or turn my attention to the gentleman's chambers in the Temple. It was a delicate point, and it widened the field of my inquiry. I fear that I bore you with these details, but I have to let you see my little difficulties, if you are to understand the situation."

"I am following you closely," I answered.

"I was still balancing the matter in my mind, when a hansom cab drove up to Briony Lodge, and a gentleman sprang out. He was a remarkably handsome man, dark, aquiline, and moustached—evidently the man of whom I had heard. He appeared to be in a great hurry, shouted to the cabman to wait, and brushed past the maid who opened the door with the air of a man who was thoroughly at home.

"He was in the house about half an hour, and I could catch glimpses of him, in the windows of the sitting-room, pacing up and down, talking excitedly and waving his arms. Of her I could see nothing. Presently he emerged, looking even more flurried than before. As he stepped up to the cab, he pulled a gold watch from his pocket and looked at it earnestly. 'Drive like the devil,' he shouted, 'first to Gross & Hankey's in Regent-street, and then to the Church of St. Monica in the Edgware Road. Half a guinea if you do it in twenty minutes!'

"Away they went, and I was just wondering whether I should not do well to follow them, when up the lane came a neat little landau, the coachman with his coat only half buttoned, and his tie under his ear, while all the tags of his harness were sticking out of the buckles. It hadn't pulled up before she shot out of the hall door and into it. I only caught a glimpse of her at the moment, but she was a lovely woman, with a face that a man might die for. 'The Church of St. Monica, John,' she cried, 'and half a sovereign if you reach it in twenty minutes.'

"This was quite too good to lose, Watson. I was just balancing whether I should run for it, or whether I should perch behind her landau, when a cab came through the street. The driver looked twice at such a shabby fare; but I jumped in before he could object. 'The Church of St. Monica,' said I, 'and half a sovereign if you reach it in twenty minutes.' It was twenty-five minutes to twelve, and of course it was clear enough what was in the wind.

"My cabby drove fast. I don't think I ever drove faster, but the others were there before us. The cab and the landau with their steaming horses were in front of the door when I arrived. I paid the man, and hurried into the church. There was not a soul there save the two whom I had followed and a surpliced clergyman, who seemed to be expostulating with them. They were all three standing in a knot in front of the altar. I lounged up the side aisle like any other idler who has dropped into a church. Suddenly, to my surprise, the three at the altar faced round to me, and Godfrey Norton came running as hard as he could towards me."

"Thank God!" he cried. "You'll do. Come! Come!"

"What then?" I asked.

"Come man, come, only three minutes, or it won't be legal."

I was half dragged up to the altar, and, before I knew where I was, I found myself mumbling responses which were whispered in my ear, and vouching for things of which I knew nothing, and generally assisting in the secure tying up of Irene Adler, spinster, to Godfrey Norton, bachelor. It was all done in an instant, and there was the gentleman thanking me on the one side and the lady on the other, while the clergyman beamed on me in front. It was the most preposterous position in which I ever found myself in my life, and it was the thought of it that started me laughing just now. It seems that there had been some informality about their license, that the clergyman absolutely refused to marry them without a witness of some sort, and that my lucky appearance saved the bridegroom from having to sally out into the streets in search of a best man. The bride gave me a sovereign, and I mean to wear it on my watch chain in memory of the occasion."

"This is a very unexpected turn of affairs," said I; "and what then?"

"Well, I found my plans very seriously menaced. It looked as if the pair might take an immediate departure, and so necessitate very prompt and energetic measures on my part. At the church door, however, they separated, he driving back to the Temple, and she to her own house. 'I shall drive out in the Park at five as usual,' she said as she left him. I heard no more. They drove away in different directions, and I went off to make my own arrangements."

"Which are?"

"Some cold beef and a glass of beer," he answered, ringing the bell. "I have been too busy to think of food, and I am likely to be busier still this evening. By the way, Doctor, I shall want your co-operation."

"I shall be delighted."

"You don't mind breaking the law?"

"Not in the least."

"Nor running a chance of arrest?"

"Not in a good cause."

"Oh, the cause is excellent!"

"Then I am your man."

"I was sure that I might rely on you."

"But what is it you wish?"

"When Mrs. Turner has brought in the tray I will make it clear to you. Now," he said, as he turned hungrily on the simple fare that our landlady had provided, "I must discuss it while I eat, for I have not much time. It is nearly five now. In two hours we must be on the scene of action. Miss Irene, or Madame, rather, returns from her drive at seven. We must be at Briony Lodge to meet her."

"And what then?"

"You must leave that to me. I have already arranged what is to occur. There is only one point on which I must insist. You must not interfere, come what may. You understand?"

"I am to be neutral?"

"To do nothing whatever. There will probably be some small unpleasantness. Do not join in it. It will end in my being conveyed into the house. Four or five minutes afterwards the sitting-room window will open. You are to station yourself close to that open window."

"Yes."

"You are to watch me, for I will be visible to you."

"Yes."

"And when I raise my hand—so—you will throw into the room what I give you to throw, and will, at the same time, raise the cry of fire. You quite follow me?"

"Entirely."

"It is nothing very formidable," he said, taking a long cigar-shaped roll from his pocket. "It is an ordinary plumber's smoke-rocket, fitted with a cap at either end to make it self-lighting. Your task is confined to that. When you raise your cry of fire, it will be taken up by quite a number of people. You may then walk to the end of the street, and I will rejoin you in ten minutes. I hope that I have made myself clear?"

"I am to remain neutral, to get near the window, to watch you, and, at the signal, to throw in this object, then to raise the cry of fire, and to wait you at the corner of the street."

"Precisely."

"Then you may entirely rely on me."

"That is excellent. I think perhaps it is almost time that I prepare for the new role I have to play." He disappeared into his bedroom, and returned in a few minutes in the character of an amiable and simple-minded Nonconformist clergyman. His broad black hat, his baggy trousers, his white tie, his sympathetic smile, and general look of peering and benevolent curiosity were such as Mr. John Hare alone could have equalled. It was not merely that Holmes changed his costume. His expression, his manner, his very soul seemed to vary with every fresh part that he assumed. The stage lost a fine actor, even as science lost an acute reasoner, when he became a specialist in crime.

It was a quarter past six when we left Baker Street, and it still wanted ten minutes to the hour when we found ourselves in Serpentine Avenue. It was already dusk, and the lamps were just being lighted as we paced up and down in front of Briony Lodge, waiting for the coming of its occupant. The house was just such as I had pictured it from Sherlock Holmes' succinct description, but the locality appeared to be less private than I expected. On the contrary, for a small street in a quiet neighbourhood, it was remarkably animated. There was a group of shabbily-dressed men smoking and laughing in a corner, a scissors grinder with his wheel, two guardsmen who were flirting with a nurse-girl, and several well-dressed young men who were lounging up and down with cigars in their mouths.

"You see," remarked Holmes, as we paced to and fro in front of the house, "this marriage rather simplifies matters. The photograph becomes a double-edged weapon now. The chances are that she would be as averse to its being seen by Mr. Godfrey Norton, as our client is to its coming to the eyes of his Princess. Now the question is: Where are we to find the photograph?"

"Where, indeed?"

"It is most unlikely that she carries it about with her. It is cabinet size. Too large for easy concealment about a woman's dress. She knows that the King is capable of having her waylaid and searched. Two attempts of the sort have already been made. We may take it then that she does not carry it about with her."

"Where, then?"

"Her banker or her lawyer. There is that double possibility. But I am inclined to think neither. Women are naturally secretive, and they like to do their own secreting. Why should she hand it over to anyone else? She could trust her own guardianship, but she could not tell what indirect or political influence might be brought to bear upon a business man. Besides, remember that she had resolved to use it within a few days. It must be where she can lay her hands upon it. It must be in her own house."

"But it has twice been burgled."

"Pshaw! They did not know how to look."

"But how will you look?"

"I will not look."

"What then?"

"I will get her to show me."

"But she will refuse."

"She will not be able to. But I hear the rumble of wheels. It is her carriage. Now carry out my orders to the letter."

As he spoke the gleam of the sidelights of a carriage came round the curve of the avenue. It was a smart little landau which rattled up to the door of Briony Lodge. As it pulled up one of the loafing men at the corner dashed forward to open the door in the hope of earning a copper, but was elbowed away by another loafer who had rushed up with the same intention. A fierce quarrel broke out, which was increased by the two guardsmen, who took sides with one of the loungers, and by the scissors grinder, who was equally hot upon the other side. A blow was struck, and in an instant the lady, who had stepped from her carriage, was the centre of a little knot of flushed and struggling men who struck savagely at each other with their fists and sticks. Holmes dashed into the crowd to protect the lady; but, just as he reached her, he gave a cry and dropped to the ground, with the blood running freely down his face. At his fall the guardsmen took to their heels in one direction and the loungers in the other, while a number of better dressed people, who had watched the scuffle without taking part in it, crowded in to help the lady and to attend to the injured man. Irene Adler, as I will still call her, had hurried up the steps; but she stood at the top with her superb figure outlined against the lights of the hall, looking back into the street.

"Is the poor gentleman much hurt?" she asked.

"He is dead," cried several voices.

"No, no, there's life in him," shouted another. "But he'll be gone before you can get him to hospital."

"He's a brave fellow," said a woman. "They would have had the lady's purse and watch if it hadn't been for him. They were a gang, and a rough one too. Ah, he's breathing now."

"He can't lie in the street. May we bring him in, marm?"

"Surely. Bring him into the sitting-room. There is a comfortable sofa. This way, please!"

Slowly and solemnly he was borne into Briony Lodge, and laid out in the principal room, while I still observed the proceedings from my post by the window. The lamps had been lit, but the blinds had not been drawn, so that I could see Holmes as he lay upon the couch. I do not know whether he was seized with compunction at that moment for the part he was playing, but I know that I never felt more heartily ashamed of myself in my life than when I saw the beautiful creature against whom I was conspiring, or the grace and kindliness with which she waited upon the injured man. And yet it would be the blackest treachery to Holmes to draw back now from the part which he had entrusted to me. I hardened my heart, and took the smoke-rocket from under my ulster. After all, I thought, we are not injuring her. We are but preventing her from injuring another.

Holmes had sat up upon the couch, and I saw him motion like a man who is in need of air. A maid rushed across and threw open the window. At the same instant I saw him raise his hand, and at the signal I tossed my rocket into the room with a cry of "Fire." The word was no sooner out of my mouth than the whole crowd of spectators, well dressed and ill—gentlemen, ostlers, and servant maids—joined in a general shriek of "Fire." Thick clouds of smoke curled through the room and out at the open window. I caught a glimpse of rushing figures, and a moment later the voice of Holmes from within, assuring them that it was a false alarm. Slipping through the shouting crowd I made my way to the corner of the street, and in ten minutes was rejoiced to find my friend's arm in mine, and to get away from the scene of uproar. He walked swiftly and in silence for some few minutes, until we had turned down one of the quiet streets which lead towards the Edgware Road.

"You did it very nicely, Doctor," he remarked. "Nothing could have been better. It is all right."

"You have the photograph!"

"I know where it is."

"And how did you find out?"

"She showed me, as I told you that she would."

"I am still in the dark."

"I do not wish to make a mystery," said he laughing. "The matter was perfectly simple. You, of course, saw that everyone in the street was an accomplice. They were all engaged for the evening."

"I guessed as much."

"Then, when the row broke out, I had a little moist red paint in the palm of my hand. I rushed forward, fell down, clapped my hand to my face, and became a piteous spectacle. It is an old trick."

"That also I could fathom."

"Then they carried me in. She was bound to have me in. What else could she do? And into her sitting-room, which was the very room which I suspected. It lay between that and her bedroom, and I was determined to see which. They laid me on a couch, I motioned for air, they were compelled to open the window, and you had your chance."

"How did that help you?"

"It was all-important. When a woman thinks that her house is on fire, her instinct is at once to rush to the thing which she values most. It is a perfectly overpowering impulse, and I have more than once taken advantage of it. In the case of the Darlington Substitution Scandal it was of use to me, and also in the Arnsworth Castle business. A married woman grabs at her baby—an unmarried one reaches for her jewel box. Now it was clear to me that our lady of today had nothing in the house more precious to her than what we are in quest of. She would rush to secure it. The alarm of fire was admirably done. The smoke and shouting were enough to shake nerves of steel. She responded beautifully. The photograph is in a recess behind a sliding panel just above the right bell pull. She was there in an instant, and I caught a glimpse of it as she half drew it out. When I cried out that it was a false alarm, she replaced it, glanced at the rocket, rushed from the room, and I have not seen her since. I rose, and, making my excuses, escaped from the house. I hesitated whether to attempt to secure the photograph at once; but the coachman had come in, and, as he was watching me narrowly, it seemed safer to wait. A little over-precipitance may ruin all."

"And now?" I asked.

"Our quest is practically finished. I shall call with the King tomorrow, and with you, if you care to come with us. We will be shown into the sitting-room to wait for the lady, but it is probable that when she comes she may find neither us nor the photograph. It might be a satisfaction to His Majesty to regain it with his own hands."

"And when will you call?"

"At eight in the morning. She will not be up, so that we shall have a clear field. Besides, we must be prompt, for this marriage may mean a complete change in her life and habits. I must wire to the King without delay."

We had reached Baker Street, and had stopped at the door. He was searching his pockets for the key, when someone passing said: "Goodnight, Mister Sherlock Holmes."

There were several people on the pavement at the time, but the greeting appeared to come from a slim youth in an ulster who had hurried by.

"I've heard that voice before," said Holmes, staring down the dimly lit street. "Now, I wonder who the deuce that could have been."

III

I slept at Baker Street that night, and we were engaged upon our toast and coffee in the morning when the King of Bohemia rushed into the room.

"You have really got it!" he cried, grasping Sherlock Holmes by either shoulder, and looking eagerly into his face.

"Not yet."

"But you have hopes?"

"I have hopes."

"Then, come. I am all impatience to be gone."

"We must have a cab."

"No, my brougham is waiting."

"Then that will simplify matters." We descended, and started off once more for Briony Lodge.

"Irene Adler is married," remarked Holmes.

"Married! When?"

"Yesterday."

"But to whom?"

"To an English lawyer named Norton."

"But she could not love him?"

"I am in hopes that she does."

"And why in hopes?"

"Because it would spare your Majesty all fear of future annoyance. If the lady loves her husband, she does not love your Majesty. If she does not love your Majesty, there is no reason why she should interfere with your Majesty's plan."

"It is true. And yet—! Well! I wish she had been of my own station! What a queen she would have made!" He relapsed into a moody silence which was not broken, until we drew up in Serpentine Avenue.

The door of Briony Lodge was open, and an elderly woman stood upon the steps. She watched us with a sardonic eye as we stepped from the brougham.

"Mr. Sherlock Holmes, I believe?" said she.

"I am Mr. Holmes," answered my companion, looking at her with a questioning and rather startled gaze.

"Indeed! My mistress told me that you were likely to call. She left this morning with her husband, by the 5:15 train from Charing Cross, for the Continent."

"What!" Sherlock Holmes staggered back, white with chagrin and surprise. "Do you mean that she has left England?"

"Never to return."

"And the papers?" asked the King, hoarsely. "All is lost."

"We shall see." He pushed past the servant, and rushed into the drawing-room, followed by the King and myself. The furniture was scattered about in every direction, with dismantled shelves, and open drawers, as if the lady had hurriedly ransacked them before her flight. Holmes rushed at the bell-pull, tore back a small sliding shutter, and, plunging in his hand, pulled out a photograph and a letter. The photograph was of Irene Adler herself in evening dress, the letter was superscribed to "Sherlock Holmes, Esq. To be left till called for." My friend tore it open, and we all three read it together. It was dated at midnight of the preceding night, and ran in this way:—

My Dear Mr. Sherlock Holmes,

You really did it very well. You took me in completely. Until after the alarm of fire, I had not a suspicion. But then, when I found how I had betrayed myself, I began to think. I had been warned against you months ago. I had been told that, if the King employed an agent, it would certainly be you. And your address had been given me. Yet, with all this, you made me reveal what you wanted to know. Even after I became suspicious, I found it hard to think evil of such a dear, kind old clergyman. But, you know, I have been trained as an actress myself. Male costume is nothing new to me. I often take advantage of the freedom which it gives. I sent John, the coachman, to watch you, ran up stairs, got into my walking clothes, as I call them, and came down just as you departed.

Well, I followed you to your door, and so made sure that I was really an object of interest to the celebrated Mr. Sherlock Holmes. Then I, rather imprudently, wished you good night, and started for the Temple to see my husband.

We both thought the best resource was flight, when pursued by so formidable an antagonist; so you will find the nest empty when you call tomorrow. As to the photograph, your client may rest in peace. I love and am loved by a better man than he. The King may do what he will without hindrance from one whom he has cruelly wronged. I keep it only to safeguard myself, and to preserve a weapon which will always secure me from any steps which he might take in the future. I leave a photograph which he might care to possess; and I remain, dear Mr. Sherlock Holmes, very truly yours,

Irene Norton, née Adler.

"What a woman—oh, what a woman!" cried the King of Bohemia, when we had all three read this epistle. "Did I not tell you how quick and resolute she was? Would she not have made an admirable queen? Is it not a pity that she was not on my level?"

"From what I have seen of the lady, she seems, indeed, to be on a very different level to your Majesty," said Holmes, coldly. "I am sorry that I have not been able to bring your Majesty's business to a more successful conclusion."

"On the contrary, my dear sir," cried the King. "Nothing could be more successful. I know that her word is inviolate. The photograph is now as safe as if it were in the fire."

"I am glad to hear your Majesty say so."

"I am immensely indebted to you. Pray tell me in what way I can reward you. This ring—" He slipped an emerald snake ring from his finger, and held it out upon the palm of his hand.

"Your Majesty has something which I should value even more highly," said Holmes.

"You have but to name it."

"This photograph!"

The King stared at him in amazement.

"Irene's photograph!" he cried. "Certainly, if you wish it."

"I thank your Majesty. Then there is no more to be done in the matter. I have the honour to wish you a very good morning." He bowed, and, turning away without observing the hand which the King had stretched out to him, he set off in my company for his chambers.

And that was how a great scandal threatened to affect the kingdom of Bohemia, and how the best plans of Mr. Sherlock Holmes were beaten by a woman's wit. He used to make merry over the cleverness of women, but I have not heard him do it of late. And when he speaks of Irene Adler, or when he refers to her photograph, it is always under the honourable title of *the* woman.

Thinking About the Story

Living in Victorian Britain, Arthur Conan Doyle was privy to the radical social, cultural, and technical changes occurring within the nation. These changes are incorporated into Conan Doyle's fiction, valuing, as he does, the primacy of logic in an unstable world. Therefore, in trying to understand Conan Doyle and his thoughts about the scientific method, it is productive to formulate some answers to the following questions: What do we mean by the term "scientific method"? Can behavior be deduced by observation and experimentation? Is it part of human nature to categorize things? In your reading, you will find it helpful to read H. G. Wells' story, "A Moth — Genus Novo" for two reasons. First, the narrator of each story is not the central protagonist. Second, contrasting the stories will lead you to examine the complexities and forms of the scientific method.

Discussion Questions

1. List the steps Holmes took to solve the case. What clues did he find? What are your thoughts on his methods?

2. Using passages of text to support your ideas, describe Holmes' friendship with Watson. What do we know about their past? What can we deduce about their working relationship?

3. Highlight some of Holmes' unique observations. Which are your favorites? Remember to explain why you feel this way.

4. In terms of dramatic tension *and* character development, analyze the importance of the scandal in both of these regards. In more specific terms, choose one of the story's characters and demonstrate how that character's action defines his personality.

5. Why is the photograph of Irene Adler important to Holmes? Describe the nature of their relationship. Do you think they will meet again?

Activities

1. Consider Sherlock Holmes' ingenious hoax on Irene Adler to reveal the photograph's location. Your task: invent another way Holmes could make Adler disclose the location.

2. Watch one of the numerous Sherlock Holmes films or television programs. Write two pages on which you prefer: the short story or the film/program. Remember to explain in detail why, and to use examples to support your opinions.

3. Create your own Sherlock Holmes mystery. Devise, develop, and write a story using Holmes, Watson, and your own characters. Choose from one of the following mediums:

   a. Short story

   b. Comic book

   c. Short film or radio drama

   d. Play

Anton Chekhov

Medicine is my lawful wedded wife, and literature my mistress.
Anton Chekhov — *Letter to A. S. Suvorin* (1888)

Emerging out of the shadow of fellow Russian author Leo Tolstoy, Anton Chekhov (1860–1904) developed the parameters of the modern short story. Chekhov was born to a middle-class family in Taganrog, a seaport in southern Russia. Growing up with his five siblings, he worked in his father's general store and in his spare time cultivated interests in music, nature, and theatre. Owing to his father's later bankruptcy, Chekhov wrote satirical pieces and newspaper columns to help with the family finances. A few years later, he attended medical school in Moscow. After he qualified as a doctor, he practiced in the provinces. Throughout his life, he devoted substantial time to both his medical and literary careers. In 1901, he married an actress, Olga Knipper, who had starred in his play, *The Seagull.* Chekhov continued to work from his home in Yalta while his wife lived in Moscow. A couple of years later, at age 44, he died of tuberculosis.

As the epigraph above demonstrates, Chekhov had a dual nature as a humanitarian and as an artist. His characters often exhibit similar tendencies, facets that deepen and instill a true-to-life moral complexity into his stories. For a short period, Chekhov wrote humorous sketches and stories. Yet in his later years, with the encouragement of the writer Dmitri Grigorovich, Chekhov took his writing seriously and focused on the short story form, publishing *Motley Tales* (1886) and *At Dusk* (1887) to great acclaim. In "The Lady with the Dog," (1899) one of his final stories, Chekhov combines psychology with subterfuge and adultery with romance. In each of the four parts, the reader is not privy to the full spectrum of character motivation or

Gurov or Anna's complete backstory. Instead, Chekhov develops the secret lives of his creations to add a human dimension to the narrative, a technique that increases the dramatic tension.

The Lady with the Dog

Anton Chekhov

Translated by Constance Garnett

I

It was said that a new person had appeared on the sea front: a lady with a little dog. Dmitri Dmitritch Gurov, who had by then been a fortnight at Yalta, and so was fairly at home there, had begun to take an interest in new arrivals. Sitting in Verney's pavilion, he saw, walking on the sea front, a fair-haired young lady of medium height, wearing a beret; a white Pomeranian dog was running behind her.

And afterwards he met her in the public gardens and in the square several times a day. She was walking alone, always wearing the same beret, and always with the same white dog; no one knew who she was, and every one called her simply "the lady with the dog."

"If she is here alone without a husband or friends, it wouldn't be amiss to make her acquaintance," Gurov reflected.

He was under forty, but he had a daughter already twelve years old, and two sons at school. He had been married young, when he was a student in his second year, and by now his wife seemed half as old again as he. She was a tall, erect woman with dark eyebrows, staid and dignified, and, as she said of herself, intellectual. She read a great deal, used phonetic spelling, called her husband, not Dmitri, but Dimitri, and he secretly considered her unintelligent, narrow, inelegant, was afraid of her, and did not like to be at home. He had begun being unfaithful to her long ago—he had been unfaithful to her often, and, probably on that account, almost always spoke ill of women, and when they were talked about in his presence, used to call them "the lower race."

It seemed to him that he had been so schooled by bitter experience that he might call them what he liked, and yet he could not get on for two days together without "the lower race." In the society of men he was bored and not himself, with them he was cold and uncommunicative; but when he was in the company of women he felt free, and knew what to say to them and how to behave; and he was at ease with them even when he was silent. In his appearance, in his character, in his whole nature, there was something attractive and elusive that allured women and disposed them in his favour; he knew that, and some force seemed to draw him, too, to them.

Experience often repeated, truly bitter experience, had taught him long ago that with decent people, especially Moscow people—always slow to move and irresolute—every intimacy, which at first so agreeably diversifies life and appears a light and charming adventure, inevitably grows into a regular problem of extreme intricacy, and in the long run the situation becomes unbearable. But at every fresh meeting with an interesting woman this experience seemed to slip out of his memory, and he was eager for life, and everything seemed simple and amusing.

One evening he was dining in the gardens, and the lady in the beret came up slowly to take the next table. Her expression, her gait, her dress, and the way she did her hair told him that she was a lady, that she was married, that she was in Yalta for the first time and alone, and that she was dull there. The stories told of the immorality in such places as Yalta are to a great extent untrue; he despised them, and knew that such stories were for the most part made up by persons who would themselves have been glad to sin if they had been able; but when the lady sat down at the next table three paces from him, he remembered these tales of easy conquests, of trips to the mountains, and the tempting thought of a swift, fleeting love affair, a romance with an unknown woman, whose name he did not know, suddenly took possession of him.

He beckoned coaxingly to the Pomeranian, and when the dog came up to him he shook his finger at it.

The Pomeranian growled: Gurov shook his finger at it again.

The lady looked at him and at once dropped her eyes.

"He doesn't bite," she said, and blushed.

"May I give him a bone?" he asked; and when she nodded he asked courteously, "Have you been long in Yalta?"

"Five days."

"And I have already dragged out a fortnight here."

There was a brief silence.

"Time goes fast, and yet it is so dull here!" she said, not looking at him.

"That's only the fashion to say it is dull here. A provincial will live in Belyov or Zhidra and not be dull, and when he comes here it's 'Oh, the dullness! Oh, the dust!' One would think he came from Grenada."

She laughed. Then both continued eating in silence, like strangers, but after dinner they walked side by side; and there sprang up between them the light jesting conversation of people who are free and satisfied, to whom it does not matter where they go or what they talk about. They walked and talked of the strange light on the sea: the water was of a soft warm lilac hue, and there was a golden streak from the moon upon it. They talked of how sultry it was after a hot day. Gurov told her that he came from Moscow, that he had taken his degree in Arts, but had a post in a bank; that he had trained as an opera-singer, but had given it up, that he owned two houses in Moscow. And from her he learnt that she had grown up in Petersburg, but had lived in S—— since her marriage two years before, that she was staying another month in Yalta, and that her husband, who needed a holiday too, might perhaps come and fetch her. She was not sure whether her husband had a post in a Crown Department or under the Provincial Council—and was amused by her own ignorance. And Gurov learnt, too, that she was called Anna Sergeyevna.

Afterwards he thought about her in his room at the hotel—thought she would certainly meet him the next day; it would be sure to happen. As he got into bed he thought how lately she had been a girl at school, doing lessons like his own daughter; he recalled the diffidence, the angularity that was still manifest in her laugh and her manner of talking with a stranger. This must have been the first time in her life she had been alone in surroundings in which she was followed, looked at, and spoken to merely from a secret motive, which she could hardly fail to guess. He recalled her slender, delicate neck, her lovely grey eyes.

"There's something pathetic about her, anyway," he thought, and fell asleep.

II

A week had passed since they had made acquaintance. It was a holiday. It was sultry indoors, while in the street the wind whirled the dust round and round, and blew people's hats off. It was a thirsty day, and Gurov often went into the pavilion, and pressed Anna Sergeyevna to have syrup and water or an ice. One did not know what to do with oneself.

In the evening when the wind had dropped a little, they went out on the groyne to see the steamer come in. There were a great many people walking about the harbour; they had gathered to welcome some one, bringing bouquets. And two peculiarities of a well-dressed Yalta crowd were very conspicuous: the elderly ladies were dressed like young ones, and there were great numbers of generals.

Owing to the roughness of the sea, the steamer arrived late, after the sun had set, and it was a long time turning about before it reached the groyne. Anna Sergeyevna looked through her lorgnette at the steamer and the passengers as though looking for acquaintances, and when she turned to Gurov her eyes were shining. She talked a great deal and asked disconnected questions, forgetting in the next moment what she had asked; then she dropped her lorgnette in the crush.

The festive crowd began to disperse; it was too dark to see people's faces. The wind had completely dropped, but Gurov and Anna Sergeyevna still stood as though waiting to see some one else come from the steamer. Anna Sergeyevna was silent now, and sniffed the flowers without looking at Gurov.

"The weather is better this evening," he said. "Where shall we go now? Shall we drive somewhere?"

She gave no answer.

Then he looked at her intently, and all at once put his arm round her and kissed her on the lips, and breathed in the moisture and the fragrance of the flowers; and he immediately looked round him, anxiously wondering whether any one had seen them.

"Let us go to your hotel," he said softly. And both walked quickly.

The room was close and smelt of the scent she had bought at the Japanese shop. Gurov looked at her and thought: "What different people one meets in the world!" From the past he preserved memories of careless, good-natured women, who loved cheerfully and were grateful to him for the happiness he gave them, however brief it might be; and of women like his wife who loved without any genuine feeling, with superfluous phrases, affectedly, hysterically, with an expression that suggested that it was not love nor passion, but something more significant; and of two or three others, very beautiful, cold women, on whose faces he had caught a glimpse of a rapacious expression—an obstinate desire to snatch from life more than it could give, and these were capricious, unreflecting, domineering, unintelligent women not in their first youth, and when Gurov grew cold to them their beauty excited his hatred, and the lace on their linen seemed to him like scales.

But in this case there was still the diffidence, the angularity of inexperienced youth, an awkward feeling; and there was a sense of consternation as though some one had suddenly knocked at the door. The attitude of Anna Sergeyevna—"the lady with the dog"—to what had happened was somehow peculiar, very grave, as though it were her fall—so it seemed, and it was strange and inappropriate. Her face dropped and faded, and on both sides of it her long hair hung down mournfully; she mused in a dejected attitude like "the woman who was a sinner" in an old-fashioned picture.

"It's wrong," she said. "You will be the first to despise me now."

There was a watermelon on the table. Gurov cut himself a slice and began eating it without haste. There followed at least half an hour of silence.

Anna Sergeyevna was touching; there was about her the purity of a good, simple woman who had seen little of life. The solitary candle burning on the table threw a faint light on her face, yet it was clear that she was very unhappy.

"How could I despise you?" asked Gurov. "You don't know what you are saying."

"God forgive me," she said, and her eyes filled with tears. "It's awful."

"You seem to feel you need to be forgiven."

"Forgiven? No. I am a bad, low woman; I despise myself and don't attempt to justify myself. It's not my husband but myself I have deceived. And not only just now; I have been deceiving myself for a long time. My husband may be a good, honest man, but he is a flunkey! I don't know what he does there, what his work is, but I know he is a flunkey! I was twenty when I was married to him. I have been tormented by curiosity; I wanted something better. 'There must be a different sort of life,' I said to myself. I wanted to live! To live, to live! I was fired by curiosity, you don't understand it, but I swear to God, I could not control myself; something happened to me: I could not be restrained. I told my husband I was ill, and came here. And here I have been walking about as though I were dazed, like a mad creature. And now I have become a vulgar, contemptible woman whom any one may despise."

Gurov felt bored already, listening to her. He was irritated by the naive tone, by this remorse, so unexpected and inopportune; but for the tears in her eyes, he might have thought she was jesting or playing a part.

"I don't understand," he said softly. "What is it you want?"

She hid her face on his breast and pressed close to him.

"Believe me, believe me, I beseech you," she said. "I love a pure, honest life, and sin is loathsome to me. I don't know what I am doing. Simple people say: 'The Evil One has beguiled me.' And I may say of myself now that the Evil One has beguiled me."

"Hush, hush!" he muttered.

He looked at her fixed, scared eyes, kissed her, talked softly and affectionately, and by degrees she was comforted, and her gaiety returned; they both began laughing.

Afterwards when they went out there was not a soul on the sea front. The town with its cypresses had quite a deathlike air, but the sea still broke noisily on the shore; a single barge was rocking on the waves, and a lantern was blinking sleepily on it.

They found a cab and drove to Oreanda.

"I found out your surname in the hall just now: it was written on the board—Von Diderits," said Gurov.

"Is your husband a German?"

"No. I believe his grandfather was a German, but he is an Orthodox Russian himself."

At Oreanda they sat on a seat not far from the church, looked down at the sea, and were silent. Yalta was hardly visible through the morning mist; white clouds stood motionless on the mountaintops. The leaves did not stir on the trees, grasshoppers chirruped, and the monotonous hollow sound of the sea rising up from below, spoke of the peace, of the eternal sleep awaiting us. So it must have sounded when there was no Yalta, no Oreanda here; so it sounds now, and it will sound as indifferently and monotonously when we are all no more. And in this constancy, in this complete indifference to the life and death of each of us, there lies hid, perhaps, a pledge of our eternal salvation, of the unceasing movement of life upon earth, of unceasing progress towards perfection. Sitting beside a young woman who in the dawn seemed so lovely, soothed and spellbound in these magical surroundings—the sea, mountains, clouds, the open sky—Gurov thought how in reality everything is beautiful in this world when one reflects: everything except what we think or do ourselves when we forget our human dignity and the higher aims of our existence.

A man walked up to them—probably a keeper—looked at them and walked away. And this detail seemed mysterious and beautiful, too. They saw a steamer come from Theodosia, with its lights out in the glow of dawn.

"There is dew on the grass," said Anna Sergeyevna, after a silence.

"Yes. It's time to go home."

They went back to the town.

Then they met every day at twelve o'clock on the sea-front, lunched and dined together, went for walks, admired the sea. She complained that she slept badly, that her heart throbbed violently; asked the same questions, troubled now by jealousy and now by the fear that he did not respect her sufficiently. And often in the square or gardens, when there was no one near them, he suddenly drew her to him and kissed her passionately. Complete idleness, these kisses in broad daylight while he looked round in dread of some one's seeing them, the heat, the smell of the sea, and the continual passing to and fro before him of idle, well-dressed, well-fed people, made a new man of him; he told Anna Sergeyevna how beautiful she was, how fascinating. He was impatiently passionate, he would not move a step away from her, while she was often pensive and continually urged him to confess that he did not respect her, did not love her in the least, and thought of her as nothing but a common woman. Rather late almost every evening they drove somewhere out of town, to Oreanda or to the waterfall; and the expedition was always a success, the scenery invariably impressed them as grand and beautiful.

They were expecting her husband to come, but a letter came from him, saying that there was something wrong with his eyes, and he entreated his wife to come home as quickly as possible. Anna Sergeyevna made haste to go.

"It's a good thing I am going away," she said to Gurov. "It's the finger of destiny!"

She went by coach and he went with her. They were driving the whole day. When she had got into a compartment of the express, and when the second bell had rung, she said:

"Let me look at you once more, look at you once again. That's right."

She did not shed tears, but was so sad that she seemed ill, and her face was quivering.

"I shall remember you—think of you," she said. "God be with you; be happy. Don't remember evil against me. We are parting forever—it must be so, for we ought never to have met. Well, God be with you."

The train moved off rapidly, its lights soon vanished from sight, and a minute later there was no sound of it, as though everything had conspired together to end as quickly as possible that sweet delirium, that madness. Left alone on the platform, and gazing into the dark distance, Gurov listened to the chirrup of the grasshoppers and the hum of the telegraph wires, feeling as though he had only just woken up. And he thought, musing, that there had been another episode or adventure in his life, and it, too, was at an end, and nothing was left of it but a memory. He was moved, sad, and conscious of a slight remorse. This young woman whom he would never meet again had not been happy with him; he was genuinely warm and affectionate with her, but yet in his manner, his tone, and his caresses there had been a shade of light irony, the coarse condescension of a happy man who was, besides, almost twice her age. All the time she had called him kind, exceptional, lofty; obviously he had seemed to her different from what he really was, so he had unintentionally deceived her.

Here at the station was already a scent of autumn; it was a cold evening.

"It's time for me to go north," thought Gurov as he left the platform. "High time!"

III

At home in Moscow everything was in its winter routine; the stoves were heated, and in the morning it was still dark when the children were having breakfast and getting ready for school, and the nurse would light the lamp for a short time. The frosts had begun already. When the first snow has fallen, on the first day of sledge driving it is pleasant to see the white earth, the white roofs, to draw soft, delicious breath, and the season brings back the days of one's youth. The old limes and birches, white with hoarfrost, have a good-natured expression; they are nearer to one's heart than cypresses and palms, and near them one doesn't want to be thinking of the sea and the mountains.

Gurov was Moscow born; he arrived in Moscow on a fine frosty day, and when he put on his fur coat and warm gloves, and walked along Petrovka, and when on Saturday evening he heard the ringing of the bells, his recent trip and the places he had seen lost all charm for him. Little by little he became absorbed in Moscow life, greedily read three newspapers a day, and declared he did not read the Moscow papers on principle! He already felt a longing to go to restaurants, clubs, dinner-parties, anniversary celebrations, and he felt flattered at entertaining distinguished lawyers and artists, and at playing cards with a professor at the doctors' club. He could already eat a whole plateful of salt fish and cabbage.

In another month, he fancied, the image of Anna Sergeyevna would be shrouded in a mist in his memory, and only from time to time would visit him in his dreams with a touching smile as others did. But more than a month passed, real winter had come, and everything was still clear in his memory as though he had parted with Anna Sergeyevna only the day before. And his memories glowed more and more vividly. When in the evening stillness he heard from his study the voices of his children, preparing their lessons, or when he listened to a song or the organ at the restaurant, or the storm howled in the chimney, suddenly everything would rise up in his memory: what had happened on the groyne, and the early morning with the mist on the mountains, and the steamer coming from Theodosia, and the kisses. He would pace a long time about his room, remembering it all and smiling; then his memories passed into dreams, and in his fancy the past was mingled with what was to come. Anna Sergeyevna did not visit him in dreams, but followed him about everywhere like a shadow and haunted him. When he shut his eyes he saw her as though she were living before him, and she seemed to him lovelier, younger, tenderer than she was; and he imagined himself finer than he had been in Yalta. In the evenings she peeped out at him from the bookcase, from the fireplace, from the corner—he heard her breathing, the caressing rustle of her dress. In the street he watched the women, looking for some one like her.

He was tormented by an intense desire to confide his memories to some one. But in his home it was impossible to talk of his love, and he had no one outside; he could not talk to his tenants nor to any one at the bank. And what had he to talk of? Had he been in love, then? Had there been anything beautiful, poetical, or edifying or simply interesting in his relations with Anna Sergeyevna? And there was nothing for him but to talk vaguely of love, of woman, and no one guessed what it meant; only his wife twitched her black eyebrows, and said:

"The part of a lady-killer does not suit you at all, Dimitri."

One evening, coming out of the doctors' club with an official with whom he had been playing cards, he could not resist saying:

"If only you knew what a fascinating woman I made the acquaintance of in Yalta!"

The official got into his sledge and was driving away, but turned suddenly and shouted:

"Dmitri Dmitritch!"

"What?"

"You were right this evening: the sturgeon was a bit too strong!"

These words, so ordinary, for some reason moved Gurov to indignation, and struck him as degrading and unclean. What savage manners, what people! What senseless nights, what uninteresting, uneventful days! The rage for card playing, the gluttony, the drunkenness, the continual talk always about the same thing. Useless pursuits and conversations always about the same things absorb the better part of one's time, the better part of one's strength, and in the end there is left a life grovelling and curtailed, worthless and trivial, and there is no escaping or getting away from it—just as though one were in a madhouse or a prison.

Gurov did not sleep all night, and was filled with indignation. And he had a headache all next day. And the next night he slept badly; he sat up in bed, thinking, or paced up and down his room. He was sick of his children, sick of the bank; he had no desire to go anywhere or to talk of anything.

In the holidays in December he prepared for a journey, and told his wife he was going to Petersburg to do something in the interests of a young friend—and he set off for S——. What for? He did not very well know himself. He wanted to see Anna Sergeyevna and to talk with her—to arrange a meeting, if possible.

He reached S—— in the morning, and took the best room at the hotel, in which the floor was covered with grey army cloth, and on the table was an inkstand, grey with dust and adorned with a figure on horseback, with its hat in its hand and its head broken off. The hotel porter gave him the necessary information; Von Diderits lived in a house of his own in Old Gontcharny Street—it was not far from the hotel: he was rich and lived in good style, and had his own horses; every one in the town knew him. The porter pronounced the name "Dridirits."

Gurov went without haste to Old Gontcharny Street and found the house. Just opposite the house stretched a long grey fence adorned with nails.

"One would run away from a fence like that," thought Gurov, looking from the fence to the windows of the house and back again.

He considered: today was a holiday, and the husband would probably be at home. And in any case it would be tactless to go into the house and upset her. If he were to send her a note it might fall into her husband's hands, and then it might ruin everything. The best thing was to trust to chance. And he kept walking up and down the street by the fence, waiting for the chance. He saw a beggar go in at the gate and dogs fly at him; then an hour later he heard a piano, and the sounds were faint and indistinct. Probably it was Anna Sergeyevna playing. The front door suddenly opened, and an old woman came out, followed by the familiar white Pomeranian. Gurov was on the point of calling to the dog, but his heart began beating violently, and in his excitement he could not remember the dog's name.

He walked up and down, and loathed the grey fence more and more, and by now he thought irritably that Anna Sergeyevna had forgotten him, and was perhaps already amusing herself with some one else, and that that was very natural in a young woman who had nothing to look at from morning till night but that confounded fence. He went back to his hotel room and sat for a long while on the sofa, not knowing what to do, then he had dinner and a long nap.

"How stupid and worrying it is!" he thought when he woke and looked at the dark windows: it was already evening. "Here I've had a good sleep for some reason. What shall I do in the night?"

He sat on the bed, which was covered by a cheap grey blanket, such as one sees in hospitals, and he taunted himself in his vexation:

"So much for the lady with the dog, so much for the adventure. You're in a nice fix."

That morning at the station a poster in large letters had caught his eye. "The Geisha" was to be performed for the first time. He thought of this and went to the theatre.

"It's quite possible she may go to the first performance," he thought.

The theatre was full. As in all provincial theatres, there was a fog above the chandelier, the gallery was noisy and restless; in the front row the local dandies were standing up before the beginning of the performance, with their hands behind them; in the Governor's box the Governor's daughter, wearing a boa, was sitting in the front seat, while the Governor himself lurked modestly behind the curtain with only his hands visible; the orchestra was a long time tuning up; the stage curtain swayed. All the time the audience were coming in and taking their seats Gurov looked at them eagerly.

Anna Sergeyevna, too, came in. She sat down in the third row, and when Gurov looked at her his heart contracted, and he understood clearly that for him there was in the whole world no creature so near, so precious, and so important to him; she, this little woman, in no way remarkable, lost in a provincial crowd, with a vulgar lorgnette in her hand, filled his whole life now, was his sorrow and his joy, the one happiness that he now desired for himself, and to the sounds of the inferior orchestra, of the wretched provincial violins, he thought how lovely she was. He thought and dreamed.

A young man with small side-whiskers, tall and stooping, came in with Anna Sergeyevna and sat down beside her; he bent his head at every step and seemed to be continually bowing. Most likely this was the husband whom at Yalta, in a rush of bitter feeling, she had called a flunkey. And there really was in his long figure, his side-whiskers, and the small bald patch on his head, something of the flunkey's obsequiousness; his smile was sugary, and in his buttonhole there was some badge of distinction like the number on a waiter.

During the first interval the husband went away to smoke; she remained alone in her stall. Gurov, who was sitting in the stalls, too, went up to her and said in a trembling voice, with a forced smile:

"Good-evening."

She glanced at him and turned pale, then glanced again with horror, unable to believe her eyes, and tightly gripped the fan and the lorgnette in her hands, evidently struggling with herself not to faint. Both were silent. She was sitting. He was standing, frightened by her confusion and not venturing to sit down beside her. The violins and the flute began tuning up. He felt suddenly frightened; it seemed as though all the people in the boxes were looking at them. She got up and went quickly to the door; he followed her, and both walked senselessly along passages, and up and down stairs, and figures in legal, scholastic, and civil service uniforms, all wearing badges, flitted before their eyes. They caught glimpses of ladies, of fur coats hanging on pegs; the draughts blew on them, bringing a smell of stale tobacco. And Gurov, whose heart was beating violently, thought:

"Oh, heavens! Why are these people here and this orchestra!"

And at that instant he recalled how when he had seen Anna Sergeyevna off at the station he had thought that everything was over and they would never meet again. But how far they were still from the end!

On the narrow, gloomy staircase over which was written "To the Amphitheatre," she stopped.

"How you have frightened me!" she said, breathing hard, still pale and overwhelmed. "Oh, how you have frightened me! I am half dead. Why have you come? Why?"

"But do understand, Anna, do understand," he said hastily in a low voice. "I entreat you to understand."

She looked at him with dread, with entreaty, with love; she looked at him intently, to keep his features more distinctly in her memory.

"I am so unhappy," she went on, not heeding him. "I have thought of nothing but you all the time; I live only in the thought of you. And I wanted to forget, to forget you; but why, oh, why, have you come?"

On the landing above them two schoolboys were smoking and looking down, but that was nothing to Gurov; he drew Anna Sergeyevna to him, and began kissing her face, her cheeks, and her hands.

"What are you doing, what are you doing!" she cried in horror, pushing him away. "We are mad. Go away today; go away at once. I beseech you by all that is sacred, I implore you. There are people coming this way!"

Some one was coming up the stairs.

"You must go away," Anna Sergeyevna went on in a whisper. "Do you hear, Dmitri Dmitritch? I will come and see you in Moscow. I have never been happy; I am miserable now, and I never, never shall be happy, never! Don't make me suffer still more! I swear I'll come to Moscow. But now let us part. My precious, good, dear one, we must part!"

She pressed his hand and began rapidly going downstairs, looking round at him, and from her eyes he could see that she really was unhappy. Gurov stood for a little while, listened, then, when all sound had died away, he found his coat and left the theatre.

IV

And Anna Sergeyevna began coming to see him in Moscow. Once in two or three months she left S——, telling her husband that she was going to consult a doctor about an internal complaint—and her husband believed her, and did not believe her. In Moscow she stayed at the Slaviansky Bazaar hotel, and at once sent a man in a red cap to Gurov. Gurov went to see her, and no one in Moscow knew of it.

Once he was going to see her in this way on a winter morning (the messenger had come the evening before when he was out). With him walked his daughter, whom he wanted to take to school; it was on the way. Snow was falling in big wet flakes.

"It's three degrees above freezing-point, and yet it is snowing," said Gurov to his daughter. "The thaw is only on the surface of the earth; there is quite a different temperature at a greater height in the atmosphere."

"And why are there no thunderstorms in the winter, Father?"

He explained that, too. He talked, thinking all the while that he was going to see her, and no living soul knew of it, and probably never would know. He had two lives: one, open, seen, and known by all who cared to know, full of relative truth and of relative falsehood, exactly like the lives of his friends and acquaintances; and another life running its course in secret. And through some strange, perhaps accidental, conjunction of circumstances, everything that was essential, of interest and of value to him, everything in which he was sincere and did not deceive himself, everything that made the kernel of his life, was hidden from other people; and all that was false in him, the sheath in which he hid himself to conceal the truth—such, for instance, as his work in the bank, his discussions at the club, his "lower race," his presence with his wife at anniversary festivities—all that was open. And he judged of others by himself, not believing in what he saw, and always believing that every man had his real, most interesting life under the cover of secrecy and under the cover of night. All personal life rested on secrecy, and possibly it was partly on that account that civilised man was so nervously anxious that personal privacy should be respected.

After leaving his daughter at school, Gurov went on to the Slaviansky Bazaar. He took off his fur coat below, went upstairs, and softly knocked at the door. Anna Sergeyevna, wearing his favourite grey dress, exhausted by the journey and the suspense, had been expecting him since the evening before. She was pale; she looked at him, and did not smile, and he had hardly come in when she fell on his breast. Their kiss was slow and prolonged, as though they had not met for two years.

"Well, how are you getting on there?" he asked. "What news?"

"Wait; I'll tell you directly. I can't talk."

She could not speak; she was crying. She turned away from him, and pressed her handkerchief to her eyes.

"Let her have her cry out. I'll sit down and wait," he thought, and he sat down in an armchair. Then he rang and asked for tea to be brought him, and while he drank his tea she remained standing at the window with her back to him. She was crying from emotion, from the miserable consciousness that their life was so hard for them; they could only meet in secret, hiding themselves from people, like thieves! Was not their life shattered?

"Come, do stop!" he said.

It was evident to him that this love of theirs would not soon be over, that he could not see the end of it. Anna Sergeyevna grew more and more attached to him. She adored him, and it was unthinkable to say to her that it was bound to have an end some day; besides, she would not have believed it!

He went up to her and took her by the shoulders to say something affectionate and cheering, and at that moment he saw himself in the looking glass.

His hair was already beginning to turn grey. And it seemed strange to him that he had grown so much older, so much plainer during the last few years. The shoulders on which his hands rested were warm and quivering. He felt compassion for this life, still so warm and lovely, but probably already not far from beginning to fade and wither like his own. Why did she love him so much? He always seemed to women different from what he was, and they loved in him not himself, but the man created by their imagination, whom they had been eagerly seeking all their lives; and afterwards, when they noticed their mistake, they loved him all the same. And not one of them had been happy with him. Time passed, he had made their acquaintance, got on with them, parted, but he had never once loved; it was anything you like, but not love.

And only now when his head was grey he had fallen properly, really in love—for the first time in his life.

Anna Sergeyevna and he loved each other like people very close and akin, like husband and wife, like tender friends; it seemed to them that fate itself had meant them for one another, and they could not understand why he had a wife and she a husband; and it was as though they were a pair of birds of passage, caught and forced to live in different cages. They forgave each other for what they were ashamed of in their past, they forgave everything in the present, and felt that this love of theirs had changed them both.

In moments of depression in the past he had comforted himself with any arguments that came into his mind, but now he no longer cared for arguments; he felt profound compassion, he wanted to be sincere and tender.

"Don't cry, my darling," he said. "You've had your cry; that's enough. Let us talk now, let us think of some plan."

Then they spent a long while taking counsel together, talked of how to avoid the necessity for secrecy, for deception, for living in different towns and not seeing each other for long at a time. How could they be free from this intolerable bondage?

"How? How?" he asked, clutching his head. "How?"

And it seemed as though in a little while the solution would be found, and then a new and splendid life would begin; and it was clear to both of them that they had still a long, long road before them, and that the most complicated and difficult part of it was only just beginning.

Thinking About the Story

In Anton Chekhov's work you will find no easy answers, no final resolutions to his stories. Instead, think about the manner in which he plays with narrative, highlighting, as he does in the story, that the end is only the beginning. In the modern age, we have a tendency to view our existence in terms of narrative, one event or action leading to another. Chekhov was aware of this phenomenon and sought to map out the drama of everyday living. Therefore, as you consider the nuances and ramifications of "The Lady with the Dog," it is advisable to read in tandem Leo Tolstoy's "How

Much Land Does a Man Need?" Although the stories examine different aspects of Russian life, both depict conflicted characters. You should draw comparisons between the two works, assessing how each writer uses storytelling to express his views on the nature of humanity.

Discussion Questions

1. The story is generally from Gurov's point of view. Does this point of view create empathy toward Gurov? How would the story change if it were told from Anna's point of view?
2. Considering Gurov's physical appearance, his speeches, and his actions, characterize his motivations and beliefs. When and how do they change over the story? Do his feelings for Anna reverse how he feels about himself?
3. What are the major conflicts for both Gurov and Anna? Are any of the conflicts resolved for either of them?
4. How is the physical environment represented? How do the landscape and people of Yalta contrast with the events and places in Moscow? What propels Gurov to leave Moscow?
5. Would you describe "Lady with the Dog" as a love story? What other categories could it fit in to? How does the ending affect your categorization of the story?

Activities

1. List the things you dislike about both Gurov and Anna. In the circumstances, are any of these traits or behaviors understandable? Write a paragraph describing how they build character in the story.
2. Write a one-sentence summary of the story. Afterward, compare and contrast with your classmate's version.
3. Create an outline of the events and action in the story. Use the outline to help you write your own part V of "The Lady with the Dog." In the new part, use the characters' pasts and personalities to create the next installment of their lives.

Charlotte Perkins Gilman

There is no female mind. The brain is not an organ of sex.
Might as well speak of a female liver.
Charlotte Perkins Gilman — *Women and Economics* (1898)

Although Charlotte Perkins Gilman's literary reputation waned during her lifetime (1860–1935), her legacy has since been recovered. In recent years, she has been celebrated as one of the most important women writers in American literature. She was born in Hartford, Connecticut, to a poor family. As a child, she was interested in social justice and the natural sciences. Later, she studied painting at the Rhode Island School of Design. In 1884, she married the artist Charles Walter Stetson and the following year they had a daughter together. After only a few years, the couple divorced, which allowed Charlotte to marry George Houghton Gilman. However, for most of her life Gilman suffered from depression, and after giving birth she regularly had episodes of postpartum psychosis. Ordered by her doctor (Dr. Weir, who also appears in the story) to a domestic rest-cure treatment, Gilman's personal experiences went on to make up the content of "The Yellow Wallpaper." In 1935, after suffering from breast cancer, Gilman used chloroform to commit suicide.

Gilman was a productive writer, completing nine novels, hundreds of poems and essays, and books of criticism and analysis, including *Human Work* (1904) and *Social Ethics* (1914). She wrote lucidly on humanism, and on the historically suppressed role women had endured over the years. Gilman's short story "The Yellow Wallpaper" (1892) is a seminal text in literature and in the history of feminism. Due to the subject matter and its strange fragmented form, the story invites questions and theories about the narrator's state of mind. Gilman compounds the ambiguity through the first-person point of view, contrasting the narrator with John's behavior and the infantile nature of the attic. Accordingly, everything in the story should be questioned: the wallpaper, the doctor, the roles of power and control. Readers will find themselves mesmerized by the wallpaper, its changing patterns and spectral manifestations. Elements of the Gothic rebound through the text, creating an unsettled atmosphere full of psychological terror and cruelty.

The Yellow Wallpaper

Charlotte Perkins Gilman

It is very seldom that mere ordinary people like John and myself secure ancestral halls for the summer.

A colonial mansion, a hereditary estate, I would say a haunted house, and reach the height of romantic felicity but that would be asking too much of fate!

Still I will proudly declare that there is something queer about it.

Else, why should it be let so cheaply? And why have stood so long untenanted?

John laughs at me, of course, but one expects that in marriage.

John is practical in the extreme. He has no patience with faith, an intense horror of superstition, and he scoffs openly at any talk of things not to be felt and seen and put down in figures.

John is a physician, and—*perhaps* (I would not say it to a living soul, of course, but this is dead paper and a great relief to my mind)—*perhaps* that is one reason I do not get well faster.

You see he does not believe I am sick!

And what can one do?

If a physician of high standing, and one's own husband, assures friends and relatives that there is really nothing the matter with one but temporary nervous depression—a slight hysterical tendency—what is one to do?

My brother is also a physician, and also of high standing, and he says the same thing.

So I take phosphates or phospites—whichever it is—and tonics, and journeys, and air, and exercise, and am absolutely forbidden to "work" until I am well again.

Personally, I disagree with their ideas.

Personally, I believe that congenial work, with excitement and change, would do me good.

But what is one to do?

I did write for a while in spite of them; but it *does* exhaust me a good deal—having to be so sly about it, or else meet with heavy opposition.

I sometimes fancy that in my condition if I had less opposition and more society and stimulus—but John says the very worst thing I can do is to think about my condition, and I confess it always makes me feel bad.

So I will let it alone and talk about the house.

The most beautiful place! It is quite alone, standing well back from the road, quite three miles from the village. It makes me think of English places that you read about, for there are hedges and walls and gates that lock, and lots of separate little houses for the gardeners and people.

There is a *delicious* garden! I never saw such a garden large and shady, full of box-bordered paths, and lined with long grape-covered arbors with seats under them.

There were greenhouses, too, but they are all broken now.

There was some legal trouble, I believe, something about the heirs and coheirs; anyhow, the place has been empty for years.

That spoils my ghostliness, I am afraid, but I don't care—there is something strange about the house—I can feel it.

I even said so to John one moonlight evening, but he said what I felt was a draught, and shut the window.

I get unreasonably angry with John sometimes. I'm sure I never used to be so sensitive. I think it is due to this nervous condition.

But John says if I feel so, I shall neglect proper self-control; so I take pains to control myself—before him, at least, and that makes me very tired.

I don't like our room a bit. I wanted one downstairs that opened on the piazza and had roses all over the window, and such pretty old-fashioned chintz hangings! but John would not hear of it.

He said there was only one window and not room for two beds, and no near room for him if he took another.

He is very careful and loving, and hardly lets me stir without special direction.

I have a schedule prescription for each hour in the day; he takes all care from me, and so I feel basely ungrateful not to value it more.

He said we came here solely on my account, that I was to have perfect rest and all the air I could get. "Your exercise depends on your strength, my dear," said he, "and your food somewhat on your appetite; but air you can absorb all the time." So we took the nursery at the top of the house.

It is a big, airy room, the whole floor nearly, with windows that look all ways, and air and sunshine galore. It was nursery first and then playroom and gymnasium, I should judge; for the windows are barred for little children, and there are rings and things in the walls.

The paint and paper look as if a boys' school had used it. It is stripped off—the paper—in great patches all around the head of my bed, about as far as I can reach, and in a great place on the other side of the room low down. I never saw a worse paper in my life.

One of those sprawling flamboyant patterns committing every artistic sin.

It is dull enough to confuse the eye in following pronounced enough to constantly irritate and provoke study, and when you follow the lame uncertain curves for a little distance they suddenly commit suicide—plunge off at outrageous angles, destroy themselves in unheard of contradictions.

The color is repellent, almost revolting; a smoldering unclean yellow, strangely faded by the slow-turning sunlight.

It is a dull yet lurid orange in some places, a sickly sulphur tint in others.

No wonder the children hated it! I should hate it myself if I had to live in this room long.

There comes John, and I must put this away—he hates to have me write a word.

* * *

We have been here two weeks, and I haven't felt like writing before, since that first day.

I am sitting by the window now, up in this atrocious nursery, and there is nothing to hinder my writing as much as I please, save lack of strength.

John is away all day, and even some nights when his cases are serious.

I am glad my case is not serious!

But these nervous troubles are dreadfully depressing.

John does not know how much I really suffer. He knows there is no reason to suffer, and that satisfies him.

Of course it is only nervousness. It does weigh on me so not to do my duty in any way!

I meant to be such a help to John, such a real rest and comfort, and here I am a comparative burden already!

Nobody would believe what an effort it is to do what little I am able—to dress and entertain, and order things.

It is fortunate Mary is so good with the baby. Such a dear baby!

And yet I *cannot* be with him, it makes me so nervous.

I suppose John never was nervous in his life. He laughs at me so about this wallpaper!

At first he meant to repaper the room, but afterwards he said that I was letting it get the better of me, and that nothing was worse for a nervous patient than to give way to such fancies.

He said that after the wallpaper was changed it would be the heavy bedstead, and then the barred windows, and then that gate at the head of the stairs, and so on.

"You know the place is doing you good," he said, "and really, dear, I don't care to renovate the house just for a three months' rental."

"Then do let us go downstairs," I said. "There are such pretty rooms there."

Then he took me in his arms and called me a blessed little goose, and said he would go down to the cellar, if I wished, and have it whitewashed into the bargain.

But he is right enough about the beds and windows and things.

It is an airy and comfortable room as any one need wish, and, of course, I would not be so silly as to make him uncomfortable just for a whim.

I'm really getting quite fond of the big room, all but that horrid paper.

Out of one window I can see the garden, those mysterious deepshaded arbors, the riotous old-fashioned flowers, and bushes and gnarly trees.

Out of another I get a lovely view of the bay and a little private wharf belonging to the estate. There is a beautiful shaded lane that runs down there from the house. I always fancy I see people walking in these numerous paths and arbors, but John has cautioned me not to give way to fancy in the least. He says that with my imaginative power and habit of story-making, a nervous weakness like mine is sure to lead to all manner of excited fancies, and that I ought to use my will and good sense to check the tendency. So I try.

I think sometimes that if I were only well enough to write a little it would relieve the press of ideas and rest me.

But I find I get pretty tired when I try.

It is so discouraging not to have any advice and companionship about my work. When I get really well, John says we will ask Cousin Henry and Julia down for a long visit; but he says he would as soon put fireworks in my pillow case as to let me have those stimulating people about now.

I wish I could get well faster.

But I must not think about that. This paper looks to me as if it knew what a vicious influence it had!

There is a recurrent spot where the pattern lolls like a broken neck and two bulbous eyes stare at you upside down.

I get positively angry with the impertinence of it and the everlastingness. Up and down and sideways they crawl, and those absurd, unblinking eyes are everywhere. There is one place where two breaths didn't match, and the eyes go all up and down the line, one a little higher than the other.

I never saw so much expression in an inanimate thing before, and we all know how much expression they have! I used to lie awake as a child and get more entertainment and terror out of blank walls and plain furniture than most children could find in a toy-store.

I remember what a kindly wink the knobs of our big, old bureau used to have, and there was one chair that always seemed like a strong friend.

I used to feel that if any of the other things looked too fierce I could always hop into that chair and be safe.

The furniture in this room is no worse than inharmonious, however, for we had to bring it all from downstairs. I suppose when this was used as a playroom they had to take the nursery things out, and no wonder! I never saw such ravages as the children have made here.

The wallpaper, as I said before, is torn off in spots, and it sticketh closer than a brother—they must have had perseverance as well as hatred.

Then the floor is scratched and gouged and splintered, the plaster itself is dug out here and there, and this great heavy bed which is all we found in the room, looks as if it had been through the wars.

But I don't mind it a bit—only the paper.

There comes John's sister. Such a dear girl as she is, and so careful of me! I must not let her find me writing.

She is a perfect and enthusiastic housekeeper, and hopes for no better profession. I verily believe she thinks it is the writing which made me sick!

But I can write when she is out, and see her a long way off from these windows.

There is one that commands the road, a lovely shaded winding road, and one that just looks off over the country. A lovely country, too, full of great elms and velvet meadows.

This wallpaper has a kind of sub-pattern in a different shade, a particularly irritating one, for you can only see it in certain lights, and not clearly then.

But in the places where it isn't faded and where the sun is just so I can see a strange, provoking, formless sort of figure, that seems to skulk about behind that silly and conspicuous front design.

There's sister on the stairs!

* * *

Well, the Fourth of July is over! The people are all gone and I am tired out. John thought it might do me good to see a little company, so we just had Mother and Nellie and the children down for a week.

Of course I didn't do a thing. Jennie sees to everything now.

But it tired me all the same.

John says if I don't pick up faster he shall send me to Weir Mitchell in the fall.

But I don't want to go there at all. I had a friend who was in his hands once, and she says he is just like John and my brother, only more so!

Besides, it is such an undertaking to go so far.

I don't feel as if it was worthwhile to turn my hand over for anything, and I'm getting dreadfully fretful and querulous.

I cry at nothing, and cry most of the time.

Of course I don't when John is here, or anybody else, but when I am alone.

And I am alone a good deal just now. John is kept in town very often by serious cases, and Jennie is good and lets me alone when I want her to.

So I walk a little in the garden or down that lovely lane, sit on the porch under the roses, and lie down up here a good deal.

I'm getting really fond of the room in spite of the wallpaper. Perhaps *because* of the wallpaper.

It dwells in my mind so!

I lie here on this great immovable bed—it is nailed down, I believe—and follow that pattern about by the hour. It is as good as gymnastics, I assure you. I start, we'll say, at the bottom, down in the corner over there where it has not been touched, and I determine for the thousandth time that I *will* follow that pointless pattern to some sort of a conclusion.

I know a little of the principle of design, and I know this thing was not arranged on any laws of I radiation, or alternation, or repetition, or symmetry, or anything else that I ever heard of.

It is repeated, of course, by the breadths, but not otherwise.

Looked at in one way each breadth stands alone, the bloated curves and flourishes—a kind of "debased Romanesque" with delirium tremens—go waddling up and down in isolated columns of fatuity.

But, on the other hand, they connect diagonally, and the sprawling outlines run off in great slanting waves of optic horror, like a lot of wallowing seaweeds in full chase.

The whole thing goes horizontally, too, at least it seems so, and I exhaust myself in trying to distinguish the order of its going in that direction.

They have used a horizontal breadth for a frieze, and that adds wonderfully to the confusion.

There is one end of the room where it is almost intact, and there, when the crosslights fade and the low sun shines directly upon it, I can almost fancy radiation after all—the interminable grotesques seem to form around a common centre and rush off in headlong plunges of equal distraction.

It makes me tired to follow it. I will take a nap I guess.

I don't know why I should write this.

I don't want to.

I don't feel able.

And I know John would think it absurd. But must say what I feel and think in some way—it is such a relief!

But the effort is getting to be greater than the relief.

* * *

Half the time now I am awfully lazy, and lie down ever so much.

John says I mustn't lose my strength, and has me take cod liver oil and lots of tonics and things, to say nothing of ale and wine and rare meat.

Dear John! He loves me very dearly, and hates to have me sick. I tried to have a real earnest reasonable talk with him the other day, and tell him how I wish he would let me go and make a visit to Cousin Henry and Julia.

But he said I wasn't able to go, nor able to stand it after I got there; and I did not make out a very good case for myself, for I was crying before I had finished.

It is getting to be a great effort for me to think straight. Just this nervous weakness I suppose.

And dear John gathered me up in his arms, and just carried me upstairs and laid me on the bed, and sat by me and read to me till it tired my head.

He said I was his darling and his comfort and all he had, and that I must take care of myself for his sake, and keep well.

He says no one but myself can help me out of it, that I must use my will and self-control and not let any silly fancies run away with me.

There's one comfort, the baby is well and happy, and does not have to occupy this nursery with the horrid wallpaper.

If we had not used it, that blessed child would have! What a fortunate escape! Why, I wouldn't have a child of mine, an impressionable little thing, live in such a room for worlds.

I never thought of it before, but it is lucky that John kept me here after all, I can stand it so much easier than a baby, you see.

Of course I never mention it to them any more—I am too wise—but I keep watch of it all the same.

There are things in that paper that nobody knows but me, or ever will.

Behind that outside pattern the dim shapes get clearer every day.

It is always the same shape, only very numerous.

And it is like a woman stooping down and creeping about behind that pattern. I don't like it a bit. I wonder—I begin to think—I wish John would take me away from here!

It is so hard to talk with John about my case, because he is so wise, and because he loves me so.

But I tried it last night.

It was moonlight. The moon shines in all around just as the sun does.

I hate to see it sometimes, it creeps so slowly, and always comes in by one window or another.

John was asleep and I hated to waken him, so I kept still and watched the moonlight on that undulating wallpaper till I felt creepy.

The faint figure behind seemed to shake the pattern, just as if she wanted to get out.

I got up softly and went to feel and see if the paper *did* move, and when I came back John was awake.

"What is it, little girl?" he said. "Don't go walking about like that—you'll get cold."

I thought it was a good time to talk, so I told him that I really was not gaining here, and that I wished he would take me away.

"Why darling!" said he, "our lease will be up in three weeks, and I can't see how to leave before.

"The repairs are not done at home, and I cannot possibly leave town just now. Of course if you were in any danger, I could and would, but you really are better, dear, whether you can see it or not. I am a doctor, dear, and I know. You are gaining flesh and color, your appetite is better, I feel really much easier about you."

"I don't weigh a bit more," said I, "nor as much; and my appetite may be better in the evening when you are here, but it is worse in the morning when you are away!"

"Bless her little heart!" said he with a big hug. "She shall be as sick as she pleases! But now let's improve the shining hours by going to sleep, and talk about it in the morning!"

"And you won't go away?" I asked gloomily.

"Why, how can I, dear? It is only three weeks more and then we will take a nice little trip of a few days while Jennie is getting the house ready. Really, dear, you are better!"

"Better in body perhaps—" I began, and stopped short, for he sat up straight and looked at me with such a stern, reproachful look that I could not say another word.

"My darling," said he, "I beg of you, for my sake and for our child's sake, as well as for your own, that you will never for one instant let that idea enter your mind! There is nothing so dangerous, so fascinating, to a temperament like yours. It is a false and foolish fancy. Can you not trust me as a physician when I tell you so?"

So of course I said no more on that score, and we went to sleep before long. He thought I was asleep first, but I wasn't, and lay there for hours trying to decide whether that front pattern and the back pattern really did move together or separately.

On a pattern like this, by daylight, there is a lack of sequence, a defiance of law, that is a constant irritant to a normal mind.

The color is hideous enough, and unreliable enough, and infuriating enough, but the pattern is torturing.

You think you have mastered it, but just as you get well underway in following, it turns a back somersault and there you are. It slaps you in the face, knocks you down, and tramples upon you. It is like a bad dream.

The outside pattern is a florid arabesque, reminding one of a fungus. If you can imagine a toadstool in joints, an interminable string of toadstools, budding and sprouting in endless convolutions—why, that is something like it.

That is, sometimes!

There is one marked peculiarity about this paper, a thing nobody seems to notice but myself and that is that it changes as the light changes.

When the sun shoots in through the east window—I always watch for that first long, straight ray—it changes so quickly that I never can quite believe it.

That is why I watch it always.

By moonlight—the moon shines in all night when there is a moon—I wouldn't know it was the same paper.

At night in any kind of light, in twilight, candlelight, lamplight, and worst of all by moonlight, it becomes bars! The outside pattern I mean, and the woman behind it is as plain as can be.

I didn't realize for a long time what the thing was that showed behind, that dim sub-pattern, but l now I am quite sure it is a woman.

By daylight she is subdued, quiet. I fancy it is the pattern that keeps her so still. It is so puzzling. It keeps me quiet by the hour.

I lie down ever so much now. John says it is good for me, and to sleep all I can.

Indeed he started the habit by making me lie down for an hour after each meal.

It is a very bad habit I am convinced, for you see I don't sleep.

And that cultivates deceit, for I don't tell them I'm awake—oh, no!

The fact is I am getting a little afraid of John.

He seems very queer sometimes, and even Jennie has an inexplicable look.

It strikes me occasionally, just as a scientific hypothesis, that perhaps it is the paper!

I have watched John when he did not know I was looking, and come into the room suddenly on the most innocent excuses, and I've caught him several times *looking at the paper!* And Jennie too. I caught Jennie with her hand on it once.

She didn't know I was in the room, and when I asked her in a quiet, a very quiet voice, with the most restrained manner possible, what she was doing with the paper—she turned around as if she had been caught stealing, and looked quite angry—asked me why I should frighten her so!

Then she said that the paper stained everything it touched, that she had found yellow smooches on all my clothes and John's, and she wished we would be more careful!

Did not that sound innocent? But I know she was studying that pattern, and I am determined that nobody shall find it out but myself!

* * *

Life is very much more exciting now than it used to be. You see I have something more to expect, to look forward to, to watch. I really do eat better, and am more quiet than I was.

John is so pleased to see me improve! He laughed a little the other day, and said I seemed to be flourishing in spite of my wallpaper.

I turned it off with a laugh. I had no intention of telling him it was *because* of the wallpaper—he would make fun of me. He might even want to take me away.

I don't want to leave now until I have found it out. There is a week more, and I think that will be enough.

I'm feeling ever so much better! I don't sleep much at night, for it is so interesting to watch developments; but I sleep a good deal in the daytime.

In the daytime it is tiresome and perplexing.

There are always new shoots on the fungus, and new shades of yellow all over it. I cannot keep count of them, though I have tried conscientiously.

It is the strangest yellow, that wallpaper! It makes me think of all the yellow things I ever saw—not beautiful ones like buttercups, but old foul, bad yellow things.

But there is something else about that paper—the smell! I noticed it the moment we came into the room, but with so much air and sun it was not bad. Now we have had a week of fog and rain, and whether the windows are open or not, the smell is here.

It creeps all over the house.

I find it hovering in the dining-room, skulking in the parlor, hiding in the hall, lying in wait for me on the stairs.

It gets into my hair.

Even when I go to ride, if I turn my head suddenly and surprise it—there is that smell!

Such a peculiar odor, too! I have spent hours in trying to analyze it, to find what it smelled like.

It is not bad—at first—and very gentle, but quite the subtlest, most enduring odor I ever met.

In this damp weather it is awful, I wake up in the night and find it hanging over me.

It used to disturb me at first. I thought seriously of burning the house—to reach the smell.

But now I am used to it. The only thing I can think of that it is like is the *color* of the paper! A yellow smell.

There is a very funny mark on this wall, low down, near the mopboard. A streak that runs round the room. It goes behind every piece of furniture, except the bed, a long, straight, even smooch, as if it had been rubbed over and over.

I wonder how it was done and who did it, and what they did it for. Round and round and round—round and round and round—it makes me dizzy!

I really have discovered something at last.

Through watching so much at night, when it changes so, I have finally found out.

The front pattern does move—and no wonder! The woman behind shakes it!

Sometimes I think there are a great many women behind, and sometimes only one, and she crawls around fast, and her crawling shakes it all over.

Then in the very bright spots she keeps still, and in the very shady spots she just takes hold of the bars and shakes them hard.

And she is all the time trying to climb through. But nobody could climb through that pattern—it strangles so; I think that is why it has so many heads.

They get through, and then the pattern strangles them off and turns them upside down, and makes their eyes white!

If those heads were covered or taken off it would not be half so bad.

I think that woman gets out in the daytime!

And I'll tell you why—privately—I've seen her!

I can see her out of every one of my windows!

It is the same woman, I know, for she is always creeping, and most women do not creep by daylight.

I see her on that long road under the trees, creeping along, and when a carriage comes she hides under the blackberry vines.

I don't blame her a bit. It must be very humiliating to be caught creeping by daylight!

I always lock the door when I creep by daylight. I can't do it at night, for I know John would suspect something at once.

And John is so queer now, that I don't want to irritate him. I wish he would take another room! Besides, I don't want anybody to get that woman out at night but myself.

I often wonder if I could see her out of all the windows at once.

But, turn as fast as I can, I can only see out of one at one time.

And though I always see her, she *may* be able to creep faster than I can turn!

I have watched her sometimes away off in the open country, creeping as fast as a cloud shadow in a high wind.

If only that top pattern could be gotten off from the under one! I mean to try it, little by little.

I have found out another funny thing, but I shan't tell it this time! It does not do to trust people too much.

There are only two more days to get this paper off, and I believe John is beginning to notice. I don't like the look in his eyes.

And I heard him ask Jennie a lot of professional questions about me. She had a very good report to give.

She said I slept a good deal in the daytime.

John knows I don't sleep very well at night, for all I'm so quiet!

He asked me all sorts of questions, too, and pretended to be very loving and kind.

As if I couldn't see through him!

Still, I don't wonder he acts so, sleeping under this paper for three months.

It only interests me, but I feel sure John and Jennie are secretly affected by it.

* * *

Hurrah! This is the last day, but it is enough. John to stay in town over night, and won't be out until this evening.

Jennie wanted to sleep with me—the sly thing! but I told her I should undoubtedly rest better for a night all alone.

That was clever, for really I wasn't alone a bit! As soon as it was moonlight and that poor thing began to crawl and shake the pattern, I got up and ran to help her.

I pulled and she shook, I shook and she pulled, and before morning we had peeled off yards of that paper.

A strip about as high as my head and half around the room.

And then when the sun came and that awful pattern began to laugh at me, I declared I would finish it today!

We go away tomorrow, and they are moving all my furniture down again to leave things as they were before.

Jennie looked at the wall in amazement, but I told her merrily that I did it out of pure spite at the vicious thing.

She laughed and said she wouldn't mind doing it herself, but I must not get tired.

How she betrayed herself that time!

But I am here, and no person touches this but me—not *alive!*

She tried to get me out of the room—it was too patent! But I said it was so quiet and empty and clean now that I believed I would lie down again and sleep all I could; and not to wake me even for dinner—I would call when I woke.

So now she is gone, and the servants are gone, and the things are gone, and there is nothing left but that great bedstead nailed down, with the canvas mattress we found on it.

We shall sleep downstairs tonight, and take the boat home tomorrow.

I quite enjoy the room, now it is bare again.

How those children did tear about here!

This bedstead is fairly gnawed!

But I must get to work.

I have locked the door and thrown the key down into the front path.

I don't want to go out, and I don't want to have anybody come in, till John comes.

I want to astonish him.

I've got a rope up here that even Jennie did not find. If that woman does get out, and tries to get away, I can tie her!

But I forgot I could not reach far without anything to stand on!

This bed will *not* move!

I tried to lift and push it until I was lame, and then I got so angry I bit off a little piece at one corner—but it hurt my teeth.

Then I peeled off all the paper I could reach standing on the floor. It sticks horribly and the pattern just enjoys it! All those strangled heads and bulbous eyes and waddling fungus growths just shriek with derision!

I am getting angry enough to do something desperate. To jump out of the window would be admirable exercise, but the bars are too strong even to try.

Besides I wouldn't do it. Of course not. I know well enough that a step like that is improper and might be misconstrued.

I don't like to *look* out of the windows even—there are so many of those creeping women, and they creep so fast.

I wonder if they all come out of that wallpaper as I did?

But I am securely fastened now by my well hidden rope—you don't get *me* out in the road there!

I suppose I shall have to get back behind the pattern when it comes night, and that is hard!

It is so pleasant to be out in this great room and creep around as I please!

I don't want to go outside. I won't, even if Jennie asks me to.

For outside you have to creep on the ground, and everything is green instead of yellow.

But here I can creep smoothly on the floor, and my shoulder just fits in that long smooch around the wall, so I cannot lose my way.

Why there's John at the door!

It is no use, young man, you can't open it!

How he does call and pound!

Now he's crying for an axe.

It would be a shame to break down that beautiful door!

"John dear!" said I in the gentlest voice. "The key is down by the front steps, under a plantain leaf!"

That silenced him for a few moments.

Then he said very quietly indeed, "Open the door, my darling!"

"I can't," said I. "The key is down by the front door under a plantain leaf!"

And then I said it again, several times, very gently and slowly, and said it so often that he had to go and see, and he got it of course, and came in. He stopped short by the door.

"What is the matter?" he cried. "For God's sake, what are you doing!"

I kept on creeping just the same, but I looked at him over my shoulder.

"I've got out at last," said I, "in spite of you and Jane. And I've pulled off most of the paper, so you can't put me back!"

Now why should that man have fainted? But he did, and right across my path by the wall, so that I had to creep over him every time!

Thinking About the Story

In "The Yellow Wallpaper," Charlotte Perkins Gilman created a narrative of psychological terror and deliberate ambiguity. The first-person point of view aids this unreliability, forcing you to question the actions and entities seen in the story. It is important, though, to contextualize the sociological aspects of the story. Accordingly, think first about the following questions: Why is it important for people to have the opportunity to express themselves? How about for nineteenth-century women? How were women's lives different then? The emphasis on self-discovery and on the understanding of the physical-mental connection is something quite vital here and can be developed through an original comparison with H. P. Lovecraft's "The Outsider." Although the stories are stylistically divergent, they share a narrator subjected to a state of child-like ignorance and enforced infantilization.

Discussion Questions

1. What function does the wallpaper have in the story? Does its role change as the narrative progresses? What's the importance of the wallpaper's color? In further evaluation of the wallpaper's symbolic importance, how do you interpret the line: "The front pattern does move—and no wonder! The woman behind shakes it!"?

2. Consider the story's style: past and present tenses, fragmentary pauses, short sentences, and brief paragraphs. Why might Gilman have written the story in this way? Do you read the story as a series of journal entries? Furthermore, what role does the writing of the story itself have for the narrator?

3. What are the major conflicts between John and his wife? Which character do you most empathize with? What is Jennie's role in the story?

4. Identify passages that describe the house. How does the narrator's description of the building reflect on her mental state? Do you think the attic was once a nursery or a room designed to house an insane person? What are the ramifications of these two possibilities?

5. What are your thoughts on the woman in the wallpaper? Do you find the narrator's testimony to be reliable? What is her mental image of herself? In what ways is the ending a victory for the narrator and in what ways is it a defeat?

Activities

1. Imagine yourself as the husband, John. Write a letter to the doctor mentioned in the story, Weir Mitchell, describing and commentating upon the events and actions John has observed in the house.

2. Highlight issues in the story that impacted on women of the day. Separately make a list of contemporary women's issues and compare and contrast the two lists.

3. Write an afterword to the story. Role-play one of the characters, either John, Dr. Weir, or the narrator, and construct what happened to the family one year later.

Edith Wharton

Silence may be as variously shaded as speech.
Edith Wharton — *The Reef* (1912)

Edith Wharton (1862–1937) was one of the great American writers of the twentieth century, winning the Pulitzer Prize for literature in 1921. Born in New York to a wealthy, upper-class family, Wharton (born Edith Jones) had a privileged childhood, alongside her two brothers. Educated by private governesses in Paris, New York, and Rhode Island, Wharton read widely, and early on in her life decided to become a writer. In 1885, she married Teddy Wharton and the two suffered an unhappy marriage. She often traveled to Europe, as she enjoyed the continental lifestyle, and spent time writing about architecture. By 1902, her mother had died and she had built a large residence, named The Mount, in Lenox, Massachusetts. Over the years, her social circle included André Gide, F. Scott Fitzgerald, Theodore Roosevelt, and Sinclair Lewis. Due to her husband's mental instability and financial indiscretions, Wharton divorced him in 1913. After the First World War she lived in France, writing her books, and traveling across Europe. Decades later, aged 75, she died at her Paris residence.

Mentored by Henry James, Wharton wrote several collections of short stories and over a dozen novels, including *The House of Mirth* (1905), *Ethan Frome* (1911), and *The Age of Innocence* (1922). Today, she is equally known for her contribution to interior architecture and design. Her important books in this field—*The Decoration of Houses* (1897) and *Italian Villas and Their Gardens* (1904)—cover innovative aspects of room design and interior symmetry. Comparatively, in her fiction writing, she was equally meticulous in her construction of narrative. Frequently, she used class sensibilities, contrasting American and European customs and morals. She also wrote incisive commentary on the role of women and their desire for freedom. These themes can be seen in her story, "The Choice" (1908). Within it there is an autobiographical suggestion of her marriage difficulties and the negative feelings she had for Teddy; however, the story transcends the limits of her personal difficulties for narrative purposes. The resultant story still resonates with modern readers, as it reveals the complexities and follies of social mores, personal bravado, and the incongruities of marriage that still plague contemporary society.

The Choice

Edith Wharton

I

Stilling, that night after dinner, had surpassed himself. He always did, Wrayford reflected, when the small fry from Highfield came to dine. He, Cobham Stilling, who had to find his bearings and keep to his level in the big heedless ironic world of New York, dilated and grew vast in the congenial medium of Highfield. The Red House was the biggest house of the Highfield summer colony, and Cobham Stilling was its biggest man. No one else within a radius of a hundred miles (on a conservative estimate) had as many horses, as many greenhouses, as many servants, and assuredly no one else had three motors and a motorboat for the lake.

The motorboat was Stilling's latest hobby, and he rode—or steered—it in and out of the conversation all the evening, to the obvious edification of every one present save his wife and his visitor, Austin Wrayford. The interest of the latter two who, from opposite ends of the drawing-room, exchanged a fleeting glance when Stilling again launched his craft on the thin current of the talk—the interest of Mrs. Stilling and Wrayford had already lost its edge by protracted contact with the subject.

But the dinner-guests—the Rector, Mr. Swordsley, his wife Mrs. Swordsley, Lucy and Agnes Granger, their brother Addison, and young

Jack Emmerton from Harvard—were all, for diverse reasons, stirred to the proper pitch of feeling. Mr. Swordsley, no doubt, was saying to himself: "If my good parishioner here can afford to buy a motorboat, in addition to all the other expenditures which an establishment like this must entail, I certainly need not scruple to appeal to him again for a contribution for our Galahad Club." The Granger girls, meanwhile, were evoking visions of lakeside picnics, not unadorned with the presence of young Mr. Emmerton; while that youth himself speculated as to whether his affable host would let him, when he came back on his next vacation, "learn to run the thing himself"; and Mr. Addison Granger, the elderly bachelor brother of the volatile Lucy and Agnes, mentally formulated the precise phrase in which, in his next letter to his cousin Professor Spildyke of the University of East Latmos, he should allude to "our last delightful trip in my old friend Cobham Stilling's ten-thousand-dollar motor-launch"—for East Latmos was still in that primitive stage of culture on which five figures impinge.

Isabel Stilling, sitting beside Mrs. Swordsley, her bead slightly bent above the needlework with which on these occasions it was her old-fashioned habit to employ herself—Isabel also had doubtless her reflections to make. As Wrayford leaned back in his corner and looked at her across the wide flower-filled drawing room he noted, first of all—for the how many hundredth time?—the play of her hands above the embroidery-frame, the shadow of the thick dark hair on her forehead, the lids over her somewhat full grey eyes. He noted all this with a conscious deliberateness of enjoyment, taking in unconsciously, at the same time, the particular quality in her attitude, in the fall of her dress and the turn of her head, which had set her for him, from the first day, in a separate world; then he said to himself: "She is certainly thinking: Where on earth will Cobham get the money to pay for it?"

Stilling, cigar in mouth and thumbs in his waistcoat pockets, was impressively perorating from his usual dominant position on the hearthrug.

"I said: 'If I have the thing at all, I want the best that can be got.' That's my way, you know, Swordsley; I suppose I'm what you'd call fastidious. Always was, about everything, from cigars to wom—" His eye met the apprehensive glance of Mrs. Swordsley, who looked like her husband with his clerical coat cut slightly lower, "So I said: 'If I have the thing at all, I want the best that can be got.' Nothing makeshift for me, no second-best. I never cared for the cheap and showy. I always say frankly to a man: 'If you can't give me a first-rate cigar, for the Lord's sake let me smoke my own.'" He paused to do so. "Well, if you have my standards, you can't buy a thing in a minute. You must look round, compare, select. I found there were lots of motorboats on the market, just as there's lots of stuff called champagne. But I said to myself: 'Ten to one there's only one fit to buy, just as there's only one champagne fit for a gentleman to drink.' Argued like a lawyer, eh, Austin?" He tossed this to Wrayford. "Take me for one of your own trade, wouldn't you? Well, I'm not such a fool as I look. I suppose you fellows who are tied to the treadmill—excuse me, Swordsley, but work's work, isn't it? I suppose you think a man like me has nothing to do but take it easy: loll through life like a woman. By George, sir, I'd like either of you to see the time it takes—I won't say the *brain*—but just the time it takes to pick out a good motorboat. Why, I went—"

Mrs. Stilling set her embroidery-frame noiselessly on the table at her side, and turned her head toward Wrayford. "Would you mind ringing for the tray?"

The interruption helped Mrs. Swordsley to waver to her feet. "I'm afraid we ought really to be going; my husband has an early service tomorrow."

Her host intervened with a genial protest. "Going already? Nothing of the sort! Why, the night's still young, as the poet says. Long way from here to the rectory? Nonsense! In our little twenty-horse car we do it in five minutes—don't we, Belle? Ah, you're walking, to be sure—"

Stilling's indulgent gesture seemed to concede that, in such a case, allowances must be made, and that he was the last man not to make them. "Well, then, Swordsley—" He held out a thick red hand that seemed to exude beneficence, and the clergyman, pressing it, ventured to murmur a suggestion.

"What, that Galahad Club again? Why, I thought my wife—Isabel, didn't we—No? Well, it must have been my mother, then. Of course, you know, anything my good mother gives is—well—virtually—You haven't asked her? Sure? I could have sworn; I get so many of these appeals. And in these times, you know, we have to go cautiously. I'm sure you recognize that yourself, Swordsley. With my obligations—here now, to show you don't bear malice, have a brandy and soda before you go. Nonsense, man! This brandy isn't liquor; it's liqueur. I picked it up last year in London—last of a famous lot from Lord St. Oswyn's cellar. Laid down here, it stood me at—Eh?" He broke off as his wife moved toward him. "Ah, yes, of course. Miss Lucy, Miss Agnes, a drop of soda water? Look here, Addison, you won't refuse my tipple, I know. Well, take a cigar, at any rate, Swordsley. And, by the way, I'm afraid you'll have to go round the long way by the avenue tonight. Sorry, Mrs. Swordsley, but I forgot to tell them to leave the gate into the lane unlocked. Well, it's a jolly night, and I daresay you won't mind the extra turn along the lake. And, by Jove, if the moon's out, you'll have a glimpse of the motorboat. She's moored just out beyond our boathouse; and it's a privilege to look at her, I can tell you!"

* * *

The dispersal of his guests carried Stilling out into the hall, where his pleasantries reverberated under the oak rafters while the Granger girls were being muffled for the drive and the carriages summoned from the stables.

By a common impulse Mrs. Stilling and Wrayford had moved together toward the fireplace, which was hidden by a tall screen from the door into the hall. Wrayford leaned his elbow against the mantelpiece, and Mrs. Stilling stood beside him, her clasped hands hanging down before her.

"Have you anything more to talk over with him?" she asked.

"No. We wound it all up before dinner. He doesn't want to talk about it any more than he can help."

"It's so bad?"

"No, but this time he's got to pull up."

She stood silent, with lowered lids. He listened a moment, catching Stilling's farewell shout; then he moved a little nearer, and laid his hand on her arm.

"In an hour?"

She made an imperceptible motion of assent.

"I'll tell you about it then. The key's as usual?"

She signed another "Yes" and walked away with her long drifting step as her husband came in from the hall.

He went up to the tray and poured himself out a tall glass of brandy and soda.

"The weather is turning queer—black as pitch. I hope the Swordsleys won't walk into the lake—involuntary immersion, eh? He'd come out a Baptist, I suppose. What'd the Bishop do in such a case? There's a problem for a lawyer, my boy!"

He clapped his hand on Wrayford's thin shoulder and then walked over to his wife, who was gathering up her embroidery silks and dropping them into her workbag. Stilling took her by the arms and swung her playfully about so that she faced the lamplight.

"What's the matter with you tonight?"

"The matter?" she echoed, coloring a little, and standing very straight in her desire not to appear to shrink from his touch.

"You never opened your lips. Left me the whole job of entertaining those blessed people. Didn't she, Austin?"

Wrayford laughed and lit a cigarette.

"There! You see even Austin noticed it. What's the matter, I say? Aren't they good enough for you? I don't say they're particularly exciting; but hang it! I like to ask them here—I like to give people pleasure."

"I didn't mean to be dull," said Isabel.

"Well, you must learn to make an effort. Don't treat people as if they weren't in the room just because they don't happen to amuse you. Do you know what they'll think? They'll think it's because you've got a bigger house and more money than they have. Shall I tell you something? My mother said she'd noticed the same thing in you lately. She said she sometimes felt you looked down on her for living in a small house. Oh, she was half joking, of course; but you see you do give people that impression. I can't understand treating any one in that way. The more I have myself, the more I want to make other people happy."

Isabel gently freed herself and laid the workbag on her embroidery-frame. "I have a headache; perhaps that made me stupid. I'm going to bed." She turned toward Wrayford and held out her hand. "Good night."

"Good night," he answered, opening the door for her.

When he turned back into the room, his host was pouring himself a third glass of brandy and soda.

"Here, have a nip, Austin? Gad, I need it badly, after the shaking up you gave me this afternoon." Stilling laughed and carried his glass to the hearth, where he took up his usual commanding position. "Why the deuce don't you drink something? You look as glum as Isabel. One would think you were the chap that had been hit by this business."

Wrayford threw himself into the chair from which Mrs. Stilling had lately risen. It was the one she usually sat in, and to his fancy a faint scent of her clung to it. He leaned back and looked up at Stilling.

"Want a cigar?" the latter continued. "Shall we go into the den and smoke?"

Wrayford hesitated. "If there's anything more you want to ask me about—"

"Gad, no! I had full measure and running over this afternoon. The deuce of it is, I don't see where the money's all gone to. Luckily I've got plenty of nerve. I'm not the kind of man to sit down and snivel because I've been touched in Wall Street."

Wrayford got to his feet again. "Then, if you don't want me, I think I'll go up to my room and put some finishing touches to a brief before I turn in. I must get back to town tomorrow afternoon."

"All right, then." Stilling set down his empty glass, and held out his hand with a tinge of alacrity. "Good night, old man."

They shook hands, and Wrayford moved toward the door.

"I say, Austin—stop a minute!" his host called after him. Wrayford turned, and the two men faced each other across the hearthrug. Stilling's eyes shifted uneasily.

"There's one thing more you can do for me before you leave. Tell Isabel about that loan; explain to her that she's got to sign a note for it."

Wrayford, in his turn, flushed slightly. "You want me to tell her?"

"Hang it! I'm soft-hearted—that's the worst of me."

Stilling moved toward the tray, and lifted the brandy decanter. "And she'll take it better from you; she'll *have* to take it from you. She's proud. You can take her out for a row tomorrow morning. Look here, take her out in the motor-launch if you like. I meant to have a spin in it myself; but if you'll tell her—"

Wrayford hesitated. "All right, I'll tell her."

"Thanks a lot, my dear fellow. And you'll make her see it wasn't my fault, eh? Women are awfully vague about money, and she'll think it's all right if you back me up."

Wrayford nodded. "As you please."

"And, Austin—there's just one more thing. You needn't say anything to Isabel about the other business. I mean about my mother's securities."

"Ah?" said Wrayford, pausing.

Stilling shifted from one foot to the other. "I'd rather put that to the old lady myself. I can make it clear to her. She idolizes me, you know—and, hang it! I've got a good record. Up to now, I mean. My mother's been in clover since I married; I may say she's been my first thought. And

I don't want her to hear of this beastly business from Isabel. Isabel's a little harsh at times and, of course, this isn't going to make her any easier to live with."

"Very well," said Wrayford.

Stilling, with a look of relief, walked toward the window that opened on the terrace. "Gad! what a queer night! Hot as the kitchen-range. Shouldn't wonder if we had a squall before morning. I wonder if that infernal skipper took in the launch's awnings before he went home."

Wrayford stopped with his hand on the door. "Yes, I saw him do it. She's shipshape for the night."

"Good! That saves me a run down to the shore."

"Good night, then," said Wrayford.

"Good night, old man. You'll tell her?"

"I'll tell her."

"And mum about my mother!" his host called after him.

II

The darkness had thinned a little when Wrayford scrambled down the steep path to the shore. Though the air was heavy the threat of a storm seemed to have vanished, and now and then the moon's edge showed above a torn slope of cloud.

But in the thick shrubbery about the boathouse the darkness was still dense, and Wrayford had to strike a match before he could find the lock and insert his key. He left the door unlatched, and groped his way in. How often he had crept into this warm pine-scented obscurity, guiding himself by the edge of the bench along the wall, and hearing the soft lap of water through the gaps in the flooring! He knew just where one had to duck one's head to avoid the two canoes swung from the rafters, and just where to put his hand on the latch of the farther door that led to the broad balcony above the lake.

The boathouse represented one of Stilling's abandoned whims. He had built it some seven years before, and for a time it had been the scene of incessant nautical exploits. Stilling had rowed, sailed, paddled indefatigably, and all Highfield had been impressed to bear him company, and to admire his versatility. Then motors had come in, and he had forsaken aquatic sports for the flying chariot. The canoes of birch-bark and canvas had been hoisted to the roof, the sailboat had rotted at her moorings, and the movable floor of the boathouse, ingeniously contrived to slide back on noiseless runners, had lain undisturbed through several seasons. Even the key of the boathouse had been mislaid—by Isabel's fault, her husband said—and the locksmith had to be called in to make a new one when the purchase of the motorboat made the lake once more the centre of Stilling's activity.

As Wrayford entered he noticed that a strange oily odor overpowered the usual scent of dry pinewood; and at the next step his foot struck an object that rolled noisily across the boards. He lighted another match, and found he had overturned a can of grease, which the boatman had no doubt been using to oil the runners of the sliding floor.

Wrayford felt his way down the length of the boathouse, and softly opening the balcony door looked out on the lake. A few yards away, he saw the launch lying at anchor in the veiled moonlight; and just below him, on the black water, was the dim outline of the skiff, which the boatman kept to paddle out to her. The silence was so intense that Wrayford fancied he heard a faint rustling in the shrubbery on the high bank behind the boathouse, and the crackle of gravel on the path descending to it.

He closed the door again and turned back into the darkness; and as he did so the other door, on the landside, swung inward, and he saw a figure in the dim opening. Just enough light entered through the round holes above the respective doors to reveal Mrs. Stilling's cloaked outline, and to guide her to him as he advanced. But before they met she stumbled and gave a little cry.

"What is it?" he exclaimed.

"My foot caught; the floor seemed to give way under me. Ah, of course," she bent down in the darkness, "I saw the men oiling it this morning."

Wrayford caught her by the arm. "Do take care! It might be dangerous if it slid too easily. The water's deep under here."

"Yes, the water's very deep. I sometimes wish—" She leaned against him without finishing her sentence, and he put both arms about her.

"Hush!" he said, his lips on hers.

Suddenly she threw her head back and seemed to listen.

"What's the matter? What do you hear?"

"I don't know." He felt her trembling. "I'm not sure this place is as safe as it used to be."

Wrayford held her to him reassuringly. "But the boatman sleeps down at the village; and who else should come here at this hour?"

"Cobham might. He thinks of nothing but the launch."

"He won't tonight. I told him I'd seen the skipper put her shipshape, and that satisfied him."

"Ah, he did think of coming, then?"

"Only for a minute, when the sky looked so black half an hour ago, and he was afraid of a squall. It's clearing now, and there's no danger."

He drew her down on the bench, and they sat a moment or two in silence, her hands in his. Then she said: "You'd better tell me."

Wrayford gave a faint laugh. "Yes, I suppose I had. In fact, he asked me to."

"He asked you to?"

"Yes."

She uttered an exclamation of contempt. "He's afraid!"

Wrayford made no reply, and she went on: "I'm not. Tell me everything, please."

"Well, he's chucked away a pretty big sum again."

"How?"

"He says he doesn't know. He's been speculating, I suppose. The madness of making him your trustee!"

She drew her hands away. "You know why I did it. When we married I didn't want to put him in the false position of the man who contributes nothing and accepts everything; I wanted people to think the money was partly his."

"I don't know what you've made people think; but you've been eminently successful in one respect. *He* thinks it's all his—and he loses it as if it were."

"There are worse things. What was it that he wished you to tell me?"

"That you've got to sign another promissory note—for fifty thousand this time."

"Is that all?"

Wrayford hesitated; then he said: "Yes, for the present."

She sat motionless, her head bent, her hand resting passively in his.

He leaned nearer. "What did you mean just now, by worse things?"

She hesitated. "Haven't you noticed that he's been drinking a great deal lately?"

"Yes, I've noticed."

They were both silent; then Wrayford broke out, with sudden vehemence: "And yet you won't—"

"Won't?"

"Put an end to it. Good God! Save what's left of your life."

She made no answer, and in the stillness the throb of the water underneath them sounded like the beat of a tormented heart.

"Isabel," Wrayford murmured. He bent over to kiss her. "Isabel! I can't stand it! Listen—"

"No, no. I've thought of everything. There's the boy—the boy's fond of him. He's not a bad father."

"Except in the trifling matter of ruining his son."

"And there's his poor old mother. He's a good son, at any rate; he'd never hurt her. And I know her. If I left him, she'd never take a penny of my money. What she has of her own is not enough to live on; and how could he provide for her? If I put him out of doors, I should be putting his mother out too."

"You could arrange that—there are always ways."

"Not for her! She's proud. And then she believes in him. Lots of people believe in him, you know. It would kill her if she ever found out."

Wrayford made an impatient movement. "It will kill you if you stay with him to prevent her finding out."

She laid her other hand on his. "Not while I have you."

"Have me? In this way?"

"In any way."

"My poor girl—poor child!"

"Unless you grow tired—unless your patience gives out."

He was silent, and she went on insistently: "Don't you suppose I've thought of that too—foreseen it?"

"Well—and then?" he exclaimed.

"I've accepted that too."

He dropped her hands with a despairing gesture. "Then, indeed, I waste my breath!"

She made no answer, and for a time they sat silent again, a little between them. At length he asked: "You're not crying?"

"No."

"I can't see your face, it's grown so dark."

"Yes. The storm must be coming." She made a motion as if to rise.

He drew close and put his arm about her. "Don't leave me yet. You know I must go tomorrow." He broke off with a laugh. "I'm to break the news to you tomorrow morning, by the way; I'm to take you out in the motor-launch and break it to you." He dropped her hands and stood up. "Good God! How can I go and leave you here with him?"

"You've done it often."

"Yes, but each time it's more damnable. And then I've always had a hope—"

She rose also. "Give it up! Give it up!"

"You've none, then, yourself?"

She was silent, drawing the folds of her cloak about her.

"None, none?" he insisted.

He had to bend his head to hear her answer. "Only one!"

"What, my dearest? What?"

"Don't touch me! That he may die!"

They drew apart again, hearing each other's quick breathing through the darkness.

"You wish that too?" he said.

"I wish it always—every day, every hour, every moment!" She paused, and then let the words break from her. "You'd better know it; you'd better know the worst of me. I'm not the saint you suppose; the duty I do is poisoned by the thoughts I think. Day by day, hour by hour, I wish him dead. When he goes out I pray for something to happen; when he comes back I say to myself: 'Are you here again?' When I hear of people being killed in accidents, I think: 'Why wasn't he there?' When I read the death-notices in the paper I say: 'So-and-so was just his age.' When I see him taking such care of his health and his diet—as he does, you know, except when he gets reckless and begins to drink too much—when I see him exercising and resting, and eating only certain things, and weighing himself, and feeling his muscles, and boasting that he hasn't gained a pound, I think of the men who die from overwork, or who throw their lives away for some great object, and I say to myself: 'What can kill a man who thinks only of himself?' And night after night I keep myself from going to sleep for fear I may dream that he's dead. When I dream that, and wake and find him there it's worse than ever."

She broke off with a sob, and the loud lapping of the water under the floor was like the beat of a rebellious heart.

"There, you know the truth!" she said.

He answered after a pause: "People do die."

"Do they?" She laughed. "Yes—in happy marriages!"

They were silent again, and Isabel turned, feeling her way toward the door. As she did so, the profound stillness was broken by the sound of a man's voice trolling out unsteadily the refrain of a music-hall song.

The two in the boathouse darted toward each other with a simultaneous movement, clutching hands as they met.

"He's coming!" Isabel said.

Wrayford disengaged his hands.

"He may only be out for a turn before he goes to bed. Wait a minute. I'll see." He felt his way to the bench, scrambled up on it, and stretching his body forward managed to bring his eyes in line with the opening above the door.

"It's as black as pitch. I can't see anything."

The refrain rang out nearer.

"Wait! I saw something twinkle. There it is again. It's his cigar. It's coming this way—down the path."

There was a long rattle of thunder through the stillness.

"It's the storm!" Isabel whispered. "He's coming to see about the launch."

Wrayford dropped noiselessly from the bench and she caught him by the arm.

"Isn't there time to get up the path and slip under the shrubbery?"

"No, he's in the path now. He'll be here in two minutes. He'll find us."

He felt her hand tighten on his arm.

"You must go in the skiff, then. It's the only way."

"And let him find you? And hear my oars? Listen, there's something I must say."

She flung her arms about him and pressed her face to his.

"Isabel, just now I didn't tell you everything. He's ruined his mother—taken everything of hers too. And he's got to tell her; it can't be kept from her."

She uttered an incredulous exclamation and drew back.

"Is this the truth? Why didn't you tell me before?"

"He forbade me. You were not to know."

Close above them, in the shrubbery, Stilling warbled:

"Nita, Juanita,

Ask thy soul if we must part!"

Wrayford held her by both arms. "Understand this: if he comes in, he'll find us. And if there's a row you'll lose your boy."

She seemed not to hear him. "You—you—you—he'll kill you!" she exclaimed.

Wrayford laughed impatiently and released her, and she stood shrinking against the wall, her hands pressed to her breast. Wrayford straightened himself and she felt that he was listening intently. Then he dropped to his knees and laid his hands against the boards of the sliding floor. It yielded at once, as if with a kind of evil alacrity; and at their feet they saw, under the motionless solid night, another darker night that moved and shimmered. Wrayford threw himself back against the opposite wall, behind the door.

A key rattled in the lock, and after a moment's fumbling the door swung open. Wrayford and Isabel saw a man's black bulk against the obscurity. It moved a step, lurched forward, and vanished out of sight. From the depths beneath them there came a splash and a long cry.

"Go! Go!" Wrayford cried out, feeling blindly for Isabel in the blackness.

"Oh—" she cried, wrenching herself away from him.

He stood still a moment, as if dazed; then she saw him suddenly plunge from her side, and heard another splash far down, and a tumult in the beaten water.

In the darkness she cowered close to the opening, pressing her face over the edge, and crying out the name of each of the two men in turn. Suddenly she began to see: the obscurity was less opaque, as if a faint moon-pallor diluted it. Isabel vaguely discerned the two shapes struggling in the black pit below her; once she saw the gleam of a face. She glanced up desperately for some means of rescue, and caught sight of the oars ranged on brackets against the wall. She snatched down the nearest, bent over the opening, and pushed the oar down into the blackness, crying out her husband's name.

The clouds had swallowed the moon again, and she could see nothing below her; but she still heard the tumult in the beaten water.

"Cobham! Cobham!" she screamed.

As if in answer, she felt a mighty clutch on the oar, a clutch that strained her arms to the breaking point as she tried to brace her knees against the runners of the sliding floor.

"Hold on! Hold on! Hold on!" a voice gasped out from below; and she held on, with racked muscles, with bleeding palms, with eyes straining from their sockets, and a heart that tugged at her as the weight was tugging at the oar.

Suddenly the weight relaxed, and the oar slipped up through her lacerated hands. She felt a wet body scrambling over the edge of the opening, and Stilling's voice, raucous and strange, groaned out, close to her: "God! I thought I was done for."

He staggered to his knees, coughing and sputtering, and the water dripped on her from his streaming clothes.

She flung herself down, again, straining over the pit. Not a sound came up from it.

"Austin! Austin! Quick! Another oar!" she shrieked.

Stilling gave a cry. "My God! Was it Austin? What in hell—Another oar? No, no. Untie the skiff, I tell you. But it's no use. Nothing's any use. I felt him lose hold as I came up."

* * *

After that she was conscious of nothing till, hours later, as it appeared to her, she became dimly aware of her husband's voice, high, hysterical and important, haranguing a group of scared lantern-struck faces that had sprung up mysteriously about them in the night.

"Poor Austin! Poor Wrayford . . . terrible loss to me . . . mysterious dispensation. Yes, I do feel gratitude—miraculous escape—but I wish old Austin could have known that I was saved!"

Thinking About the Story

Social nuance, especially in terms of class and economic privilege, loom large in Edith Wharton's story. Although "The Choice" is one of her early, more forthright stories, perhaps what makes it so engaging is the underlying use of irony. Moreover, in regard to Wharton's work, you should think about the human experience and the role of love, particularly in how the complexities of irony manifest themselves. Accordingly, try to formulate some conclusions about the following: What makes something ironic? Can you give examples of social, verbal, and dramatic irony? After answering these questions, it is essential that you look to Kate Chopin's "The Story of an Hour" for other ways that irony is used. Examine how both writers use this technique to amplify meaning within their stories.

Discussion Questions

1. The two men—Cobham Stilling and Austin Wrayford—are cleverly contrasted. Assess this contrast as fully as possible, making sure to reference each character's actions, socio-economic status, and morals and values.
2. When does Mrs. Stilling find out about Cobham Stilling's past behavior? Do her feelings toward her husband change over the course of the story?
3. Compare and contrast the events at the dinner party with the meeting in the boathouse. What do these scenes suggest about social class and economic prosperity?
4. Analyze the nature of Austin Wrayford and Mrs. Stilling's relationship. Do you think they are having an affair? What clues can you find in the text to support your opinion?
5. What types of irony exist in the story? Locate several examples and discuss them with a partner. Evaluate how important irony is to the final effect of the story.

Activities

1. In the guise of Mrs. Stilling, compose a letter to the relatives of Austin Wrayford, explaining the circumstances surrounding his death.
2. Extend the story by writing a new final scene. What happens next?
3. Imagine you're hosting a dinner party. Select six writers and/or fictional characters you would invite. Next write a paragraph on the following:
   a. Explain the reason behind each of your choices.
   b. Speculate on possible conversation topics.

O. Henry

The true adventurer goes forth aimless and uncalculating
to meet and greet unknown fate.
O. Henry — "The Green Door" (1906)

At the end of the nineteenth century, O. Henry—the pen name for William Sydney Porter (1862–1910)—was established as one of America's most popular writers. He was born in Greensboro, North Carolina. As a young man he suffered health problems, prompting Porter after high school, to move to a dry air climate. He chose Texas, and by 1882, he was working on a cattle ranch. A couple of years later, he relocated to Austin, gaining employment as a drug clerk. He married Athol Estes Roach in 1887, and later they had a daughter. Porter next became a bank teller and after work he ran a small press that produced a weekly humorous tract named *Rolling Stone*. The magazine's loss-making operation enticed him to embezzle funds from his bank. Faced with a trial, he fled to Honduras, but came back in 1897 to be near his dying wife. During his time in prison, he created the O. Henry persona. After his release he drank and wasted money on indulgences and easy living. At the height of his commercial appeal and public fame, he married a childhood friend, Sarah Coleman. By 1910, his life's excesses took hold and he died of heart complications and cirrhosis of the liver.

The last decade of O. Henry's life was his most productive and successful. Several of his stories were published in national magazines like *McClure's* and *Smart Set*, and later in collections such as *Cabbages and Kings* (1904), *The Four Million* (1906), and *The Gentle Grafter* (1908). Popular with the American public, O. Henry's stories became an in-demand commodity, due in part to his colorful, engaging characters. His stories are further distinguished by their plot twists, situational ironies, landscape depictions, and vivid humor. Many of these features are present in "The Ransom of Red Chief" (1910); a story that juxtaposes rich and poor characters, and raises questions about the role of fate and predestination. The voice of the narrator, Sam, with his colloquialisms and dialect, drive the story on, as he relays the events of the kidnapping with regional eloquence and comedic timing. Further within the story, tensions arise in various opposing guises: authority and rebellion, crime and punishment, and sin and redemption.

The Ransom of Red Chief

O. Henry

It looked like a good thing: but wait till I tell you. We were down South, in Alabama—Bill Driscoll and myself—when this kidnapping idea struck us. It was, as Bill afterward expressed it, "during a moment of temporary mental apparition"; but we didn't find that out till later.

There was a town down there, as flat as a flannel cake, and called Summit, of course. It contained inhabitants of as undeleterious and self-satisfied a class of peasantry as ever clustered around a Maypole.

Bill and me had a joint capital of about six hundred dollars, and we needed just two thousand dollars more to pull off a fraudulent town-lot scheme in Western Illinois. We talked it over on the front steps of the hotel. Philoprogenitiveness, says we, is strong in semi-rural communities therefore, and for other reasons, a kidnapping project ought to do better there than in the radius of newspapers that send reporters out in plain clothes to stir up talk about such things. We knew that Summit couldn't get after us with anything stronger than constables and, maybe, some lackadaisical bloodhounds and a diatribe or two in the *Weekly Farmers' Budget*. So, it looked good.

We selected for our victim the only child of a prominent citizen named Ebenezer Dorset. The father was respectable and tight, a mortgage fancier and a stern, upright collection-plate passer and forecloser. The kid was a boy of ten, with bas-relief freckles, and hair the color of the cover of the magazine you buy at the newsstand when you want to catch a train. Bill and me figured that Ebenezer would melt down for a ransom of two thousand dollars to a cent. But wait till I tell you.

About two miles from Summit was a little mountain, covered with a dense cedar brake. On the rear elevation of this mountain was a cave. There we stored provisions.

One evening after sundown, we drove in a buggy past old Dorset's house. The kid was in the street, throwing rocks at a kitten on the opposite fence.

"Hey, little boy!" says Bill, "would you like to have a bag of candy and a nice ride?"

The boy catches Bill neatly in the eye with a piece of brick.

"That will cost the old man an extra five hundred dollars," says Bill, climbing over the wheel.

That boy put up a fight like a welterweight cinnamon bear; but, at last, we got him down in the bottom of the buggy and drove away. We took him up to the cave, and I hitched the horse in the cedar brake. After dark I drove the buggy to the little village, three miles away, where we had hired it, and walked back to the mountain.

Bill was pasting court plaster over the scratches and bruises on his features. There was a fire burning behind the big rock at the entrance of the cave, and the boy was watching a pot of boiling coffee, with two buzzard tail feathers stuck in his red hair. He points a stick at me when I come up, and says:

"Ha! cursed paleface, do you dare to enter the camp of Red Chief, the terror of the plains?"

"He's all right now," says Bill, rolling up his trousers and examining some bruises on his shins. "We're playing Indian. We're making Buffalo Bill's show look like magic-lantern views of Palestine in the town hall. I'm Old Hank, the Trapper, Red Chief's captive, and I'm to be scalped at daybreak. By Geronimo! That kid can kick hard."

Yes, sir, that boy seemed to be having the time of his life. The fun of camping out in a cave had made him forget that he was a captive himself. He immediately christened me Snake-eye, the Spy, and announced that, when his braves returned from the warpath, I was to be broiled at the stake at the rising of the sun.

Then we had supper; and he filled his mouth full of bacon and bread and gravy, and began to talk. He made a during-dinner speech something like this:

"I like this fine. I never camped out before; but I had a pet 'possum once, and I was nine last birthday. I hate to go to school. Rats ate up sixteen of Jimmy Talbot's aunt's speckled hen's eggs. Are there any real Indians in these woods? I want some more gravy. Does the trees moving make the wind blow? We had five puppies. What makes your nose so red, Hank? My father has lots of money. Are the stars hot? I whipped Ed Walker twice, Saturday. I don't like girls. You dassent catch toads unless with a string. Do oxen make any noise? Why are oranges round? Have you got beds to sleep on in this cave? Amos Murray has got six toes. A parrot can talk, but a monkey or a fish can't. How many does it take to make twelve?"

Every few minutes he would remember that he was a pesky redskin, and pick up his stick rifle and tiptoe to the mouth of the cave to rubber for the scouts of the hated paleface. Now and then he would let out a war-whoop that made Old Hank the Trapper shiver. That boy had Bill terrorized from the start.

"Red Chief," says I to the kid, "would you like to go home?"

"Aw, what for?" says he. "I don't have any fun at home. I hate to go to school. I like to camp out. You won't take me back home again, Snake-eye, will you?"

"Not right away," says I. "We'll stay here in the cave a while."

"All right!" says he. "That'll be fine. I never had such fun in all my life."

We went to bed about eleven o'clock. We spread down some wide blankets and quilts and put Red Chief between us. We weren't afraid he'd run away. He kept us awake for three hours, jumping up and reaching for his rifle and screeching: "Hist! pard," in mine and Bill's ears, as the fancied crackle of a twig or the rustle of a leaf revealed to his young imagination the stealthy approach of the outlaw band. At last, I fell into a troubled sleep, and dreamed that I had been kidnapped and chained to a tree by a ferocious pirate with red hair.

Just at daybreak, I was awakened by a series of awful screams from Bill. They weren't yells, or howls, or shouts, or whoops, or yawps, such as you'd expect from a manly set of vocal organs—they were simply indecent, terrifying, humiliating screams, such as women emit when they see ghosts or caterpillars. It's an awful thing to hear a strong, desperate, fat man scream incontinently in a cave at daybreak.

I jumped up to see what the matter was. Red Chief was sitting on Bill's chest, with one hand twined in Bill's hair. In the other he had the sharp case knife we used for slicing bacon; and he was industriously and realistically trying to take Bill's scalp, according to the sentence that had been pronounced upon him the evening before.

I got the knife away from the kid and made him lie down again. But, from that moment, Bill's spirit was broken. He laid down on his side of the bed, but he never closed an eye again in sleep as long as that boy was with us. I dozed off for a while, but along toward sun-up I remembered that Red Chief had said I was to be burned at the stake at the rising of the sun. I wasn't nervous or afraid; but I sat up and lit my pipe and leaned against a rock.

"What you getting up so soon for, Sam?" asked Bill.

"Me?" says I. "Oh, I got a kind of a pain in my shoulder. I thought sitting up would rest it."

"You're a liar!" says Bill. "You're afraid. You was to be burned at sunrise, and you was afraid he'd do it. And he would, too, if he could find a match. Ain't it awful, Sam? Do you think anybody will pay out money to get a little imp like that back home?"

"Sure," said I. "A rowdy kid like that is just the kind that parents dote on. Now, you and the Chief get up and cook breakfast, while I go up on the top of this mountain and reconnoitre."

I went up on the peak of the little mountain and ran my eye over the contiguous vicinity. Over toward Summit I expected to see the sturdy yeomanry of the village armed with scythes and pitchforks beating the countryside for the dastardly kidnappers. But what I saw was a peaceful landscape dotted with one man plowing with a dun mule. Nobody was dragging the creek; no couriers dashed hither and yon, bringing tidings of no news to the distracted parents. There was a sylvan attitude of somnolent sleepiness pervading that section of the external outward surface of Alabama that lay exposed to my view.

"Perhaps," says I to myself, "it has not yet been discovered that the wolves have borne away the tender lambkin from the fold. Heaven help the wolves!" says I, and I went down the mountain to breakfast.

When I got to the cave I found Bill backed up against the side of it, breathing hard, and the boy threatening to smash him with a rock half as big as a coconut.

"He put a red-hot boiled potato down my back," explained Bill, "and then mashed it with his foot; and I boxed his ears. Have you got a gun about you, Sam?"

I took the rock away from the boy and kind of patched up the argument. "I'll fix you," says the kid to Bill. "No man ever yet struck the Red Chief but what he got paid for it. You better beware!"

After breakfast the kid takes a piece of leather with strings wrapped around it out of his pocket and goes outside the cave unwinding it.

"What's he up to now?" says Bill, anxiously. "You don't think he'll run away, do you, Sam?"

"No fear of it," says I. "He don't seem to be much of a home body. But we've got to fix up some plan about the ransom. There don't seem to be much excitement around Summit on account of his disappearance; but maybe they haven't realized yet that he's gone. His folks may think he's spending the night with Aunt Jane or one of the neighbors. Anyhow, he'll be missed today. Tonight we must get a message to his father demanding the two thousand dollars for his return."

Just then we heard a kind of war-whoop, such as David might have emitted when he knocked out the champion Goliath. It was a sling that Red Chief had pulled out of his pocket, and he was whirling it around his head.

I dodged, and heard a heavy thud and a kind of a sigh from Bill, like a horse gives out when you take his saddle off. A dark rock the size of an egg had caught Bill just behind his left ear. He loosened himself all over and fell in the fire across the frying pan of hot water for washing the dishes. I dragged him out and poured cold water on his head for half an hour.

By and by, Bill sits up and feels behind his ear and says: "Sam, do you know who my favorite Biblical character is?"

"Take it easy," says I. "You'll come to your senses presently."

"King Herod," says he. "You won't go away and leave me here alone, will you, Sam?"

I went out and caught that boy and shook him until his freckles rattled.

"If you don't behave," says I, "I'll take you straight home. Now, are you going to be good, or not?"

"I was only funning," says he sullenly. "I didn't mean to hurt Old Hank. But what did he hit me for? I'll behave, Snake-eye, if you won't send me home, and if you'll let me play the Black Scout today."

"I don't know the game," says I. "That's for you and Mr. Bill to decide. He's your playmate for the day. I'm going away for a while, on business. Now, you come in and make friends with him and say you are sorry for hurting him, or home you go, at once."

I made him and Bill shake hands, and then I took Bill aside and told him I was going to Poplar Cove, a little village three miles from the cave, and find out what I could about how the kidnapping had been regarded in Summit. Also, I thought it best to send a peremptory letter to old man Dorset that day, demanding the ransom and dictating how it should be paid.

"You know, Sam," says Bill, "I've stood by you without batting an eye in earthquakes, fire and flood—in poker games, dynamite outrages, police raids, train robberies and cyclones. I never lost my nerve yet till we kidnapped that two-legged skyrocket of a kid. He's got me going. You won't leave me long with him, will you, Sam?"

"I'll be back some time this afternoon," says I. "You must keep the boy amused and quiet till I return. And now we'll write the letter to old Dorset."

Bill and I got paper and pencil and worked on the letter while Red Chief, with a blanket wrapped around him, strutted up and down, guarding the mouth of the cave. Bill begged me tearfully to make the ransom fifteen hundred dollars instead of two thousand. "I ain't attempting," says he, "to decry the celebrated moral aspect of parental affection, but we're dealing with humans, and it ain't human for anybody to give up two thousand dollars for that forty-pound chunk of freckled wildcat. I'm willing to take a chance at fifteen hundred dollars. You can charge the difference up to me."

So, to relieve Bill, I acceded, and we collaborated a letter that ran this way:

> *Ebenezer Dorset, Esq.:*
>
> We have your boy concealed in a place far from Summit. It is useless for you or the most skilful detectives to attempt to find him. Absolutely, the only terms on which you can have him restored to you are these: We demand fifteen hundred dollars in large bills for his return; the money to be left at midnight to-night at the same spot and in the same box as your reply—as hereinafter described. If you agree to these terms, send your answer in writing by a solitary messenger tonight at half-past eight o'clock. After

crossing Owl Creek, on the road to Poplar Cove, there are three large trees about a hundred yards apart, close to the fence of the wheat field on the right-hand side. At the bottom of the fence-post, opposite the third tree, will be found a small pasteboard box.

The messenger will place the answer in this box and return immediately to Summit.

If you attempt any treachery or fail to comply with our demand as stated, you will never see your boy again.

If you pay the money as demanded, he will be returned to you safe and well within three hours. These terms are final, and if you do not accede to them no further communication will be attempted.

TWO DESPERATE MEN.

I addressed this letter to Dorset, and put it in my pocket. As I was about to start, the kid comes up to me and says:

"Aw, Snake-eye, you said I could play the Black Scout while you was gone."

"Play it, of course," says I. "Mr. Bill will play with you. What kind of a game is it?"

"I'm the Black Scout," says Red Chief, "and I have to ride to the stockade to warn the settlers that the Indians are coming. I'm tired of playing Indian myself. I want to be the Black Scout."

"All right," says I. "It sounds harmless to me. I guess Mr. Bill will help you foil the pesky savages."

"What am I to do?" asks Bill, looking at the kid suspiciously.

"You are the hoss," says Black Scout. "Get down on your hands and knees. How can I ride to the stockade without a hoss?"

"You'd better keep him interested," said I, "till we get the scheme going. Loosen up."

Bill gets down on his all fours, and a look comes in his eye like a rabbit's when you catch it in a trap.

"How far is it to the stockade, kid?" he asks, in a husky manner of voice.

"Ninety miles," says the Black Scout. "And you have to hump yourself to get there on time. Whoa, now!"

The Black Scout jumps on Bill's back and digs his heels in his side.

"For Heaven's sake," says Bill, "hurry back, Sam, as soon as you can. I wish we hadn't made the ransom more than a thousand. Say, you quit kicking me or I'll get up and warm you good."

I walked over to Poplar Cove and sat around the post office and store, talking with the chawbacons that came in to trade. One whiskerando says that he hears Summit is all upset on account of Elder Ebenezer Dorset's boy having been lost or stolen. That was all I wanted to know. I bought some smoking tobacco, referred casually to the price of black-eyed peas, posted my letter surreptitiously and came away. The postmaster said the mail carrier would come by in an hour to take the mail on to Summit.

When I got back to the cave Bill and the boy were not to be found. I explored the vicinity of the cave, and risked a yodel or two, but there was no response.

So I lighted my pipe and sat down on a mossy bank to await developments.

In about half an hour I heard the bushes rustle, and Bill wabbled out into the little glade in front of the cave. Behind him was the kid, stepping softly like a scout, with a broad grin on his face. Bill stopped, took off his hat and wiped his face with a red handkerchief. The kid stopped about eight feet behind him.

"Sam," says Bill, "I suppose you'll think I'm a renegade, but I couldn't help it. I'm a grown person with masculine proclivities and habits of self-defense, but there is a time when all systems of egotism and predominance fail. The boy is gone. I have sent him home. All is off. There was martyrs in old times," goes on Bill, "that suffered death rather than give up the particular graft they enjoyed. None of 'em ever was subjugated to such supernatural tortures as I have been. I tried to be faithful to our articles of depredation; but there came a limit."

"What's the trouble, Bill?" I asks him.

"I was rode," says Bill, "the ninety miles to the stockade, not barring an inch. Then, when the settlers was rescued, I was given oats. Sand ain't a palatable substitute. And then, for an hour I had to try to explain to him why there was nothin' in holes, how a road can run both ways and what makes the grass green. I tell you, Sam, a human can only stand so much. I takes him by the neck of his clothes and drags him down the mountain. On the way he kicks my legs black-and-blue from the knees down; and I've got two or three bites on my thumb and hand cauterized.

"But he's gone"—continues Bill—"gone home. I showed him the road to Summit and kicked him about eight feet nearer there at one kick. I'm sorry we lose the ransom; but it was either that or Bill Driscoll to the madhouse."

Bill is puffing and blowing, but there is a look of ineffable peace and growing content on his rose-pink features.

"Bill," says I, "there isn't any heart disease in your family, is there?"

"No," says Bill, "nothing chronic except malaria and accidents. Why?"

"Then you might turn around," says I, "and have a look behind you."

Bill turns and sees the boy, and loses his complexion and sits down plump on the ground and begins to pluck aimlessly at grass and little sticks. For an hour I was afraid for his mind. And then I told him that my scheme was to put the whole job through immediately and that we would get the ransom and be off with it by midnight if old Dorset fell in with our proposition. So Bill braced up enough to give the kid a weak sort of a smile and a promise to play the Russian in a Japanese war with him as soon as he felt a little better.

I had a scheme for collecting that ransom without danger of being caught by counterplots that ought to commend itself to professional kidnappers. The tree under which the answer was to be left—and the money later on—was close to the road fence with big, bare fields on all sides. If a gang of constables should be watching for any one to come for the note they could see him a long way off crossing the fields or in the road. But no, sirree! At half-past eight I was up in that tree as well hidden as a tree toad, waiting for the messenger to arrive.

Exactly on time, a half-grown boy rides up the road on a bicycle, locates the pasteboard box at the foot of the fencepost, slips a folded piece of paper into it and pedals away again back toward Summit.

I waited an hour and then concluded the thing was square. I slid down the tree, got the note, slipped along the fence till I struck the woods, and was back at the cave in another half an hour. I opened the note, got near the lantern and read it to Bill. It was written with a pen in a crabbed hand, and the sum and substance of it was this:

> *Two Desperate Men.*
> Gentlemen: I received your letter today by post, in regard to the ransom you ask for the return of my son. I think you are a little high in your demands, and I hereby make you a counter-proposition,

which I am inclined to believe you will accept. You bring Johnny home and pay me two hundred and fifty dollars in cash, and I agree to take him off your hands. You had better come at night, for the neighbors believe he is lost, and I couldn't be responsible for what they would do to anybody they saw bringing him back.

Very respectfully,
Ebenezer Dorset.

"Great pirates of Penzance!" says I; "of all the impudent—"

But I glanced at Bill, and hesitated. He had the most appealing look in his eyes I ever saw on the face of a dumb or a talking brute.

"Sam," says he, "what's two hundred and fifty dollars, after all? We've got the money. One more night of this kid will send me to a bed in Bedlam. Besides being a thorough gentleman, I think Mr. Dorset is a spendthrift for making us such a liberal offer. You ain't going to let the chance go, are you?"

"Tell you the truth, Bill," says I, "this little he ewe lamb has somewhat got on my nerves too. We'll take him home, pay the ransom and make our get-away."

We took him home that night. We got him to go by telling him that his father had bought a silver-mounted rifle and a pair of moccasins for him, and we were going to hunt bears the next day.

It was just twelve o'clock when we knocked at Ebenezer's front door. Just at the moment when I should have been abstracting the fifteen hundred dollars from the box under the tree, according to the original proposition, Bill was counting out two hundred and fifty dollars into Dorset's hand.

When the kid found out we were going to leave him at home he started up a howl like a calliope and fastened himself as tight as a leech to Bill's leg. His father peeled him away gradually, like a porous plaster.

"How long can you hold him?" asks Bill.

"I'm not as strong as I used to be," says old Dorset, "but I think I can promise you ten minutes."

"Enough," says Bill. "In ten minutes I shall cross the Central, Southern, and Middle Western States, and be legging it trippingly for the Canadian border."

And, as dark as it was, and as fat as Bill was, and as good a runner as I am, he was a good mile and a half out of Summit before I could catch up with him.

Thinking About the Story

O. Henry once wrote, "Write what you like; there is no other rule." When analyzing "The Ransom of Red Chief" it is instructive to keep his words in mind. O. Henry created a formula for his fiction, one that relied on voice and plot, but also a heavy use of situational and dramatic ironies, which confounded his readers' expectations. Bearing this in mind, you should assess whether you find this story to be formulaic. You may want to think about how you classify this story. Is it commercial, genre, or literary fiction? Consider where the story's emphasis lies: plot, character, language, or something else? In your quest to differentiate between distinct forms of fiction, consider the other so-called genre stories in this collection: H. P. Lovecraft's "The Outsider," Arthur Conan Doyle's "A Scandal in Bohemia," and Robert E. Howard's "Circus Fists."

Discussion Questions

1. Identify the protagonist(s) and antagonist(s) in the story. What are the conflicts for each of them?

2. In what ways do hyperbole and exaggeration function in the story? Do they add or subtract from your enjoyment and understanding of the story?

3. Discuss the story's voice, tone, and use of dialect. In particular, consider each character's education and social position. Does the story offer any commentary, whether implicit or explicit, on either?

4. How do you assess Bill and Sam's friendship? What is it based on? Do you consider the friendship to be strong or weak? Explain your

reasons using examples from the text. In the end, why do Bill and Sam accept Mr. Dorset's deal? Can you find foreshadowing evidence for this reversal?

5. Is the primary emphasis of the story on character, theme, or plot? Is this a story of entertainment or interpretation?

Activities

1. Imagine you are Johnny and that throughout the kidnapping you have kept a secret journal. Write a journal entry for each of the days he was in captivity.
2. List several humorous and/or ironic scenarios. Pick one scenario and write a story in which Bill and Sam are the central characters. You can choose which of the two men will be the first-person narrator ("I").
3. Using the characters and events from the story, create the fictional front page of a newspaper article. Format the article appropriately: single-spaced, columns, headings, and headlines.

Rudyard Kipling

All the people like us are We, and everyone else is They.
Rudyard Kipling — "We and They" (1926)

Forever associated with the British Empire, Rudyard Kipling (1865–1936) was a novelist, poet, and children's writer, who won the Nobel Prize for literature in 1907. Born in Bombay, India, to English parents, Kipling and his sister, Alice, were sent to England as young children to live with foster-parents and to be educated in the British tradition. At school, Kipling wrote poems and stories, and with his friends developed his love of action and adventure. In 1882, he sailed for India to edit an English-language newspaper based in Lahore. When Kipling returned to England in 1889, he found himself honored by the public and his literary peers for the books he had published while in India. Within a couple of years, he married Carrie Balestier. Soon after they moved to Vermont, where they raised two daughters. In the early years of the twentieth century they lived in England, where Kipling wrote many of his later books. Friends with Henry James and Cecil Rhodes, Kipling's final years were a heady mix of literature and politics. At the age of 70 he died and his ashes were interred in Westminster Abbey.

Best remembered today for *The Jungle Book* (1894), *Kim* (1901), and *Just So Stories* (1902), Kipling was a prolific and serious artist of his age. Although much of his output is connected to the jingoistic impulses of the British Empire and the largess of imperial domain, Kipling remains important as a writer of Anglo-Indian and children's literature. Throughout his writing on India are sensual descriptions and myth-narratives that often contrast with his depictions of England. Perhaps lacking psychological depth in his minor works, Kipling does in his finest writing achieve an emotional connection with the reader. "Mowgli's Brothers" is the first story in

The Jungle Book and contains some of Kipling's most visceral depictions. The colorful jungle, the exotic animals, and the strange dialogue interweave with each other, lending the story a fable quality. Yet inside these childlike constructions lay important questions about Mowgli's unusual upbringing and the complexities of human nature.

Mowgli's Brothers

Rudyard Kipling

Now Rann the Kite brings home the night
That Mang the Bat sets free —
The herds are shut in byre and hut
For loosed till dawn are we.
This is the hour of pride and power,
Talon and tush and claw.
Oh, hear the call! — Good hunting all
That keep the Jungle Law!
Night-Song in the Jungle

It was seven o'clock of a very warm evening in the Seeonee hills when Father Wolf woke up from his day's rest, scratched himself, yawned, and spread out his paws one after the other to get rid of the sleepy feeling in their tips. Mother Wolf lay with her big gray nose dropped across her four tumbling, squealing cubs, and the moon shone into the mouth of the cave where they all lived. "Augrh!" said Father Wolf. "It is time to hunt again." He was going to spring down hill when a little shadow with a bushy tail crossed the threshold and whined: "Good luck go with you, O Chief of the Wolves. And good luck and strong white teeth go with noble children that they may never forget the hungry in this world."

It was the jackal—Tabaqui, the Dish-licker—and the wolves of India despise Tabaqui because he runs about making mischief, and telling tales, and eating rags and pieces of leather from the village rubbish-heaps. But they are afraid of him too, because Tabaqui, more than anyone else in the jungle, is apt to go mad, and then he forgets that he was ever afraid of anyone, and runs through the forest biting everything in his way. Even the tiger runs and hides when little Tabaqui goes mad, for madness is the most disgraceful thing that can overtake a wild creature. We call it hydrophobia, but they call it *dewanee*—the madness—and run.

"Enter, then, and look," said Father Wolf stiffly, "but there is no food here."

"For a wolf, no," said Tabaqui, "but for so mean a person as myself a dry bone is a good feast. Who are we, the Gidur-log [the jackal people], to pick and choose?" He scuttled to the back of the cave, where he found the bone of a buck with some meat on it, and sat cracking the end merrily.

"All thanks for this good meal," he said, licking his lips. "How beautiful are the noble children! How large are their eyes! And so young too! Indeed, indeed, I might have remembered that the children of kings are men from the beginning."

Now, Tabaqui knew as well as anyone else that there is nothing so unlucky as to compliment children to their faces. It pleased him to see Mother and Father Wolf look uncomfortable.

Tabaqui sat still, rejoicing in the mischief that he had made, and then he said spitefully:

"Shere Khan, the Big One, has shifted his hunting grounds. He will hunt among these hills for the next moon, so he has told me."

Shere Khan was the tiger who lived near the Waingunga River, twenty miles away.

"He has no right!" Father Wolf began angrily. "By the Law of the Jungle he has no right to change his quarters without due warning. He will frighten every head of game within ten miles, and I—I have to kill for two, these days."

"His mother did not call him Lungri [the Lame One] for nothing," said Mother Wolf quietly. "He has been lame in one foot from his birth. That is why he has only killed cattle. Now the villagers of the Waingunga are angry with him, and he has come here to make *our* villagers angry. They will scour the jungle for him when he is far away, and we and our children must run when the grass is set alight. Indeed, we are very grateful to Shere Khan!"

"Shall I tell him of your gratitude?" said Tabaqui.

"Out!" snapped Father Wolf. "Out and hunt with thy master. Thou hast done harm enough for one night."

"I go," said Tabaqui quietly. "Ye can hear Shere Khan below in the thickets. I might have saved myself the message."

Father Wolf listened, and below in the valley that ran down to a little river he heard the dry, angry, snarly, singsong whine of a tiger who has caught nothing and does not care if all the jungle knows it.

"The fool!" said Father Wolf. "To begin a night's work with that noise! Does he think that our buck are like his fat Waingunga bullocks?"

"H'sh. It is neither bullock nor buck he hunts tonight," said Mother Wolf. "It is Man."

The whine had changed to a sort of humming purr that seemed to come from every quarter of the compass. It was the noise that bewilders woodcutters and gypsies sleeping in the open, and makes them run sometimes into the very mouth of the tiger.

"Man!" said Father Wolf, showing all his white teeth. "Faugh! Are there not enough beetles and frogs in the tanks that he must eat Man, and on our ground too!"

The Law of the Jungle, which never orders anything without a reason, forbids every beast to eat Man except when he is killing to show his children how to kill, and then he must hunt outside the hunting grounds of his pack or tribe. The real reason for this is that man-killing means, sooner or later, the arrival of white men on elephants, with guns, and hundreds of brown men with gongs and rockets and torches. Then everybody in the jungle suffers. The reason the beasts give among themselves is that Man is the weakest and most defenseless of all living things, and it is unsportsmanlike to touch him. They say too—and it is true—that man-eaters become mangy, and lose their teeth.

The purr grew louder, and ended in the full-throated "Aaarh!" of the tiger's charge.

Then there was a howl—an untigerish howl—from Shere Khan. "He has missed," said Mother Wolf. "What is it?"

Father Wolf ran out a few paces and heard Shere Khan muttering and mumbling savagely as he tumbled about in the scrub.

"The fool has had no more sense than to jump at a woodcutter's campfire, and has burned his feet," said Father Wolf with a grunt. "Tabaqui is with him."

"Something is coming uphill," said Mother Wolf, twitching one ear. "Get ready."

The bushes rustled a little in the thicket, and Father Wolf dropped with his haunches under him, ready for his leap. Then, if you had been watching, you would have seen the most wonderful thing in the world—the wolf checked in mid-spring. He made his bound before he saw what it was he was jumping at, and then he tried to stop himself. The result was that he shot up straight into the air for four or five feet, landing almost where he left ground.

"Man!" he snapped. "A man's cub. Look!"

Directly in front of him, holding on by a low branch, stood a naked brown baby who could just walk—as soft and as dimpled a little atom as ever came to a wolf's cave at night. He looked up into Father Wolf's face, and laughed.

"Is that a man's cub?" said Mother Wolf. "I have never seen one. Bring it here."

A Wolf accustomed to moving his own cubs can, if necessary, mouth an egg without breaking it, and though Father Wolf's jaws closed right on the child's back not a tooth even scratched the skin as he laid it down among the cubs.

"How little! How naked, and—how bold!" said Mother Wolf softly. The baby was pushing his way between the cubs to get close to the warm hide. "Ahai! He is taking his meal with the others. And so this is a man's cub. Now, was there ever a wolf that could boast of a man's cub among her children?"

"I have heard now and again of such a thing, but never in our Pack or in my time," said Father Wolf.

"He is altogether without hair, and I could kill him with a touch of my foot. But see, he looks up and is not afraid."

The moonlight was blocked out of the mouth of the cave, for Shere Khan's great square head and shoulders were thrust into the entrance. Tabaqui, behind him, was squeaking: "My lord, my lord, it went in here!"

"Shere Khan does us great honor," said Father Wolf, but his eyes were very angry. "What does Shere Khan need?"

"My quarry. A man's cub went this way," said Shere Khan. "Its parents have run off. Give it to me."

Shere Khan had jumped at a woodcutter's campfire, as Father Wolf had said, and was furious from the pain of his burned feet. But Father Wolf knew that the mouth of the cave was too narrow for a tiger to come in by. Even where he was, Shere Khan's shoulders and forepaws were cramped for want of room, as a man's would be if he tried to fight in a barrel.

"The Wolves are a free people," said Father Wolf. "They take orders from the Head of the Pack, and not from any striped cattle-killer. The man's cub is ours—to kill if we choose."

"Ye choose and ye do not choose! What talk is this of choosing? By the bull that I killed, am I to stand nosing into your dog's den for my fair dues? It is I, Shere Khan, who speak!"

The tiger's roar filled the cave with thunder. Mother Wolf shook herself clear of the cubs and sprang forward, her eyes, like two green moons in the darkness, facing the blazing eyes of Shere Khan.

"And it is I, Raksha [The Demon], who answers. The man's cub is mine, Lungri—mine to me! He shall not be killed. He shall live to run with the Pack and to hunt with the Pack; and in the end, look you, hunter of little naked cubs—frog-eater—fish-killer—he shall hunt *thee!* Now get hence, or by the Sambhur that I killed (*I* eat no starved cattle), back thou goest to thy mother, burned beast of the jungle, lamer than ever thou camest into the world! Go!"

Father Wolf looked on amazed. He had almost forgotten the days when he won Mother Wolf in fair fight from five other wolves, when she ran in the Pack and was not called The Demon for compliment's sake. Shere Khan might have faced Father Wolf, but he could not stand up against Mother Wolf, for he knew that where he was she had all the advantage of the ground, and would fight to the death. So he backed out of the cave mouth growling, and when he was clear he shouted:

"Each dog barks in his own yard! We will see what the Pack will say to this fostering of man-cubs. The cub is mine, and to my teeth he will come in the end, O bush-tailed thieves!"

Mother Wolf threw herself down panting among the cubs, and Father Wolf said to her gravely:

"Shere Khan speaks this much truth. The cub must be shown to the Pack. Wilt thou still keep him, Mother?"

"Keep him!" she gasped. "He came naked, by night, alone and very hungry; yet he was not afraid!

"Look, he has pushed one of my babes to one side already. And that lame butcher would have killed him and would have run off to the Waingunga while the villagers here hunted through all our lairs in revenge! Keep him? Assuredly I will keep him. Lie still, little frog. O thou Mowgli—for Mowgli the Frog I will call thee—the time will come when thou wilt hunt Shere Khan as he has hunted thee."

"But what will our Pack say?" said Father Wolf.

The Law of the Jungle lays down very clearly that any wolf may, when he marries, withdraw from the Pack he belongs to. But as soon as his cubs are old enough to stand on their feet he must bring them to the Pack Council, which is generally held once a month at full moon, in order that the other wolves may identify them. After that inspection the cubs are free to run where they please, and until they have killed their first buck no excuse is accepted if a grown wolf of the Pack kills one of them. The punishment is death where the murderer can be found; and if you think for a minute you will see that this must be so.

Father Wolf waited till his cubs could run a little, and then on the night of the Pack Meeting took them and Mowgli and Mother Wolf to the Council Rock—a hilltop covered with stones and boulders where a hundred wolves could hide. Akela, the great gray Lone Wolf, who led all the Pack by strength and cunning, lay out at full length on his rock, and below him sat forty or more wolves of every size and color, from badger-colored veterans who could handle a buck alone to young black three-year-olds who thought they could. The Lone Wolf had led them for a year now. He had fallen twice into a wolf trap in his youth, and once he had been beaten and left for dead; so he knew the manners and customs of men. There was very little talking at the Rock. The cubs tumbled over each other in the center of the circle where their mothers and fathers sat, and now and again a senior wolf would go quietly up to a cub, look at him carefully, and return to his place on noiseless feet. Sometimes a mother would push her cub far out into the moonlight to be sure that he had not been overlooked. Akela from his rock would cry: "Ye know the Law—ye know the Law. Look well, O Wolves!" And the anxious mothers would take up the call: "Look—look well, O Wolves!"

At last—and Mother Wolf's neck bristles lifted as the time came—Father Wolf pushed "Mowgli the Frog," as they called him, into the center, where he sat laughing and playing with some pebbles that glistened in the moonlight.

Akela never raised his head from his paws, but went on with the monotonous cry: "Look well!" A muffled roar came up from behind the rocks—the voice of Shere Khan crying: "The cub is mine. Give him to me. What have the Free People to do with a man's cub?" Akela never even twitched his ears. All he said was: "Look well, O Wolves! What have the Free People to do with the orders of any save the Free People? Look well!"

There was a chorus of deep growls, and a young wolf in his fourth year flung back Shere Khan's question to Akela: "What have the Free People to do with a man's cub?" Now, the Law of the Jungle lays down that if there is any dispute as to the right of a cub to be accepted by the Pack, he must be spoken for by at least two members of the Pack who are not his father and mother.

"Who speaks for this cub?" said Akela. "Among the Free People who speaks?" There was no answer and Mother Wolf got ready for what she knew would be her last fight, if things came to fighting.

Then the only other creature who is allowed at the Pack Council—Baloo, the sleepy brown bear who teaches the wolf cubs the Law of the Jungle: old Baloo, who can come and go where he pleases because he eats only nuts and roots and honey—rose upon his hind quarters and grunted.

"The man's cub—the man's cub?" he said. "*I* speak for the man's cub. There is no harm in a man's cub. I have no gift of words, but I speak the truth. Let him run with the Pack, and be entered with the others. I myself will teach him."

"We need yet another," said Akela. "Baloo has spoken, and he is our teacher for the young cubs. Who speaks besides Baloo?"

A black shadow dropped down into the circle. It was Bagheera the Black Panther, inky black all over, but with the panther markings showing up in certain lights like the pattern of watered silk. Everybody knew Bagheera, and nobody cared to cross his path; for he was as cunning as Tabaqui, as bold as the wild buffalo, and as reckless as the wounded elephant. But he had a voice as soft as wild honey dripping from a tree, and a skin softer than down.

"O Akela, and ye the Free People," he purred, "I have no right in your assembly, but the Law of the Jungle says that if there is a doubt which is not a killing matter in regard to a new cub, the life of that cub may be bought at a price. And the Law does not say who may or may not pay that price. Am I right?"

"Good! Good!" said the young wolves, who are always hungry. "Listen to Bagheera. The cub can be bought for a price. It is the Law."

"Knowing that I have no right to speak here, I ask your leave."

"Speak then," cried twenty voices.

"To kill a naked cub is shame. Besides, he may make better sport for you when he is grown. Baloo has spoken in his behalf. Now to Baloo's word I will add one bull, and a fat one, newly killed, not half a mile from here, if ye will accept the man's cub according to the Law. Is it difficult?"

There was a clamor of scores of voices, saying: "What matter? He will die in the winter rains. He will scorch in the sun. What harm can a naked frog do us? Let him run with the Pack. Where is the bull, Bagheera? Let him be accepted." And then came Akela's deep bay, crying: "Look well—look well, O Wolves!"

Mowgli was still deeply interested in the pebbles, and he did not notice when the wolves came and looked at him one by one. At last they all went down the hill for the dead bull, and only Akela, Bagheera, Baloo, and Mowgli's own wolves were left. Shere Khan roared still in the night, for he was very angry that Mowgli had not been handed over to him.

"Ay, roar well," said Bagheera, under his whiskers, "for the time will come when this naked thing will make thee roar to another tune, or I know nothing of man."

"It was well done," said Akela. "Men and their cubs are very wise. He may be a help in time."

"Truly, a help in time of need; for none can hope to lead the Pack forever," said Bagheera.

Akela said nothing. He was thinking of the time that comes to every leader of every pack when his strength goes from him and he gets feebler and feebler, till at last he is killed by the wolves and a new leader comes up—to be killed in his turn.

"Take him away," he said to Father Wolf, "and train him as befits one of the Free People."

And that is how Mowgli was entered into the Seeonee Wolf Pack for the price of a bull and on Baloo's good word.

Now you must be content to skip ten or eleven whole years, and only guess at all the wonderful life that Mowgli led among the wolves, because if it were written out it would fill ever so many books. He grew up with the cubs, though they, of course, were grown wolves almost before he was a child. And Father Wolf taught him his business, and the meaning of things in the jungle, till every rustle in the grass, every breath of the warm night air, every note of the owls above his head, every scratch of a bat's claws as it roosted for a while in a tree, and every splash of every little fish jumping in a pool meant just as much to him as the work of his office means to a business man. When he was not learning he sat out in the sun and slept, and ate and went to sleep again. When he felt dirty or hot he swam in the forest pools; and when he wanted honey (Baloo told him that honey and nuts were just as pleasant to eat as raw meat) he climbed up for it, and that Bagheera showed him how to do. Bagheera would lie out on a branch and call, "Come along, Little Brother," and at first Mowgli would cling like the sloth, but afterward he would fling himself through the branches almost as boldly as the gray ape. He took his place at the Council Rock, too, when the Pack met, and there he discovered that if he stared hard at any wolf, the wolf would be forced to drop his eyes, and so he used to stare for fun. At other times he would pick the long thorns out of the pads of his friends, for wolves suffer terribly from thorns and burs in their coats. He would go down the hillside into the cultivated lands by night, and look very curiously at the villagers in their huts, but he had a mistrust of men because Bagheera showed him a square box with a drop gate so cunningly hidden in the jungle that he nearly walked into it, and told him that it was a trap. He loved better than anything else to go with Bagheera into the dark warm heart of the forest, to sleep all through the drowsy day, and at night see how Bagheera did his killing. Bagheera killed right and left as he felt hungry, and so did Mowgli—with one exception. As soon as he was old enough to understand things, Bagheera told him that he must never touch cattle because he had been bought into the Pack at the price of a bull's life. "All the jungle is thine," said Bagheera, "and thou canst kill everything that thou art strong enough to kill; but for the sake of the bull that bought thee thou must never kill or eat any cattle young or old. That is the Law of the Jungle." Mowgli obeyed faithfully.

And he grew and grew strong as a boy must grow who does not know that he is learning any lessons, and who has nothing in the world to think of except things to eat.

Mother Wolf told him once or twice that Shere Khan was not a creature to be trusted, and that some day he must kill Shere Khan. But though a young wolf would have remembered that advice every hour, Mowgli forgot it because he was only a boy—though he would have called himself a wolf if he had been able to speak in any human tongue.

Shere Khan was always crossing his path in the jungle, for as Akela grew older and feebler the lame tiger had come to be great friends with the younger wolves of the Pack, who followed him for scraps, a thing

Akela would never have allowed if he had dared to push his authority to the proper bounds. Then Shere Khan would flatter them and wonder that such fine young hunters were content to be led by a dying wolf and a man's cub. "They tell me," Shere Khan would say, "that at Council ye dare not look him between the eyes." And the young wolves would growl and bristle.

Bagheera, who had eyes and ears everywhere, knew something of this, and once or twice he told Mowgli in so many words that Shere Khan would kill him some day. Mowgli would laugh and answer: "I have the Pack and I have thee; and Baloo, though he is so lazy, might strike a blow or two for my sake. Why should I be afraid?"

It was one very warm day that a new notion came to Bagheera—born of something that he had heard. Perhaps Ikki the Porcupine had told him; but he said to Mowgli when they were deep in the jungle, as the boy lay with his head on Bagheera's beautiful black skin, "Little Brother, how often have I told thee that Shere Khan is thy enemy?"

"As many times as there are nuts on that palm," said Mowgli, who, naturally, could not count. "What of it? I am sleepy, Bagheera, and Shere Khan is all long tail and loud talk—like Mao, the Peacock."

"But this is no time for sleeping. Baloo knows it; I know it; the Pack know it; and even the foolish, foolish deer know. Tabaqui has told thee too."

"Ho! ho!" said Mowgli. "Tabaqui came to me not long ago with some rude talk that I was a naked man's cub and not fit to dig pig-nuts. But I caught Tabaqui by the tail and swung him twice against a palm-tree to teach him better manners."

"That was foolishness, for though Tabaqui is a mischief-maker, he would have told thee of something that concerned thee closely. Open those eyes, Little Brother. Shere Khan dare not kill thee in the jungle. But remember, Akela is very old, and soon the day comes when he cannot kill his buck, and then he will be leader no more. Many of the wolves that looked thee over when thou wast brought to the Council first are old too, and the young wolves believe, as Shere Khan has taught them, that a man-cub has no place with the Pack. In a little time thou wilt be a man."

"And what is a man that he should not run with his brothers?" said Mowgli. "I was born in the jungle. I have obeyed the Law of the Jungle, and there is no wolf of ours from whose paws I have not pulled a thorn. Surely they are my brothers!"

Bagheera stretched himself at full length and half shut his eyes. "Little Brother," said he, "feel under my jaw."

Mowgli put up his strong brown hand, and just under Bagheera's silky chin, where the giant rolling muscles were all hid by the glossy hair, he came upon a little bald spot.

"There is no one in the jungle that knows that I, Bagheera, carry that mark—the mark of the collar; and yet, Little Brother, I was born among men, and it was among men that my mother died—in the cages of the king's palace at Oodeypore. It was because of this that I paid the price for thee at the Council when thou wast a little naked cub. Yes, I too was born among men. I had never seen the jungle. They fed me behind bars from an iron pan till one night I felt that I was Bagheera—the Panther—and no man's plaything, and I broke the silly lock with one blow of my paw and came away. And because I had learned the ways of men, I became more terrible in the jungle than Shere Khan. Is it not so?"

"Yes," said Mowgli, "all the jungle fear Bagheera—all except Mowgli."

"Oh, *thou* art a man's cub," said the Black Panther very tenderly. "And even as I returned to my jungle, so thou must go back to men at last—to the men who are thy brothers—if thou art not killed in the Council."

"But why—but why should any wish to kill me?" said Mowgli.

"Look at me," said Bagheera. And Mowgli looked at him steadily between the eyes. The big panther turned his head away in half a minute.

"*That* is why," he said, shifting his paw on the leaves. "Not even I can look thee between the eyes, and I was born among men, and I love thee, Little Brother. The others they hate thee because their eyes cannot meet thine; because thou art wise; because thou hast pulled out thorns from their feet—because thou art a man."

"I did not know these things," said Mowgli sullenly, and he frowned under his heavy black eyebrows.

"What is the Law of the Jungle? Strike first and then give tongue. By thy very carelessness they know that thou art a man. But be wise. It is in my heart that when Akela misses his next kill—and at each hunt it costs him more to pin the buck—the Pack will turn against him and against thee. They will hold a jungle Council at the Rock, and then—and then—I have it!" said Bagheera, leaping up. "Go thou down quickly to the men's huts in the valley, and take some of the Red Flower which they grow there, so that when the time comes thou mayest have even a stronger friend than I or Baloo or those of the Pack that love thee. Get the Red Flower."

By Red Flower Bagheera meant fire, only no creature in the jungle will call fire by its proper name. Every beast lives in deadly fear of it, and invents a hundred ways of describing it.

"The Red Flower?" said Mowgli. "That grows outside their huts in the twilight. I will get some."

"There speaks the man's cub," said Bagheera proudly. "Remember that it grows in little pots. Get one swiftly, and keep it by thee for time of need."

"Good!" said Mowgli. "I go. But art thou sure, O my Bagheera." He slipped his arm around the splendid neck and looked deep into the big eyes, "Art thou sure that all this is Shere Khan's doing?"

"By the Broken Lock that freed me, I am sure, Little Brother."

"Then, by the Bull that bought me, I will pay Shere Khan full tale for this, and it may be a little over," said Mowgli, and he bounded away.

"That is a man. That is all a man," said Bagheera to himself, lying down again. "Oh, Shere Khan, never was a blacker hunting than that frog-hunt of thine ten years ago!"

Mowgli was far and far through the forest, running hard, and his heart was hot in him. He came to the cave as the evening mist rose, and drew breath, and looked down the valley. The cubs were out, but Mother Wolf, at the back of the cave, knew by his breathing that something was troubling her frog.

"What is it, Son?" she said.

"Some bat's chatter of Shere Khan," he called back. "I hunt among the plowed fields tonight," and he plunged downward through the bushes, to the stream at the bottom of the valley. There he checked, for he heard the yell of the Pack hunting, heard the bellow of a hunted Sambhur, and the snort as the buck turned at bay. Then there were wicked, bitter howls from the young wolves: "Akela! Akela! Let the Lone Wolf show his strength. Room for the leader of the Pack! Spring, Akela!"

The Lone Wolf must have sprung and missed his hold, for Mowgli heard the snap of his teeth and then a yelp as the Sambhur knocked him over with his forefoot.

He did not wait for anything more, but dashed on; and the yells grew fainter behind him as he ran into the croplands where the villagers lived.

"Bagheera spoke truth," he panted, as he nestled down in some cattle fodder by the window of a hut.

"Tomorrow is one day both for Akela and for me."

Then he pressed his face close to the window and watched the fire on the hearth. He saw the husbandman's wife get up and feed it in the night with black lumps. And when the morning came and the mists were all white and cold, he saw the man's child pick up a wicker pot plastered inside with earth, fill it with lumps of red-hot charcoal, put it under his blanket, and go out to tend the cows in the byre.

"Is that all?" said Mowgli. "If a cub can do it, there is nothing to fear." So he strode round the corner and met the boy, took the pot from his hand, and disappeared into the mist while the boy howled with fear.

"They are very like me," said Mowgli, blowing into the pot as he had seen the woman do. "This thing will die if I do not give it things to eat"; and he dropped twigs and dried bark on the red stuff. Halfway up the hill he met Bagheera with the morning dew shining like moonstones on his coat.

"Akela has missed," said the Panther. "They would have killed him last night, but they needed thee also. They were looking for thee on the hill."

"I was among the plowed lands. I am ready. See!" Mowgli held up the fire-pot.

"Good! Now, I have seen men thrust a dry branch into that stuff, and presently the Red Flower blossomed at the end of it. Art thou not afraid?"

"No. Why should I fear? I remember now—if it is not a dream—how, before I was a Wolf, I lay beside the Red Flower, and it was warm and pleasant."

All that day Mowgli sat in the cave tending his fire pot and dipping dry branches into it to see how they looked. He found a branch that satisfied him, and in the evening when Tabaqui came to the cave and told him rudely enough that he was wanted at the Council Rock, he laughed till Tabaqui ran away. Then Mowgli went to the Council, still laughing.

Akela the Lone Wolf lay by the side of his rock as a sign that the leadership of the Pack was open, and Shere Khan with his following of scrap-fed wolves walked to and fro openly being flattered. Bagheera lay close to Mowgli, and the fire pot was between Mowgli's knees. When they were all gathered together, Shere Khan began to speak—a thing he would never have dared to do when Akela was in his prime.

"He has no right," whispered Bagheera. "Say so. He is a dog's son. He will be frightened."

Mowgli sprang to his feet. "Free People," he cried, "does Shere Khan lead the Pack? What has a tiger to do with our leadership?"

"Seeing that the leadership is yet open, and being asked to speak—" Shere Khan began.

"By whom?" said Mowgli. "Are we *all* jackals, to fawn on this cattle butcher? The leadership of the Pack is with the Pack alone."

There were yells of "Silence, thou man's cub!" "Let him speak. He has kept our Law"; and at last the seniors of the Pack thundered: "Let the Dead Wolf speak." When a leader of the Pack has missed his kill, he is called the Dead Wolf as long as he lives, which is not long.

Akela raised his old head wearily:

"Free People, and ye too, jackals of Shere Khan, for twelve seasons I have led ye to and from the kill, and in all that time not one has been trapped or maimed. Now I have missed my kill. Ye know how that plot was made. Ye know how ye brought me up to an untried buck to make my weakness known. It was cleverly done. Your right is to kill me here on the Council Rock, now. Therefore, I ask, who comes to make an end of the Lone Wolf? For it is my right, by the Law of the Jungle, that ye come one by one."

There was a long hush, for no single wolf cared to fight Akela to the death. Then Shere Khan roared: "Bah! What have we to do with this toothless fool? He is doomed to die! It is the man-cub who has lived too long. Free People, he was my meat from the first. Give him to me. I am weary of this man-wolf folly. He has troubled the jungle for ten seasons. Give me the man-cub, or I will hunt here always, and not give you one bone. He is a man, a man's child, and from the marrow of my bones I hate him!"

Then more than half the Pack yelled: "A man! A man! What has a man to do with us? Let him go to his own place."

"And turn all the people of the villages against us?" clamored Shere Khan. "No, give him to me. He is a man, and none of us can look him between the eyes."

Akela lifted his head again and said, "He has eaten our food. He has slept with us. He has driven game for us. He has broken no word of the Law of the Jungle."

"Also, I paid for him with a bull when he was accepted. The worth of a bull is little, but Bagheera's honor is something that he will perhaps fight for," said Bagheera in his gentlest voice.

"A bull paid ten years ago!" the Pack snarled. "What do we care for bones ten years old?"

"Or for a pledge?" said Bagheera, his white teeth bared under his lip. "Well are ye called the Free People!"

"No man's cub can run with the people of the jungle," howled Shere Khan. "Give him to me!"

"He is our brother in all but blood," Akela went on, "and ye would kill him here! In truth, I have lived too long. Some of ye are eaters of cattle, and of others I have heard that, under Shere Khan's teaching, ye go by dark night and snatch children from the villager's doorstep. Therefore I know ye to be cowards, and it is to cowards I speak. It is certain that I must die, and my life is of no worth, or I would offer that in the man-cub's place. But for the sake of the Honor of the Pack—a little matter that by being without a leader ye have forgotten—I promise that if ye let the man-cub go to his own place, I will not, when my time comes to die, bare one tooth against ye. I will die without fighting. That will at least save the Pack three lives. More I cannot do; but if ye will, I can save ye the shame that comes of killing a brother against whom there is no fault—a brother spoken for and bought into the Pack according to the Law of the Jungle."

"He is a man—a man—a man!" snarled the Pack. And most of the wolves began to gather round Shere Khan, whose tail was beginning to switch.

"Now the business is in thy hands," said Bagheera to Mowgli. "*We* can do no more except fight."

Mowgli stood upright—the fire pot in his hands. Then he stretched out his arms, and yawned in the face of the Council; but he was furious with rage and sorrow, for, wolflike, the wolves had never told him how they hated him. "Listen you!" he cried. "There is no need for this dog's jabber. Ye have told me so often tonight that I am a man (and indeed I would have been a wolf with you to my life's end) that I feel your words are true. So I do not call ye my brothers any more, but *sag* [dogs], as a man should. What ye will do, and what ye will not do, is not yours to say. That matter is with *me;* and that we may see the matter more plainly, I, the man, have brought here a little of the Red Flower which ye, dogs, fear."

He flung the fire pot on the ground, and some of the red coals lit a tuft of dried moss that flared up, as all the Council drew back in terror before the leaping flames.

Mowgli thrust his dead branch into the fire till the twigs lit and crackled, and whirled it above his head among the cowering wolves.

"Thou art the master," said Bagheera in an undertone. "Save Akela from the death. He was ever thy friend."

Akela, the grim old wolf who had never asked for mercy in his life, gave one piteous look at Mowgli as the boy stood all naked, his long black hair tossing over his shoulders in the light of the blazing branch that made the shadows jump and quiver.

"Good!" said Mowgli, staring round slowly. "I see that ye are dogs. I go from you to my own people—if they be my own people. The jungle is shut to me, and I must forget your talk and your companionship. But I will be more merciful than ye are. Because I was all but your brother in blood, I promise that when I am a man among men I will not betray ye to men as ye have betrayed me." He kicked the fire with his foot, and the sparks flew up. "There shall be no war between any of us in the Pack. But here is a debt to pay before I go." He strode forward to where Shere Khan sat blinking stupidly at the flames, and caught him by the tuft on his chin. Bagheera followed in case of accidents.

"Up, dog!" Mowgli cried. "Up, when a man speaks, or I will set that coat ablaze!"

Shere Khan's ears lay flat back on his head, and he shut his eyes, for the blazing branch was very near.

"This cattle-killer said he would kill me in the Council because he had not killed me when I was a cub.

Thus and thus, then, do we beat dogs when we are men. Stir a whisker, Lungri, and I ram the Red Flower down thy gullet!" He beat Shere Khan over the head with the branch, and the tiger whimpered and whined in an agony of fear.

"Pah! Singed jungle cat—go now! But remember when next I come to the Council Rock, as a man should come, it will be with Shere Khan's hide on my head. For the rest, Akela goes free to live as he pleases. Ye will *not* kill him, because that is not my will. Nor do I think that ye will sit here any longer, lolling out your tongues as though ye were somebodies, instead of dogs whom I drive out—thus! Go!"

The fire was burning furiously at the end of the branch, and Mowgli struck right and left round the circle, and the wolves ran howling with the sparks burning their fur. At last there were only Akela, Bagheera, and perhaps ten wolves that had taken Mowgli's part. Then something began to hurt Mowgli inside him, as he had never been hurt in his life before, and he caught his breath and sobbed, and the tears ran down his face.

"What is it? What is it?" he said. "I do not wish to leave the jungle, and I do not know what this is. Am I dying, Bagheera?"

"No, Little Brother. That is only tears such as men use," said Bagheera. "Now I know thou art a man, and a man's cub no longer. The jungle is shut indeed to thee henceforward. Let them fall, Mowgli. They are only tears." So Mowgli sat and cried as though his heart would break; and he had never cried in all his life before.

"Now," he said, "I will go to men. But first I must say farewell to my mother." And he went to the cave where she lived with Father Wolf, and he cried on her coat, while the four cubs howled miserably.

"Ye will not forget me?" said Mowgli.

"Never while we can follow a trail," said the cubs. "Come to the foot of the hill when thou art a man, and we will talk to thee; and we will come into the croplands to play with thee by night."

"Come soon!" said Father Wolf. "Oh, wise little frog, come again soon; for we be old, thy mother and I."

"Come soon," said Mother Wolf, "little naked son of mine. For, listen, child of man, I loved thee more than ever I loved my cubs."

"I will surely come," said Mowgli. "And when I come it will be to lay out Shere Khan's hide upon the Council Rock. Do not forget me! Tell them in the jungle never to forget me!"

The dawn was beginning to break when Mowgli went down the hillside alone, to meet those mysterious things that are called men.

Thinking About the Story

Rudyard Kipling's writing helped to establish and popularize the short story in Britain. "Mowgli's Brothers" is a fine example of why this was the case. Kipling's portrayal of jungle life, an imaginative blending of the natural world and the fantastic, perfectly renders a classically structured story into a timeless fable. With foresight, then, you should think about the interplay of the human and the animal worlds. In particular, consider how you feel about the anthropomorphizing of the jungle animals? What role does language play in the story and how you understand its themes?

Furthermore, reading "Mowgli's Brothers" as a coming-of-age story, it is productive to compare Kipling's fiction to James Joyce's "Araby" and to Sarah Orne Jewett's "A White Heron." You can use adolescence as a touchstone to evaluate how the three stories handle each protagonist's self-awareness and transformation. In reference to the latter story, you can further analyze the role of animals in this arena, too.

Discussion Questions

1. What stylistic devices does Kipling use to create the impression that "Mowgli's Brothers" is a children's story? Do you think the story should be read as a fable?

2. With reference to the text, describe Mowgli and Bagheera's relationship. How does Akela feel about Mowgli? For Akela, what does Mowgli represent?

3. Characterize Shere Khan's dealings with the wolf pack. In what ways is Khan a character foil for Mowgli?

4. List three themes you find in the story. For each theme, explain in detail how each one manifests itself throughout the text.

5. At the story's end, what is the symbolic importance of fire? What insights into the human condition can you gauge from Mowgli leaving the jungle?

Activities

1. In the style of Kipling, continue the story on for a page or two. Consider what happens when Mowgli meets the other humans.

2. Write your own short story that has animals as the principle characters. One condition: instead of the jungle, use a different setting.

3. Roleplay as a defender of Shere Khan's behavior and write a letter to the wolf pack leader, Akela, which supports Khan's actions.

H. G. Wells

Adapt or perish, now as ever, is nature's inexorable imperative.
H. G. Wells — *Mind at the End of Its Tether* (1945)

The writing of Herbert George Wells (1866–1946) has maintained its relevance to the analyzing and forecasting of social systems, while providing insight into the most successful elements of speculative fiction. Wells was born in Bromley, England, to an impoverished family. His education was frequently hampered by expensive fees, his wavering interests, and later, a serious football injury. He did not complete his higher education until 1890, when he earned his bachelor's degree in zoology from the University of London. After graduation he became a tutor and a freelance journalist, and he married his cousin, Isabel. In a purposeful manner, he spent the next few years on his literary output. As a result, his marriage disintegrated and he married his student, Amy Robbins, with whom he later had two sons. Ill health plagued Wells, and he moved his family from London to Sandwell in hopes of recuperation. By 1909, they moved back to London and Wells became increasingly political. He stood once in 1922 for the Labour Party, but he was unsuccessful. In later years, his philosophy became more pessimistic as he criticized the ideologies behind both World Wars. He died in 1946.

By the end of his career, Wells had written over a dozen books. He made his name with *The Time Machine* (1895), *The Island of Doctor Moreau* (1896), and *The War of the Worlds* (1898). In subsequent years, he continued to produce challenging texts, such as *The New Machiavelli* (1911) and *The Outline of History* (1920). In his novels, short stories, and essays, he combined the romantic and the scientific. He investigated the nature and allure of the utopian, often highlighting the dystopian repercussions of such an enterprise. His interest in scientific possibility is a hallmark of

Wells' work. Often his characters, immured with science, exhibit obsessive personalities and self-destructive tendencies. In "A Moth — Genus Novo" (1895) Wells uses an unknown narrator to tell the story. Familiar with the events and the particular milieu of the characters' lives, the narrator retells the relationship between Hapley and Pawkins. Adroit with humor, pathos, and narrative drive, the story explores the borderland between objective and subjective experiences.

A Moth — Genus Novo

H. G. Wells

Probably you have heard of Hapley—not W. T. Hapley, the son, but the celebrated Hapley, the Hapley of *Periplaneta Hapliia*, Hapley the entomologist. If so, you know at least of the great feud between Hapley and Professor Pawkins, though certain of its consequences may be new to you. For those who have not, a word or two of explanation is necessary, which the idle reader may go over with a glancing eye, if his indolence so incline him.

It is amazing how very widely diffused is the ignorance of such really important matters as this Hapley-Pawkins feud. Those epoch-making controversies, again, that have convulsed the Geological Society are, I verily believe, almost entirely unknown outside the fellowship of that body. I have heard men of fair general education even refer to the great scenes at these meetings as vestry-meeting squabbles. Yet the great hate of the English and Scotch geologists has lasted now half a century, and has "left deep and abundant marks upon the body of the science." And this Hapley-Pawkins business, though perhaps a more personal affair, stirred passions as profound, if not profounder. Your common man has no conception of the zeal that animates a scientific investigator, the fury of contradiction you can arouse in him. It is the *odium theologicum* in a new form. There are men, for instance, who would gladly burn Professor

Ray Lankester at Smithfield for his treatment of the Mollusca in the Encyclopaedia. That fantastic extension of the Cephalopods to cover the Pteropods . . . But I wander from Hapley and Pawkins.

It began years and years ago, with a revision of the Microlepidoptera (whatever these may be) by Pawkins, in which he extinguished a new species created by Hapley. Hapley, who was always quarrelsome, replied by a stinging impeachment of the entire classification of Pawkins. Pawkins in his "Rejoinder" suggested that Hapley's microscope was as defective as his power of observation, and called him an "irresponsible meddler"—Hapley was not a professor at that time. Hapley in his retort, spoke of "blundering collectors," and described, as if inadvertently, Pawkins' revision as a "miracle of ineptitude." It was war to the knife. However, it would scarcely interest the reader to detail how these two great men quarrelled, and how the split between them widened until from the Microlepidoptera they were at war upon every open question in entomology. There were memorable occasions. At times the Royal Entomological Society meetings resembled nothing so much as the Chamber of Deputies. On the whole, I fancy Pawkins was nearer the truth than Hapley. But Hapley was skilful with his rhetoric, had a turn for ridicule rare in a scientific man, was endowed with vast energy, and had a fine sense of injury in the matter of the extinguished species; while Pawkins was a man of dull presence, prosy of speech, in shape not unlike a water-barrel, over conscientious with testimonials, and suspected of jobbing museum appointments. So the young men gathered round Hapley and applauded him. It was a long struggle, vicious from the beginning and growing at last to pitiless antagonism. The successive turns of fortune, now an advantage to one side and now to another—now Hapley tormented by some success of Pawkins, and now Pawkins outshone by Hapley, belong rather to the history of entomology than to this story.

But in 1891 Pawkins, whose health had been bad for some time, published some work upon the "mesoblast" of the Death's Head Moth. What the mesoblast of the Death's Head Moth may be does not matter a rap in this story. But the work was far below his usual standard, and gave Hapley an opening he had coveted for years. He must have worked night and day to make the most of his advantage.

In an elaborate critique he rent Pawkins to tatters—one can fancy the man's disordered black hair, and his queer dark eyes flashing as he went for his antagonist—and Pawkins made a reply, halting, ineffectual, with painful gaps of silence, and yet malignant. There was no mistaking his will to wound Hapley, nor his incapacity to do it. But few of those who heard him—I was absent from that meeting—realised how ill the man was.

Hapley got his opponent down, and meant to finish him. He followed with a simply brutal attack upon Pawkins, in the form of a paper upon the development of moths in general, a paper showing evidence of a most extraordinary amount of mental labour, and yet couched in a violently controversial tone. Violent as it was, an editorial note witnesses that it was modified. It must have covered Pawkins with shame and confusion of face. It left no loophole; it was murderous in argument, and utterly contemptuous in tone; an awful thing for the declining years of a man's career.

The world of entomologists waited breathlessly for the rejoinder from Pawkins. He would try one, for Pawkins had always been game. But when it came it surprised them. For the rejoinder of Pawkins was to catch influenza, proceed to pneumonia, and die.

It was perhaps as effectual a reply as he could make under the circumstances, and largely turned the current of feeling against Hapley. The very people who had most gleefully cheered on those gladiators became serious at the consequence. There could be no reasonable doubt the fret of the defeat had contributed to the death of Pawkins. There was a limit even to scientific controversy, said serious people. Another crushing attack was already in the press and appeared on the day before the funeral. I don't think Hapley exerted himself to stop it. People remembered how Hapley had hounded down his rival, and forgot that rival's defects. Scathing satire reads ill over fresh mould. The thing provoked comment in the daily papers. This it was that made me think that you had probably heard of Hapley and this controversy. But, as I have already remarked, scientific workers live very much in a world of their own; half the people, I dare say, who go along Piccadilly to the Academy every year, could not tell you where the learned societies abide. Many even think that research is a kind of happy-family cage in which all kinds of men lie down together in peace.

In his private thoughts Hapley could not forgive Pawkins for dying. In the first place, it was a mean dodge to escape the absolute pulverisation Hapley had in hand for him, and in the second, it left Hapley's mind with a queer gap in it. For twenty years he had worked hard, sometimes far into the night, and seven days a week, with microscope, scalpel, collecting-net, and pen, and almost entirely with reference to Pawkins. The European reputation he had won had come as an incident in that great antipathy. He had gradually worked up to a climax in this last controversy. It had killed Pawkins, but it had also thrown Hapley out of gear, so to speak, and his doctor advised him to give up work for a time, and rest. So Hapley went down into a quiet village in Kent, and thought day and night of Pawkins, and good things it was now impossible to say about him.

At last Hapley began to realise in what direction the pre-occupation tended. He determined to make a fight for it, and started by trying to read novels. But he could not get his mind off Pawkins, white in the face and making his last speech—every sentence a beautiful opening for Hapley. He turned to fiction—and found it had no grip on him. He read *Island Nights' Entertainments* until his "sense of causation" was shocked beyond endurance by the Bottle Imp. Then he went to Kipling, and found he "proved nothing," besides being irreverent and vulgar. These scientific people have their limitations. Then unhappily, he tried Besant's *Inner House*, and the opening chapter set his mind upon learned societies and Pawkins at once.

So Hapley turned to chess, and found it a little more soothing. He soon mastered the moves and the chief gambits and commoner closing positions, and began to beat the Vicar. But then the cylindrical contours of the opposite king began to resemble Pawkins standing up and gasping ineffectually against check-mate, and Hapley decided to give up chess.

Perhaps the study of some new branch of science would after all be better diversion. The best rest is change of occupation. Hapley determined to plunge at diatoms, and had one of his smaller microscopes and Halibut's monograph sent down from London. He thought that perhaps if he could get up a vigorous quarrel with Halibut, he might be able to begin life afresh and forget Pawkins. And very soon he was hard at work in his habitual strenuous fashion, at these microscopic denizens of the way-side pool.

It was on the third day of the diatoms that Hapley became aware of a novel addition to the local fauna. He was working late at the microscope, and the only light in the room was the brilliant little lamp with the special form of green shade. Like all experienced microscopists, he kept both eyes open. It is the only way to avoid excessive fatigue. One eye was over the instrument, and bright and distinct before that was the circular field of the microscope, across which a brown diatom was slowly moving. With the other eye Hapley saw, as it were, without seeing. He was only dimly conscious of the brass side of the instrument, the illuminated part of the table-cloth, a sheet of note-paper, the foot of the lamp, and the darkened room beyond.

Suddenly his attention drifted from one eye to the other. The table-cloth was of the material called tapestry by shopmen, and rather brightly coloured. The pattern was in gold, with a small amount of crimson and pale blue upon a greyish ground. At one point the pattern seemed displaced, and there was a vibrating movement of the colours at this point.

Hapley suddenly moved his head back and looked with both eyes. His mouth fell open with astonishment.

It was a large moth or butterfly; its wings spread in butterfly fashion!

It was strange it should be in the room at all, for the windows were closed. Strange that it should not have attracted his attention when fluttering to its present position. Strange that it should match the table-cloth. Stranger far that to him, Hapley, the great entomologist, it was altogether unknown. There was no delusion. It was crawling slowly towards the foot of the lamp.

"New Genus, by heavens! And in England!" said Hapley, staring.

Then he suddenly thought of Pawkins. Nothing would have maddened Pawkins more . . . And Pawkins was dead!

Something about the head and body of the insect became singularly suggestive of Pawkins, just as the chess king had been.

"Confound Pawkins!" said Hapley. "But I must catch this." And looking round him for some means of capturing the moth, he rose slowly out of his chair. Suddenly the insect rose, struck the edge of the lampshade—Hapley heard the "ping"—and vanished into the shadow.

In a moment Hapley had whipped off the shade, so that the whole room was illuminated. The thing had disappeared, but soon his practised eye detected it upon the wallpaper near the door. He went towards it poising the lamp-shade for capture. Before he was within striking distance, however, it had risen and was fluttering round the room. After the fashion of its kind, it flew with sudden starts and turns, seeming to vanish here and reappear there. Once Hapley struck, and missed; then again.

The third time he hit his microscope. The instrument swayed, struck and overturned the lamp, and fell noisily upon the floor. The lamp turned over on the table and, very luckily, went out. Hapley was left in the dark. With a start he felt the strange moth blunder into his face.

It was maddening. He had no lights. If he opened the door of the room the thing would get away. In the darkness he saw Pawkins quite distinctly laughing at him. Pawkins had ever an oily laugh. He swore furiously and stamped his foot on the floor.

There was a timid rapping at the door.

Then it opened, perhaps a foot, and very slowly. The alarmed face of the landlady appeared behind a pink candle flame; she wore a night-cap over her grey hair and had some purple garment over her shoulders. "What *was* that fearful smash?" she said. "Has anything—" The strange moth appeared fluttering about the chink of the door. "Shut that door!" said Hapley, and suddenly rushed at her.

The door slammed hastily. Hapley was left alone in the dark. Then in the pause he heard his landlady scuttle upstairs, lock her door, and drag something heavy across the room and put against it.

It became evident to Hapley that his conduct and appearance had been strange and alarming. Confound the moth! And Pawkins! However, it was a pity to lose the moth now. He felt his way into the hall and found the matches, after sending his hat down upon the floor with a noise like a drum. With the lighted candle he returned to the sitting-room. No moth was to be seen. Yet once for a moment it seemed that the thing was fluttering round his head. Hapley very suddenly decided to give up the moth and go to bed. But he was excited. All night long his sleep was broken by dreams of the moth, Pawkins, and his landlady. Twice in the night he turned out and soused his head in cold water.

One thing was very clear to him. His landlady could not possibly understand about the strange moth, especially as he had failed to catch it. No one but an entomologist would understand quite how he felt. She was probably frightened at his behaviour, and yet he failed to see how he could explain it. He decided to say nothing further about the events of last night. After breakfast he saw her in her garden, and decided to go out and talk to reassure her. He talked to her about beans and potatoes, bees, caterpillars, and the price of fruit. She replied in her usual manner, but she looked at him a little suspiciously, and kept walking as he walked, so that there was always a bed of flowers, or a row of beans, or something of the sort, between them. After a while he began to feel singularly irritated at this, and to conceal his vexation went indoors and presently went out for a walk.

The moth, or butterfly, trailing an odd flavour of Pawkins with it, kept coming into that walk, though he did his best to keep his mind off it. Once he saw it quite distinctly, with its wings flattened out, upon the old stone wall that runs along the west edge of the park, but going up to it he found it was only two lumps of grey and yellow lichen. "This," said Hapley, "is the reverse of mimicry. Instead of a butterfly looking like a stone, here is a stone looking like a butterfly!" Once something hovered and fluttered round his head, but by an effort of will he drove that impression out of his mind again.

In the afternoon Hapley called upon the Vicar, and argued with him upon theological questions. They sat in the little arbour covered with briar, and smoked as they wrangled. "Look at that moth!" said Hapley, suddenly, pointing to the edge of the wooden table.

"Where?" said the Vicar.

"You don't see a moth on the edge of the table there?" said Hapley.

"Certainly not," said the Vicar.

Hapley was thunderstruck. He gasped. The Vicar was staring at him. Clearly the man saw nothing. "The eye of faith is no better than the eye of science," said Hapley awkwardly.

"I don't see your point," said the Vicar, thinking it was part of the argument.

That night Hapley found the moth crawling over his counterpane. He sat on the edge of the bed in his shirt sleeves and reasoned with himself. Was it pure hallucination? He knew he was slipping, and he battled for his sanity with the same silent energy he had formerly displayed against Pawkins. So persistent is mental habit, that he felt as if it were still a struggle with Pawkins. He was well versed in psychology. He knew that such visual illusions do come as a result of mental strain. But the point was, he did not only *see* the moth, he had heard it when it touched the edge of the lampshade, and afterwards when it hit against the wall, and he had felt it strike his face in the dark.

He looked at it. It was not at all dreamlike, but perfectly clear and solid-looking in the candle-light. He saw the hairy body, and the short feathery antennae, the jointed legs, even a place where the down was rubbed from the wing. He suddenly felt angry with himself for being afraid of a little insect.

His landlady had got the servant to sleep with her that night, because she was afraid to be alone. In addition she had locked the door, and put the chest of drawers against it. They listened and talked in whispers after they had gone to bed, but nothing occurred to alarm them. About eleven they had ventured to put the candle out, and had both dozed off to sleep. They woke up with a start, and sat up in bed, listening in the darkness.

Then they heard slippered feet going to and fro in Hapley's room. A chair was overturned, and there was a violent dab at the wall. Then a china mantel ornament smashed upon the fender. Suddenly the door of the room opened, and they heard him upon the landing. They clung to one another, listening. He seemed to be dancing upon the staircase. Now he would go down three or four steps quickly, then up again, then hurry down into the hall. They heard the umbrella stand go over, and the fanlight break. Then the bolt shot and the chain rattled. He was opening the door.

They hurried to the window. It was a dim grey night; an almost unbroken sheet of watery cloud was sweeping across the moon, and the hedge and trees in front of the house were black against the pale roadway. They saw Hapley, looking like a ghost in his shirt and white trousers, running to and fro in the road, and beating the air. Now he would stop, now he would dart very rapidly at something invisible, now he would move upon it with stealthy strides. At last he went out of sight up the road towards the down. Then, while they argued who should go down and lock the door, he returned. He was walking very fast, and he came straight into the house, closed the door carefully, and went quietly up to his bedroom. Then everything was silent.

"Mrs. Colville," said Hapley, calling down the staircase next morning, "I hope I did not alarm you last night."

"You may well ask that!" said Mrs. Colville.

"The fact is, I am a sleep-walker, and the last two nights I have been without my sleeping mixture. There is nothing to be alarmed about, really. I am sorry I made such an ass of myself. I will go over the down to Shoreham, and get some stuff to make me sleep soundly. I ought to have done that yesterday."

But half-way over the down, by the chalk pits, the moth came upon Hapley again. He went on, trying to keep his mind upon chess problems, but it was no good. The thing fluttered into his face, and he struck at it with his hat in self-defence. Then rage, the old rage—the rage he had so often felt against Pawkins—came upon him again. He went on, leaping and striking at the eddying insect. Suddenly he trod on nothing, and fell headlong.

There was a gap in his sensations, and Hapley found himself sitting on the heap of flints in front of the opening of the chalk-pits, with a leg twisted back under him. The strange moth was still fluttering round his head. He struck at it with his hand, and turning his head saw two men approaching him. One was the village doctor. It occurred to Hapley that this was lucky. Then it came into his mind with extraordinary vividness, that no one would ever be able to see the strange moth except himself, and that it behoved him to keep silent about it.

Late that night, however, after his broken leg was set, he was feverish and forgot his self-restraint. He was lying flat on his bed, and he began to run his eyes round the room to see if the moth was still about. He tried not to do this, but it was no good. He soon caught sight of the thing resting close to his hand, by the night-light, on the green table-cloth. The wings quivered. With a sudden wave of anger he smote at it with his fist, and the nurse woke up with a shriek. He had missed it.

"That moth!" he said; and then, "It was fancy. Nothing!"

All the time he could see quite clearly the insect going round the cornice and darting across the room, and he could also see that the nurse saw nothing of it and looked at him strangely. He must keep himself in hand. He knew he was a lost man if he did not keep himself in hand. But as the night waned the fever grew upon him, and the very dread he had of seeing the moth made him see it. About five, just as the dawn was grey, he tried to get out of bed and catch it, though his leg was afire with pain. The nurse had to struggle with him.

On account of this, they tied him down to the bed. At this the moth grew bolder, and once he felt it settle in his hair. Then, because he struck out violently with his arms, they tied these also. At this the moth came and crawled over his face, and Hapley wept, swore, screamed, prayed for them to take it off him, unavailingly.

The doctor was a blockhead, a just-qualified general practitioner, and quite ignorant of mental science. He simply said there was no moth. Had he possessed the wit, he might still, perhaps, have saved Hapley from his fate by entering into his delusion, and covering his face with gauze, as he prayed might be done. But, as I say, the doctor was a blockhead, and until the leg was healed Hapley was kept tied to his bed, and with the imaginary moth crawling over him. It never left him while he was awake and it grew to a monster in his dreams. While he was awake he longed for sleep, and from sleep he awoke screaming.

So now Hapley is spending the remainder of his days in a padded room, worried by a moth that no one else can see. The asylum doctor calls it hallucination; but Hapley, when he is in his easier mood, and can talk, says it is the ghost of Pawkins, and consequently a unique specimen and well worth the trouble of catching.

Thinking About the Story

As you have read in several of the stories in this collection, death figures heavily as a plot contrivance and as a spur for character action. In H. G. Wells' story, you again see death working in both these regards. Moreover, you should note that the scientific obsessions of the Victorian era are merged with the speculative nature of the afterlife. For you, then, how do you understand the term *supernatural*? Can it measured by scientific means? Do you agree that perception is reality? Or is there an objective world that we interpret? Similar questions to these were tackled by the authors of this period and occasionally, as in Wells' story, led to an obsessive search for truth. Indeed, you can compare, on these terms, "A Moth — Genus Novo" with both Edgar Allan Poe's "The Man of the Crowd" and Mark Twain's "The Californian's Tale."

Discussion Questions

1. Speculate on who is narrating the events of the story. What clues can you find to support your answer? Do you think the narrator is reliable?

2. How would you characterize the relationship between Hapley and Pawkins? And between Hapley and the vicar? What can you deduce about the motivations of each character?

3. Using passages of text to support your views, explain the thematic concerns of science and the supernatural in the story. Furthermore, explain Hapley's outburst: "The eye of faith is no better than the eye of science."

4. Analyze the changes in Hapley before and after Pawkins' death. What might the moth symbolize for Hapley?
5. Do you agree that Hapley should have been imprisoned in the asylum? Do you think the moth existed or was it a figment of Hapley's imagination?

Activities

1. Research the life and work of H. G. Wells. Read another one of his short stories and explain the premise and the inherent themes. In your conclusions, assess how the themes relate to his life and personal interests.
2. Rewrite a scene from another character's perspective. Choose one of the following:
   a. Hapley.
   b. The vicar.
   c. The landlady.
3. Re-imagine the story with a different specialized field (for example, art history, mathematics, archeology, etc.): list pertinent details, including vocabulary and appropriate settings. Pitch the new version of the story to a fellow student. Compare and contrast the results.

Stephen Crane

Let a thing become a tradition, and it becomes half a lie.
Stephen Crane — *Maggie* (1893)

Dead before the age of 30, Stephen Crane (1871–1900) was a highly regarded poet and prose stylist who influenced the next generation of American writers. Born in Newark, New Jersey, as the fourteenth child of Reverend Jonathan Crane and Mary Crane, Stephen grew up in a strict Methodist household. His father was a religious author, but died when Crane was eight years old. Often in ill health himself, Crane had time to read voraciously and compose poems. Following his brother Townley's career path, Crane became a journalist, working for several local and national newspapers over his career. In 1897, while on assignment to Cuba, his boat sank. While recuperating from the incident in Florida, he met a brothel owner, Cora Taylor. They later traveled together to Greece, where they both reported on the Greco-Turkish War. By the summer of 1897 they moved to London to live as husband and wife. After several more journalist assignments in Cuba and Puerto Rico, Crane returned to England. There he developed friendships with H. G. Wells and Joseph Conrad. The following year he traveled to a German sanitarium, where he soon died of tuberculosis.

Crane is a noted nonfiction writer; however, his legacy lies in his poetry and fiction. In Crane's fiction persists an innovative synergy of Naturalism and Literary Realism that embodies many traits seen in later Modernist writing. His most successful works—*Maggie* (1893), *The Red Badge of Courage* (1895), and *The Open Boat and Other Tales of Adventure* (1898)—have in common sensuous imagery and thematic intensity. In particular, death and violence are evoked emblems, renewed each time with devastating horror and awe. In this arena sits the long story "The Open Boat" (1897), composed after the sinking of the *Commodore*. The story is a milestone in the development of American fiction. It is based on Crane's experiences and often he is identified with the Correspondent character. The story is balanced between Realism and allegory, perfectly nuanced between the two forms to increase the sense of isolation and despair.

The Open Boat

Stephen Crane

A tale intended to be after the fact, being the experience of four men from the sunk steamer *Commodore*.

I

None of them knew the color of the sky. Their eyes glanced level, and were fastened upon the waves that swept toward them. These waves were of the hue of slate, save for the tops, which were of foaming white, and all of the men knew the colors of the sea. The horizon narrowed and widened, and dipped and rose, and at all times its edge was jagged with waves that seemed thrust up in points like rocks.

Many a man ought to have a bath-tub larger than the boat which here rode upon the sea. These waves were most wrongfully and barbarously abrupt and tall, and each froth-top was a problem in small boat navigation.

The cook squatted in the bottom and looked with both eyes at the six inches of gunwale which separated him from the ocean. His sleeves were rolled over his fat forearms, and the two flaps of his unbuttoned vest dangled as he bent to bail out the boat. Often he said: "Gawd! That was a narrow clip." As he remarked it he invariably gazed eastward over the broken sea.

The oiler, steering with one of the two oars in the boat, sometimes raised himself suddenly to keep clear of water that swirled in over the stern. It was a thin little oar and it seemed often ready to snap.

The correspondent, pulling at the other oar, watched the waves and wondered why he was there. The injured captain, lying in the bow, was at this time buried in that profound dejection and indifference which comes, temporarily at least, to even the bravest and most enduring when, willy nilly, the firm fails, the army loses, the ship goes down. The mind of the master of a vessel is rooted deep in the timbers of her, though he command for a day or a decade, and this captain had on him the stern impression of a scene in the grays of dawn of seven turned faces, and later a stump of a top-mast with a white ball on it that slashed to and fro at the waves, went low and lower, and down. Thereafter there was something strange in his voice. Although steady, it was deep with mourning, and of a quality beyond oration or tears.

"Keep'er a little more south, Billie," said he.

"'A little more south,' sir," said the oiler in the stern.

A seat in this boat was not unlike a seat upon a bucking broncho, and, by the same token, a broncho is not much smaller. The craft pranced and reared, and plunged like an animal. As each wave came, and she rose for it, she seemed like a horse making at a fence outrageously high. The manner of her scramble over these walls of water is a mystic thing, and, moreover, at the top of them were ordinarily these problems in white water, the foam racing down from the summit of each wave, requiring a new leap, and a leap from the air. Then, after scornfully bumping a crest, she would slide, and race, and splash down a long incline and arrive bobbing and nodding in front of the next menace.

A singular disadvantage of the sea lies in the fact that after successfully surmounting one wave you discover that there is another behind it just as important and just as nervously anxious to do something effective in the way of swamping boats. In a ten-foot dinghy one can get an idea of the resources of the sea in the line of waves that is not probable to the average experience, which is never at sea in a dinghy. As each slaty wall of water approached, it shut all else from the view of the men in the boat, and it was not difficult to imagine that this particular wave was the final outburst of the ocean, the last effort of the grim water. There was a terrible grace in the move of the waves, and they came in silence, save for the snarling of the crests.

In the wan light, the faces of the men must have been gray. Their eyes must have glinted in strange ways as they gazed steadily astern. Viewed from a balcony, the whole thing would doubtlessly have been weirdly picturesque. But the men in the boat had no time to see it, and if they had had leisure there were other things to occupy their minds. The sun swung steadily up the sky, and they knew it was broad day because the color of the sea changed from slate to emerald-green, streaked with amber lights, and the foam was like tumbling snow. The process of the breaking day was unknown to them. They were aware only of this effect upon the color of the waves that rolled toward them.

In disjointed sentences the cook and the correspondent argued as to the difference between a life-saving station and a house of refuge. The cook had said: "There's a house of refuge just north of the Mosquito Inlet Light, and as soon as they see us, they'll come off in their boat and pick us up."

"As soon as who see us?" said the correspondent.

"The crew," said the cook.

"Houses of refuge don't have crews," said the correspondent. "As I understand them, they are only places where clothes and grub are stored for the benefit of shipwrecked people. They don't carry crews."

"Oh, yes, they do," said the cook.

"No, they don't," said the correspondent.

"Well, we're not there yet, anyhow," said the oiler, in the stern.

"Well," said the cook, "perhaps it's not a house of refuge that I'm thinking of as being near Mosquito Inlet Light. Perhaps it's a life-saving station."

"We're not there yet," said the oiler, in the stern.

II

As the boat bounced from the top of each wave, the wind tore through the hair of the hatless men, and as the craft plopped her stern down again the spray slashed past them. The crest of each of these waves was a hill, from the top of which the men surveyed, for a moment, a broad tumultuous expanse; shining and wind-riven. It was probably splendid. It was probably glorious, this play of the free sea, wild with lights of emerald and white and amber.

"Bully good thing it's an on-shore wind," said the cook. "If not, where would we be? Wouldn't have a show."

"That's right," said the correspondent.

The busy oiler nodded his assent.

Then the captain, in the bow, chuckled in a way that expressed humor, contempt, tragedy, all in one. "Do you think we've got much of a show, now, boys?" said he.

Whereupon the three were silent, save for a trifle of hemming and hawing. To express any particular optimism at this time they felt to be childish and stupid, but they all doubtless possessed this sense of the situation in their mind. A young man thinks doggedly at such times. On the other hand, the ethics of their condition was decidedly against any open suggestion of hopelessness. So they were silent.

"Oh, well," said the captain, soothing his children, "we'll get ashore all right."

But there was that in his tone which made them think, so the oiler quoth: "Yes! If this wind holds!"

The cook was bailing: "Yes! If we don't catch hell in the surf."

Canton flannel gulls flew near and far. Sometimes they sat down on the sea, near patches of brown sea-weed that rolled over the waves with a movement like carpets on line in a gale. The birds sat comfortably in groups, and they were envied by some in the dinghy, for the wrath of the sea was no more to them than it was to a covey of prairie chickens a thousand miles inland. Often they came very close and stared at the men with black bead-like eyes. At these times they were uncanny and sinister in their unblinking scrutiny, and the men hooted angrily at them, telling them to be gone. One came, and evidently decided to alight on the top of the captain's head. The bird flew parallel to the boat and did not circle, but made short sidelong jumps in the air in chicken-fashion. His black eyes were wistfully fixed upon the captain's head. "Ugly brute," said the oiler to the bird. "You look as if you were made with a jack-knife." The cook and the correspondent swore darkly at the creature. The captain naturally wished to knock it away with the end of the heavy painter, but he did not dare do it, because anything resembling an emphatic gesture would have capsized this freighted boat, and so with his open hand, the captain gently and carefully waved the gull away. After it had been discouraged from the pursuit the captain breathed easier on account of his hair, and others breathed easier because the bird struck their minds at this time as being somehow gruesome and ominous.

In the meantime the oiler and the correspondent rowed. And also they rowed.

They sat together in the same seat, and each rowed an oar. Then the oiler took both oars; then the correspondent took both oars; then the oiler; then the correspondent. They rowed and they rowed. The very ticklish part of the business was when the time came for the reclining one in the stern to take his turn at the oars. By the very last star of truth, it is easier to steal eggs from under a hen than it was to change seats in the dinghy. First the man in the stern slid his hand along the thwart and moved with care, as if he were of Sevres. Then the man in the rowing seat slid his hand along the other thwart. It was all done with the most extraordinary care. As the two sidled past each other, the whole party kept watchful eyes on the coming wave, and the captain cried:

"Look out now! Steady there!"

The brown mats of sea-weed that appeared from time to time were like islands, bits of earth. They were travelling, apparently, neither one way nor the other. They were, to all intents, stationary. They informed the men in the boat that it was making progress slowly toward the land.

The captain, rearing cautiously in the bow, after the dinghy soared on a great swell, said that he had seen the lighthouse at Mosquito Inlet. Presently the cook remarked that he had seen it. The correspondent was at the oars, then, and for some reason he too wished to look at the lighthouse, but his back was toward the far shore and the waves were important, and for some time he could not seize an opportunity to turn his head. But at last there came a wave more gentle than the others, and when at the crest of it he swiftly scoured the western horizon.

"See it?" said the captain.

"No," said the correspondent, slowly, "I didn't see anything."

"Look again," said the captain. He pointed. "It's exactly in that direction."

At the top of another wave, the correspondent did as he was bid, and this time his eyes chanced on a small still thing on the edge of the swaying horizon. It was precisely like the point of a pin. It took an anxious eye to find a lighthouse so tiny.

"Think we'll make it, captain?"

"If this wind holds and the boat don't swamp, we can't do much else," said the captain.

The little boat, lifted by each towering sea, and splashed viciously by the crests, made progress that in the absence of sea-weed was not apparent to those in her. She seemed just a wee thing wallowing, miraculously, top-up, at the mercy of five oceans. Occasionally, a great spread of water, like white flames, swarmed into her.

"Bail her, cook," said the captain, serenely.

"All right, captain," said the cheerful cook.

III

It would be difficult to describe the subtle brotherhood of men that was here established on the seas. No one said that it was so. No one mentioned it. But it dwelt in the boat, and each man felt it warm him. They were a captain, an oiler, a cook, and a correspondent, and they were friends, friends in a more curiously iron-bound degree than may be common. The hurt captain, lying against the water-jar in the bow, spoke always in a low voice and calmly, but he could never command a more ready and swiftly obedient crew than the motley three of the dinghy. It was more than a mere recognition of what was best for the common safety. There was surely in it a quality that was personal and heartfelt. And after this devotion to the commander of the boat there was this comradeship that the correspondent, for instance, who had been taught to be cynical of men, knew even at the time was the best experience of his life. But no one said that it was so. No one mentioned it.

"I wish we had a sail," remarked the captain. "We might try my overcoat on the end of an oar and give you two boys a chance to rest." So the cook and the correspondent held the mast and spread wide the overcoat. The oiler steered, and the little boat made good way with her new rig. Sometimes the oiler had to scull sharply to keep a sea from breaking into the boat, but otherwise sailing was a success.

Meanwhile the light-house had been growing slowly larger. It had now almost assumed color, and appeared like a little gray shadow on the sky. The man at the oars could not be prevented from turning his head rather often to try for a glimpse of this little gray shadow.

At last, from the top of each wave the men in the tossing boat could see land. Even as the light-house was an upright shadow on the sky, this land seemed but a long black shadow on the sea. It certainly was thinner than paper. "We must be about opposite New Smyrna," said the cook, who had coasted this shore often in schooners. "Captain, by the way, I believe they abandoned that life-saving station there about a year ago."

"Did they?" said the captain.

The wind slowly died away. The cook and the correspondent were not now obliged to slave in order to hold high the oar. But the waves continued their old impetuous swooping at the dinghy, and the little craft, no longer under way, struggled woundily over them. The oiler or the correspondent took the oars again.

Shipwrecks are apropos of nothing. If men could only train for them and have them occur when the men had reached pink condition, there would be less drowning at sea. Of the four in the dinghy none had slept any time worth mentioning for two days and two nights previous to embarking in the dinghy, and in the excitement of clambering about the deck of a foundering ship they had also forgotten to eat heartily.

For these reasons, and for others, neither the oiler nor the correspondent was fond of rowing at this time. The correspondent wondered ingenuously how in the name of all that was sane could there be people who thought it amusing to row a boat. It was not an amusement; it was a diabolical punishment, and even a genius of mental aberrations could never conclude that it was anything but a horror to the muscles and a crime against the back. He mentioned to the boat in general how the amusement of rowing struck him, and the weary-faced oiler smiled in full sympathy. Previously to the foundering, by the way, the oiler had worked double-watch in the engine-room of the ship.

"Take her easy, now, boys," said the captain. "Don't spend yourselves. If we have to run a surf you'll need all your strength, because we'll sure have to swim for it. Take your time."

Slowly the land arose from the sea. From a black line it became a line of black and a line of white, trees, and sand. Finally, the captain said that he could make out a house on the shore.

"That's the house of refuge, sure," said the cook. "They'll see us before long, and come out after us."

The distant light-house reared high. "The keeper ought to be able to make us out now, if he's looking through a glass," said the captain. "He'll notify the life-saving people."

"None of those other boats could have got ashore to give word of the wreck," said the oiler, in a low voice. "Else the life-boat would be out hunting us."

Slowly and beautifully the land loomed out of the sea. The wind came again. It had veered from the northeast to the southeast. Finally, a new sound struck the ears of the men in the boat. It was the low thunder of the surf on the shore. "We'll never be able to make the light-house now," said the captain. "Swing her head a little more north, Billie," said the captain.

"A little more north, sir," said the oiler.

Whereupon the little boat turned her nose once more down the wind, and all but the oarsman watched the shore grow. Under the influence of this expansion doubt and direful apprehension was leaving the minds of the men. The management of the boat was still most absorbing, but it could not prevent a quiet cheerfulness. In an hour, perhaps, they would be ashore.

Their back-bones had become thoroughly used to balancing in the boat and they now rode this wild colt of a dinghy like circus men. The correspondent thought that he had been drenched to the skin, but happening to feel in the top pocket of his coat, he found therein eight cigars. Four of them were soaked with sea-water; four were perfectly scatheless. After a search, somebody produced three dry matches, and thereupon the four waifs rode in their little boat, and with an assurance of an impending rescue shining in their eyes, puffed at the big cigars and judged well and ill of all men. Everybody took a drink of water.

IV

"Cook," remarked the captain, "there don't seem to be any signs of life about your house of refuge."

"No," replied the cook. "Funny they don't see us!"

A broad stretch of lowly coast lay before the eyes of the men. It was of low dunes topped with dark vegetation. The roar of the surf was plain, and sometimes they could see the white lip of a wave as it spun up the beach. A tiny house was blocked out black upon the sky. Southward, the slim light-house lifted its little gray length.

Tide, wind, and waves were swinging the dinghy northward. "Funny they don't see us," said the men.

The surf's roar was here dulled, but its tone was, nevertheless, thunderous and mighty. As the boat swam over the great rollers, the men sat listening to this roar. "We'll swamp sure," said everybody.

It is fair to say here that there was not a life-saving station within twenty miles in either direction, but the men did not know this fact and in consequence they made dark and opprobrious remarks concerning the eyesight of the nation's life-savers. Four scowling men sat in the dinghy and surpassed records in the invention of epithets.

"Funny they don't see us."

The light-heartedness of a former time had completely faded. To their sharpened minds it was easy to conjure pictures of all kinds of incompetency and blindness and indeed, cowardice. There was the shore of the populous land, and it was bitter and bitter to them that from it came no sign.

"Well," said the captain, ultimately, "I suppose we'll have to make a try for ourselves. If we stay out here too long, we'll none of us have strength left to swim after the boat swamps."

And so the oiler, who was at the oars, turned the boat straight for the shore. There was a sudden tightening of muscles. There was some thinking.

"If we don't all get ashore—" said the captain. "If we don't all get ashore, I suppose you fellows know where to send news of my finish?"

They then briefly exchanged some addresses and admonitions. As for the reflections of the men, there was a great deal of rage in them. Perchance they might be formulated thus: "If I am going to be drowned—if I am going to be drowned—if I am going to be drowned, why, in the name of the seven mad gods who rule the sea, was I allowed to come thus far and contemplate sand and trees? Was I brought here merely to have my nose dragged away as I was about to nibble the sacred cheese of life? It is preposterous. If this old ninny-woman, Fate, cannot do better than this, she should be deprived of the management of men's fortunes. She is an old hen who knows not her intention. If she has decided to drown me, why did she not do it in the beginning and save me all this trouble. The whole affair is absurd. . . . But, no, she cannot mean to drown me. She dare not drown me. She cannot drown me. Not after all this work." Afterward the man might have had an impulse to shake his fist at the clouds: "Just you drown me, now, and then hear what I call you!"

The billows that came at this time were more formidable. They seemed always just about to break and roll over the little boat in a turmoil of foam. There was a preparatory and long growl in the speech of them. No mind unused to the sea would have concluded that the dinghy could ascend these sheer heights in time. The shore was still afar. The oiler was a wily surfman. "Boys," he said, swiftly, "she won't live three minutes more and we're too far out to swim. Shall I take her to sea again, captain?"

"Yes! Go ahead!" said the captain.

This oiler, by a series of quick miracles, and fast and steady oarsmanship, turned the boat in the middle of the surf and took her safely to sea again.

There was a considerable silence as the boat bumped over the furrowed sea to deeper water. Then somebody in gloom spoke. "Well, anyhow, they must have seen us from the shore by now."

The gulls went in slanting flight up the wind toward the gray desolate east. A squall, marked by dingy clouds, and clouds brick-red, like smoke from a burning building, appeared from the southeast.

"What do you think of those life-saving people? Ain't they peaches?"

"Funny they haven't seen us."

"Maybe they think we're out here for sport! Maybe they think we're fishin'. Maybe they think we're damned fools."

It was a long afternoon. A changed tide tried to force them southward, but wind and wave said northward. Far ahead, where coast-line, sea, and sky formed their mighty angle, there were little dots which seemed to indicate a city on the shore.

"St. Augustine?"

The captain shook his head. "Too near Mosquito Inlet."

And the oiler rowed, and then the correspondent rowed. Then the oiler rowed. It was a weary business. The human back can become the seat of more aches and pains than are registered in books for the composite anatomy of a regiment. It is a limited area, but it can become the theatre of innumerable muscular conflicts, tangles, wrenches, knots, and other comforts.

"Did you ever like to row, Billie?" asked the correspondent.

"No," said the oiler. "Hang it."

When one exchanged the rowing-seat for a place in the bottom of the boat, he suffered a bodily depression that caused him to be careless of everything save an obligation to wiggle one finger. There was cold sea-water swashing to and fro in the boat, and he lay in it. His head, pillowed on a thwart, was within an inch of the swirl of a wave crest, and sometimes a particularly obstreperous sea came in-board and drenched him once more. But these matters did not annoy him. It is almost certain that if the boat had capsized he would have tumbled comfortably out upon the ocean as if he felt sure it was a great soft mattress.

"Look! There's a man on the shore!"

"Where?"

"There! See 'im? See 'im?"

"Yes, sure! He's walking along."

"Now he's stopped. Look! He's facing us!"

"He's waving at us!"

"So he is! By thunder!"

"Ah, now, we're all right! Now we're all right! There'll be a boat out here for us in half an hour."

"He's going on. He's running. He's going up to that house there."

The remote beach seemed lower than the sea, and it required a searching glance to discern the little black figure. The captain saw a floating stick and they rowed to it. A bath-towel was by some weird chance in the boat, and, tying this on the stick, the captain waved it. The oarsman did not dare turn his head, so he was obliged to ask questions.

"What's he doing now?"

"He's standing still again. He's looking, I think. . . . There he goes again. Toward the house. . . .

Now he's stopped again."

"Is he waving at us?"

"No, not now! He was, though."

"Look! There comes another man!"

"He's running."

"Look at him go, would you."

"Why, he's on a bicycle. Now he's met the other man. They're both waving at us. Look!"

"There comes something up the beach."

"What the devil is that thing?"

"Why, it looks like a boat."

"Why, certainly it's a boat."

"No, it's on wheels."

"Yes, so it is. Well, that must be the life-boat. They drag them along shore on a wagon."

"That's the life-boat, sure."

"No, by——, it's—it's an omnibus."

"I tell you it's a life-boat."

"It is not! It's an omnibus. I can see it plain. See? One of these big hotel omnibuses."

"By thunder, you're right. It's an omnibus, sure as fate. What do you suppose they are doing with an omnibus? Maybe they are going around collecting the life-crew, hey?"

"That's it, likely. Look! There's a fellow waving a little black flag. He's standing on the steps of the omnibus. There come those other two fellows. Now they're all talking together. Look at the fellow with the flag. Maybe he ain't waving it."

"That ain't a flag, is it? That's his coat. Why, certainly, that's his coat."

"So it is. It's his coat. He's taken it off and is waving it around his head. But would you look at him swing it."

"Oh, say, there isn't any life-saving station there. That's just a winter resort hotel omnibus that has brought over some of the boarders to see us drown."

"What's that idiot with the coat mean? What's he signaling, anyhow?"

"It looks as if he were trying to tell us to go north. There must be a life-saving station up there."

"No! He thinks we're fishing. Just giving us a merry hand. See? Ah, there, Willie."

"Well, I wish I could make something out of those signals. What do you suppose he means?"

"He don't mean anything. He's just playing."

"Well, if he'd just signal us to try the surf again, or to go to sea and wait, or go north, or go south, or go to hell—there would be some reason in it. But look at him. He just stands there and keeps his coat revolving like a wheel. The ass!"

"There come more people."

"Now there's quite a mob. Look! Isn't that a boat?"

"Where? Oh, I see where you mean. No, that's no boat."

"That fellow is still waving his coat."

"He must think we like to see him do that. Why don't he quit it. It don't mean anything."

"I don't know. I think he is trying to make us go north. It must be that there's a life-saving station there somewhere."

"Say, he ain't tired yet. Look at 'im wave."

"Wonder how long he can keep that up. He's been revolving his coat ever since he caught sight of us. He's an idiot. Why aren't they getting men to bring a boat out. A fishing boat—one of those big yawls—could come out here all right. Why don't he do something?"

"Oh, it's all right, now."

"They'll have a boat out here for us in less than no time, now that they've seen us."

A faint yellow tone came into the sky over the low land. The shadows on the sea slowly deepened. The wind bore coldness with it, and the men began to shiver.

"Holy smoke!" said one, allowing his voice to express his impious mood, "if we keep on monkeying out here! If we've got to flounder out here all night!"

"Oh, we'll never have to stay here all night! Don't you worry. They've seen us now, and it won't be long before they'll come chasing out after us."

The shore grew dusky. The man waving a coat blended gradually into this gloom, and it swallowed in the same manner the omnibus and the group of people. The spray, when it dashed uproariously over the side, made the voyagers shrink and swear like men who were being branded.

"I'd like to catch the chump who waved the coat. I feel like soaking him one, just for luck."

"Why? What did he do?"

"Oh, nothing, but then he seemed so damned cheerful."

In the meantime the oiler rowed, and then the correspondent rowed, and then the oiler rowed. Gray-faced and bowed forward, they mechanically, turn by turn, plied the leaden oars. The form of the lighthouse had vanished from the southern horizon, but finally a pale star appeared, just lifting from the sea. The streaked saffron in the west passed before the all-merging darkness, and the sea to the east was black. The land had vanished, and was expressed only by the low and drear thunder of the surf.

"If I am going to be drowned—if I am going to be drowned—if I am going to be drowned, why, in the name of the seven mad gods, who rule the sea, was I allowed to come thus far and contemplate sand and trees? Was I brought here merely to have my nose dragged away as I was about to nibble the sacred cheese of life?"

The patient captain, drooped over the water-jar, was sometimes obliged to speak to the oarsman.

"Keep her head up! Keep her head up!"

"'Keep her head up,' sir." The voices were weary and low.

This was surely a quiet evening. All save the oarsman lay heavily and listlessly in the boat's bottom. As for him, his eyes were just capable of noting the tall black waves that swept forward in a most sinister silence, save for an occasional subdued growl of a crest.

The cook's head was on a thwart, and he looked without interest at the water under his nose. He was deep in other scenes. Finally he spoke. "Billie," he murmured, dreamfully, "what kind of pie do you like best?"

V

"Pie!" said the oiler and the correspondent, agitatedly. "Don't talk about those things, blast you!"

"Well," said the cook, "I was just thinking about ham sandwiches, and—"

A night on the sea in an open boat is a long night. As darkness settled finally, the shine of the light, lifting from the sea in the south, changed to full gold. On the northern horizon a new light appeared, a small bluish gleam on the edge of the waters. These two lights were the furniture of the world. Otherwise there was nothing but waves.

Two men huddled in the stern, and distances were so magnificent in the dinghy that the rower was enabled to keep his feet partly warmed by thrusting them under his companions. Their legs indeed extended far under the rowing-seat until they touched the feet of the captain forward. Sometimes, despite the efforts of the tired oarsman, a wave came piling into the boat, an icy wave of the night, and the chilling water soaked them anew. They would twist their bodies for a moment and groan, and sleep the dead sleep once more, while the water in the boat gurgled about them as the craft rocked.

The plan of the oiler and the correspondent was for one to row until he lost the ability, and then arouse the other from his sea-water couch in the bottom of the boat.

The oiler plied the oars until his head drooped forward, and the overpowering sleep blinded him. And he rowed yet afterward. Then he touched a man in the bottom of the boat, and called his name. "Will you spell me for a little while?" he said, meekly.

"Sure, Billie," said the correspondent, awakening and dragging himself to a sitting position. They exchanged places carefully, and the oiler, cuddling down to the sea-water at the cook's side, seemed to go to sleep instantly.

The particular violence of the sea had ceased. The waves came without snarling. The obligation of the man at the oars was to keep the boat headed so that the tilt of the rollers would not capsize her, and to preserve her from filling when the crests rushed past. The black waves were silent and hard to be seen in the darkness. Often one was almost upon the boat before the oarsman was aware.

In a low voice the correspondent addressed the captain. He was not sure that the captain was awake, although this iron man seemed to be always awake. "Captain, shall I keep her making for that light north, sir?"

The same steady voice answered him. "Yes. Keep it about two points off the port bow."

The cook had tied a life-belt around himself in order to get even the warmth which this clumsy cork contrivance could donate, and he seemed almost stove-like when a rower, whose teeth invariably chattered wildly as soon as he ceased his labor, dropped down to sleep.

The correspondent, as he rowed, looked down at the two men sleeping under foot. The cook's arm was around the oiler's shoulders, and, with their fragmentary clothing and haggard faces, they were the babes of the sea, a grotesque rendering of the old babes in the wood.

Later he must have grown stupid at his work, for suddenly there was a growling of water, and a crest came with a roar and a swash into the boat, and it was a wonder that it did not set the cook afloat in his life-belt. The cook continued to sleep, but the oiler sat up, blinking his eyes and shaking with the new cold.

"Oh, I'm awful sorry, Billie," said the correspondent, contritely.

"That's all right, old boy," said the oiler, and lay down again and was asleep.

Presently it seemed that even the captain dozed, and the correspondent thought that he was the one man afloat on all the oceans. The wind had a voice as it came over the waves, and it was sadder than the end.

There was a long, loud swishing astern of the boat, and a gleaming trail of phosphorescence, like blue flame, was furrowed on the black waters. It might have been made by a monstrous knife.

Then there came a stillness, while the correspondent breathed with the open mouth and looked at the sea.

Suddenly there was another swish and another long flash of bluish light, and this time it was alongside the boat, and might almost have been reached with an oar. The correspondent saw an enormous fin speed like a shadow through the water, hurling the crystalline spray and leaving the long glowing trail.

The correspondent looked over his shoulder at the captain. His face was hidden, and he seemed to be asleep. He looked at the babes of the sea. They certainly were asleep. So, being bereft of sympathy, he leaned a little way to one side and swore softly into the sea.

But the thing did not then leave the vicinity of the boat. Ahead or astern, on one side or the other, at intervals long or short, fled the long sparkling streak, and there was to be heard the whiroo of the dark fin. The speed and power of the thing was greatly to be admired. It cut the water like a gigantic and keen projectile.

The presence of this biding thing did not affect the man with the same horror that it would if he had been a picnicker. He simply looked at the sea dully and swore in an undertone.

Nevertheless, it is true that he did not wish to be alone with the thing. He wished one of his companions to awaken by chance and keep him company with it. But the captain hung motionless over the water-jar and the oiler and the cook in the bottom of the boat were plunged in slumber.

VI

"If I am going to be drowned—if I am going to be drowned—if I am going to be drowned, why, in the name of the seven mad gods, who rule the sea, was I allowed to come thus far and contemplate sand and trees?"

During this dismal night, it may be remarked that a man would conclude that it was really the intention of the seven mad gods to drown him, despite the abominable injustice of it. For it was certainly an abominable injustice to drown a man who had worked so hard, so hard. The man felt it would be a crime most unnatural. Other people had drowned at sea since galleys swarmed with painted sails, but still—

When it occurs to a man that nature does not regard him as important, and that she feels she would not maim the universe by disposing of him, he at first wishes to throw bricks at the temple, and he hates deeply the fact that there are no bricks and no temples. Any visible expression of nature would surely be pelleted with his jeers.

Then, if there be no tangible thing to hoot he feels, perhaps, the desire to confront a personification and indulge in pleas, bowed to one knee, and with hands supplicant, saying: "Yes, but I love myself."

A high cold star on a winter's night is the word he feels that she says to him. Thereafter he knows the pathos of his situation.

The men in the dinghy had not discussed these matters, but each had, no doubt, reflected upon them in silence and according to his mind. There was seldom any expression upon their faces save the general one of complete weariness. Speech was devoted to the business of the boat.

To chime the notes of his emotion, a verse mysteriously entered the correspondent's head. He had even forgotten that he had forgotten this verse, but it suddenly was in his mind.

A soldier of the Legion lay dying in Algiers;
There was lack of woman's nursing, there was dearth
    of woman's tears;
But a comrade stood beside him, and he took that
    comrade's hand,
And he said, "I shall never see my own, my
    native land."

In his childhood, the correspondent had been made acquainted with the fact that a soldier of the Legion lay dying in Algiers, but he had never regarded the fact as important. Myriads of his school-fellows had informed him of the soldier's plight, but the dinning had naturally ended by making him perfectly indifferent. He had never considered it his affair that a soldier of the Legion lay dying in Algiers, nor had it appeared to him as a matter for sorrow. It was less to him than breaking of a pencil's point.

Now, however, it quaintly came to him as a human, living thing. It was no longer merely a picture of a few throes in the breast of a poet, meanwhile drinking tea and warming his feet at the grate; it was an actuality—stern, mournful, and fine.

The correspondent plainly saw the soldier. He lay on the sand with his feet out straight and still. While his pale left hand was upon his chest in an attempt to thwart the going of his life, the blood came between his fingers. In the far Algerian distance, a city of low square forms was set against a sky that was faint with the last sunset hues. The correspondent, plying the oars and dreaming of the slow and slower movements of the lips of the soldier, was moved by a profound and perfectly impersonal comprehension. He was sorry for the soldier of the Legion who lay dying in Algiers.

The thing which had followed the boat and waited had evidently grown bored at the delay. There was no longer to be heard the slash of the cut-water, and there was no longer the flame of the long trail. The light in the north still glimmered, but it was apparently no nearer to the boat. Sometimes the boom of the surf rang in the correspondent's ears, and he turned the craft seaward then and rowed harder. Southward, someone had evidently built a watch-fire on the beach. It was too low and too far to be seen, but it made a shimmering, roseate reflection upon the bluff back of it, and this could be discerned from the boat. The wind came stronger, and sometimes a wave suddenly raged out like a mountain-cat and there was to be seen the sheen and sparkle of a broken crest.

The captain, in the bow, moved on his water-jar and sat erect. "Pretty long night," he observed to the correspondent. He looked at the shore. "Those life-saving people take their time."

"Did you see that shark playing around?"

"Yes, I saw him. He was a big fellow, all right."

"Wish I had known you were awake."

Later the correspondent spoke into the bottom of the boat.

"Billie!" There was a slow and gradual disentanglement. "Billie, will you spell me?"

"Sure," said the oiler.

As soon as the correspondent touched the cold comfortable sea-water in the bottom of the boat, and had huddled close to the cook's life-belt he was deep in sleep, despite the fact that his teeth played all the popular airs. This sleep was so good to him that it was but a moment before he heard a voice call his name in a tone that demonstrated the last stages of exhaustion. "Will you spell me?"

"Sure, Billie."

The light in the north had mysteriously vanished, but the correspondent took his course from the wide-awake captain.

Later in the night they took the boat farther out to sea, and the captain directed the cook to take one oar at the stern and keep the boat facing the seas. He was to call out if he should hear the thunder of the surf. This plan enabled the oiler and the correspondent to get respite together.

"We'll give those boys a chance to get into shape again," said the captain. They curled down and, after a few preliminary chatterings and trembles, slept once more the dead sleep. Neither knew they had bequeathed to the cook the company of another shark, or perhaps the same shark.

As the boat caroused on the waves, spray occasionally bumped over the side and gave them a fresh soaking, but this had no power to break their repose. The ominous slash of the wind and the water affected them as it would have affected mummies.

"Boys," said the cook, with the notes of every reluctance in his voice, "she's drifted in pretty close. I guess one of you had better take her to sea again." The correspondent, aroused, heard the crash of the toppled crests.

As he was rowing, the captain gave him some whiskey and water, and this steadied the chills out of him. "If I ever get ashore and anybody shows me even a photograph of an oar—"

At last there was a short conversation.

"Billie. . . . Billie, will you spell me?"

"Sure," said the oiler.

VII

When the correspondent again opened his eyes, the sea and the sky were each of the gray hue of the dawning. Later, carmine and gold was painted upon the waters. The morning appeared finally, in its splendor with a sky of pure blue, and the sunlight flamed on the tips of the waves.

On the distant dunes were set many little black cottages, and a tall white wind-mill reared above them. No man, nor dog, nor bicycle appeared on the beach. The cottages might have formed a deserted village.

The voyagers scanned the shore. A conference was held in the boat. "Well," said the captain, "if no help is coming, we might better try a run through the surf right away. If we stay out here much longer we will be too weak to do anything for ourselves at all." The others silently acquiesced in this reasoning. The boat was headed for the beach. The correspondent wondered if none ever ascended the tall wind-tower, and if then they never looked seaward. This tower was a giant, standing with its back to the plight of the ants. It represented in a degree, to the correspondent, the serenity of nature amid the struggles of the individual—nature in the wind, and nature in the vision of men. She did not seem cruel to him, nor beneficent, nor treacherous, nor wise. But she was indifferent, flatly indifferent. It is, perhaps, plausible that a man in this situation, impressed with the unconcern of the universe, should see the innumerable flaws of his life and have them taste wickedly in his mind and wish for another chance. A distinction between right and wrong seems absurdly clear to him, then, in this new ignorance of the grave-edge, and he understands that if he were given another opportunity he would mend his conduct and his words, and be better and brighter during an introduction, or at a tea.

"Now, boys," said the captain, "she is going to swamp sure. All we can do is to work her in as far as possible, and then when she swamps, pile out and scramble for the beach. Keep cool now and don't jump until she swamps sure."

The oiler took the oars. Over his shoulders he scanned the surf. "Captain," he said, "I think I'd better bring her about, and keep her head-on to the seas and back her in."

"All right, Billie," said the captain. "Back her in." The oiler swung the boat then and, seated in the stern, the cook and the correspondent were obliged to look over their shoulders to contemplate the lonely and indifferent shore.

The monstrous inshore rollers heaved the boat high until the men were again enabled to see the white sheets of water scudding up the slanted beach. "We won't get in very close," said the captain. Each time a man could wrest his attention from the rollers, he turned his glance toward the shore, and in the expression of the eyes during this contemplation there was a singular quality.

The correspondent, observing the others, knew that they were not afraid, but the full meaning of their glances was shrouded.

As for himself, he was too tired to grapple fundamentally with the fact. He tried to coerce his mind into thinking of it, but the mind was dominated at this time by the muscles, and the muscles said they did not care. It merely occurred to him that if he should drown it would be a shame.

There were no hurried words, no pallor, no plain agitation. The men simply looked at the shore.

"Now, remember to get well clear of the boat when you jump," said the captain. Seaward the crest of a roller suddenly fell with a thunderous crash, and the long white comber came roaring down upon the boat.

"Steady now," said the captain. The men were silent. They turned their eyes from the shore to the comber and waited. The boat slid up the incline, leaped at the furious top, bounced over it, and swung down the long back of the waves. Some water had been shipped and the cook bailed it out.

But the next crest crashed also. The tumbling boiling flood of white water caught the boat and whirled it almost perpendicular. Water swarmed in from all sides. The correspondent had his hands on the gunwale at this time, and when the water entered at that place he swiftly withdrew his fingers, as if he objected to wetting them.

The little boat, drunken with this weight of water, reeled and snuggled deeper into the sea.

"Bail her out, cook! Bail her out," said the captain.

"All right, captain," said the cook.

"Now, boys, the next one will do for us, sure," said the oiler. "Mind to jump clear of the boat."

The third wave moved forward, huge, furious, implacable. It fairly swallowed the dinghy, and almost simultaneously the men tumbled into the sea. A piece of life-belt had lain in the bottom of the boat, and as the correspondent went overboard he held this to his chest with his left hand.

The January water was icy, and he reflected immediately that it was colder than he had expected to find it off the coast of Florida. This appeared to his dazed mind as a fact important enough to be noted at the time. The coldness of the water was sad; it was tragic. This fact was somehow mixed and confused with his opinion of his own situation that it seemed almost a proper reason for tears. The water was cold.

When he came to the surface he was conscious of little but the noisy water. Afterward he saw his companions in the sea. The oiler was ahead in the race. He was swimming strongly and rapidly. Off to the correspondent's left, the cook's great white and corked back bulged out of the water, and in the rear the captain was hanging with his one good hand to the keel of the overturned dinghy.

There is a certain immovable quality to a shore, and the correspondent wondered at it amid the confusion of the sea.

It seemed also very attractive, but the correspondent knew that it was a long journey, and he paddled leisurely. The piece of life-preserver lay under him, and sometimes he whirled down the incline of a wave as if he were on a hand-sled.

But finally he arrived at a place in the sea where travel was beset with difficulty. He did not pause swimming to inquire what manner of current had caught him, but there his progress ceased. The shore was set before him like a bit of scenery on a stage, and he looked at it and understood with his eyes each detail of it.

As the cook passed, much farther to the left, the captain was calling to him, "Turn over on your back, cook! Turn over on your back and use the oar."

"All right, sir!" The cook turned on his back, and, paddling with an oar, went ahead as if he were a canoe.

Presently the boat also passed to the left of the correspondent with the captain clinging with one hand to the keel. He would have appeared like a man raising himself to look over a board fence, if it were not for the extraordinary gymnastics of the boat. The correspondent marveled that the captain could still hold to it.

They passed on, nearer to shore—the oiler, the cook, the captain—and following them went the water-jar, bouncing gaily over the seas.

The correspondent remained in the grip of this strange new enemy—a current. The shore, with its white slope of sand and its green bluff, topped with little silent cottages, was spread like a picture before him. It was very near to him then, but he was impressed as one who in a gallery looks at a scene from Brittany or Algiers.

He thought: "I am going to drown? Can it be possible? Can it be possible? Can it be possible?"

Perhaps an individual must consider his own death to be the final phenomenon of nature.

But later a wave perhaps whirled him out of this small deadly current, for he found suddenly that he could again make progress toward the shore. Later still, he was aware that the captain, clinging with one hand to the keel of the dinghy, had his face turned away from the shore and toward him, and was calling his name. "Come to the boat! Come to the boat!"

In his struggle to reach the captain and the boat, he reflected that when one gets properly wearied, drowning must really be a comfortable arrangement, a cessation of hostilities accompanied by a large degree of relief, and he was glad of it, for the main thing in his mind for some moments had been horror of the temporary agony. He did not wish to be hurt.

Presently he saw a man running along the shore. He was undressing with most remarkable speed. Coat, trousers, shirt, everything flew magically off him.

"Come to the boat," called the captain.

"All right, captain." As the correspondent paddled, he saw the captain let himself down to bottom and leave the boat. Then the correspondent performed his one little marvel of the voyage. A large wave caught him and flung him with ease and supreme speed completely over the boat and far beyond it. It struck him even then as an event in gymnastics, and a true miracle of the sea. An overturned boat in the surf is not a plaything to a swimming man.

The correspondent arrived in water that reached only to his waist, but his condition did not enable him to stand for more than a moment. Each wave knocked him into a heap, and the under-tow pulled at him.

Then he saw the man who had been running and undressing, and undressing and running, come bounding into the water. He dragged ashore the cook, and then waded toward the captain, but the captain waved him away, and sent him to the correspondent. He was naked, naked as a tree in winter, but a halo was about his head, and he shone like a saint. He gave a strong pull, and a long drag, and a bully heave at the correspondent's hand. The correspondent, schooled in the minor formulae, said: "Thanks, old man." But suddenly the man cried: "What's that?" He pointed a swift finger. The correspondent said: "Go."

In the shallows, face downward, lay the oiler. His forehead touched sand that was periodically, between each wave, clear of the sea.

The correspondent did not know all that transpired afterward. When he achieved safe ground he fell, striking the sand with each particular part of his body. It was as if he had dropped from a roof, but the thud was grateful to him.

It seems that instantly the beach was populated with men with blankets, clothes, and flasks, and women with coffee-pots and all the remedies sacred to their minds. The welcome of the land to the men from the sea was warm and generous, but a still and dripping shape was carried slowly up the beach, and the land's welcome for it could only be the different and sinister hospitality of the grave.

When it came night, the white waves paced to and fro in the moonlight, and the wind brought the sound of the great sea's voice to the men on shore, and they felt that they could then be interpreters.

Thinking About the Story

Stephen Crane's story lingers for almost ten thousand words on the four men in the boat. The uncertainty as to what will happen to the characters drives the narrative onward, causing questions to arise: Who are the people on the shore? Why do they seem so incapable of helping the men in the boat? What is the relationship between humans and nature? In formulating your thoughts, you should ruminate on the lack of romanticism and the bleak portrayal of the men's situation. You may find John Ruskin's concept of the "pathetic fallacy" valuable in your discussions. Ruskin's idea argued that artists were mistaken in giving nature and non-sentient things human consciousness or emotions. As well as considering Ruskin's views, useful avenues of intellectual scholarship can be found in reading Sarah Orne Jewett's "A White Heron" and Rudyard Kipling's "Mowgli's Brothers." With the three stories read, you can examine the varying manifestations in which humanity's complex entente with the environment is represented and explored.

Discussion Questions

1. Crane prefaces his story as "A tale intended to be after the fact." Does the story's real event origins change your reading of it? Are facts and fiction compatible? Are there any ethical implications?

2. How do you interpret the first line: "None of them knew the color of the sky." How does the story's first paragraph foreshadow later events?

3. Comment on the dinghy's crew: specifically focus on their occupations, personalities, and the way each views the situation. Is each character

given an equal place in the story? Are some characters more developed, more complex than others? Is the point of view more closely aligned with one of the characters?

4. Using passages of text to support your thoughts, describe the relationship between nature and man in the story. Discuss how this relationship pertains to the story's pessimism.

5. What is the significance(s) of the last line? What are the connotations for the story as a whole?

Activities

1. Look through a newspaper and find a story that piques your interest. Fictionalize the real event(s) and person(s), making sure to alter names and specifics. In other words, use the material to write a short story. Feel free to deviate from the actual events to increase the drama and the depth of characterization.

2. Use the Internet to track down Crane's original newspaper article, "Stephen Crane's Own Story," which describes in journalistic detail the sinking of the *Commodore* and the aftermath. Once you have located a copy, analyze the ways in which the article and the story overlap and also where both pieces diverge.

3. The lighthouse in the story can be read as a symbol of hope, of land, or of civilization. Create a list of notable and prominent buildings, such as the Cathedral of Learning in Pittsburgh, the Eiffel Tower in Paris, or the Statue of Liberty in New York. Go through your own list and note down several symbolic possibilities for each one. Compare and contrast your thoughts with a fellow student.

Willa Cather

Most of the basic material a writer works with is acquired before the age of fifteen.
Willa Cather — *Bookman Interview* (1921)

Willa Cather (1873–1947) is best remembered for her novels set in Nebraska—books that examined frontier life and the pioneers who settled in the American West. Born in Back Creek, Virginia, Cather's family moved to Red Cloud, Nebraska, when she was nine years old. Later schooled at the University of Nebraska-Lincoln, Cather discovered journalism and wrote for several newspapers. Hired by *Home Monthly* in 1896, she moved to Pittsburgh to become the magazine's managing editor. After five years she left to teach high school Latin and English. Simultaneously, she published a book of poems and one of short stories. In 1906, Cather went back to journalism, working for the prestigious *McClure's Magazine.* By 1912 she had moved to Greenwich Village in New York City, where she shared an apartment with her close friend, Edith Lewis. Over the next few years Cather traveled to Nebraska and Wyoming for novel research, and visited post-war France. The next two decades of her life were taken up with writing, further travels across the US and overseas, and receiving numerous awards and honorary degrees. At her residence in New York, she died from a cerebral hemorrhage.

Mentored by Sarah Orne Jewett, Cather became one of America's leading writers in the early part of the twentieth century. She wrote poetry, essays, short stories, and several influential novels, including *O Pioneers!* (1913), *My Ántonia* (1918), and *Death Comes for the Archbishop* (1927). Moreover, she won the Pulitzer Prize in 1922 for her First World War novel, *One of Ours*. In Cather's fiction she often deals with the frontier and the immigrants who settled in it. In her early work, such as the story

"A Wagner Matinee" (included as part of her first short story collection, *The Troll Garden*, in 1905), she paints Nebraska with bleak color and eviscerating description. Cather draws Aunt Georgiana as a sad figure of the pioneer period, a character who evokes pathos and revulsion. Clark, on the other hand, is Georgiana's foil, a well-meaning but wrong-headed young man. The story's beauty emerges from the role of music: it unites the two characters in present and past. Yet, through the power of Wagner's compositions, the memories of another life are brought to the fore, causing dangerous emotions to surface.

A Wagner Matinee

Willa Cather

I received one morning a letter, written in pale ink on glassy, blue-lined notepaper, and bearing the postmark of a little Nebraska village. This communication, worn and rubbed, looking as though it had been carried for some days in a coat pocket that was none too clean, was from my Uncle Howard and informed me that his wife had been left a small legacy by a bachelor relative who had recently died, and that it would be necessary for her to go to Boston to attend to the settling of the estate. He requested me to meet her at the station and render her whatever services might prove necessary. On examining the date indicated as that of her arrival, I found it no later than tomorrow. He had characteristically delayed writing until, had I been away from home for a day, I must have missed the good woman altogether.

The name of my Aunt Georgiana called up not alone her own figure, at once pathetic and grotesque, but opened before my feet a gulf of recollections so wide and deep, that, as the letter dropped from my hand, I felt suddenly a stranger to all the present conditions of my existence, wholly ill at ease and out of place amid the surroundings of my study. I became, in short, the gangling farm boy my aunt had known, scourged with chilblains and bashfulness, my hands cracked and raw from the corn husking. I felt the knuckles of my thumb tentatively, as though they were raw again. I sat again before her parlor organ, fumbling the scales with my stiff, red hands, while she, beside me, made canvas mittens for the huskers.

The next morning, after preparing my landlady somewhat, I set out for the station. When the train arrived I had some difficulty in finding my aunt. She was the last of the passengers to alight, and it was not until I got her into the carriage that she seemed really to recognize me. She had come all the way in a day coach; her linen duster had become black with soot and her black bonnet grey with dust during the journey. When we arrived at my boardinghouse the landlady put her to bed at once and I did not see her again until the next morning.

Whatever shock Mrs. Springer experienced at my aunt's appearance, she considerately concealed. As for myself, I saw my aunt's misshapen figure with that feeling of awe and respect with which we behold explorers who have left their ears and fingers north of Franz-Joseph Land, or their health somewhere along the Upper Congo. My Aunt Georgiana had been a music teacher at the Boston Conservatory, somewhere back in the latter sixties. One summer, while visiting in the little village among the Green Mountains where her ancestors had dwelt for generations, she had kindled the callow fancy of the most idle and shiftless of all the village lads, and had conceived for this Howard Carpenter one of those extravagant passions which a handsome country boy of twenty-one sometimes inspires in an angular, spectacled woman of thirty. When she returned to her duties in Boston, Howard followed her, and the upshot of this inexplicable infatuation was that she eloped with him, eluding the reproaches of her family and the criticisms of her friends by going with him to the Nebraska frontier. Carpenter, who, of course, had no money, had taken a homestead in Red Willow County, fifty miles from the railroad. There they had measured off their quarter section themselves by driving across the prairie in a wagon, to the wheel of which they had tied a red cotton handkerchief, and counting off its revolutions. They built a dugout in the red hillside, one of those cave dwellings whose inmates so often reverted to primitive conditions. Their water they got from the lagoons where the buffalo drank, and their slender stock of provisions was always at the mercy of bands of roving Indians. For thirty years my aunt had not been further than fifty miles from the homestead.

But Mrs. Springer knew nothing of all this, and must have been considerably shocked at what was left of my kinswoman. Beneath the soiled linen duster which, on her arrival, was the most conspicuous feature of her costume, she wore a black stuff dress whose ornamentation showed that she had surrendered herself unquestioningly into the hands of a country dressmaker. My poor aunt's figure, however, would have presented astonishing difficulties to any dressmaker. Originally stooped, her shoulders were almost bent together over her sunken chest. She wore no stays, and her gown, which trailed unevenly behind, rose in a sort of peak over her abdomen. She wore ill-fitting false teeth, and her skin was as yellow as a Mongolian's from constant exposure to a pitiless wind and to the alkaline water which hardens the most transparent cuticle into a sort of flexible leather.

I owed to this woman most of the good that ever came my way in my boyhood, and had a reverential affection for her. During the years when I was riding herd for my uncle, my aunt, after cooking the three meals—the first of which was ready at six o'clock in the morning—and putting the six children to bed, would often stand until midnight at her ironing-board, with me at the kitchen table beside her, hearing me recite Latin declensions and conjugations, gently shaking me when my drowsy head sank down over a page of irregular verbs. It was to her, at her ironing or mending, that I read my first Shakespeare, and her old textbook on mythology was the first that ever came into my empty hands. She taught me my scales and exercises, too—on the little parlor organ, which her husband had bought her after fifteen years, during which she had not so much as seen any instrument, but an accordion that belonged to one of the Norwegian farm-hands. She would sit beside me by the hour, darning and counting while I struggled with the "Joyous Farmer," but she seldom talked to me about music, and I understood why. She was a pious woman; she had the consolation of religion and, to her at least, her martyrdom was not wholly sordid. Once when I had been doggedly beating out some easy passages from an old score of *Euryanthe* I had found among her music books, she came up to me and, putting her hands over my eyes, gently drew my head back upon her shoulder, saying tremulously, "Don't love it so well, Clark, or it may be taken from you. Oh! dear boy, pray that whatever your sacrifice may be, it be not that."

When my aunt appeared on the morning after her arrival, she was still in a semi-somnambulant state. She seemed not to realize that she was in the city where she had spent her youth, the place longed for hungrily half a lifetime. She had been so wretchedly train-sick throughout the journey that she had no recollection of anything but her discomfort, and, to all intents and purposes, there were but a few hours of nightmare between the farm in Red Willow County and my study on Newbury Street. I had planned a little pleasure for her that afternoon, to repay her for some of the glorious moments she had given me when we used to milk together in the straw-thatched cowshed and she, because I was more than usually tried, or because her husband had spoken sharply to me, would tell me of the splendid performance of the *Huguenots* she had seen in Paris, in her youth. At two o'clock the Symphony Orchestra was to give a Wagner program, and I intended to take my aunt; though, as I conversed with her I grew doubtful about her enjoyment of it. Indeed, for her own sake, I could only wish her taste for such things quite dead, and the long struggle mercifully ended at last. I suggested our visiting the Conservatory and the Common before lunch, but she seemed altogether too timid to wish to venture out. She questioned me absently about various changes in the city, but she was chiefly concerned that she had forgotten to leave instructions about feeding half-skimmed milk to a certain weakling calf. "Old Maggie's calf, you know, Clark," she explained, evidently having forgotten how long I had been away. She was further troubled because she had neglected to tell her daughter about the freshly-opened kit of mackerel in the cellar, that would spoil if it were not used directly.

I asked her whether she had ever heard any of the Wagnerian operas, and found that she had not, though she was perfectly familiar with their respective situations, and had once possessed the piano score of *The Flying Dutchman*. I began to think it would have been best to get her back to Red Willow County without waking her, and regretted having suggested the concert.

From the time we entered the concert hall, however, she was a trifle less passive and inert, and for the first time seemed to perceive her surroundings. I had felt some trepidation lest she might become aware of the absurdities of her attire, or might experience some painful embarrassment at stepping suddenly into the world to which she had been dead for a quarter of a century. But, again, I found how superficially I had judged her. She sat looking about her with eyes as impersonal, almost as stony, as those with which the granite Rameses in a museum watches the froth and fret that ebbs and flows about his pedestal—separated from it by the lonely stretch of centuries. I have seen this same aloofness in old miners who drift into the Brown Hotel at Denver, their pockets full of bullion, their linen soiled, their haggard faces unshaven; standing in the thronged corridors as solitary as though they were still in a frozen camp on the Yukon, conscious that certain experiences have isolated them from their fellows by a gulf no haberdasher could bridge.

We sat at the extreme left of the first balcony, facing the arc of our own and the balcony above us, veritable hanging gardens, brilliant as tulip beds. The matinée audience was made up chiefly of women. One lost the contour of faces and figures, indeed any effect of line whatever, and there was only the color of bodices past counting the shimmer of fabrics soft and firm, silky and sheer; red, mauve, pink, blue, lilac, purple, ecru, rose, yellow, cream, and white, all the colors that an impressionist finds in a sunlit landscape, with here and there the dead shadow of a frock coat. My Aunt Georgiana regarded them as though they had been so many daubs of tube-paint on a palette.

When the musicians came out and took their places, she gave a little stir of anticipation, and looked with quickening interest down over the rail at that invariable grouping, perhaps the first wholly familiar thing that had greeted her eye since she had left old Maggie and her weakling calf. I could feel how all those details sank into her soul, for I had not forgotten how they had sunk into mine when I came fresh from plowing forever and forever between green aisles of corn, where, as in a treadmill, one might walk from daybreak to dusk without perceiving a shadow of change. The clean profiles of the musicians, the gloss of their linen, the dull black of their coats, the beloved shapes of the instruments, the patches of yellow light thrown by the green shaded lamps on the smooth, varnished bellies of the 'cellos and the bass viols in the rear, the restless, wind-tossed forest of fiddle necks and bows—I recalled how, in the first orchestra I had ever heard, those long bow strokes seemed to draw the heart out of me, as a conjurer's stick reels out yards of paper ribbon from a hat.

The first number was the *Tannhauser* overture. When the horns drew out the first strain of the Pilgrim's chorus, my Aunt Georgiana clutched my coat sleeve. Then it was that I first realized that for her this broke a silence of thirty years; the inconceivable silence of the plains. With the battle between the two motives, with the frenzy of the Venusberg theme and its ripping of strings, there came to me an overwhelming sense of the waste and wear we are so powerless to combat; and I saw again the tall, naked house on the prairie, black and grim as a wooden fortress; the black pond where I had learned to swim, its margin pitted with sun-dried cattle tracks; the rain gullied clay banks about the naked house, the four dwarf ash seedlings where the dishcloths were always hung to dry before the kitchen door. The world there was the flat world of the ancients; to the east, a cornfield that stretched to daybreak; to the west, a corral that stretched to sunset; between, the conquests of peace, dearer bought than those of war.

The overture closed, my aunt released my coat sleeve, but she said nothing. She sat staring at the orchestra through a dullness of thirty years, through the films made little by little by each of the three hundred and sixty-five days in every one of them. What, I wondered, did she get from it? She had been a good pianist in her day I knew, and her musical education had been broader than that of most music teachers of a quarter of a century ago. She had often told me of Mozart's operas and Meyerbeer's, and I could remember hearing her sing, years ago, certain melodies of Verdi's. When I had fallen ill with a fever in her house she used to sit by my cot in the evening—when the cool, night wind blew in through the faded mosquito netting tacked over the window and I lay watching a certain bright star that burned red above the cornfield—and sing "Home to our mountains, O, let us return!" in a way fit to break the heart of a Vermont boy near dead of homesickness already.

I watched her closely through the prelude to *Tristan and Isolde*, trying vainly to conjecture what that seething turmoil of strings and winds might mean to her, but she sat mutely staring at the violin bows that drove obliquely downward, like the pelting streaks of rain in a summer shower. Had this music any message for her? Had she enough left to at all comprehend this glory which had kindled the world since she had left it? I was in a fever of curiosity, but Aunt Georgiana sat silent upon her peak in Darien. She preserved this utter immobility throughout the number from *The Flying Dutchman*, though her fingers worked mechanically upon her black dress, as though, of themselves, they were recalling the piano score they had once played. Poor old hands! They had been stretched and twisted into mere tentacles to hold and lift and knead with; the palm, unduly swollen, the fingers bent and knotted—on one of them a thin, worn band that had once been a wedding ring. As I pressed and gently quieted one of those groping hands, I remembered with quivering eyelids their services for me in other days.

Soon after the tenor began the "Prize Song," I heard a quick drawn breath and turned to my aunt. Her eyes were closed, but the tears were glistening on her cheeks, and I think, in a moment more, they were in my eyes as well. It never really died, then—the soul that can suffer so excruciatingly and so interminably; it withers to the outward eye only; like that strange moss which can lie on a dusty shelf half a century and yet, if placed in water, grows green again. She wept so throughout the development and elaboration of the melody.

During the intermission before the second half of the concert, I questioned my aunt and found that the "Prize Song" was not new to her. Some years before there had drifted to the farm in Red Willow County a young German, a tramp cow puncher, who had sung in the chorus at Beyruth, when he was a boy, along with the other peasant boys and girls. Of a Sunday morning he used to sit on his gingham-sheeted bed in the hands' bedroom which opened off the kitchen, cleaning the leather of his boots and saddle, singing the "Prize Song," while my aunt went about her work in the kitchen. She had hovered about him until she had prevailed upon him to join the country church, though his sole fitness for this step, in so far as I could gather, lay in his boyish face and his possession of this divine melody. Shortly afterward he had gone to town on the Fourth of July, been drunk for several days, lost his money at a faro table, ridden a saddled Texan steer on a bet, and disappeared with a fractured collar-bone. All this my aunt told me huskily, wanderingly, as though she were talking in the weak lapses of illness.

"Well, we have come to better things than the old *Trovatore* at any rate, Aunt Georgie?" I queried, with a well meant effort at jocularity.

Her lip quivered and she hastily put her handkerchief up to her mouth. From behind it she murmured, "And you have been hearing this ever since you left me, Clark?" Her question was the gentlest and saddest of reproaches.

The second half of the program consisted of four numbers from the *Ring*, and closed with Siegfried's funeral march. My aunt wept quietly, but almost continuously, as a shallow vessel overflows in a rainstorm. From time to time her dim eyes looked up at the lights which studded the ceiling, burning softly under their dull glass globes; doubtless they were stars in truth to her. I was still perplexed as to what measure of musical comprehension was left to her, she who had heard nothing but the singing of Gospel Hymns at Methodist services in the square frame school-house on Section Thirteen for so many years. I was unable to gauge how much of it had been dissolved in soapsuds, or worked into bread, or milked into the bottom of a pail.

The deluge of sound poured on and on; I never knew what she found in the shining current of it; I never knew how far it bore her, or past what happy islands. From the trembling of her face I could well believe that before the last numbers she had been carried out where the myriad graves are, into the grey, nameless burying grounds of the sea; or into some world of death vaster yet, where, from the beginning of the world, hope has lain down with hope and dream with dream and, renouncing, slept.

The concert was over; the people filed out of the hall chattering and laughing, glad to relax and find the living level again, but my kinswoman made no effort to rise. The harpist slipped its green felt cover over his instrument; the flute-players shook the water from their mouthpieces; the men of the orchestra went out one by one, leaving the stage to the chairs and music stands, empty as a winter cornfield.

I spoke to my aunt. She burst into tears and sobbed pleadingly. "I don't want to go, Clark, I don't want to go!"

I understood. For her, just outside the door of the concert hall, lay the black pond with the cattle-tracked bluffs; the tall, unpainted house, with weather-curled boards; naked as a tower, the crook-backed ash seedlings where the dishcloths hung to dry; the gaunt, molting turkeys picking up refuse about the kitchen door.

Thinking About the Story

In considering the ideas within Willa Cather's story, it is useful to first think about forms of art (for example, music, painting, film) and then reflect upon art's purposes, namely: Why does art exist? For whose benefit is it created? What does it reveal about the society in which it was produced and the society it is later shown in? Spend a few minutes reviewing these questions, and formulating responses, before moving onto the questions and activities below. You may also find it productive to compare and contrast "A Wagner Matinee" with Edgar Allan Poe's "The Man of the Crowd" and James Joyce's "Araby." In particular, you should examine how each writer depicts modernity and civilization and come to some conclusions on each author's treatment of these notions in his or her story.

Discussion Questions

1. How old is Aunt Georgiana? What are the circumstances of her visit to Boston? Why does she warn Clark with the words: "Oh! dear boy, pray that whatever your sacrifice may be, it be not that"?

2. Underline the physical descriptions of Aunt Georgiana. In what ways do the descriptions reveal Aunt Georgiana's personality and behavior? Describe Clark's relationship with his aunt. How does he feel about her past in relation to how she is now?

3. In reference to the story, examine the relationship between the notions of "civilization" and "art" (in this case, music). How are these notions linked to both Nebraska and Boston? What role does Wagner's music play?

4. Define the conflicts facing both Aunt Georgiana and Clark. How does each character respond to the other's conflict?

5. Speculate on the reason(s) why Aunt Georgiana does not want to leave the concert. How does she feel about music? How has she changed over the course of the story?

Activities

1. Choose your favorite part of the story and rewrite it from Aunt Georgiana's point of view. You may choose the first- or third-person.

2. Locate a piece of Richard Wagner's music; be sure to cite its title in your notebook. After listening, write a one page emotional and/or intellectual response to the piece.

3. Compile research on nineteenth-century women's lives in Nebraska. Use the Internet or visit your local library to assist you. Possible topics could include: historical events, landscape and farming, family life, and courting rituals. Next, assemble the research into a ten-minute class presentation. This can be in the form of a handout, a talk, or a PowerPoint presentation.

James Joyce

A nation is the same people living in the same place.
James Joyce — *Ulysses* (1922)

James Joyce (1882–1941) was one of the most significant and innovative writers of his day. He was born in Dublin to strict Catholic parents and grew up in a tumultuous and politically charged Ireland, a country that at the time sought independence from Britain. As a child, he studied at a Jesuit school and then on scholarship he continued his education at Belvedere College and University College Dublin. Though a talented writer, he moved in 1903 to Paris to study medicine. Financial hardship meant he soon left the college; however, during this period he developed his concept of the epiphany: a sudden realization of the self or the social situation. On his return to Ireland a year later, he met Nora Barnacle, a woman with whom he enjoyed a long relationship and subsequent marriage in 1931. The couple and their two children lived in Zurich, Trieste, and Paris. In 1940 they moved back to Zurich, but the following year Joyce suffered a perforated ulcer and soon died in hospital of surgical complications.

In the first decades of the twentieth century Joyce became a central figure in the rise of Modernist literature, a form of writing often associated with pessimism, fragmentation, and explorations of the mundane. Although these themes regularly occur in Joyce's oeuvre, his realist prose later shifts to a language-focused style, which could best be described as stream of consciousness. In particular, this inclination is seen in *Ulysses* (1922) and *Finnegans Wake* (1939). "Araby" is part of Joyce's short story collection *Dubliners* (1914) and fits into his early realist mode, displaying working-class drudgery and vivid details of urban Dublin life. On the sentence level, the story contains accurate evocations of a boy's mind. The reader is drawn into the obsessions of first love, the boundaries of childish frustration, and a quest for the exotic. Within a few thousand words, Joyce manages to convey the intricacies of adolescent drama in a manner imbibed with youthful enthusiasm and mature pathos. The resolution of this classic coming-of-age narrative culminates in a Joycean epiphany that surprises and invites heady discussion.

Araby

James Joyce

North Richmond Street, being blind, was a quiet street except at the hour when the Christian Brothers' School set the boys free. An uninhabited house of two storeys stood at the blind end, detached from its neighbours in a square ground. The other houses of the street, conscious of decent lives within them, gazed at one another with brown imperturbable faces.

The former tenant of our house, a priest, had died in the back drawing-room. Air, musty from having been long enclosed, hung in all the rooms, and the waste room behind the kitchen was littered with old useless papers. Among these I found a few paper-covered books, the pages of which were curled and damp: *The Abbot*, by Walter Scott, *The Devout Communicant*, and *The Memoirs of Vidocq*. I liked the last best because its leaves were yellow. The wild garden behind the house contained a central apple-tree and a few straggling bushes, under one of which I found the late tenant's rusty bicycle-pump. He had been a very charitable priest; in his will he had left all his money to institutions and the furniture of his house to his sister.

When the short days of winter came, dusk fell before we had well eaten our dinners. When we met in the street the houses had grown sombre. The space of sky above us was the colour of ever-changing violet and towards it the lamps of the street lifted their feeble lanterns. The cold air stung us and we played till our bodies glowed. Our shouts echoed in the silent street. The career of our play brought us through the dark muddy lanes behind the houses, where we ran the gauntlet of the rough tribes from the cottages, to the back doors of the dark dripping gardens where odours arose from the ashpits, to the dark odorous stables where a coachman smoothed and combed the horse or shook music from the buckled harness. When we returned to the street, light from the kitchen windows had filled the areas. If my uncle was seen turning the corner, we hid in the shadow until we had seen him safely housed. Or if Mangan's sister came out on the doorstep to call her brother in to his tea, we watched her from our shadow peer up and down the street. We waited to see whether she would remain or go in and, if she remained, we left our shadow and walked up to Mangan's steps resignedly. She was waiting for us, her figure defined by the light from the half-opened door. Her brother always teased her before he obeyed, and I stood by the railings looking at her. Her dress swung as she moved her body, and the soft rope of her hair tossed from side to side.

Every morning I lay on the floor in the front parlour watching her door. The blind was pulled down to within an inch of the sash so that I could not be seen. When she came out on the doorstep my heart leaped. I ran to the hall, seized my books and followed her. I kept her brown figure always in my eye and, when we came near the point at which our ways diverged, I quickened my pace and passed her. This happened morning after morning. I had never spoken to her, except for a few casual words, and yet her name was like a summons to all my foolish blood.

Her image accompanied me even in places the most hostile to romance. On Saturday evenings when my aunt went marketing I had to go to carry some of the parcels. We walked through the flaring streets, jostled by drunken men and bargaining women, amid the curses of labourers, the shrill litanies of shop-boys who stood on guard by the barrels of pigs' cheeks, the nasal chanting of street-singers, who sang a *come-all-you* about O'Donovan Rossa, or a ballad about the troubles in our native land. These noises converged in a single sensation of life for me: I imagined that I bore my chalice safely through a throng of foes. Her name sprang to my lips at moments in strange prayers and praises which I myself did not understand. My eyes were often full of tears (I could not tell why) and at times a flood from my heart seemed to pour itself out into my bosom. I thought little of the future. I did not know whether I would ever speak to her or not or, if I spoke to her, how I could tell her of my confused adoration. But my body was like a harp and her words and gestures were like fingers running upon the wires.

One evening I went into the back drawing-room in which the priest had died. It was a dark rainy evening and there was no sound in the house. Through one of the broken panes I heard the rain impinge upon the earth, the fine incessant needles of water playing in the sodden beds. Some distant lamp or lighted window gleamed below me. I was thankful that I could see so little. All my senses seemed to desire to veil themselves and, feeling that I was about to slip from them, I pressed the palms of my hands together until they trembled, murmuring: "*O love! O love!*" many times.

At last she spoke to me. When she addressed the first words to me I was so confused that I did not know what to answer. She asked me was I going to *Araby*. I forgot whether I answered yes or no. It would be a splendid bazaar; she said she would love to go.

"And why can't you?" I asked.

While she spoke she turned a silver bracelet round and round her wrist. She could not go, she said, because there would be a retreat that week in her convent. Her brother and two other boys were fighting for their caps, and I was alone at the railings. She held one of the spikes, bowing her head towards me. The light from the lamp opposite our door caught the white curve of her neck, lit up her hair that rested there and, falling, lit up the hand upon the railing. It fell over one side of her dress and caught the white border of a petticoat, just visible as she stood at ease.

"It's well for you," she said.

"If I go," I said, "I will bring you something."

What innumerable follies laid waste my waking and sleeping thoughts after that evening! I wished to annihilate the tedious intervening days. I chafed against the work of school. At night in my bedroom and by day in the classroom her image came between me and the page I strove to read. The syllables of the word *Araby* were called to me through the silence in which my soul luxuriated and cast an Eastern enchantment over me. I asked for leave to go to the bazaar on Saturday night. My aunt was surprised, and hoped it was not some Freemason affair. I answered few questions in class. I watched my master's face pass from amiability to sternness; he hoped I was not beginning to idle. I could not call my wandering thoughts together. I had hardly any patience with the serious work of life which, now that it stood between me and my desire, seemed to me child's play, ugly monotonous child's play.

On Saturday morning I reminded my uncle that I wished to go to the bazaar in the evening. He was fussing at the hallstand, looking for the hat-brush, and answered me curtly:

"Yes, boy, I know."

As he was in the hall I could not go into the front parlour and lie at the window. I felt the house in bad humour and walked slowly towards the school. The air was pitilessly raw and already my heart misgave me.

When I came home to dinner my uncle had not yet been home. Still it was early. I sat staring at the clock for some time and, when its ticking began to irritate me, I left the room. I mounted the staircase and gained the upper part of the house. The high, cold, empty, gloomy rooms liberated me and I went from room to room singing. From the front window I saw my companions playing below in the street. Their cries reached me weakened and indistinct and, leaning my forehead against the cool glass, I looked over at the dark house where she lived. I may have stood there for an hour, seeing nothing but the brown-clad figure cast by my imagination, touched discreetly by the lamplight at the curved neck, at the hand upon the railings and at the border below the dress.

When I came downstairs again I found Mrs. Mercer sitting at the fire. She was an old, garrulous woman, a pawnbroker's widow, who collected used stamps for some pious purpose. I had to endure the gossip of the tea-table. The meal was prolonged beyond an hour and still my uncle did not come. Mrs. Mercer stood up to go: she was sorry she couldn't wait any longer, but it was after eight o'clock and she did not like to be out late, as the night air was bad for her. When she had gone I began to walk up and down the room, clenching my fists. My aunt said:

"I'm afraid you may put off your bazaar for this night of Our Lord."

At nine o'clock I heard my uncle's latchkey in the hall door. I heard him talking to himself and heard the hallstand rocking when it had received the weight of his overcoat. I could interpret these signs. When he was midway through his dinner I asked him to give me the money to go to the bazaar. He had forgotten.

"The people are in bed and after their first sleep now," he said.

I did not smile. My aunt said to him energetically:

"Can't you give him the money and let him go? You've kept him late enough as it is."

My uncle said he was very sorry he had forgotten. He said he believed in the old saying: "All work and no play makes Jack a dull boy." He asked me where I was going and, when I told him a second time, he asked me did I know *The Arab's Farewell to his Steed*. When I left the kitchen he was about to recite the opening lines of the piece to my aunt.

I held a florin tightly in my hand as I strode down Buckingham Street towards the station. The sight of the streets thronged with buyers and glaring with gas recalled to me the purpose of my journey. I took my seat in a third-class carriage of a deserted train. After an intolerable delay the train moved out of the station slowly. It crept onward among ruinous houses and over the twinkling river. At Westland Row Station a crowd of people pressed to the carriage doors; but the porters moved them back, saying that it was a special train for the bazaar. I remained alone in the bare carriage. In a few minutes the train drew up beside an improvised wooden platform. I passed out on to the road and saw by the lighted dial of a clock that it was ten minutes to ten. In front of me was a large building which displayed the magical name.

I could not find any sixpenny entrance and, fearing that the bazaar would be closed, I passed in quickly through a turnstile, handing a shilling to a weary-looking man. I found myself in a big hall girded at half its height by a gallery. Nearly all the stalls were closed and the greater part of the hall was in darkness. I recognized a silence like that which pervades a church after a service. I walked into the centre of the bazaar timidly. A few people were gathered about the stalls which were still open. Before a curtain, over which the words *Café Chantant* were written in coloured lamps, two men were counting money on a salver. I listened to the fall of the coins.

Remembering with difficulty why I had come, I went over to one of the stalls and examined porcelain vases and flowered tea-sets. At the door of the stall a young lady was talking and laughing with two young gentlemen. I remarked their English accents and listened vaguely to their conversation.

"O, I never said such a thing!"

"O, but you did!"

"O, but I didn't!"

"Didn't she say that?"

"Yes. I heard her."

"O, there's a . . . fib!"

Observing me, the young lady came over and asked me did I wish to buy anything. The tone of her voice was not encouraging; she seemed to have spoken to me out of a sense of duty. I looked humbly at the great jars that stood like eastern guards at either side of the dark entrance to the stall and murmured:

"No, thank you."

The young lady changed the position of one of the vases and went back to the two young men. They began to talk of the same subject. Once or twice the young lady glanced at me over her shoulder.

I lingered before her stall, though I knew my stay was useless, to make my interest in her wares seem the more real. Then I turned away slowly and walked down the middle of the bazaar. I allowed the two pennies to fall against the sixpence in my pocket. I heard a voice call from one end of the gallery that the light was out. The upper part of the hall was now completely dark.

Gazing up into the darkness I saw myself as a creature driven and derided by vanity; and my eyes burned with anguish and anger.

Thinking About the Story

In his story, James Joyce sets up a fictionalized picture of his early life in Dublin. This rendering provides a context for the narrator—existing at some point in the future—to reflect back upon his childhood. Accordingly, one useful manner in which to view the story is as a classic coming-of-age narrative. The period of adolescence, the transitional period between childhood and adulthood is a rich area in literary history. For you, what do you consider special about this point in life? What conflicts do teenagers face? How does active decision making (often called "agency") relate to the construction of identity? To broaden the scope of your answers, factor in Sarah Orne Jewett's "A White Heron." Using gender differences as a starting point, assess each story's protagonist and his or her understanding of the complications of love and desire.

Discussion Questions

1. Consider how the story being in the past tense and in the first-person point of view affects your reading of the narrative. If either of these variables were changed, what would be the result?

2. How do the boy's descriptions of his Dublin neighborhood contrast against his later experiences at the bazaar? What can you deduce about the kind of house and the type of neighborhood the boy lives in?

3. Why do you think the narrator lives with his aunt and uncle? Do these circumstances change your understanding of the boy? Further evaluate the role of absence, including death, in the story.

4. Assess the roles of the female characters in the story. What are your feelings about the boy's relationship with his aunt? What connections can be made between Mangan's sister and the woman at the bazaar?

5. Evaluate the following line and consider the repercussions it has for the rest of the story: "Gazing up into the darkness I saw myself as a creature driven and derided by vanity; and my eyes burned with anguish and anger." What is the boy's epiphany? Which other passages support your contention? Did the ending seem abrupt? If so, why did you feel that way?

Activities

1. Read again Joyce's details of urban Dublin life. What can you infer about the role of social class and gender at the beginning of the twentieth century?

2. Choose one line from the story that ably sums up each of the following characters:

   a. The boy (narrator).

   b. His uncle.

   c. His aunt.

   d. Mangan's sister.

   e. The woman at the bazaar.

3. Think of a time when you were in love or liked someone a great deal. Write a two to three page story fictionalizing that experience. Remember to include details of setting and character. As this is fiction, shape your recollections to give them a narrative arc, one that emphasizes drama and epiphany.

H. P. Lovecraft

It is only the inferior thinker who hastens to explain the singular and the complex by the primitive shortcut of supernaturalism.
H. P. Lovecraft — "The Temple" (1925)

Howard Phillips Lovecraft (1890–1937) was a divergent and original voice in twentieth-century horror fiction. Yet his position in the canon is maligned by his personal affinities with racism and anti-Semitism. Born in Providence, Rhode Island, Lovecraft, at age three, saw his father hospitalized for syphilis-induced psychosis and paranoia. Raised by his mother and other relatives living in the house, the family's income eroded to a point of near-poverty, and Lovecraft, often sick, was kept home from school. An enthusiastic and creative boy, he read widely, especially Roman and Greek mythology, astronomy, and chemistry. He wrote on these subjects for local newspapers and published articles in several periodicals. Over his lifetime, he continued his work as an amateur journalist parallel to his fiction and ghostwriting work. His mother's death in 1921 left Lovecraft depressed. Soon after the funeral, he met Sonia Greene—a Russian Jew seven years his senior—and, despite his political views, the couple married two years later. By 1926, though, Lovecraft had left her and moved back to Providence, leading to their eventual divorce in 1929. Until his death of intestinal cancer in 1937, he lived in Rhode Island, carrying on lengthy correspondences with the writers Robert E. Howard and Robert Bloch.

Influenced by Edgar Allan Poe, Algernon Blackwood, and Lord Dunsany, Lovecraft reworked the Gothic and macabre writing of his forebears into a new, peculiar form that encompassed madness, isolation, and decay. His stories were published in pulp magazines like *Weird Tales* and *Amazing Stories*. Within his claustrophobic and lonely narratives, he formulated the mythologies later referred to as the "Cthulhu Mythos."

Often Lovecraft returned to squalid urban landscapes and pernicious cults, underworlds that contained characters who reflected his ideas of racial difference. Nevertheless, "The Outsider" (written in 1921; published in 1926) is a gloriously strange tale that questions the nature of childhood and its aftereffects. Questions of identity plague the story, drawing attention to the narrator's relationship with his interior and exterior worlds. The individual's estrangement from the outside is strikingly apparent to readers, as is the breakdown of his quest for acceptance into a dreamscape of nightmarish madness.

The Outsider

H. P. Lovecraft

Unhappy is he to whom the memories of childhood bring only fear and sadness. Wretched is he who looks back upon lone hours in vast and dismal chambers with brown hangings and maddening rows of antique books, or upon awed watches in twilight groves of grotesque, gigantic, and vine-encumbered trees that silently wave twisted branches far aloft. Such a lot the gods gave to me—to me, the dazed, the disappointed; the barren, the broken. And yet I am strangely content and cling desperately to those sere memories, when my mind momentarily threatens to reach beyond to *the other*.

I know not where I was born, save that the castle was infinitely old and infinitely horrible, full of dark passages and having high ceilings where the eye could find only cobwebs and shadows. The stones in the crumbling corridors seemed always hideously damp, and there was an accursed smell everywhere, as of the piled-up corpses of dead generations. It was never light, so that I used sometimes to light candles and gaze steadily at them for relief, nor was there any sun outdoors, since the terrible trees grew high above the topmost accessible tower. There was one black tower which reached above the trees into the unknown outer sky, but that was partly ruined and could not be ascended save by a well-nigh impossible climb up the sheer wall, stone by stone.

I must have lived years in this place, but I cannot measure the time. Beings must have cared for my needs, yet I cannot recall any person except myself, or anything alive but the noiseless rats and bats and spiders. I think that whoever nursed me must have been shockingly aged, since my first conception of a living person was that of somebody mockingly like myself, yet distorted, shrivelled, and decaying like the castle. To me there was nothing grotesque in the bones and skeletons that strewed some of the stone crypts deep down among the foundations. I fantastically associated these things with everyday events, and thought them more natural than the coloured pictures of living beings which I found in many of the mouldy books. From such books I learned all that I know. No teacher urged or guided me, and I do not recall hearing any human voice in all those years—not even my own; for although I had read of speech, I had never thought to try to speak aloud. My aspect was a matter equally unthought of, for there were no mirrors in the castle, and I merely regarded myself by instinct as akin to the youthful figures I saw drawn and painted in the books. I felt conscious of youth because I remembered so little.

Outside, across the putrid moat and under the dark mute trees, I would often lie and dream for hours about what I read in the books; and would longingly picture myself amidst gay crowds in the sunny world beyond the endless forests. Once I tried to escape from the forest, but as I went farther from the castle the shade grew denser and the air more filled with brooding fear; so that I ran frantically back lest I lose my way in a labyrinth of nighted silence.

So through endless twilights I dreamed and waited, though I knew not what I waited for. Then in the shadowy solitude my longing for light grew so frantic that I could rest no more, and I lifted entreating hands to the single black ruined tower that reached above the forest into the unknown outer sky. And at last I resolved to scale that tower, fall though I might; since it were better to glimpse the sky and perish, than to live without ever beholding day.

In the dank twilight I climbed the worn and aged stone stairs till I reached the level where they ceased, and thereafter clung perilously to small footholds leading upward. Ghastly and terrible was that dead, stairless cylinder of rock; black, ruined, and deserted, and sinister with startled bats whose wings made no noise. But more ghastly and terrible still was the slowness of my progress; for climb as I might, the darkness overhead grew no thinner, and a new chill as of haunted and venerable mould assailed me. I shivered as I wondered why I did not reach the light, and would have looked down had I dared. I fancied that night had come suddenly upon me, and vainly groped with one free hand for a window embrasure, that I might peer out and above, and try to judge the height I had once attained.

All at once, after an infinity of awesome, sightless, crawling up that concave and desperate precipice, I felt my head touch a solid thing, and I knew I must have gained the roof, or at least some kind of floor. In the darkness I raised my free hand and tested the barrier, finding it stone and immovable. Then came a deadly circuit of the tower, clinging to whatever holds the slimy wall could give; till finally my testing hand found the barrier yielding, and I turned upward again, pushing the slab or door with my head as I used both hands in my fearful ascent. There was no light revealed above, and as my hands went higher I knew that my climb was for the nonce ended; since the slab was the trapdoor of an aperture leading to a level stone surface of greater circumference than the lower tower, no doubt the floor of some lofty and capacious observation chamber. I crawled through carefully, and tried to prevent the heavy slab from falling back into place, but failed in the latter attempt. As I lay exhausted on the stone floor I heard the eerie echoes of its fall, hoped when necessary to pry it up again.

Believing I was now at prodigious height, far above the accursed branches of the wood, I dragged myself up from the floor and fumbled about for windows, that I might look for the first time upon the sky, and the moon and stars of which I had read. But on every hand I was disappointed; since all that I found were vast shelves of marble, bearing odious oblong boxes of disturbing size. More and more I reflected, and wondered what hoary secrets might abide in this high apartment so many aeons cut off from the castle below. Then unexpectedly my hands came upon a doorway, where hung a portal of stone, rough with strange chiselling. Trying it, I found it locked; but with a supreme burst of strength I overcame all obstacles and dragged it open inward. As I did so there came to me the purest ecstasy I have ever known; for shining tranquilly through an ornate grating of iron, and down a short stone passageway of steps that ascended from the newly found doorway, was the radiant full moon, which I had never before seen save in dreams and in vague visions I dared not call memories.

Fancying now that I had attained the very pinnacle of the castle, I commenced to rush up the few steps beyond the door; but the sudden veiling of the moon by a cloud caused me to stumble, and I felt my way more slowly in the dark. It was still very dark when I reached the grating—which I tried carefully and found unlocked, but which I did not open for fear of falling from the amazing height to which I had climbed. Then the moon came out.

Most demoniacal of all shocks is that of the abysmally unexpected and grotesquely unbelievable. Nothing I had before undergone could compare in terror with what I now saw; with the bizarre marvels that sight implied. The sight itself was as simple as it was stupefying, for it was merely this: instead of a dizzying prospect of treetops seen from a lofty eminence, there stretched around me on the level through the grating nothing less than *the solid ground,* decked and diversified by marble slabs and columns, and overshadowed by an ancient stone church, whose ruined spire gleamed spectrally in the moonlight.

Half unconscious, I opened the grating and staggered out upon the white gravel path that stretched away in two directions. My mind, stunned and chaotic as it was, still held the frantic craving for light; and not even the fantastic wonder which had happened could stay my course. I neither knew nor cared whether my experience was insanity, dreaming, or magic; but was determined to gaze on brilliance and gaiety at any cost. I knew not who I was or what I was, or what my surroundings might be; though as I continued to stumble along I became conscious of a kind of fearsome latent memory that made my progress not wholly fortuitous. I passed under an arch out of that region of slabs and columns, and wandered through the open country; sometimes following the visible road, but sometimes leaving it curiously to tread across meadows where only occasional ruins bespoke the ancient presence of a forgotten road. Once I swam across a swift river where crumbling, mossy masonry told of a bridge long vanished.

Over two hours must have passed before I reached what seemed to be my goal, a venerable ivied castle in a thickly wooded park, maddeningly familiar, yet full of perplexing strangeness to me. I saw that the moat was filled in, and that some of the well-known towers were demolished, whilst new wings existed to confuse the beholder. But what I observed with chief interest and delight were the open windows—gorgeously ablaze with light and sending forth sound of the gayest revelry. Advancing to one of these I looked in and saw an oddly dressed company indeed; making merry, and speaking brightly to one another. I had never, seemingly, heard human speech before and could guess only vaguely what was said. Some of the faces seemed to hold expressions that brought up incredibly remote recollections, others were utterly alien.

I now stepped through the low window into the brilliantly lighted room, stepping as I did so from my single bright moment of hope to my blackest convulsion of despair and realization. The nightmare was quick to come, for as I entered, there occurred immediately one of the most terrifying demonstrations I had ever conceived. Scarcely had I crossed the sill when there descended upon the whole company a sudden and unheralded fear of hideous intensity, distorting every face and evoking the most horrible screams from nearly every throat. Flight was universal, and in the clamour and panic several fell in a swoon and were dragged away by their madly fleeing companions. Many covered their eyes with their hands, and plunged blindly and awkwardly in their race to escape, overturning furniture and stumbling against the walls before they managed to reach one of the many doors.

The cries were shocking; and as I stood in the brilliant apartment alone and dazed, listening to their vanishing echoes, I trembled at the thought of what might be lurking near me unseen. At a casual inspection the room seemed deserted, but when I moved towards one of the alcoves I thought I detected a presence there—a hint of motion beyond the golden-arched doorway leading to another and somewhat similar room. As I approached the arch I began to perceive the presence more clearly; and then, with the first and last sound I ever uttered—a ghastly ululation that revolted me almost as poignantly as its noxious cause—I beheld in full, frightful vividness the inconceivable, indescribable, and unmentionable monstrosity which had by its simple appearance changed a merry company to a herd of delirious fugitives.

I cannot even hint what it was like, for it was a compound of all that is unclean, uncanny, unwelcome, abnormal, and detestable. It was the ghoulish shade of decay, antiquity, and dissolution; the putrid, dripping eidolon of unwholesome revelation, the awful baring of that which the merciful earth should always hide. God knows it was not of this world—or no longer of this world—yet to my horror I saw in its eaten-away and bone-revealing outlines a leering, abhorrent travesty on the human shape; and in its mouldy, disintegrating apparel an unspeakable quality that chilled me even more.

I was almost paralysed, but not too much so to make a feeble effort towards flight; a backward stumble which failed to break the spell in which the nameless, voiceless monster held me. My eyes bewitched by the glassy orbs which stared loathsomely into them, refused to close; though they were mercifully blurred, and showed the terrible object but indistinctly after the first shock. I tried to raise my hand to shut out the sight, yet so stunned were my nerves that my arm could not fully obey my will. The attempt, however, was enough to disturb my balance; so that I had to stagger forward several steps to avoid falling. As I did so I became suddenly and agonizingly aware of the *nearness* of the carrion thing, whose hideous hollow breathing I half fancied I could hear. Nearly mad, I found myself yet able to throw out a hand to ward off the foetid apparition which pressed so close; when in one cataclysmic second of cosmic nightmarishness and hellish accident *my fingers touched the rotting outstretched paw of the monster beneath the golden arch.*

I did not shriek, but all the fiendish ghouls that ride the nightwind shrieked for me as in that same second there crashed down upon my mind a single fleeting avalanche of soul-annihilating memory. I knew in that second all that had been; I remembered beyond the frightful castle and the trees, and recognized the altered edifice in which I now stood; I recognized, most terrible of all, the unholy abomination that stood leering before me as I withdrew my sullied fingers from its own.

But in the cosmos there is balm as well as bitterness, and that balm is nepenthe. In the supreme horror of that second I forgot what had horrified me, and the burst of black memory vanished in a chaos of echoing images. In a dream I fled from that haunted and accursed pile, and ran swiftly and silently in the moonlight. When I returned to the churchyard place of marble and went down the steps I found the stone trap-door immovable; but I was not sorry, for I had hated the antique castle and the trees. Now I ride with the mocking and friendly ghouls on the night-wind, and play by day amongst the catacombs of Nephren-Ka in the sealed and unknown valley of Hadoth by the Nile. I know that light is not for me, save that of the moon over the rock tombs of Neb, nor any gaiety save the unnamed feasts of Nitokris beneath the Great Pyramid; yet in my new wildness and freedom I almost welcome the bitterness of alienage.

For although nepenthe has calmed me, I know always that I am an outsider; a stranger in this century and among those who are still men. This I have known ever since I stretched out my fingers to the abomination within that great gilded frame; stretched out my fingers and touched *a cold and unyielding surface of polished glass.*

Thinking About the Story

H. P. Lovecraft's story explores the complexities of identity loss and memory in a strange, Gothic landscape. He achieves this complexity through vivid, yet occasionally melodramatic prose that builds to create terrifying imagery. You should analyze why there is this insistence upon the visual in the story. Indeed, you can investigate the specific instances of narratorial confusion and draw out the psychological aspects of the distorted self. In addition, you will find it helpful to position the story within a genre framework: Do you view it as a piece of horror or fantastical fiction? Or as a narrative of psychological terror? To follow these latter thematic avenues of obsession and madness read "The Outsider" in conjunction Edgar Allan Poe's "The Man of the Crowd," and evaluate how each story handles these themes.

Discussion Questions

1. In your opinion, *who* or *what* is the narrator? How does the story's first paragraph relate to the narrator's identity? How do you understand the line: "And yet I am strangely content and cling desperately to those sere memories, when my mind momentarily threatens to reach beyond to the other"?

2. How do you interpret the title of the story? In which scenes could you apply the title to the action and events of the story?

3. Identity archetypal images within the story. Are these features of the Gothic? How does your understanding of the Gothic pertain to this story?

4. In what regard is the setting important in establishing the tone and atmosphere of the story?

5. How does the narrator truly feel about "the bitterness of alienage"? How does this relate to your understanding of the story's end? How could the mirror scene be interpreted?

Activities

1. Write a few paragraphs that continue the story. What happens next to the narrator?
2. Facing a mirror write a long descriptive passage of what you can see. In essence, create a written self-portrait.
3. Draw a picture of what you think the narrator looks like. Don't worry too much about your artistic skills. Instead, focus on the details you can glean from the story and how you present them visually. Lastly, write a page to explain your depiction of the narrator.

F. Scott Fitzgerald

Show me a hero and I'll write you a tragedy.
F. Scott Fitzgerald — *The Crack-Up* (1945)

Francis Scott Fitzgerald (1896–1940) was one of the great literary talents of the twentieth century. Born in St. Paul, Minnesota, Fitzgerald was the third child of his parents (the other two died as infants). He attended a Catholic boys' school before entering Princeton in 1913 as an English major. A poor student, he left in 1917 for military training; however, the First World War ended before he could actively serve. The next year he met Zelda Sayre at a dance in her hometown of Montgomery, Alabama. The couple had a tumultuous engagement, often disrupted by Zelda's insistence on Fitzgerald achieving success. With the financial income from his first novel, *This Side of Paradise* (1920), the two of them married, and the following year they had a daughter. Over the subsequent decade, Fitzgerald's so-called "Jazz Era," the couple became celebrities, living in New York and Paris. After returning from France, they moved to a mansion in Delaware. Here, Zelda studied ballet. Her training took them back to Paris; however, she had a physical breakdown. By 1936, Fitzgerald was debt-ridden and suffering from alcoholism. After a short stint in Hollywood and a relationship with a film columnist, Fitzgerald later died from a heart attack.

Inside a copy of *Princeton Alumni Weekly* are Fitzgerald's last scribbled words: "Good prose." This phrase, aimed at a football article, is useful in understanding the majesty of his ability. A contemporary of James Joyce and Ernest Hemingway, Fitzgerald was a language stylist of the highest caliber. Moreover, although he was a competent screenwriter and playwright, Fitzgerald's talents only fully emerged in his fiction. In both his short stories and his novels, such as *The Great Gatsby* (1925), and

Tender is the Night (1934), exquisite descriptions are coupled with elegiac writing. His lyrical impulses are often tinged with nostalgia, a literary memory of how he wanted things to be. In "Winter Dreams" (1922), as in *The Great Gatsby*, there is a sense of longing for the past. The story points to transcendence: the escape of lower-class origins for the world of the rich and the elite. Fitzgerald embodies this American ideal in Dexter Green, a protagonist mired by his blighted relationship with Judy Jones.

Winter Dreams

F. Scott Fitzgerald

I

Some of the caddies were poor as sin and lived in one-room houses with a neurasthenic cow in the front yard, but Dexter Green's father owned the second best grocery-store in Black Bear—the best one was "The Hub," patronized by the wealthy people from Sherry Island—and Dexter caddied only for pocket-money.

In the fall when the days became crisp and gray, and the long Minnesota winter shut down like the white lid of a box, Dexter's skis moved over the snow that hid the fairways of the golf course. At these times the country gave him a feeling of profound melancholy—it offended him that the links should lie in enforced fallowness, haunted by ragged sparrows for the long season. It was dreary, too, that on the tees where the gay colors fluttered in summer there were now only the desolate sand-boxes knee-deep in crusted ice. When he crossed the hills the wind blew cold as misery, and if the sun was out he tramped with his eyes squinted up against the hard dimensionless glare.

In April the winter ceased abruptly. The snow ran down into Black Bear Lake scarcely tarrying for the early golfers to brave the season with red and black balls. Without elation, without an interval of moist glory, the cold was gone.

Dexter knew that there was something dismal about this Northern spring, just as he knew there was something gorgeous about the fall. Fall made him clinch his hands and tremble and repeat idiotic sentences to himself, and make brisk abrupt gestures of command to imaginary audiences and armies. October filled him with hope which November raised to a sort of ecstatic triumph, and in this mood the fleeting brilliant impressions of the summer at Sherry Island were ready grist to his mill. He became a golf champion and defeated Mr. T. A. Hedrick in a marvelous match played a hundred times over the fairways of his imagination, a match each detail of which he changed about untiringly—sometimes he won with almost laughable ease, sometimes he came up magnificently from behind. Again, stepping from a Pierce-Arrow automobile, like Mr. Mortimer Jones, he strolled frigidly into the lounge of the Sherry Island Golf Club—or perhaps, surrounded by an admiring crowd, he gave an exhibition of fancy diving from the spring-board of the club raft. Among those who watched him in open-mouthed wonder was Mr. Mortimer Jones.

And one day it came to pass that Mr. Jones—himself and not his ghost—came up to Dexter with tears in his eyes and said that Dexter was the best caddy in the club, and wouldn't he decide not to quit if Mr. Jones made it worth his while, because every other caddy in the club lost one ball a hole for him regularly.

"No, sir," said Dexter decisively, "I don't want to caddy any more." Then, after a pause: "I'm too old."

"You're not more than fourteen. Why the devil did you decide just this morning that you wanted to quit? You promised that next week you'd go over to the State tournament with me."

"I decided I was too old."

Dexter handed in his "A Class" badge, collected what money was due him from the caddy master, and walked home to Black Bear Village.

"The best caddy I ever saw," shouted Mr. Mortimer Jones over a drink that afternoon. "Never lost a ball! Willing! Intelligent! Quiet! Honest! Grateful!"

The little girl who had done this was eleven—beautifully ugly as little girls are apt to be who are destined after a few years to be inexpressibly lovely and bring no end of misery to a great number of men. The spark, however, was perceptible. There was a general ungodliness in the way her lips twisted down at the corners when she smiled, and in the—Heaven help us!—in the almost passionate quality of her eyes. Vitality is born early in such women. It was utterly in evidence now, shining through her thin frame in a sort of glow.

She had come eagerly out on to the course at nine o'clock with a white linen nurse and five small new golf-clubs in a white canvas bag which the nurse was carrying. When Dexter first saw her she was standing by the caddy house, rather ill at ease and trying to conceal the fact by engaging her nurse in an obviously unnatural conversation graced by startling and irrelevant grimaces from herself.

"Well, it's certainly a nice day, Hilda," Dexter heard her say. She drew down the corners of her mouth, smiled, and glanced furtively around, her eyes in transit falling for an instant on Dexter.

Then to the nurse:

"Well, I guess there aren't very many people out here this morning, are there?"

The smile again—radiant, blatantly artificial—convincing.

"I don't know what we're supposed to do now," said the nurse, looking nowhere in particular.

"Oh, that's all right. I'll fix it up."

Dexter stood perfectly still, his mouth slightly ajar. He knew that if he moved forward a step his stare would be in her line of vision—if he moved backward he would lose his full view of her face. For a moment he had not realized how young she was. Now he remembered having seen her several times the year before in bloomers.

Suddenly, involuntarily, he laughed, a short abrupt laugh—then, startled by himself, he turned and began to walk quickly away.

"Boy!"

Dexter stopped.

"Boy—"

Beyond question he was addressed. Not only that, but he was treated to that absurd smile, that preposterous smile—the memory of which at least a dozen men were to carry into middle age.

"Boy, do you know where the golf teacher is?"

"He's giving a lesson."

"Well, do you know where the caddy-master is?"

"He isn't here yet this morning."

"Oh." For a moment this baffled her. She stood alternately on her right and left foot.

"We'd like to get a caddy," said the nurse. "Mrs. Mortimer Jones sent us out to play golf, and we don't know how without we get a caddy."

Here she was stopped by an ominous glance from Miss Jones, followed immediately by the smile.

"There aren't any caddies here except me," said Dexter to the nurse, "and I got to stay here in charge until the caddy-master gets here."

"Oh."

Miss Jones and her retinue now withdrew, and at a proper distance from Dexter became involved in a heated conversation, which was concluded by Miss Jones taking one of the clubs and hitting it on the ground with violence. For further emphasis she raised it again and was about to bring it down smartly upon the nurse's bosom, when the nurse seized the club and twisted it from her hands.

"You damn little mean old *thing!*" cried Miss Jones wildly.

Another argument ensued. Realizing that the elements of the comedy were implied in the scene, Dexter several times began to laugh, but each time restrained the laugh before it reached audibility. He could not resist the monstrous conviction that the little girl was justified in beating the nurse.

The situation was resolved by the fortuitous appearance of the caddy-master, who was appealed to immediately by the nurse.

"Miss Jones is to have a little caddy, and this one says he can't go."

"Mr. McKenna said I was to wait here till you came," said Dexter quickly.

"Well, he's here now." Miss Jones smiled cheerfully at the caddy-master. Then she dropped her bag and set off at a haughty mince toward the first tee.

"Well?" The caddy-master turned to Dexter. "What you standing there like a dummy for? Go pick up the young lady's clubs."

"I don't think I'll go out today," said Dexter.

"You don't—"

"I think I'll quit."

The enormity of his decision frightened him. He was a favorite caddy, and the thirty dollars a month he earned through the summer were not to be made elsewhere around the lake. But he had received a strong emotional shock, and his perturbation required a violent and immediate outlet.

It is not so simple as that, either. As so frequently would be the case in the future, Dexter was unconsciously dictated to by his winter dreams.

II

Now, of course, the quality and the seasonability of these winter dreams varied, but the stuff of them remained. They persuaded Dexter several years later to pass up a business course at the State university—his father, prospering now, would have paid his way—for the precarious advantage of attending an older and more famous university in the East, where he was bothered by his scanty funds. But do not get the impression, because his winter dreams happened to be concerned at first with musings on the rich, that there was anything merely snobbish in the boy. He wanted not association with glittering things and glittering people—he wanted the glittering things themselves. Often he reached out for the best without knowing why he wanted it—and sometimes he ran up against the mysterious denials and prohibitions in which life indulges. It is with one of those denials and not with his career as a whole that this story deals.

He made money. It was rather amazing. After college he went to the city from which Black Bear Lake draws its wealthy patrons. When he was only twenty-three and had been there not quite two years, there were already people who liked to say: "Now *there's* a boy—" All about him rich men's sons were peddling bonds precariously, or investing patrimonies precariously, or plodding through the two dozen volumes of the "George Washington Commercial Course," but Dexter borrowed a thousand dollars on his college degree and his confident mouth, and bought a partnership in a laundry.

It was a small laundry when he went into it but Dexter made a specialty of learning how the English washed fine woolen golf-stockings without shrinking them, and within a year he was catering to the trade that wore knickerbockers. Men were insisting that their Shetland hose and sweaters go to his laundry just as they had insisted on a caddy who could find golf balls. A little later he was doing their wives' lingerie as well—and running five branches in different parts of the city. Before he was twenty-seven he owned the largest string of laundries in his section of the country. It was then that he sold out and went to New York. But the part of his story that concerns us goes back to the days when he was making his first big success.

When he was twenty-three Mr. Hart—one of the gray-haired men who like to say, "Now there's a boy"—gave him a guest card to the Sherry Island Golf Club for a week-end. So he signed his name one day on the register, and that afternoon played golf in a foursome with Mr. Hart and Mr. Sandwood and Mr. T. A. Hedrick. He did not consider it necessary to remark that he had once carried Mr. Hart's bag over this same links, and that he knew every trap and gully with his eyes shut—but he found himself glancing at the four caddies who trailed them, trying to catch a gleam or gesture that would remind him of himself, that would lessen the gap which lay between his present and his past.

It was a curious day, slashed abruptly with fleeting, familiar impressions. One minute he had the sense of being a trespasser—in the next he was impressed by the tremendous superiority he felt toward Mr. T. A. Hedrick, who was a bore and not even a good golfer any more.

Then, because of a ball Mr. Hart lost near the fifteenth green, an enormous thing happened. While they were searching the stiff grasses of the rough there was a clear call of "Fore!" from behind a hill in their rear. And as they all turned abruptly from their search a bright new ball sliced abruptly over the hill and caught Mr. T. A. Hedrick in the abdomen.

"By Gad!" cried Mr. T. A. Hedrick, "they ought to put some of these crazy women off the course. It's getting to be outrageous."

A head and a voice came up together over the hill:

"Do you mind if we go through?"

"You hit me in the stomach!" declared Mr. Hedrick wildly.

"Did I?" The girl approached the group of men. "I'm sorry. I yelled, *Fore!*"

Her glance fell casually on each of the men—then scanned the fairway for her ball.

"Did I bounce into the rough?"

It was impossible to determine whether this question was ingenuous or malicious. In a moment, however, she left no doubt, for as her partner came up over the hill she called cheerfully:

"Here I am! I'd have gone on the green except that I hit something."

As she took her stance for a short mashie shot, Dexter looked at her closely. She wore a blue gingham dress, rimmed at throat and shoulders with a white edging that accentuated her tan. The quality of exaggeration, of thinness, which had made her passionate eyes and down-turning mouth absurd at eleven, was gone now. She was arrestingly beautiful. The color in her cheeks was centered like the color in a picture—it was not a "high" color, but a sort of fluctuating and feverish warmth, so shaded that it seemed at any moment it would recede and disappear. This color and the mobility of her mouth gave a continual impression of flux, of intense life, of passionate vitality—balanced only partially by the sad luxury of her eyes.

She swung her mashie impatiently and without interest, pitching the ball into a sand-pit on the other side of the green. With a quick, insincere smile and a careless "Thank you!" she went on after it.

"That Judy Jones!" remarked Mr. Hedrick on the next tee, as they waited—some moments—for her to play on ahead. "All she needs is to be turned up and spanked for six months and then to be married off to an old fashioned cavalry captain."

"My God, she's good-looking!" said Mr. Sandwood, who was just over thirty.

"Good-looking!" cried Mr. Hedrick contemptuously, "she always looks as if she wanted to be kissed! Turning those big cow-eyes on every calf in town!"

It was doubtful if Mr. Hedrick intended a reference to the maternal instinct.

"She'd play pretty good golf if she'd try," said Mr. Sandwood.

"She has no form," said Mr. Hedrick solemnly.

"She has a nice figure," said Mr. Sandwood.

"Better thank the Lord she doesn't drive a swifter ball," said Mr. Hart, winking at Dexter.

Later in the afternoon the sun went down with a riotous swirl of gold and varying blues and scarlets, and left the dry, rustling night of Western summer. Dexter watched from the veranda of the Golf Club, watched the even overlap of the waters in the little wind, silver molasses under the harvest-moon. Then the moon held a finger to her lips and the lake became a clear pool, pale and quiet. Dexter put on his bathing-suit and swam out to the farthest raft, where he stretched dripping on the wet canvas of the springboard.

There was a fish jumping and a star shining and the lights around the lake were gleaming. Over on a dark peninsula a piano was playing the songs of last summer and of summers before that—songs from "Chin-Chin" and "The Count of Luxemburg" and "The Chocolate Soldier"—and because the sound of a piano over a stretch of water had always seemed beautiful to Dexter he lay perfectly quiet and listened.

The tune the piano was playing at that moment had been gay and new five years before when Dexter was a sophomore at college. They had played it at a prom once when he could not afford the luxury of proms, and he had stood outside the gymnasium and listened. The sound of the tune precipitated in him a sort of ecstasy and it was with that ecstasy he viewed what happened to him now. It was a mood of intense appreciation, a sense that, for once, he was magnificently attune to life and that everything about him was radiating a brightness and a glamour he might never know again.

A low, pale oblong detached itself suddenly from the darkness of the Island, spitting forth the reverberate sound of a racing motor-boat. Two white streamers of cleft water rolled themselves out behind it and almost immediately the boat was beside him, drowning out the hot tinkle of the piano in the drone of its spray. Dexter raising himself on his arms was aware of a figure standing at the wheel, of two dark eyes regarding him over the lengthening space of water—then the boat had gone by and was sweeping in an immense and purposeless circle of spray round and round in the middle of the lake. With equal eccentricity one of the circles flattened out and headed back toward the raft.

"Who's that?" she called, shutting off her motor. She was so near now that Dexter could see her bathing-suit, which consisted apparently of pink rompers.

The nose of the boat bumped the raft, and as the latter tilted rakishly he was precipitated toward her. With different degrees of interest they recognized each other.

"Aren't you one of those men we played through this afternoon?" she demanded.

He was.

"Well, do you know how to drive a motor-boat? Because if you do I wish you'd drive this one so I can ride on the surf-board behind. My name is Judy Jones"—she favored him with an absurd smirk—rather, what tried to be a smirk, for, twist her mouth as she might, it was not grotesque, it was merely beautiful—"and I live in a house over there on the Island, and in that house there is a man waiting for me. When he drove up at the door I drove out of the dock because he says I'm his ideal."

There was a fish jumping and a star shining and the lights around the lake were gleaming. Dexter sat beside Judy Jones and she explained how her boat was driven. Then she was in the water, swimming to the floating surfboard with a sinuous crawl. Watching her was without effort to the eye, watching a branch waving or a sea-gull flying. Her arms, burned to butternut, moved sinuously among the dull platinum ripples, elbow appearing first, casting the forearm back with a cadence of falling water, then reaching out and down, stabbing a path ahead.

They moved out into the lake; turning, Dexter saw that she was kneeling on the low rear of the now uptilted surf-board.

"Go faster," she called, "fast as it'll go."

Obediently he jammed the lever forward and the white spray mounted at the bow. When he looked around again the girl was standing up on the rushing board, her arms spread wide, her eyes lifted toward the moon.

"It's awful cold," she shouted. "What's your name?"

He told her.

"Well, why don't you come to dinner tomorrow night?"

His heart turned over like the fly-wheel of the boat, and, for the second time, her casual whim gave a new direction to his life.

III

Next evening while he waited for her to come downstairs, Dexter peopled the soft deep summer room and the sun-porch that opened from it with the men who had already loved Judy Jones. He knew the sort of men they were—the men who when he first went to college had entered from the great prep schools with graceful clothes and the deep tan of healthy summers. He had seen that, in one sense, he was better than these men. He was newer and stronger. Yet in acknowledging to himself that he wished his children to be like them he was admitting that he was but the rough, strong stuff from which they eternally sprang.

When the time had come for him to wear good clothes, he had known who were the best tailors in America, and the best tailors in America had made him the suit he wore this evening. He had acquired that particular reserve peculiar to his university, that set it off from other universities. He recognized the value to him of such a mannerism and he had adopted it; he knew that to be careless in dress and manner required more confidence than to be careful. But carelessness was for his children. His mother's name had been Krimslich. She was a Bohemian of the peasant class and she had talked broken English to the end of her days. Her son must keep to the set patterns.

At a little after seven Judy Jones came downstairs. She wore a blue silk afternoon dress, and he was disappointed at first that she had not put on something more elaborate. This feeling was accentuated when, after a brief greeting, she went to the door of a butler's pantry and pushing it open called: "You can serve dinner, Martha." He had rather expected that a butler would announce dinner, that there would be a cocktail. Then he put these thoughts behind him as they sat down side by side on a lounge and looked at each other.

"Father and mother won't be here," she said thoughtfully.

He remembered the last time he had seen her father, and he was glad the parents were not to be here tonight—they might wonder who he was. He had been born in Keeble, a Minnesota village fifty miles farther north, and he always gave Keeble as his home instead of Black Bear Village. Country towns were well enough to come from if they weren't inconveniently in sight and used as footstools by fashionable lakes.

They talked of his university, which she had visited frequently during the past two years, and of the near-by city which supplied Sherry Island with its patrons, and whither Dexter would return next day to his prospering laundries.

During dinner she slipped into a moody depression which gave Dexter a feeling of uneasiness. Whatever petulance she uttered in her throaty voice worried him. Whatever she smiled at—at him, at a chicken liver, at nothing—it disturbed him that her smile could have no root in mirth, or even in amusement. When the scarlet corners of her lips curved down, it was less a smile than an invitation to a kiss.

Then, after dinner, she led him out on the dark sun-porch and deliberately changed the atmosphere.

"Do you mind if I weep a little?" she said.

"I'm afraid I'm boring you," he responded quickly.

"You're not. I like you. But I've just had a terrible afternoon. There was a man I cared about, and this afternoon he told me out of a clear sky that he was poor as a church-mouse. He'd never even hinted it before. Does this sound horribly mundane?"

"Perhaps he was afraid to tell you."

"Suppose he was," she answered. "He didn't start right. You see, if I'd thought of him as poor—well, I've been mad about loads of poor men, and fully intended to marry them all. But in this case, I hadn't thought of him that way, and my interest in him wasn't strong enough to survive the shock. As if a girl calmly informed her fiancé that she was a widow. He might not object to widows, but—

"Let's start right," she interrupted herself suddenly. "Who are you, anyhow?"

For a moment Dexter hesitated. Then:

"I'm nobody," he announced. "My career is largely a matter of futures."

"Are you poor?"

"No," he said frankly, "I'm probably making more money than any man my age in the Northwest. I know that's an obnoxious remark, but you advised me to start right."

There was a pause. Then she smiled and the corners of her mouth drooped and an almost imperceptible sway brought her closer to him, looking up into his eyes. A lump rose in Dexter's throat, and he waited breathless for the experiment, facing the unpredictable compound that would form mysteriously from the elements of their lips. Then he saw— she communicated her excitement to him, lavishly, deeply, with kisses that were not a promise but a fulfillment. They aroused in him not hunger demanding renewal but surfeit that would demand more surfeit kisses that were like charity, creating want by holding back nothing at all.

It did not take him many hours to decide that he had wanted Judy Jones ever since he was a proud, desirous little boy.

IV

It began like that—and continued, with varying shades of intensity, on such a note right up to the dénouement. Dexter surrendered a part of himself to the most direct and unprincipled personality with which he had ever come in contact. Whatever Judy wanted, she went after with the full pressure of her charm. There was no divergence of method, no jockeying for position or premeditation of effects—there was a very little mental side to any of her affairs. She simply made men conscious to the highest degree of her physical loveliness. Dexter had no desire to change her. Her deficiencies were knit up with a passionate energy that transcended and justified them.

When, as Judy's head lay against his shoulder that first night, she whispered, "I don't know what's the matter with me. Last night I thought I was in love with a man and tonight I think I'm in love with you."

It seemed to him a beautiful and romantic thing to say. It was the exquisite excitability that for the moment he controlled and owned. But a week later he was compelled to view this same quality in a different light. She took him in her roadster to a picnic supper, and after supper she disappeared, likewise in her roadster, with another man. Dexter became enormously upset and was scarcely able to be decently civil to the other people present. When she assured him that she had not kissed the other man, he knew she was lying—yet he was glad that she had taken the trouble to lie to him.

He was, as he found before the summer ended, one of a varying dozen who circulated about her. Each of them had at one time been favored above all others—about half of them still basked in the solace of occasional sentimental revivals. Whenever one showed signs of dropping out through long neglect, she granted him a brief honeyed hour, which encouraged him to tag along for a year or so longer. Judy made these forays upon the helpless and defeated without malice, indeed half unconscious that there was anything mischievous in what she did.

When a new man came to town every one dropped out—dates were automatically cancelled.

The helpless part of trying to do anything about it was that she did it all herself. She was not a girl who could be "won" in the kinetic sense—she was proof against cleverness, she was proof against charm; if any of these assailed her too strongly she would immediately resolve the affair to a physical basis, and under the magic of her physical splendor the strong as well as the brilliant played her game and not their own. She was entertained only by the gratification of her desires and by the direct exercise of her own charm. Perhaps from so much youthful love, so many youthful lovers, she had come, in self-defense, to nourish herself wholly from within.

Succeeding Dexter's first exhilaration came restlessness and dissatisfaction. The helpless ecstasy of losing himself in her was opiate rather than tonic. It was fortunate for his work during the winter that those moments of ecstasy came infrequently. Early in their acquaintance it had seemed for a while that there was a deep and spontaneous mutual attraction that first August, for example—three days of long evenings on her dusky veranda, of strange wan kisses through the late afternoon, in shadowy alcoves or behind the protecting trellises of the garden arbors, of mornings when she was fresh as a dream and almost shy at meeting him in the clarity of the rising day. There was all the ecstasy of an engagement about it, sharpened by his realization that there was no engagement.

It was during those three days that, for the first time, he had asked her to marry him. She said "maybe some day," she said "kiss me," she said "I'd like to marry you," she said "I love you." She said nothing.

The three days were interrupted by the arrival of a New York man who visited at her house for half September. To Dexter's agony, rumor engaged them. The man was the son of the president of a great trust company. But at the end of a month it was reported that Judy was yawning. At a dance one night she sat all evening in a motor-boat with a local beau, while the New Yorker searched the club for her frantically. She told the local beau that she was bored with her visitor, and two days later he left. She was seen with him at the station, and it was reported that he looked very mournful indeed.

On this note the summer ended. Dexter was twenty-four, and he found himself increasingly in a position to do as he wished. He joined two clubs in the city and lived at one of them. Though he was by no means an integral part of the stag-lines at these clubs, he managed to be on hand at dances where Judy Jones was likely to appear. He could have gone out socially as much as he liked—he was an eligible young man, now, and popular with down-town fathers. His confessed devotion to Judy Jones had rather solidified his position. But he had no social aspirations and rather despised the dancing men who were always on tap for the Thursday or Saturday parties and who filled in at dinners with the younger married set. Already he was playing with the idea of going East to New York. He wanted to take Judy Jones with him. No disillusion as to the world in which she had grown up could cure his illusion as to her desirability.

Remember that—for only in the light of it can what he did for her be understood.

Eighteen months after he first met Judy Jones he became engaged to another girl. Her name was Irene Scheerer, and her father was one of the men who had always believed in Dexter. Irene was light-haired and sweet and honorable, and a little stout, and she had two suitors whom she pleasantly relinquished when Dexter formally asked her to marry him.

Summer, fall, winter, spring, another summer, another fall—so much he had given of his active life to the incorrigible lips of Judy Jones. She had treated him with interest, with encouragement, with malice, with indifference, with contempt. She had inflicted on him the innumerable little slights and indignities possible in such a case—as if in revenge for having ever cared for him at all. She had beckoned him and yawned at him and beckoned him again and he had responded often with bitterness and narrowed eyes. She had brought him ecstatic happiness and intolerable agony of spirit. She had caused him untold inconvenience and not a little trouble. She had insulted him, and she had ridden over him, and she had played his interest in her against his interest in his work—for fun. She had done everything to him except to criticize him—this she had not done—it seemed to him only because it might have sullied the utter indifference she manifested and sincerely felt toward him.

When autumn had come and gone again it occurred to him that he could not have Judy Jones. He had to beat this into his mind but he convinced himself at last. He lay awake at night for a while and argued it over. He told himself the trouble and the pain she had caused him, he enumerated her glaring deficiencies as a wife. Then he said to himself that he loved her, and after a while he fell asleep. For a week, lest he imagined her husky voice over the telephone or her eyes opposite him at lunch, he worked hard and late, and at night he went to his office and plotted out his years.

At the end of a week he went to a dance and cut in on her once. For almost the first time since they had met he did not ask her to sit out with him or tell her that she was lovely. It hurt him that she did not miss these things—that was all. He was not jealous when he saw that there was a new man tonight. He had been hardened against jealousy long before.

He stayed late at the dance. He sat for an hour with Irene Scheerer and talked about books and about music. He knew very little about either. But he was beginning to be master of his own time now, and he had a rather priggish notion that he—the young and already fabulously successful Dexter Green—should know more about such things.

That was in October, when he was twenty-five. In January, Dexter and Irene became engaged. It was to be announced in June, and they were to be married three months later.

The Minnesota winter prolonged itself interminably, and it was almost May when the winds came soft and the snow ran down into Black Bear Lake at last. For the first time in over a year Dexter was enjoying a certain tranquility of spirit. Judy Jones had been in Florida, and afterward in Hot Springs, and somewhere she had been engaged, and somewhere she had broken it off. At first, when Dexter had definitely given her up, it had made him sad that people still linked them together and asked for news of her, but when he began to be placed at dinner next to Irene Scheerer people didn't ask him about her any more—they told him about her. He ceased to be an authority on her.

May at last. Dexter walked the streets at night when the darkness was damp as rain, wondering that so soon, with so little done, so much of ecstasy had gone from him. May one year back had been marked by Judy's poignant, unforgivable, yet forgiven turbulence—it had been one of those rare times when he fancied she had grown to care for him. That old penny's worth of happiness he had spent for this bushel of content. He knew that Irene would be no more than a curtain spread behind him, a hand moving among gleaming tea-cups, a voice calling to children. Fire and loveliness were gone, the magic of nights and the wonder of the varying hours and seasons, slender lips, down-turning, dropping to his lips and bearing him up into a heaven of eyes. The thing was deep in him. He was too strong and alive for it to die lightly.

In the middle of May when the weather balanced for a few days on the thin bridge that led to deep summer he turned in one night at Irene's house. Their engagement was to be announced in a week now—no one would be surprised at it. And tonight they would sit together on the lounge at the University Club and look on for an hour at the dancers. It gave him a sense of solidity to go with her—she was so sturdily popular, so intensely "great."

He mounted the steps of the brownstone house and stepped inside.

"Irene," he called.

Mrs. Scheerer came out of the living-room to meet him.

"Dexter," she said, "Irene's gone upstairs with a splitting headache. She wanted to go with you but I made her go to bed."

"Nothing serious, I—"

"Oh, no. She's going to play golf with you in the morning. You can spare her for just one night, can't you, Dexter?"

Her smile was kind. She and Dexter liked each other. In the living-room he talked for a moment before he said good-night.

Returning to the University Club, where he had rooms, he stood in the doorway for a moment and watched the dancers. He leaned against the door-post, nodded at a man or two—yawned.

"Hello, darling."

The familiar voice at his elbow startled him. Judy Jones had left a man and crossed the room to him—Judy Jones, a slender enamelled doll in cloth of gold: gold in a band at her head, gold in two slipper points at her dress's hem. The fragile glow of her face seemed to blossom as she smiled at him. A breeze of warmth and light blew through the room. His hands in the pockets of his dinner-jacket tightened spasmodically. He was filled with a sudden excitement.

"When did you get back?" he asked casually.

"Come here and I'll tell you about it."

She turned and he followed her. She had been away—he could have wept at the wonder of her return. She had passed through enchanted streets, doing things that were like provocative music. All mysterious happenings, all fresh and quickening hopes, had gone away with her, come back with her now.

She turned in the doorway.

"Have you a car here? If you haven't, I have."

"I have a Coupé."

In then, with a rustle of golden cloth. He slammed the door. Into so many cars she had stepped like this, like that, her back against the leather, so her elbow resting on the door, waiting. She would have been soiled long since had there been anything to soil her—except herself—but this was her own self outpouring.

With an effort he forced himself to start the car and back into the street. This was nothing, he must remember. She had done this before, and he had put her behind him, as he would have crossed a bad account from his books.

He drove slowly down-town and, affecting abstraction, traversed the deserted streets of the business section, peopled here and there where a movie was giving out its crowd or where consumptive or pugilistic youth lounged in front of pool halls. The clink of glasses and the slap of hands on the bars issued from saloons, cloisters of glazed glass and dirty yellow light.

She was watching him closely and the silence was embarrassing, yet in this crisis he could find no casual word with which to profane the hour. At a convenient turning he began to zigzag back toward the University Club.

"Have you missed me?" she asked suddenly.

"Everybody missed you."

He wondered if she knew of Irene Scheerer. She had been back only a day—her absence had been almost contemporaneous with his engagement.

"What a remark!" Judy laughed sadly—without sadness. She looked at him searchingly. He became absorbed in the dashboard.

"You're handsomer than you used to be," she said thoughtfully. "Dexter, you have the most rememberable eyes."

He could have laughed at this, but he did not laugh. It was the sort of thing that was said to sophomores. Yet it stabbed at him.

"I'm awfully tired of everything, darling." She called every one darling, endowing the endearment with careless, individual camaraderie. "I wish you'd marry me."

The directness of this confused him. He should have told her now that he was going to marry another girl, but he could not tell her. He could as easily have sworn that he had never loved her.

"I think we'd get along," she continued, on the same note, "unless probably you've forgotten me and fallen in love with another girl."

Her confidence was obviously enormous. She had said, in effect, that she found such a thing impossible to believe, that if it were true he had merely committed a childish indiscretion—and probably to show off. She would forgive him, because it was not a matter of any moment but rather something to be brushed aside lightly.

"Of course you could never love anybody but me," she continued. "I like the way you love me. Oh, Dexter, have you forgotten last year?"

"No, I haven't forgotten."

"Neither have I!"

Was she sincerely moved—or was she carried along by the wave of her own acting?

"I wish we could be like that again," she said, and he forced himself to answer:

"I don't think we can."

"I suppose not. I hear you're giving Irene Scheerer a violent rush."

There was not the faintest emphasis on the name, yet Dexter was suddenly ashamed.

"Oh, take me home," cried Judy suddenly; "I don't want to go back to that idiotic dance—with those children."

Then, as he turned up the street that led to the residence district, Judy began to cry quietly to herself. He had never seen her cry before.

The dark street lightened, the dwellings of the rich loomed up around them, he stopped his Coupé in front of the great white bulk of the Mortimer Joneses house, somnolent, gorgeous, drenched with the splendor of the damp moonlight. Its solidity startled him. The strong walls, the steel of the girders, the breadth and beam and pomp of it were there only to bring out the contrast with the young beauty beside him. It was sturdy to accentuate her slightness—as if to show what a breeze could be generated by a butterfly's wing.

He sat perfectly quiet, his nerves in wild clamor, afraid that if he moved he would find her irresistibly in his arms. Two tears had rolled down her wet face and trembled on her upper lip.

"I'm more beautiful than anybody else," she said brokenly, "why can't I be happy?" Her moist eyes tore at his stability—her mouth turned slowly downward with an exquisite sadness: "I'd like to marry you if you'll have me, Dexter. I suppose you think I'm not worth having, but I'll be so beautiful for you, Dexter."

A million phrases of anger, pride, passion, hatred, tenderness fought on his lips. Then a perfect wave of emotion washed over him, carrying off with it a sediment of wisdom, of convention, of doubt, of honor. This was his girl who was speaking, his own, his beautiful, his pride.

"Won't you come in?" He heard her draw in her breath sharply.

Waiting.

"All right," his voice was trembling, "I'll come in."

V

It was strange that neither when it was over nor a long time afterward did he regret that night. Looking at it from the perspective of ten years, the fact that Judy's flare for him endured just one month seemed of little importance. Nor did it matter that by his yielding he subjected himself to a deeper agony in the end and gave serious hurt to Irene Scheerer and to Irene's parents, who had befriended him. There was nothing sufficiently pictorial about Irene's grief to stamp itself on his mind.

Dexter was at bottom hard-minded. The attitude of the city on his action was of no importance to him, not because he was going to leave the city, but because any outside attitude on the situation seemed superficial. He was completely indifferent to popular opinion. Nor, when he had seen that it was no use, that he did not possess in himself the power to move fundamentally or to hold Judy Jones, did he bear any malice toward her. He loved her, and he would love her until the day he was too old for loving—but he could not have her. So he tasted the deep pain that is reserved only for the strong, just as he had tasted for a little while the deep happiness.

Even the ultimate falsity of the grounds upon which Judy terminated the engagement that she did not want to "take him away" from Irene—Judy, who had wanted nothing else—did not revolt him. He was beyond any revulsion or any amusement.

He went East in February with the intention of selling out his laundries and settling in New York—but the war came to America in March and changed his plans. He returned to the West, handed over the management of the business to his partner, and went into the first officers' training-camp in late April. He was one of those young thousands who greeted the war with a certain amount of relief, welcoming the liberation from webs of tangled emotion.

VI

This story is not his biography, remember, although things creep into it which have nothing to do with those dreams he had when he was young. We are almost done with them and with him now. There is only one more incident to be related here, and it happens seven years farther on.

It took place in New York, where he had done well—so well that there were no barriers too high for him. He was thirty-two years old, and, except for one flying trip immediately after the war, he had not been West in seven years. A man named Devlin from Detroit came into his office to see him in a business way, and then and there this incident occurred, and closed out, so to speak, this particular side of his life.

"So you're from the Middle West," said the man Devlin with careless curiosity. "That's funny—I thought men like you were probably born and raised on Wall Street. You know, the wife of one of my best friends in Detroit came from your city. I was an usher at the wedding."

Dexter waited with no apprehension of what was coming.

"Judy Simms," said Devlin with no particular interest; "Judy Jones she was once."

"Yes, I knew her." A dull impatience spread over him. He had heard, of course, that she was married—perhaps deliberately he had heard no more.

"Awfully nice girl," brooded Devlin meaninglessly, "I'm sort of sorry for her."

"Why?" Something in Dexter was alert, receptive, at once.

"Oh, Lud Simms has gone to pieces in a way. I don't mean he ill-uses her, but he drinks and runs around."

"Doesn't she run around?"

"No. Stays at home with her kids."

"Oh."

"She's a little too old for him," said Devlin.

"Too old!" cried Dexter. "Why, man, she's only twenty-seven."

He was possessed with a wild notion of rushing out into the streets and taking a train to Detroit. He rose to his feet spasmodically.

"I guess you're busy," Devlin apologized quickly. "I didn't realize—"

"No, I'm not busy," said Dexter, steadying his voice. "I'm not busy at all. Not busy at all. Did you say she was twenty-seven? No, I said she was twenty-seven."

"Yes, you did," agreed Devlin dryly.

"Go on, then. Go on."

"What do you mean?"

"About Judy Jones."

Devlin looked at him helplessly.

"Well, that's, I told you all there is to it. He treats her like the devil. Oh, they're not going to get divorced or anything. When he's particularly outrageous she forgives him. In fact, I'm inclined to think she loves him. She was a pretty girl when she first came to Detroit."

A pretty girl! The phrase struck Dexter as ludicrous.

"Isn't she—a pretty girl, anymore?"

"Oh, she's all right."

"Look here," said Dexter, sitting down suddenly, "I don't understand. You say she was a *pretty girl* and now you say she's *all right*. I don't understand what you mean. Judy Jones wasn't a pretty girl, at all. She was a great beauty. Why, I knew her, I knew her. She was—"

Devlin laughed pleasantly.

"I'm not trying to start a row," he said. "I think Judy's a nice girl and I like her. I can't understand how a man like Lud Simms could fall madly in love with her, but he did." Then he added: "Most of the women like her."

Dexter looked closely at Devlin, thinking wildly that there must be a reason for this, some insensitivity in the man or some private malice.

"Lots of women fade just like that," Devlin snapped his fingers. "You must have seen it happen. Perhaps I've forgotten how pretty she was at her wedding. I've seen her so much since then, you see. She has nice eyes."

A sort of dullness settled down upon Dexter. For the first time in his life he felt like getting very drunk. He knew that he was laughing loudly at something Devlin had said, but he did not know what it was or why it was funny. When, in a few minutes, Devlin went he lay down on his lounge and looked out the window at the New York sky-line into which the sun was sinking in dull lovely shades of pink and gold.

He had thought that having nothing else to lose he was invulnerable at last—but he knew that he had just lost something more, as surely as if he had married Judy Jones and seen her fade away before his eyes.

The dream was gone. Something had been taken from him. In a sort of panic he pushed the palms of his hands into his eyes and tried to bring up a picture of the waters lapping on Sherry Island and the moonlit veranda, and gingham on the golf-links and the dry sun and the gold color of her neck's soft down. And her mouth damp to his kisses and her eyes plaintive with melancholy and her freshness like new fine linen in the morning. Why, these things were no longer in the world! They had existed and they existed no longer.

For the first time in years the tears were streaming down his face. But they were for himself now. He did not care about mouth and eyes and moving hands. He wanted to care, and he could not care. For he had gone away and he could never go back any more. The gates were closed, the sun was gone down, and there was no beauty but the gray beauty of steel that withstands all time. Even the grief he could have borne was left behind in the country of illusion, of youth, of the richness of life, where his winter dreams had flourished.

"Long ago," he said, "long ago, there was something in me, but now that thing is gone. Now that thing is gone, that thing is gone. I cannot cry. I cannot care. That thing will come back no more."

Thinking About the Story

F. Scott Fitzgerald's story shares some of the themes of his novel *The Great Gatsby*. He prefigures both Jay Gatsby and Daisy Buchanan in Dexter Green and Judy Jones. Furthermore, both are narratives steeped in romantic possibility, featuring complicated relationships and social nuances that sully the outcome for all involved. If you have not read Fitzgerald's masterpiece, then you should determine what you think the themes of "Winter Dreams" are in isolation. After this, consider the following: What role does the past play in fiction? What is the relationship between nostalgia and sentimentality? How does Fitzgerald avoid the latter? In further analyzing "Winter Dreams," read again Anton Chekhov's "The Lady with the Dog." See if you can ascertain how each author uses his characters to examine lifestyles of the trivial and the significant—and then how this examination fits in with the rest of the story.

Discussion Questions

1. What are Dexter Green's "winter dreams"? How are they influenced by Dexter's love for Judy Jones? Speculate on why Fitzgerald chose "winter" and not one of the other seasons.
2. What are your thoughts on the story's narrative structure? How about the prose style? Does Fitzgerald's execution of these elements enhance your enjoyment of the story?
3. Compare and the contrast the lives, personalities, and behaviors of Judy Jones and Irene Scheerer. Does Judy's outlook on life change when she becomes an adult? What criteria does Judy use to find herself a husband?
4. Why does Dexter quit his caddying job? What does Dexter think about rich people? Do his views change over the story? How do you interpret the following quote: "Often he reached out for the best without knowing why he wanted it—and sometimes he ran up against the mysterious denials and prohibitions in which life indulges. It is with one of those denials and not with his career as a whole that this story deals"?
5. How do you interpret the end of the story? How would you describe the "thing" that is now "gone" from Dexter's life?"

Activities

1. Fitzgerald often uses alliteration (the repetition of a certain sound in a close series of words) in his writing. Underline some good examples

of this technique in the story. Next, write detailed responses to the following:

a. What are your thoughts on the pros and cons of alliteration?

b. Compose five of your own alliterative phrases or sentences.

2. Write your own short story, emulating "Winter Dreams." Include a hope or dream, a sport, and a flawed relationship that progresses throughout the story.

3. Locate and listen to a selection of 1920s jazz music; be sure to cite the pieces in your notebook. After listening, write a one page emotional and/or intellectual response to the music.

Robert E. Howard

I have not been a success, and probably never will be.
Robert E. Howard — *Letter to H. P. Lovecraft* (1933)

Early in the twentieth century, Robert Ervin Howard (1906–1936) made a lasting contribution to the strange and popular world of pulp fiction. Born in Peaster, Texas, Howard grew up as an only child and he spent much of his time reading. In his teens, his family moved to Cross Plains in central Texas. There he was bullied, so he took up bodybuilding and boxing to fend off unwanted attention. After high school, Howard briefly attended college, studying stenography at his father's expense. While writing and sending stories out for publication, Howard worked at a drugstore. In the late 1920s, Howard published dozens of stories and made a reasonable income from these sales. Due to this change in his fortunes, Howard quit his job and began to write full-time. He spent his spare-time watching sports, particularly boxing, and heavily corresponded with H. P. Lovecraft. In 1933, he met an old high school friend, Novalyne Price, and the two became romantically involved. Three years later, Howard committed suicide after hearing that his mother's tuberculosis was terminal. He was thirty years old.

In Howard's brief career he produced hundreds of stories, many of which were reprinted in book form several years after his death. The novel *Conan the Conqueror* (1950) started the resurgent interest in Howard's work. Over the following decades, dozens of short story collections were released. These books showcased the breadth, and also the variable quality, of Howard's genre output: western, fantasy, science fiction, gothic, detective, and adventure. Like his contemporary and friend, H. P. Lovecraft, many of Howard's stories first emerged in pulp magazines, like *Weird Tales, Argosy,* and *Cowboy Stories.* Within these pages are action-driven, masculine narratives that draw on—yet surpass in terms of directness and candor—his influences: Jack London, Rudyard Kipling, and Harold Lamb. The story "Circus Fists" (1931) is an adrenalin-fueled piece, filled with acts of physical strength and brutal violence. The brash, colloquial style with which Howard presents Sailor Steve Costigan invites and entertains: he is a drunkard and a fighter. Costigan is driven by his primitive passions and emotions; so much so, that his charm and courage demands the reader take his side.

Circus Fists

Robert E. Howard

Me and the Old Man had a most violent row whilst the *Sea Girl* was tied up at the docks of a small seaport on the West Coast. Somebody put a polecat in the Old Man's bunk, and he accused me of doing it. I denied it indignantly, and asked him where he reckoned I would get a polecat, and he said well, it was a cinch *somebody* had got a polecat, because there it was, and it was his opinion that I was the only man of the crew which was low-down enough to do a trick like that.

This irritated me, and I told him he oughta know it wasn't me, because I had the reputation of being kind to animals, and I wouldn't put a decent skunk where it would have to associate with a critter like the Old Man.

This made him so mad that he busted a bottle of good rye whiskey over my head. Annoyed at such wanton waste of good licker, I grabbed the old walrus and soused him in a horse-trough—us being on the docks at the time.

The Old Man ariz like Neptune from the deep, and, with whiskers dripping, he shook his fists at me and yelled, "Don't never darken my decks again, Steve Costigan. If you ever try to come aboard the *Sea Girl,* I'll fill you fulla buckshot, you mutineerin' pirate!"

"Go set on a marlin-spike," I sneered. "I wouldn't sail with you again for ten bucks a watch and plum duff every mess. I'm through with the sea, anyhow. You gimme a bad taste for the whole business. A landman's life is the life for me, by golly. Me and Mike is goin' to fare forth and win fame and fortune ashore."

And so saying, I swaggered away with my white bulldog, follered clean outa sight by the Old Man's sincere maledictions.

Casting about for amusement, I soon come onto a circus which was going full blast at the edge of town. I seen a side-show poster which said, *Battling Bingo, Champion of the West Coast*. So I went in and they was considerable of a crowd there and a big dumb-looking mutt in tights standing up in a ring, flexing his arms and showing off his muscles.

"Gents," yelled the barker, a flashy-dressed young feller with a diamond horseshoe stickpin, "the management offers fifty dollars to any man which can stay four rounds with this tiger of the ring! Five minutes ago I made the same offer on the platform outside, and some gent took me up. But now he seems to have got cold feet, and is nowhere to be found. So here and now I again make the original proposition—fifty round, bright iron men to any guy which can stay four rounds with this man-killin' terror, this fire-breathin' murderer, this iron-fisted man-mountain, Battling Bingo, the Terror of the Rockies!"

The crowd whooped, and three or four fellers made a move like they was going to take up the challenge, but I brushed 'em scornfully aside and bellered, "I'll take that dough, mate!"

I bounced into the ring, and the barker said, "You realize that the management ain't responsible for life or limb?"

"Aw, stow that guff and gimme them gloves," I roared, ripping off my shirt. "Get ready, champeen. I'm goin' to knock your crown off!"

The gong sounded, and we went for each other. They wasn't no canvas stretched across the back of the ring where Bingo couldst shove me up against to be blackjacked by somebody behind it, so I knowed very well he had a iron knuckle-duster on one of his hands, and, from the way he dangled his right, I knowed that was the hand. So I watched his right, and, when he throwed it, I stepped inside of his swing and banged him on the whiskers with a left and a right hook which tucked him away for the evening.

The crowd roared in huge approval, and I jerked the wad of greenbacks outa the barker's hand and started away when he stopped me.

"Say," he said, "I reckernize you now. You're Sailor Costigan. How'd you like to take this tramp's place? We'll pay you good wages."

"All I got to do is flatten jobbies?" I said, and he said it was. So that's how I come to start working in Flash Larney's Gigantic Circus and Animal Show.

Each night I'd appear in fighting tights before the multitude, and the barker, Joe Beemer, wouldst go through the usual ballyhoo, and then all I had to do was to knock the blocks offa the saps which tried to collect the fifty. I wouldn't use the knuckle-duster. I wouldn't of used it even if I'd of needed it, which I didn't. If I can't sock a palooka to sleep, fair and above-board, with my own personal knuckles, then they ain't no use in trying to dint him with a load of iron.

* * *

We worked up and down the West Coast and inland, and it was mostly easy. The men which tried to lick me was practically all alley-fighters—big strong fellers, but they didn't know nothing. Mostly farmers, blacksmiths, sailors, longshoremen, miners, cowpunchers, barroom bouncers.

All I had to do was to hit 'em. More'n once I knocked out three or four men in one night.

I always got action because the crowd was always against me, just like they was against Battling Bingo when I flattened him. A crowd is always against the carnival fighter, whether they know his opponent or not. And when the opponent is some well-known local boy, they nearly have hydrophobia in their excitement.

You oughta heered the cheers they'd give their home-town pride, and the dirty remarks they'd yell at me. No matter how hard I was fighting, I generally found time to reply to their jeers with choice insults I had picked up all over the seven seas, with the result that the maddened mob wouldst spew forth more raging sluggers to be slaughtered. Some men can't fight their best when the crowd's against 'em, but I always do better, if anything. It makes me mad, and I take it out on my opponent.

When I wasn't performing in the ring, I was driving stakes, setting up or taking down tents, and fighting with my circus-mates. Larney's outfit had the name of being the toughest on the Coast, and it was. The fights I had in the ring wasn't generally a stitch to them I had on the lot.

Well, I always makes it a point to be the champeen of whatever outfit I'm with, and I done so in this case. The first day I was with the show I licked three razor-backs, the lion-tamer and a side-show barker, and from then on it was a battle practically every day till them mutts realized I was the best man on the lot.

Fighting all the time like I was, I got so hard and mean I surprised myself. They wasn't a ounce of flesh on me that wasn't like iron, and I believe I could of run ten miles at top speed without giving out. The Dutch weight-lifter figgered to give me a close scrimmage, but he was way too slow. The toughest scrap I had was with a big Japanese acrobat. We fought all over the lot one morning, and everybody postponed the parade for an hour to watch. I was about all in when I finally put the heathen away, but, with my usual recuperative powers, I was able to go on that night as usual, and flatten a farm hand, a piano-mover and a professional football player.

Some trouble was had with Mike, which always set in my corner and bit anybody which tried to hit me through the ropes, as often happened when the local boy started reeling. Larney wanted to shave him and tattoo him and put him in a sideshow.

"The tattooed dog!" said Larney. "That would draw 'em! A novelty! Can't you see the crowds flockin' through the gates for a look at him?"

"I can see me bustin' you in the snoot," I growled. "You let Mike alone."

"Well," said Larney, "we got to make him more presentable. He looks kinda crude and uncultured alongside our trained poodles."

So the lion-trainer bathed Mike and combed him and perfumed him, and put on a little fool dog blanket with straps and gilt buckles, and tied a big bow ribbon on his stump tail. But Mike seen himself in a mirror and tore off all that rigging and bit the lion-tamer.

Well, they had an old decrepit lion by the name of Oswald which didn't have no teeth, and Mike got to sleeping in his cage. So they fixed a place where Mike couldst get in and out without Oswald getting out, and made a kind of act out of it.

Larney advertised Mike as the dog which laid down with the lion, and wouldst have Mike and Oswald in the cage together, and spiel about how ferocious Oswald was, and how unusual it was for a friendship to spring up between such natural enemies. But the reason Mike slept in the cage was that they put more straw in it than they did in the other cages on account of Oswald being old and thin-blooded, and Mike liked a soft bed.

Larney was afraid Mike would hurt Oswald, but the only critters Mike couldn't get along with was Amir, a big African leopard which had already kilt three men, and Sultan, the man-eating tiger. They was the meanest critters in the show, and was always trying to get out and claw Mike up. But he wasn't afeard of 'em.

* * *

Well, I was having a lot of fun. I thrives in a rough environment like that, though I'll admit I sometimes got kinda homesick for the *Sea Girl* and the sea, and wondered what Bill O'Brien and Mushy Hanson and Red O'Donnell was doing. But I got my pride, and I wouldn't go back after the Old Man had practically kicked me out to shift for myself.

Anyway, it was a lot of fun. I'd stand out on the platform in front of the tent with my massive arms folded and a scowl on my battered face, whilst Joe Beemer wouldst cock his derby back on his head and start the ballyhoo.

He'd whoop and yell and interjuice me to the crowd as "Sailor Costigan, the Massive Man-mauler of the Seven Seas!" And I'd do strongman stunts—twisting horseshoes in two and bending coins between my fingers and etc. Then he'd rare back and holler, "Is they any man in this fair city courageous enough to try and stay four rounds with this slashin' slugger? Take a chance, boys—he's been drivin' stakes all day and maybe he's tired and feeble—heh! heh! heh!"

Then generally some big ham wouldst jump outa the crowd and roar, "I'll fight the so-and-so." And Joe wouldst rub his hands together and say under his breath, "Money, roll in! I need groceries!" And he'd holler, "Right this way, gents! Right through the door to the left. Ten cents admission—one dime! See the battle of the century! Don't crowd, folks. Don't crowd."

The tent was nearly always packed with raging fans which honed at the top of their voices for their local hope to knock my iron skull off. However small a tank-town might be, it generally had at least one huge roughneck with a reputation of some kind.

One time we hit a town in the throes of a rassling carnival. Nobody couldst be found to box with me, but a big Polack came forward claiming to be the rassling champeen of the West—I ain't never seen a rassler which wasn't champeen of something—and wanted me to rassle him. Beemer refused, and the crowd hissed, and the rassler said I was yeller.

I seen red and told him I wasn't no rassler but I'd give him more'n he could tote home. He figgered I was easy, but he got fooled. I don't know a lot about scientific rassling, but I know plenty rough-and-tumble, and I was so incredibly hard and tough, and played so rough that I broke his arm and dislocated his shoulder. And after that nobody ast me to rassle.

It wasn't long after that when we blowed into a mining town by the name of Ironville, up in the Nevada hills, and from the looks of the populace I figgered I'd have plenty of competition that night. I wasn't fooled none, neither, believe me.

Long before we was ready to start the show, a huge crowd of tough-looking mugs in boots and whiskers was congregated around the athaletic tent, which wasn't showing no interest whatever in the main-top nor the freaks nor the animals.

Joe hadn't hardly got started on his ballyhoo when through the crowd come a critter which looked more like a grizzly than a man—a big black-headed feller with shoulders as broad as a door, and arms like a bear's paw. From the way the crowd all swarmed around him, I figgered he was a man of some importance in Ironville.

I was right.

"You don't need to say no more, pard," he rumbled in a voice like a bull. "I'll take a whirl at yore tramp!"

Joe looked at the black-browed giant, and he kinda got cold feet for the first time in his career.

"Who are you?" he demanded, uneasily.

The big feller grinned wolfishly and said, "Who, me? Oh, I'm just a blacksmith around here." And the crowd all whooped and yelled and laughed like he'd said something very funny.

"Somethin's fishy about this, Steve," whispered Joe to me. "I don't like the looks of it."

About that time the crowd begun to hiss and boo, and the big feller said nastily, "Well, what's the matter—you hombres gettin' yeller?"

I seen red. "Get into this tent, you black-muzzled palooka!" I roared. "I'll show you who's yeller!

"Shut up, Joe. Ain't I always said I barred nobody? What's the matter with you, anyhow?"

"I tell you, Steve," he said, wiping his forehead with his bandanner, "I seen this big punk somewheres, and if he's a simple blacksmith I'm a Bohemian!"

"Gahhh!" I snorted disgustfully. "When I get through with him, he'll look like a carpet. Have I lost you a penny since I joined the show? Naw! Come on!"

And so saying, I swaggered into the tent and bounded into the ring while the crowd gathered around, packing the place solid, applauding their man and howling insults at me, which I returned with interest, that being a game at which I ain't no amateur myself.

Joe started to lead the big feller to the dressing room that was partitioned off with a curtain in one corner of the tent, but he snorted and began ripping off his clothes then and there, revealing ring togs under 'em. Ah, thought I, he come here with the intention of going on with me. Some local battler, no doubtless.

When he clumb into the ring, they was several men with him—one a tall cold-faced man which looked like a high-class gambler, and who they called Brelen, and three or four tough mugs which was to act as seconds. They had the game writ all over their flat noses and tin ears. In fact, it looked to me like the big feller had a right elaborate follering, even if he was a local white hope.

"Who referee's?" asked Brelen, the poker-faced gent.

"Oh, I referee," said Joe.

"Not this time you don't," said Brelen. "The crowd chooses a referee who'll give my boy a square deal, see?"

"It's against the rules of the management—" began Joe, and the crowd rumbled and begun to surge forward. "All right, all right," said Joe, hurriedly. "It's okay with me."

Brelen grinned kinda thin-like, and turned to the crowd and said, "Well, boys, who do you want to referee?"

"Honest Jim Donovan!" they roared, and pushed forward a bald-headed old sea-lion which had the crookedest face I ever seen on a human. Joe give him a look and clasped his head and groaned. The crowd was nasty—itching for trouble. Joe was kinda white around the gills, and my handlers was uneasy. I was glad I'd locked Mike up in Oswald's cage before the show started, being suspicious of the customers. Mike ain't got much discretion; when the crowd starts throwing things at me, he's likely to go for 'em.

"Gents," yelled Joe, who, being a natural-born barker, couldn't keep his mouth shut if he swung for it, "you are now about to witness the battle of the centu-ree, wherein the Fighting Blacksmith of your fair city endeavors to stay four actual rounds with Sailor Costigan, the Terror of the Seven Seas—"

"Aw, shut up and get out of this ring," snarled Brelen. "Let the massacre commence!"

The gong sounded and the Blacksmith come swinging outa his corner. Jerusha, he was a man! He stood six feet one and a quarter and weighed not less than two hundred and ten pounds to my six feet and one ninety. With a broad chest matted with black hair, arms knotted with muscles like full-sized cables, legs like trees, a heavy jutting jaw, a broad fighting face with wicked gray eyes glittering from under thick black brows, and a shock of coarse black hair piled up on top of his low, broad forehead—I wanta tell you I ain't never seen a more formidable-looking fighter in my life!

We rushed together like a pair of mad bulls. *Bang!* In a shower of stars I felt myself flying through the air, and I landed on my shoulders with a jolt that shook the ring. Zowie! I sprawled about, almost petrified with dumfoundment. The crowd was whooping and cheering and laughing like all get-out.

I glared in wild amazement at the black-headed giant which was standing almost over me, with a nasty grin on his lips. A light dawned.

"Blacksmith my eye!" I roared, leaping up at him. "They ain't but one man in the world can hit a lick like that—*Bill Cairn*!"

I heard Joe's despairing howl as I slashed into my foe. *Wham! Wham!* I was on the resin again before I even got a chance to connect. The yells sounded kinda jumbled this time, and I shook my head violently, cussing fervently as I got my feet under me. Ironville. I oughta knowed—Bill Cairn, which they called the Ironville Blacksmith, the hardest hitter in the game! This was his hometown, and this was him!

Fighting mad, I bounded up, but Cairn was so close to me that he reached me with one of his pile-driving left hooks before I was balanced, and down I went again. Now the yelling was kinda dim and the lights was quaking and rocking. I crouched, taking a count which Honest Jim was reeling off a lot faster than necessary. Bill Cairn! The kayo king of the heavyweights, with thirty or forty knockouts in a row, and never been socked off his feet, himself. He was in line for a crack at the champ, and I was supposed to flatten this grizzly in four rounds!

I was up at nine, and, ducking a savage drive for the face, I clinched. By golly, it was like tying up a grizzly. But I ain't no chicken myself. I gripped him in a desperate bear-hug whilst him and the referee cussed and strained, and the crowd begged him to shake me loose and kill me.

"You side-show rat!" he gritted between his teeth. "Leggo whilst I rip yore head off! How can I show my best stuff with you hangin' on like a leech?"

"This is cheap stuff for a headliner like you!" I snarled, red-eyed.

"Givin' my home town folks a free show," he grinned, nastily. "It was just my luck to have a mug like you blow in whilst I was visitin' back home."

Oh, I see the idee all right. It was a big joke with him to knock me off and give his friends a treat —show off before the home-folks! He was laughing at me and so was all them Ironville lubbers. Well, I thought, grinding my teeth with red rage, they's many a good man punched hisself into fistic oblivion on my iron jaw.

I let go of Cairn and throwed my right at his jaw like it was a hammer. He pulled away from it and—*bang!* It mighta been a left hook to the head. It felt like a handspike. And the next instant, whilst my eyes was still full of stars, I felt another jolt like a concentrated earthquake.

Purty soon I heered somebody say, "Seven!" and I instinctively clumb up and looked about for my foe. I didn't locate him, as he was evidently standing behind me, but I did locate a large gloved mauler which crashed under my ear and nearly unjinted my neck. I done a beautiful dive, ploughing my nose vigorously into the resin, whilst the crowd wept with delight, and then I heered a noise like a sleigh-bell and was aware of being dragged to my corner.

A snifter of ammonia brung me to myself, and I discovered I was propped on my stool and being worked over by my handlers and Joe, who was bleeding from a cut over the temple.

"How'd you get that?" I asked groggily.

"One of these eggs hit me with a bottle," he said. "They claim I jerked the gong too soon. Listen at 'em! Toughest crowd I ever seen."

They sure was. They was rumbling and growling, just seething for a scrap, but stopping now and then to cheer Cairn, which was bowing and smirking in his corner.

"I knew I'd seen him," said Joe, "and Ace Brelen, his manager. The lousy chiselers! You ain't got a chance, Steve—"

At this moment a rough-whiskered mug stuck his head through the ropes and waved a coil of rope at Joe.

"We're on to you, you rat!" he bellered. "None of your side-show tricks, understand? If you try anything dirty, we'll stretch your neck. And that goes for you, too, you tin-eared gorilla!"

"So's your old man!" I roared, kicking out with all my might. My heel crunched solid on his jaw, and he shot back into the first row amongst a tangle of busted seats and cussing customers, from which he emerged bleeding at the mouth and screaming with rage. He was fumbling for a gun in his shirt, but just then the gong sounded and me and Cairn went for each other.

I come in fast, and figgered on beating him to the punch, but he was too quick for me. He wasn't so clever, but he moved like a big cat, and the very power of his punches was a swell defense. No man couldst keep his balance under them thundering smashes, even if they didn't land on no vital spot. Just trying to block 'em numbed my arms.

Zip! His left whizzed past my jaw like a red-hot brick. *Zinggg!* His right burned my ear as it went by. I seen a opening and shot my right with everything I had. But I was too eager; my arm looped over his shoulder and he banged his left into my ribs, which I distinctly felt bend almost to the breaking point as my breath went outa me in a explosive grunt.

I throwed my arms about him in a vain effort to clinch, but he pushed me away and slammed a full-armed right to my jaw. *Crash!* I felt myself turning a complete somersault in the air, and I landed on my belly with my head sticking out under the ropes and ogling glassily down at the ecstatic customers. One of these riz up and slashed his thigh with his hat and, sticking his face almost into mine, yelled, "Well, you carnival punk, how do you like *those?*"

"Like this!" I roared, catching him on the whiskers with a unexpected bash that sunk his nose in the sawdust. I then rolled over on my back and, observing that the referee had rapidly counted up to nine, I ariz and, abandoning my scanty boxing skill, started slugging wild and ferocious in the hope of landing a haymaker.

But that was Cairn's game; he blocked my punches for a second or so, then *bang!* he caught me square on the chin with one of them thunderbolt rights which shot me back into the ropes, and I rebounded from 'em square into a whistling left hook that dropped me face-down in the resin.

I couldst dimly hear the crowd yelling like wolves. When the average man falls face-first he's through, but nobody never accused me of being a average man. At nine I was up as usual, reeling, and Cairn approached me with a look of disgust on his brutal face.

"Will you stay down?" he gritted, and, measuring me with a left, he crashed his right square into my mouth, and I went down like a pole-axed ox.

"That finishes him!" I heered somebody yelp, and evidently Cairn thought so too, because he give a scornful laugh and started toward his corner where his manager was getting his bathrobe ready. But I got my legs under me and at nine I staggered up, as is my habit.

"Come back here, you big sissy!" I roared groggily, spitting out fragments of a tooth. "This fight ain't over by a devil of a ways!"

The mob screamed with amazement, and Cairn, swearing ferociously, turned and rushed at me like a tiger. But though I reeled on buckling knees, I didn't go down under his smashing left hooks.

"Why don't you get an ax, you big false-alarm?" I sneered, trying to shake the blood outa my eyes.

"What you got in them gloves—powder puffs?"

At that he give a roar which made the ring lights shimmy, and brought one up from the canvas which hung me over the top rope just as the gong sounded. Joe and his merry men untangled my limp carcass and held me on the stool while they worked despairingly over me.

"Drop it, Steve," urged Joe. "Cairn will kill you."

"How many times was I on the canvas that round?" I asked.

"How should I know?" he returned, peevishly, wringing the gore out of my towel. "I ain't no adding machine."

"Well, try to keep count, willya?" I requested. "It's important; I can tell how much he's weakenin' if you check up on the knockdowns from round to round."

Joe dropped the sponge he was fixing to throw into the ring.

"Ye gods! Are you figgerin' on continuin' the massakree?"

"He can't keep this pace all night," I growled. "Lookit Brelen talkin' to his baby lamb!"

Ace was gesticulating purty emphatic, and Cairn was growling back at him and glaring at me and kneading his gloves like he wisht it was my goozle. I knowed that Brelen was telling him this scrap was getting beyond the point of a joke, and that it wasn't helping his reputation none for me to keep getting up on him, and for him to make it another quick kayo. Ha, ha, thought I grimly, shaking the blood outa my mangled ear, let's see how quick a kayo Bill Cairn can make where so many other iron-fisted sluggers has failed.

At the gong I was still dizzy and bleeding copiously, but that's a old story to me.

Cairn, infuriated at not having finished me, rushed outa his corner and throwed over a terrible right, which I seen coming like a cannonball, and ducked. His arm looped over my shoulder and his shoulder rammed into my neck with such force that we both crashed to the canvas.

Cairn untangled hisself with a snarl of irritation, and, assisted by the fair-minded referee, arose, casually kicking me in the face as he done so. I ariz likewise, and, enraged by my constant position on the canvas, looped a whistling left at his head that would of undoubtedly decapitated him hadst it landed—but luck was against me as usual. My foot slipped in a smear of my own blood, my swing was wild, and I run smack into his ripping right.

I fell into Cairn, ignoring an uppercut which loosened all my lower teeth, and tied him up.

"Leggo, you tin-eared baboon!" he snarled, heaving and straining. "Try to show me up, wouldja? Try to make a monkey outa me, wouldja?"

"Nature's already attended to that, you lily-fingered tap-dancer," I croaked. "A flapper with a powder-puff couldst do more damage than you can with them chalk-knuckled bread-hooks."

"So!" he yelled, jerking away and crashing his right to my jaw with every ounce of his huge frame behind it. I revolved in the air like a spin-wheel, felt the ropes scrape my back, and realized that I was falling through space. *Crash!* My fall was cushioned by a mass of squirming, cussing fans, else I would of undoubtedly broke my back.

I looked up, and high above me, it seemed, I seen the referee leaning over the ropes and counting down at me. I began to kick and struggle, trying to get up, and a number of willing hands—and a few hob-nailed boots—hoisted me offa the squawking fans, and I grabbed the ropes and swung up.

Somebody had a grip on my belt, and I heard a guy growl. "You're licked, you fool! Take the count. Do you want to get slaughtered?"

"Leggo!" I roared, kicking out furiously. "I ain't never licked!"

I tore loose and crawled through the ropes—it looked like I'd never make it—and hauled myself up just as the referee was lifting his arm to bring it down on "Ten!" Cairn didn't rush this time; he was scowling, and I noticed that sweat was streaming down his face, and his huge chest was heaving.

Some of the crowd yelled, "Stop it!" but most of 'em whooped, "Now you got him, Bill. Polish him off!"

Cairn measured me, and smashed his right into my face. The top-rope snapped as I crashed back against it, but I didn't fall. Cairn swore in amazement, and drawed back his right again, when the gong sounded. He hesitated, then lemme have it anyway—a pile-driving smash that nearly lifted me offa my feet. And the crowd cheered the big egg. My handlers jostled him aside and, as they pulled me offa the ropes, Cairn sneered and walked slowly to his corner.

Supported on my stool, I seen Joe pick up a sponge stealthily.

"Drop that sponge!" I roared, and Joe, seeing the baleful light in my one good eye, done so like it was red-hot.

"Lemme catch you throwin' a sponge in for me!" I growled. "Gimme ammonia! Dump that bucket of water over me! Slap the back of my neck with a wet towel! One more round to go, and I gotta save that fifty bucks!"

Swearing dumfoundedly, my handlers did as they was bid, and I felt better and stronger every second. Even they couldn't understand how I couldst take such a beating and come back for more. But any slugger which depends on his ruggedness to win his fights understands it. We got to be solid iron, and we are.

Besides, my recent rough-and-ready life hadst got me into condition such as few men ever gets in, even athaletes. This, coupled with my amazing recuperative powers, made me just about unbeatable. Cairn could, and had, battered me from pillar to post, knocked me down repeatedly, and had me groggy and glassy-eyed, but he hadn't sapped the real reservoir of my vitality. Being groggy and being weak is two different things. Cairn hadn't weakened me. The minute my head cleared under the cold water and ammonia, I was as good as ever. Well, just about, anyhow.

So I come out for the fourth round raring to go. Cairn didn't rush as usual. In fact, he looked a little bit sick of his job. He walked out and lashed at my head with his left. He connected solid, but I didn't go down.

And for the first time I landed squarely. *Bang*. My right smashed under his ear, and his head rocked on his bull's neck.

With a roar of fury, he come back with a thundering right to the head, but it only knocked me to my knees, and I was up in a instant. I was outlasting him! His blows was losing their dynamite!

This realization electrified me, and I bored in, slashing with both hands.

A left to the face staggered but didn't stop me, and I ripped a terrific left hook under his heart. He grunted and backed away. He wasn't near as good at taking punishment as he was at handing it out. I slashed both hands to his head, and the blood flew. With a deafening roar, he sunk his right mauler clean outa sight in my belly.

I thought for a second that my spine was broke, as I curled up on the canvas, gasping. The referee sprang forward and began counting, and I looked for Cairn, expecting to see him standing almost astraddle of me, as usual, waiting to slug me down as I got up. He wasn't; but was over against the ropes, holding onto 'em with one mitt whilst he wiped the blood and sweat outa his eyes with the other'n. And I seen his great chest heaving, his belly billowing out and in, and his leg muscles quivering.

Grinning wolfishly, I drawed in great gulps of air and beat the count by a second. Cairn lurched offa the ropes at me, swinging a wide left, but I went under it and crashed my right to his heart. He rolled like a ship in a heavy gale, and I knowed I had him. That last punch which had floored me had been his dying effort. He'd fought hisself clean out on me, as so many a man had didst. Strategy, boy, strategy!

I went after him like a tiger after a bull, amid a storm of yells and curses and threats. The crowd, at first dumfounded, was now leaping up and down and shaking their fists and busting chairs and threatening me with torture and sudden death if I licked their hero. But I was seeing red. Wait'll you've took the beating I'd took and then get a chance to even it up! I ripped both hands to Cairn's quivering belly and swaying head, driving him to the ropes, off of which he rolled drunkenly.

I heered a gong sounding frantically; Brelen hadst knocked the timekeeper stiff with a blackjack and was trying to save his man. Also the referee was grabbing at me, trying to push me away. But I give no heed. A left and right under the heart buckled Cairn's knees, and a blazing right to the temple glazed his eyes. He reeled, and a trip-hammer left hook to the jaw that packed all my beef sent him crashing to the canvas, just as the crowd come surging into the ring, tearing down the ropes. I seen Joe take it on the run, ducking out under the wall of the tent, and yelling,

"Hey, Rube!"

Then me and the handlers was engulfed. Half a hundred hands grabbed at me, and fists, boots and chairs swung for me. But I ducked, ripping off my gloves, and come up fighting like a wild man.

I swung my fists like they was topping-mauls, and ribs snapped and noses and jaw-bones cracked, whilst through the melee I caught glimpses of Brelen and his men carrying out their battered gladiator. He was still limp.

Just as the sheer number of maddened citizens was dragging me down, a gang of frothing razor-backs come through the tent like a whirlwind, swinging pick handles and tent-stakes.

Well, I ain't seen many free-for-alls to equal that 'un! The circus war-whoop of "Hey, Rube!" mingled with the bloodthirsty yells of the customers. The Iron-villians outnumbered us, but we give 'em a bellyful. In about three seconds the ring was tore to pieces and the storm of battle surged into the tent-wall, which collapsed under the impact.

Knives was flashing and a few guns barking, and all I wonder is that somebody wasn't kilt. The athaletic tent was literally ripped plumb to ribbons, and the battle surged out onto the grounds and raged around the other tents and booths.

Then a wild scream went up: "Fire!" And over everything was cast a lurid glow. Somehow or other the main top hadst caught in the melee—or maybe some fool set it on fire. A strong wind was fanning the flames, which mounted higher each second. In a instant the fight was abandoned. Everything was in a tumult, men running and yelling, children squalling, women screaming. The circus-people was running and hauling the cages and wagons outa the animal tent, which was just catching. The critters was bellering and howling in a most hair-raising way, and I remembered Mike in Oswald's cage. I started for there on the run, when there riz a most fearful scream above all the noise: "The animals are loose!"

Everybody hollered and tore their hair and ran, and here come the elephants like a avalanche! They crashed over wagons and cages and booths, trumpeting like Judgment Day, and thundered on into the night. How they got loose nobody never exactly knowed. Anything can happen in a fire. But, in stampeding, they'd bumped into and busted open some more cages, letting loose the critters inside.

And here *they* come roaring—Sultan, the tiger, and Amir, the leopard, killers both of 'em. A crowd of screaming children rushed by me, and right after them come that striped devil, Sultan, his eyes blazing. I grabbed up a heavy tent-stake and leaped betweenst him and the kids. He roared and leaped with his talons spread wide, and I braced my feet and met him in mid-air with a desperate smash that had every ounce of my beef behind it. The impact nearly knocked me offa my feet, and the stake splintered in my hand, but Sultan rolled to the ground with a shattered skull.

And almost simultaneously a terrible cry from the people made me wheel just in time to see Amir racing toward me like a black shadder with balls of fire for eyes. And, just as I turned, he soared from the ground straight at my throat. I didn't have time to do nothing. He crashed full on my broad breast, and his claws ripped my hide as the impact dashed me to the earth. And at the same instant I felt another shock which knocked him clear of me.

I scrambled up to see a squat white form tearing and worrying at the limp body of the big cat. Again Mike had saved my worthless life. When Amir hit me, he hit Amir and broke his neck with one crunch of his iron jaws. He'd squoze out between the bars of Oswald's cage and come looking for me.

He lolled out his tongue, grinning, and vibrated his stump tail, and all to once I heered my name called in a familiar voice. Looking around, I seen a battered figger crawl out from under the ruins of a bandwagon, and, in the lurid light of the burning tents, I reckernized him.

"Jerusha!" I said. "The Old Man! What you doin' under that wagon?"

"I crawled under there to keep from bein' trampled by the mob," he said, working his legs to see if they was broke. "And it was a good idee, too, till a elephant run over the wagon. By gad, if I ever get safe to sea once more I'll never brave the perils of the land again, I wanta tell ya!"

"Did you see me lick Bill Cairn?" I asked.

"I ain't see nothin' but a passel of luneyticks," he snapped. "I arrived just as the free-for-all was ragin'. I don't mind a roughhouse, but when they drags in a fire and a stampede of jungle-critters, I'm ready to weigh anchor! And you!" he added, accusingly. "A merry chase you've led me, you big sea-lion! I've come clean from Frisco, and it looked for a while like I wouldn't never find this blame circus."

"What you wanta find it for?" I growled, the thought of my wrongs renewing itself.

"Steve," said the Old Man, "I done you a injustice! It was the cabin-boy which put that polecat in my bunk—I found it out after he jumped ship. Steve, as champeen of the old *Sea Girl*, I asks you—let bygones be gone-byes! Steve, me and the crew has need of your mallet-like fists. At Seattle, a few weeks ago, I shipped on a fiend in human form by the name of Monagan, which immediately set hisself up as the bully of the fo'c'le. I had to put in Frisco because of shortage of hands. Even now, Mate O'Donnell, Mushy Hanson and Jack Lynch lies groanin' in their bunks from his man-handlin', and he has likewise licked Bill O'Brien, Maxie Heimer and Sven Larsen. He has threatened to hang me on my own bowsprit by my whiskers. I dast not fire him, for fear of my life. Steve!" the Old Man's voice trembled with emotion, "I asks you—forgive and forget! Come back to the *Sea Girl* and demonstrate the eternal brotherhood of man by knockin' the devil outa this demon Monagan before he destroys us all! Show the monster who's the real champeen of the craft!"

"Well," I said, "I got some money comin' to me from Larney—but let it go. He'll need it repairin' his show. Monagan, of Seattle—bah! I hammered him into a pulp in Tony Vitello's poolroom three years ago, and I can do it again. Calls hisself champeen of the *Sea Girl*, huh? Well, when I kick his battered carcass onto the wharf, he'll know who's champeen of the craft. They never was, and they ain't now, and they never will be but one champeen of her, and that's Steve Costigan, A. B. Let's go! I wasn't never cut out for no peaceful landlubber's existence, nohow."

Thinking About the Story

Set clearly within the pulp tradition, Robert E. Howard's story is a signature example of the action-adventure genre. It displays the classic features: the emphasis on plot and action, and exaggerated characterization. However, there is more. Placing the story within the realm of male, working-class literature, one concept to consider is the "homosocial." As in the stories of Ernest Hemingway, the idea in Howard's fiction is that of a male-only sphere. In this space, men interact with men, creating a narrative of gendered action, where men prove themselves to each other. Accordingly, come to some conclusions as to why certain stories are like this? What does the absence of women reveal about the story and the author? With Howard's "Circus Fists" you can draw three distinct comparisons: to Edith Wharton's "The Choice" you can contrast the role of class, to O. Henry's "The Ransom of Red Chief" you can examine the similarities in terms of dialect and voice, and to H. P. Lovecraft's "The Outsider" you can analyze the different qualities of pulp fiction.

Discussion Questions

1. Describe Steve Costigan's personality. Do you find him to be likeable? Support your answer with quotes from the text.
2. What effect does Costigan's use of slang have on the story? Next, research the history of the term "pulp fiction." Does this story match your criteria for "pulp" status? Explain why or why not. If not, how would you categorize this story?
3. Speculate on the reasons why Steve Costigan keeps getting up from the ring floor. How would you define these qualities? In what ways does machismo function in the story?
4. Comment on the intended audience for this story. Is there a gender or age bias? What are your reasons for believing there is or is not a bias? Do you think the audience has changed since the story was first published?
5. Do you find the ending to be contrived? How would you improve it?

Activities

1. Rewrite your favorite part of the story from one of the following perspectives:
   a. Joe.
   b. Bill Cairn.
   c. Brelen.

2. Use the details of the big fight between Costigan and Cairn to create your own newspaper article that neutrally reports the action and the outcome. Remember to format it appropriately and to include "interviews" from the principle characters.

3. Choose a sport and make a list of the sport's attributes and the persons who play it. Without stereotyping, develop a fictional character (detailing his or her personality) and write a scene in which he or she plays that sport.

Copyrights

Ambrose Bierce. "An Occurrence at Owl Creek Bridge." From *San Francisco Examiner* (July 1890).

Willa Cather. "A Wagner Matinee." First published in *Everybody's Magazine* (February 1904).

Anton Chekhov. "The Lady with the Dog." First published in *Russkaya Mysl* (1899). Translated by Constance Garrett (1917). Edited by Christopher Linforth (2010).

Kate Chopin. "The Story of an Hour." First published in *Vogue* (1894).

Stephen Crane. "The Open Boat." First published in *Scribner's Magazine* (June 1897).

Arthur Conan Doyle. "A Scandal in Bohemia." First published in *The Strand Magazine* (July 1891).

F. Scott Fitzgerald. "Winter Dreams." First published in *Metropolitan Magazine* (December 1922).

Charlotte Perkins Gilman. "The Yellow Wallpaper." First published in *New England Magazine.* (January 1892).

Nathaniel Hawthorne. "Young Goodman Brown." First published in *New England Magazine* (April 1835).

O. Henry. "The Ransom of Red Chief." From *Whirligigs* by O. Henry (1910).

Robert E. Howard. "Circus Fists." First published in *Fight Stories* (December 1931).

Sarah Orne Jewett. "A White Heron." From *A White Heron and Other Stories* (1886).

James Joyce. "Araby." From *Dubliners* by James Joyce (1916).

Rudyard Kipling. "Mowgli's Brothers." From *The Jungle Book* by Rudyard Kipling (1894).

H. P. Lovecraft. "The Outsider." First published in *Weird Tales* (April 1926).

Edgar Allan Poe. "The Man of the Crowd." First published in *Burton's Gentleman's Magazine* (December 1840).

Leo Tolstoy. "How Much Land Does a Man Need?" From *What Men Live By and Other Tales* by Leo Tolstoy. Translated by Louise and Aylmer Maude (1887). Edited by Christopher Linforth (2010).

Mark Twain. "The Californian's Tale." From *The First Book of the Author's Club, Liber Scriptorium* (1893).

H. G. Wells. "A Moth — Genus Novo." From *The Stolen Bacillus, and Other Incidents* by H. G. Wells (1895).

Edith Wharton. "The Choice." First published in *Scribner's Magazine* (1916).

Glossary of Literary Terms

allegory A narrative of symbolic ideas and concepts expressed through events, places, objects, and characters.

antagonist The character that opposes, and seeks to negate, the interests and desires of the protagonist.

atmosphere A tonal background in which characters operate. Often, the atmosphere consists of setting, mood, and weather.

backstory Significant past events or actions that are related to the ongoing narrative.

climax The point of greatest tension in the narrative and usually the point in which the conflict is resolved.

complication A tension-building twist that develops the conflict.

conflict An obstacle thrust upon the protagonist by another character or by a situation.

dénouement The falling action that occurs after the climax.

dramatic irony The reader's awareness of certain information, which is not yet known by the character.

epigraph A quotation at the beginning of a story that relates to its theme.

epiphany A sudden realization by the character about himself or his social situation.

figurative language Words and phrases—often consisting of metaphors and similes—that go beyond the literal to evoke new sensations and insights about a character, object, event, or action.

flashback A narrative leap to an earlier incident or scene.

foreshadowing The introduction of images, events, and words into the narrative that becomes significant later on in the story.

monologue A single character's long speech.

narrator The teller of the story. Often a character within—or existing outside of—the story, the narrator is either a *frame* (or *peripheral*) narrator or a *central* narrator. A notable exception is the *omniscient* narrator, which results in a God-like telling of the story.

plot A story's sequence of events.

point of view The person or vantage point from which the narrative is told. There are several established forms: first-person, the narrator telling a story in which he is involved. This comes in the singular, *I*, and the plural, *we*. Second-person narration often comes in the imperative; that is, *you* plus a directive. Third-person narration is the most diverse point of view. It comes in third-person *close* or *intimate*, which entails the *he* or *she* (*they*, if it's plural) being the character of focus and the one to whom the reader is privy to his or her thoughts and feelings. The involvement of a separate narrator and/or displaying knowledge of a few characters is termed third-person *limited*. Finally, third-person *omniscient*, which is the God-like perspective. Here, the point of view moves freely between characters and has knowledge of every person's actions, thoughts, and motivations.

protagonist The main character or hero of the story.

realism A mode of writing that attempts to portray the world and its inhabitants in a realistic manner.

rising action Events and incidences that raise a story's tension and build toward the climax.

setting The time and place in which a story takes place.

stream of consciousness A stylized point of view that can be in the first- or third-person. This narrative technique seeks to reproduce the memories, thoughts, and impressions that flow through a character's mind.

symbol A person, object, or event that is representative of a larger idea or concept.

tale An early form of the short story that covers several variants: the tall tale, the cautionary tale, the folk tale, the fairytale, and the fable.

theme A unifying idea or abstraction that emerges from the narrative.

Lightning Source UK Ltd.
Milton Keynes UK
UKOW050019160312

189035UK00001B/15/P

9 780857 287694